SHADOWS OF SHAME

ISBN-13 978-0692733943
ISBN-10 0692733949.

This book is dedicated to my father, Harold Ashkenas

SHADOWS OF SHAME

BRUCE ASHKENAS

CHAPTER ONE
A WORKING WOMAN

A woman shall not wear that which pertains to a man
And a man shall not wear the garment of a woman for
Whosoever doeth these things is an abomination to the
Lord.

—Deuteronomy 22:5

IS THIS WHAT it takes to get a story these days? Harold Apple wondered as he looked at his companions in the dank holding cell in the cellar of police headquarters. They were hardscrabble women, some used up and some still pretty, but all dressed in the short-skirted uniform of the hooker. So was Harold. He sat on a splintery jail bench, watching his breath form in the fetid air. The winter cold penetrated his filmy red dress and cheap stockings. His short brown hair was hidden under a platinum wig and his clean cut face was covered by cracked makeup streaked with rouge.

Forty prostitutes had been rounded up on the streets of the Tenderloin—New York's meanest red-light district, herded into paddy wagons, and dumped in the holding pen of the jail at two in the morning. Harold, posing as a woman, was among them.

The cops were taking the women out of the cell, one at a time, for arraignment before a night court judge. Harold's mind raced. *Will they do a strip search? I don't think so. I hope I find what I'm looking for soon. My beard will start showing in a couple of days.*

Hazy light reflected dimly off rhinestones and glitter on the hooker uniforms, making a muddy rainbow on the floor of the large cell. One of the girls, her long silk legs extending from a slinky black gown, shouted into the night. "Come and get me copper. Ha! A real man would know what to do."

Harold sat with his back against cold stone. *I've got to be a prostitute to get this story. I've got to be bold and brassy. I can do that, but I can't be a girl. How long before they find me out?*

Harold contemplated the words of Aaron, his editor at the paper. "We've all heard rumors of what happens at the women's jail—wild parties, guards whipping naked prisoners, the whole sadistic thing. I don't want to send a girl reporter into that. But you're slightly built; we can dress you up and get you in, no problem. C'mon Apple, you're a good reporter. Don't you smell a story?" The twenty-six-year-old couldn't resist such pleading; he could get any story, the more dangerous the better.

Harold settled in on the cold bench, waiting for his turn before the judge. He could barely breathe, hemmed in by the sickly sweet odor of the hookers. Light-headed, he remembered another time when he was overwhelmed by the smell of bad perfume. He was six years old and had to sit with the women in the synagogue. "Ma, I want to go sit with Daddy," he said.

"No, Daddy is reading from the Torah."

His daddy, reading the Torah? Daddy never read the Torah. The women, their big bosoms covered by lace, pressed all around him. Above him was a forest of big hats and hat pins. The smell of toilet water, sickly-sweet, overcame him. Harold puked. The thought of throw-up brought another story to mind, one his father used to tell.

❧

Sam Appel, Harold's father, knew puking. He had puked every day when his high school classmates beat him because he was a Jew. Born in Frankfurt, Germany in 1882, Sam grew up in a world that did not want him. The school he attended, the Gymnasium Friedrich the Great, required a course in political philosophy, taught by the most august scholar on the faculty, Professor Jacobus von Dingell. The great man would swish into class, his thick horn-rim glasses steaming from an intellectual confrontation or a lecture to a wayward student. He would shed his long frock coat, and, in vest and shirt sleeves, ample belly hanging over rumpled trousers, stringy hair flying, quiz the class on the thought of the great philosopher, Friedrich Nietzsche, and his theory of the 'blond Teutonic beast' as superior to all dark-haired sub-races. Small and dark, Sam met the criteria for sub-human but it was not until the class began to study Houston Stewart Chamberlain that his life became a living hell. Chamberlain, in his history of the Aryan race, showed scorn for the wealthy German Jew. The only other Jew in the class was the handsome Bernhard Kreutzer, star of the upper form football team, immune to all criticism, which instead fell on Sam's narrow shoulders. He was the son of that bloodsucking Jew who owned the department store. He must be evil also. There was no way Sam was going to avoid his daily beating.

And there was no way Sam was going to stay in Germany. It's America for me, he thought, as soon as I finish school and am able to leave. He didn't even protest when he got off the boat at Ellis Island and found his name changed from Appel to Apple. With this name, he exalted, I'll be free as Johnny Appleseed. I'll be free to travel the country from the cities of the east to the prairies of the west. And when I get tired I can go to that city in the middle, Cleveland it's called, and work for my brother Leo.

❧

Harold sat on the bench in the cold cell, his thoughts wandering as he waited his turn before the judge. *When I was little I had a cowboy suit that my dad bought me. He wanted me to be a real American. I loved that suit—chaps and vest and wide-brimmed cowboy hat. It never crossed my mind that I'd be dressed up like a hooker, waiting my day in court. The things I do for that newspaper.*

The newspaper was the *New York World Journal*, where Harold had found a job running copy from the city room to the compositors in the printing plant. It wasn't much of a job for a journalism school grad, only 23 years old, but times were tough, and it was New York, where twenty dailies competed for the latest news, the most sensational story. For Harold it felt like the center of the universe. Then he got a break. City Editor Arnold Aaron, a sharp-eyed man who saw everything in his empire, noticed him scribbling notes for a reporter who showed up for work drunk as a skunk. Harold's reward was a desk next to the drunk, rewriting copy phoned in by beat men. But Harold wasn't satisfied rewriting the words of others. He pleaded with Aaron to give him stories of his own. He wanted to be a reporter.

As time went by Aaron gave in and Harold got better and better assignments. His story on graft in subway construction caused so much of an uproar among the public that the Mayor fired the Commissioner of Streets. After that Aaron went around the city room crowing, "I know talent when I see it."

Harold smiled and asked for a raise. The reporter became a fixture at City Hall, hated by the Tammany poohbahs but a darling of the reformers who took power with Fiorello LaGuardia in 1933. But now Harold was sitting in a dank jail cell surrounded by hookers. "Why the fuck am I here?" he muttered to his seatmate, a skinny blond named Trudy. "Because Aaron asked me, damn him."

"Yeah, they all ask me too, honey," Trudy said. "That's the business." And she held her hands out, palms down, to examine her fingernails, which Harold noticed had some big chips in the polish.

"Candy Apple," a large matron called from the door. Harold stood up. Two male guards entered the cell and surrounded him closely. One of them put a hand on his ass and shoved him forward.

"Be careful honey," Trudy cautioned in her thick New York accent. "See ya on the streets."

The guards marched Harold out of the cell-block. One of the hookers yelled after them, "Jeb, leave some of that ass for me." The guard squeezed harder. Harold squirmed beneath the prodding.

He's leaving a bruise on my butt the size of New Jersey. He's going to be the first one canned when I get out of here.

≈

It was ten months later, and the woman's jail expose had created a sensation in the city. Harold's story of sexual abuse and physical assault made heads roll in the Department of Corrections, from the Chief of Corrections to that guard with the wandering hands. But in the newspaper business it was, 'what have you done for me lately.'

"Apple, get in here," Aaron stood at his office door and yelled out over the din of the city room.

What now? Harold picked his way between old desks covered by overflowing ashtrays and empty coffee cups, typewriter stands, and the teletype machine clacking away, surrounded by overflowing wastebaskets full of ignored dispatches from around the world.

"I've got a job only you can do," Aaron said, whipping sweat from his bald head with a big handkerchief he always carried. It was November and the steam heat in the city room was turned up. Aaron liked it that way. "This is big and absolutely hush-hush."

I've heard that before. Harold rolled his eyes as he sat, slouched in front of his editor's desk. The odor of Aaron, sweat mixed with cologne and printer's ink, made Harold pugnacious. He wanted to fight the little man. Instead he argued, "No more dressing up boss. Remember the trouble you had getting me out of the women's prison. The warden wouldn't listen when you told him I was a man. Then they thought I was a transvestite or some kind of pervert. When they finally realized the kind of trouble they were in they didn't want to let me go."

"I know Harold," Aaron said with all the confidence of a man who usually gets his way. "But you got out and wrote the story, and the bad guys got fired and may even go to jail themselves. Now I've got a more straightforward job for you. But you still have to act. I want you to pretend to be German and infiltrate the Bund."

Everyone in New York knew about the German American Bund. They called themselves the Nazis of America. They were Jew-hating bastards just like their German brethren, but unlike the National Socialists in Germany, the Bund was more of a clown act. No one took them seriously.

Aaron went on, his wire-rim glasses moving up and down the slope of his nose as he bobbed and weaved like a fighter in the ring. "I've been jonesing to expose the stinking Nazis for months, before they amount to anything. Hitler was a joke in Germany for years before he won the election. We've got to nip them in the bud. Corkwright approved the story, but only if I give you the assignment.

"Why me?" Harold was astounded that publisher Clinton Corkwright even knew who he was.

"I've been talking you up, Harold. You're a damn good writer and you speak German like you were born in Dusseldorf. Remember that translating you did when you were a copyboy? Corkwright remembers. Besides, we need something new. The War of the Worlds stuff is wearing thin."

"Damn it Boss, I'm not going to write about Nazis from Mars. Either you're serious or I'm not doing the job." He stood up from his chair and paced the floor. "What kind of cover do you have for me? Those Bund boys are tough."

᳗

These schmucks were real authentic Nazis despite their clownish reputation, Harold ruminated while walking to the subway after work. The crowd on the sidewalk carried him along. People rushing who knows where but many had *World Journals* under their arms. Harold smiled at them. He wrote for them. They were all his friends. It was a crowd of familiar strangers, men in drab overcoats, women in brighter colors. There were no uniforms, no Nazi insignia, no swastikas. This was New York, not Germany. Nazis had no place here.

Harold knew a UPI stringer, a reporter who worked in Berlin. Krauss had told him exactly what the streets of Germany were like. People walked with fear, fear of brown shirts and black shirts and the swastika. Krauss had seen Jewish storekeepers pulled out of their shops and taken away by the Gestapo. He'd seen looting and burning encouraged by the Party and unanswered by the police. He told Harold of a reporter for the *Tagblatt* who had disappeared in the middle of the night after writing an article intimating fat Hermann Goering was a drug addict. Krauss was afraid to return to Germany, but he went. Harold hadn't heard from him in months.

He knew the Nazis in Germany were strong; they took over a whole country. It was quite possible his friend Krauss had been tossed in a prison camp. The Bund members were foreigners and didn't hold the sway in the U.S. that their counterparts held in their homeland. Not yet anyway.

It didn't matter how strong they were because there was just one Harold. He had to watch his step, not let anyone find out he was a reporter or a Jew. It could be deadly for him if his cover was blown at the wrong time or place. *Whew! I hate danger. Then why oh why do I get in so many tight spots? That damn newspaper.*

CHAPTER TWO

YORKVILLE CALLS

"I'VE GOT TO convince the Bund that I'm a German," Harold said while spearing a large piece of beef brisket off the serving plate. He was sitting down to dinner with his girlfriend Sally, and her family. "I've got to be one of them." His one and only knew he was a daring reporter who would do almost anything for a story. At least that's what he hoped she knew and supported.

Her big brown eyes opened wider as she tossed her head back in a gesture Harold knew well. He thought of it as the flying page-boy and it meant she doubted what he was saying.

"How are you going to do that? Go live with them?" After dating Harold for nearly 4 years, she knew he took risks, and she didn't like it.

"That's right." Harold was glad his love had deduced it herself. "Aaron says I have to live in Yorkville. He's the boss." *It's my job. I don't have to feel guilty about doing my job. I don't have to ask her permission to go away for a week, or even a month.* He looked up, right at Sally. There it was, that telltale wrinkle between her brown eyes that only bothered her gentle face when she was fighting her emotions, trying not to cry. He knew she'd been expecting him to pop the question and here he was, going off on newspaper business again. But then, she'd been expecting him to propose for years and he never did. Harold placed his hand atop Sally's, hoping to appease her. He loved her, he really did, but he was a coward. He could face crooked politicians, brutal jail guards, even Nazis, but he couldn't face a wife, a life-long commitment to one woman scared him more than anything. *I would disappoint her.* He stole a look and saw trembling tears forming in the corners of her eyes.

The reporter was saved by Saul, Sally's flame-haired younger brother, who, not noticing his sister's distress, cried out in excitement at Harold's revelation. "Harold, you're going underground again, like in the woman's jail story! Will it be dangerous this time too?"

"Only if the Nazis find out I'm Jewish," Harold told the teenager. "I'll have an apartment in Yorkville, a German birth certificate, immigration documents, and a job as a typesetter at the paper."

"Harold will be safe," Israel Schwartz, Sally's craggy-faced father, told his son. "Mr. Aaron wouldn't have him take risks."

"Well, I think you're crazy. *Me ken ge'herget verein*, you could get killed Harold," exclaimed Sarah, Sally's mother, her broad Yiddish accent spilling out of thin lips in an otherwise full face. "Those people, if you can call Nazis people, hate us. They'd as soon kill a Jew as spit on him."

"My wife, who knows everything, is right this time Harold," Israel said with just a hint of an eastern-European accent. "I know about Jew haters. When I grew up in Glusk we had to be very careful around the *goyim*. A man who lived near us fixed watches for a living. A captain in the army brought him an heirloom clock to fix. The clock couldn't be fixed without a special spring from Switzerland. When the captain heard this he flew into a rage and killed the watchmaker, then told the police he had been cheated. A pogrom was organized, and three more Jews were killed before it was over. Jewish life was very cheap in the old country. But this is New York. Harold will be safe."

"I talked this over with Aaron," Harold snuck a peak at Sally to see how she was taking in all that he was revealing. "My number one priority will be having an unbreakable cover. That means living in Yorkville. Number two will be gaining the trust of the Nazis. I'll even have a different last name, Appel instead of Apple." *Number three is getting out of here without hearing any more of Izzy's story.* Harold pushed the food around on his plate with his fork while examining the faces of the Schwartz family. Sally's face was still scrunched up but she'd managed to control her tears. Saul had a big smile, as if he couldn't wait to be old enough to do daring deeds. Sarah looked placid. Her potential son-in-law was doing something dangerous and unnecessary but she couldn't stop him so why worry. Izzy was more complicated. The long wrinkles on either side of his face from the corners of his mouth to the top of his jaw jumped up and down while he talked, telling another story. His yarmulke was perched rakishly to one side, revealing thin brown hair on a balding head. He looked like Major Hoople in the funnies. If he'd stayed in Russia he would have been a rabbi, but here he was a candy-store philosopher, serving up Biblical morsels, Talmud tidbits, and tales of Glusk with every bag of jawbreakers.

"How long will you be gone this time, Harold?" Sally asked, her whole brow wrinkled now.

I'm a cad, Harold thought, *but I can't really tell her because this is an open-ended story.* "I don't know Sally."

Sarah steered the conversation to safe ground, gossiping about people they all knew in the building. No one brought up the subject of Nazis through the brisket, salad, potato *knishes*. cake, fruit, and coffee. But the way Sally forced her words during the few times she joined the dinner table talk told Harold that she was eaten up inside by his Yorkville announcement. He wasn't happy either, although he took part in the conversation. Sally's long silences wore on him even as he tried to fill the slack. *I love her, damn it. And she loves me too. But we never tell. Instead we torture one another.*

Saul, sitting across the table from Harold, was the only one who wanted to talk about Nazis. "It's not an adventure, kiddo," the reporter said to the 17-year-old. "I could get hurt. And I really, really, really want to come back to Sally."

Sally turned, grabbed his face, and pulled him to her for a big kiss.

❧

Harold emerged from the subway at the corner of York Ave. and East 85th St., looking at a sea of grey and brown buildings cascading down to the East River. The houses looked the same as anywhere in the city but the atmosphere was different. Not the air but the sounds, no English being spoken, only German. The signs on the buildings were all in German. *Hell, I can almost see men prancing around in lederhosen. But Germans are people, real people like Frenchmen, or Russians, or Chinese. Only the language is different.* He was standing right next to a bakery, a German bakery from the signs in the window, but the bread smelled the same as in The Bronx. A yeasty, doughy smell with hints of cinnamon wafted out whenever the door was opened. *Why do I feel uncomfortable when I hear German, when I speak German? It didn't used to be this way, when I spoke German with my dad. It's because of the politics, because of the Nazis.* Harold stared at a building across the street, a big building with a big sign. *Amerikadeutscher Volksbund*, it said. The sign was accompanied by a blood-red swastika flag. The headquarters of the German American Bund was not just another nondescript Yorkville building. The sign transformed it into a malevolent monster of a building, occupied by death and destruction. The flag, hanging dead-center over the entrance, was the mouth, dripping scarlet gore from swastika fangs.

෯

On a raw Saturday afternoon in early November, under a slate-grey sky with the air offering the cold promise of winter, Harold found an apartment in Yorkville. A fourth floor walk-up, it had been listed in the *World Journal* classified by the superintendent of the larger building next door. A plump man whose heavy jowls shook, he introduced himself in a pronounced German accent. "My *namen* is Georg Willknecht. Let us go look at the apartment. It is at the top of this fire escape." He pointed out the window of his first floor flat to the metal stairs which led to the top of the neighboring tenement. "I won't make you use the outside stairs the first time." He laughed, his belly shimmering while a few strands of thin blond hair jumped up and down on his mostly bald head.

"Of course, *Herr* Willknecht," Harold began, his German accent faltering a bit from nerves, "I am only a young man from Germany who has not been in New York many months, but those stairs would be *schwer* in this weather." His accent grew steadier as he became calmer, but did he need it? Throwing in a few German words like *schwer*, difficult, might be enough. *This super, Willknecht, does not appear to be an educated man.*

"*Nein, nein, Herr* Appel," Willknecht said. The big man continued to chuckle as the two walked outside and entered the building next door. "I made a joke. Please call me Georg. Where are you from in Germany? How long have you been in this country?"

"I came from Frankfurt nine months ago. I could find no work there, but I was not happy to leave. These are exciting times in Germany."

"*Ja*, I wish I was there," Willknecht said, switching to broken German as he let Harold into a tiny loft apartment, converted from an attic. "I lived in Frankfurt for two years, Herr Appel. It was after the war but I have fond memories. Did you ever go to *Das Spritzerhaus*? Now there was a proper beerhall. I wonder if it still exists."

"*Bitte* Georg, call me Harold. I don't recall a place by that name but I did not like beer when I was younger." He looked through the small flat, opening the icebox, examining the tiny oven, opening and closing the door to the white-tiled bathroom with modern fixtures, all the while deliberately avoiding further questions about Frankfurt, a city he knew only from his father's rambling reminisces. "Some work has been done in here recently," he said, pointing to the toilet.

"Yes, the owner decided to expand the number of rentals in the building. I personally did the tile work in the bathroom," the super said proudly. Harold, I am glad that you have chosen to live in the midst of Germans," Willknecht said while watching the reporter sign the three month lease. "It is easy in this country to lose the spirit of the Fatherland. Too easy, as I have seen even in my own family." His high forehead furrowed for a moment, then smoothed as if stormy memories had passed.

What is that all about? Harold wondered. *It might be worthwhile to get to know this man, to find out about troubles in German paradise.*

"There are several good beerhalls in Yorkville," Willknecht continued. "We will have to sample them if you are interested now."

"I'll look forward to that. I took a room in New Jersey when I first came to America. I was surrounded by Italians, Irishmen, and Polish. It has been so long since I was in the company of good German men, and women too, of course.

"Ha ha, yes, we must not forget the *frauleins*," Willknecht guffawed.

He then stared at the younger man—quizzically, Harold thought. *Oh no, is this where he says I'm no German? Is it my accent? What did I do wrong?*

"*Herr* Appel, have you become acquainted with the *Amerika-deutscher Volksbund* during your short time in this country?"

"I know of the Bund," Harold replied with great relief. "I went to a meeting of the *Ortsgruppe* Hudson County during my time in New Jersey. But I knew I wanted to live in Yorkville so I did not join.

"You will be welcome to join our group, upon verification of your German ancestry, of course," Willknecht said properly.

"Of course. There are procedures, as there should be. My papers are in order."

"I am sure they are," replied the Bund member. "Our next event is an Armistice Day parade for veterans of the *Reichsheer* living in New York. The authorities do not like German troops marching, but it is a solemn day for Germans as much as Americans."

"Are there enough veterans of the German army to have an impressive march?" Harold said. "I myself was not old enough to have fought in the war."

"*Ja*, there are thousands of us in Yorkville. There are many veterans in the Bund and we all long for Germany. I know you are young, but you must miss the Fatherland as we do. I must go now, Comrade Harold. *Heil* Hitler."

"*Heil* Hitler," Harold replied, momentarily startled by the seeming commonplaceness of the salutation. It wasn't routine for him and never would be, but he was certain he would be 'heiling' often. *All part of the job. I don't have to like it.*

The following Saturday morning was Harold's last in The Bronx. With the morning sun warming the air, the idea of moving was almost bearable. He was taking only those pieces of furniture he absolutely needed, his bed, some tables, a few chairs, some lamps, his typewriter, loading them all into the big Buick Roadmaster he had borrowed for the day.

Sally was helping, wrapping lightbulbs in newspaper and placing his lamps in the trunk while he fit his mattress into the wide back seat. "I know you'll be back soon," she said, embracing Harold from the rear, her arms locking about his waist. "And all in one piece, or else. Let's go upstairs. You make a pot of coffee while I finish putting your dishes in boxes. Then we can have those bagels

I brought. They're your favorites, from Glickman's." Kissing his shoulder, she reluctantly let him go.

The coffee was ready. Sally poured the steaming brew while Harold sliced the bagels and spread them with cream cheese. He carried the tray to the living room and placed it on the floor where the coffee table had been. Sally was quiet as she sat on the far end of the sofa.

Harold could sense her sadness, her fear of losing him. It tugged at his heartstrings and made him realize he too was afraid of losing her. "Sally, marry me," he whispered, forcing out the words.

Harold's proposal, so long awaited yet so unexpected, startled Sally, causing her to spill hot coffee all over the two of them. "Ow!" she yelped. "Yes, yes, I'll marry you, my darling." Stepping over the cup now sitting on the floor, she gave him a hot, wet hug.

"Look at us. We're soaked," laughed Harold.

"Let's get out of these wet things," Sally said. "We can lay them over the radiator. The clothes will be dry in an hour." She quickly lifted her sweater over her head and shimmied out of her plaid skirt to stand proudly in her bra and panties.

"What a loose woman," Harold said. "She undresses at the drop of a hat, or the tip of a cup. Come here doll. You're trembling."

"Not until you get out of those wet trousers, I won't."

Quickly taking off his pants, Harold held the slight brunette. Their mouths met and they fell as one onto the couch. They had made love on Harold's sofa before but never with such fervor. Their remaining clothes flew all over the room as they embraced front and back, up and down, backwards and forward. Never had they been closer, never filled with such passion. "Why did I wait so long to ask you to marry me? Harold cried.

"I've been asking myself the same thing," Sally answered.

❧

"Today is November sixth," Harold said, cuddling into his fiancée on the well-used sofa. "Let's get married in March, on your birthday. I can finish this Nazi story before then."

"I'll have time to plan everything. It's perfect," Sally smiled. "I can't wait to tell Mother."

Warning bells, not wedding bells, went off in Harold's head. Engagement notices in all the papers, with pictures. A demure bride standing next to a Nazi storm trooper, both giving the Hitler salute, was what he saw. The headline read 'Young Bund member takes Jewish bride' or 'Undercover reporter blows assignment under covers.' Sally couldn't tell her mother, or anyone else.

"Sally, doll, let's make it our secret for now. I don't want any announcement in the newspapers."

"Harold, do you really want to get married?" Sally tensed up. The cuddle they had shared on the sofa turned frozen, stiff, as she scrambled out of his arms.

"With all my heart Doll. But you're going to have to be patient with me until this Nazi thing is over. Please understand."

"I can't plan a wedding if I can't tell anyone," Sally said slowly and deliberately. "If it were any other kind of story I'd be mad as hell. But how can I be mad when you're going after Nazis?"

"You can't be mad," Harold said with relief although he knew, from the way she reacted, that she was hurt. His impulsive act, asking his girl to marry him, could have ruined his new story, not to mention endangered both their lives. Thank goodness Sally was a level-headed girl. She had waited a long time for him to pop the question. Now she'd have to wait a little longer to spread the good news. He'd make it up to her, somehow, he silently vowed.

They stiffly kissed, but Harold's mind was elsewhere. This story could be the big one, the one that won him a Pulitzer.

CHAPTER THREE

A SACRIFICE FOR THE FATHERLAND

MONDAY MORNING, HAROLD'S first in Yorkville, he woke before dawn, dressed in his work clothes, slouched down three flights, and headed toward the subway. At Second Avenue and 96th the smell of bacon wafting out of a dingy looking coffee shop captured him. *Jaeger's* flashed intermittently in dispirited purple neon above the door. He bought a copy of the paper from a newsboy out front and slipped inside. The headline screamed at him, "Germany to break Czechoslovakia." He slumped at a back table, ordered bacon and eggs, and scanned the article for any Nazi news.

"We've never had a leader like Hitler," said the white-haired waitress bringing his food. "If only there was one like him during the War."

Harold ate quickly and left the restaurant. *Do I look German? I don't want to look German.* He thought about what the old crone had said all through his train ride downtown. *Hitler, everything is about Hitler.*

ક

Al Scudari, Harold's new boss and the only one in the pressroom who knew his true identity, called him aside when he arrived for work. "I won't be hard on you, Apple, seeing as how you actually work across the street."

Harold knew the guys on the production side of the paper, the pressroom and circulation gang, looked at the reporters as pantywaists, not fit for an honest day's work. "Hey Scudari, I want you to treat me like an ordinary joe. I know the machinery. I worked at the Cleveland *Plain Dealer,* as a typesetter, in the summers, when I was in school."

"Then I won't worry about you," the supervisor said. The two men walked onto the floor of the printing plant to examine the different pieces of machinery, from the rumbling presses to the modern cutter-folder, which did the work of ten men.

"Who's this, Al?" a loud voice called out from out of the bowels of a broken down press.

"Max, come meet the new man," Scudari said to the giant who appeared, one segment at a time, on the oily floor. Feet emerged, great work shoe shod clodhoppers, then massive legs, attached to a thick waist and a hard belly. Broad shoulders clad in dirty brown came next, along with rolled-up sleeves barely surrounding two muscular biceps and forearms. A brown-haired bullet head followed, standing high over Harold.

Harold, startled by this apparition, could only mumble, "heeello."

"Max, this is Harold Appel, the new typesetter," Scudari said in a dismissive manner, as if the giant didn't matter in the hierarchy of the pressroom.

"Harold, Finnhandlerr will be your foreman," Scudari continued. "You go to him if you have any problems with the work."

Now why would Scudari make a guy like that a foreman? Harold wondered.

"Come. I *vill* show you *der* machine," the foreman growled in a thick German accent.

Aha, Finnhandlerr was German. Maybe the pressroom boss didn't like Germans. He followed the big man across the room to the typesetting machinery. The bench, where the operator sat in front of a big keyboard, was covered with wooden boxes. Harold tried to move one but the box, full of ink-encrusted lead type, was too heavy to lift. The foreman pushed Harold aside and swept the box to the floor with one swipe of his great arm. He was so fast that the old type barely rattled against the side of the box.

"*Ve vill* have to clean this," the giant grumbled.

"You are very strong, *Herr* Finnhandlerr," Harold said in his best German accent as he sat on the vacated bench.

Appel, it's time for you to go across the street and finish your paperwork," Scudari called. "Come back after lunch and we'll see how you do on the machine."

≪⑤

Harold crossed the street to the World Journal Building but instead of going to personnel he made for the eighth floor and the city room, where he slipped into Arnold Aaron's office. "*Guten morgen, Herr* Aaron. *Wo bist du? Heil Hitler*," he said in his best New York German accent.

"Knock it off Apple," replied the editor, annoyance showing in his voice. "Everyone knows how much you love *der Fuehrer*. How's it going in Yorkville? Have you made any contacts yet?" Aaron leaned back in his chair and pushed his reading glasses down his long nose, the better to see the annoying reporter standing in front of his cluttered desk.

"One day on the job and I've already been invited to a Bund meeting," boasted Harold. "Am I good or what?"

"When can I expect the first story then, hotshot?"

"In about a week, Chief. Right after the Bund Armistice Day march. After all, the World War ended on the eleventh hour, of the eleventh day, of the eleventh month for everyone, not just the

Americans, British, and French. At least that's the way Willknecht, my source for everything German, explained it to me."

"The krauts are celebrating the armistice. They're crazy. They lost the war."

"That's true, Chief," Harold replied. "But they don't see it that way. Are you ready for this? Willknecht says the Jews caused them to lose the War. And my biggest problem is going to be right here at the paper. The guy I'm working for in the pressroom is German."

"Scudari's not German. He's Italian."

"Yeah. He's the big boss, but my foreman is as German as they come and if he hates Jews as much as Willknecht does I could be in for some rough sledding."

"Can you handle him, Apple?"

"Yeah, I can handle him Chief." But Harold had doubts. He didn't know if he could manipulate so rough and tough a man. He had worked on other tough men throughout his reporting career, and had indeed persuaded Aaron, the toughest of them all, into giving him a shot at the job of reporter. *Yeah, I'm a real charmer,* Harold thought as he said goodbye to his real boss. He ought to be able to get along with a German giant.

On his way out of the newsroom Harold stopped at the wire service ticker. The international service had an item from France. It read 'Ernst vom Rath, third secretary of the German Embassy in Paris, was shot this morning by a Polish Jew. The German Government and Party view this provocation seriously. *Reichsfuehrer* Hitler vows revenge against the Jewish enemy of the *Reich.*' Harold read the dispatch over quickly, then again slowly, carefully, alert for nuance. *Hitler vows revenge,* he thought. *He means it too. But will it play in New York?*

Harold took the elevator to the lobby, deep in thought about the German response to the shooting of a very minor diplomat. "This is just the excuse Hitler wants," he muttered to himself.

"An excuse for what?"

"Huh." Harold woke from a daze and found himself in the lobby face to face with his old friend and fellow reporter, Pat O'Rourke.

"Hitler doesn't need any excuses," O'Rourke said. "We all know he's crazy. You, on the other hand, do need an excuse. You didn't show up for work this morning. I had to rewrite the weekend police reports all by myself. And you look a mess. Don't they teach you how to dress in The Bronx? I was going to ask you to join me for lunch but they don't serve derelicts in the places I go."

Harold; dressed in old pants, a blue flannel shirt, and an old overcoat against the cold; could never have competed with his friend's natty ways even at the best of times. "I'm just dressed for honest labor, old son. I don't wear my paycheck on my back, like some people I know." And he slapped his pal on the back.

O'Rourke, wearing a fine, camelhair coat over an expensive grey suit and an impeccably knotted red silk tie, pushed his stylishly cut black hair off his forehead in a practiced gesture and said in a light brogue, "I just want to make this a classier place to work."

"Let's get a corned beef at Ozzie's," Harold said. "It's fast and you don't have to be dressed to the nines to get in."

"All right, my sneaky friend, what's going on?" O'Rourke asked after they got their food and found a table. "I saw you slinking out of Aaron's office and making a beeline for the elevator. If you hadn't stopped to read the ticker I'd never have caught up with you."

"It's a new assignment, Pat. It came right from the top, Corkwright himself. I'm infiltrating the German American Bund. And I'm working in the pressroom as a cover."

"Hey, I know about the Bund," O'Rourke exclaimed. "I have a friend from college whose old man is mixed up with them. He's the lawyer you read about in the paper, always bailing Nazis out of jail."

"Aha, a lead already. When can I talk to your buddy?" Harold looked at his watch and hurried to finish his sandwich. "I've got to get back to my cover job in the pressroom. I'll talk to you later."

❧

"Hello Doll. How was your day?" Harold spoke to Sally in a low voice, his hand cupped around the receiver while standing, back to the door, in a closed phone booth built into the rear wall of Jaeger's Restaurant. He knew calling her from Yorkville was risky, but his need to hear her voice outweighed the risk.

"Oh Harold, it was the hardest day of my life. I wanted to tell everyone about us and *couldn't*," Sally wailed. "That was a mean thing you did, making me promise not to tell. When I got to work Pam Baker was blabbing about her wedding plans and I couldn't say a word!"

"It's just for a few more days, doll," Harold said in what he hoped was a soothing tone. "I'm making real progress. I'm already an official German, so anointed by the superintendent of my building, who wants me to join the Bund."

"Please be careful Harold," Sally pleaded.

"Don't worry Sal. I'm in Yorkville, not Germany." Harold knew the edge of enthusiasm was in his voice, but he couldn't help it.

Harold left the phone booth and the restaurant, heading up York Avenue to 89th. He turned in at the entrance to the larger building next door to his brownstone, the building where he was known as a loyal German, and knocked on Willknecht's door.

"*Herr* Appel. What can I do for you tonight?" the super said in heavily accented English, upon opening his door. "Is everything correct in your flat?"

Harold hesitated. Willknecht seemed stiff and formal, not at all the gregarious German of Saturday. "Yes everything is fine," he reassured. "You were so kind to me before. I had hoped to have a moment of your time this evening."

"But of course." Suddenly the man seemed hospitable. "Come in. We are all in the kitchen. Will you have some coffee and cake?"

Harold walked into Willknecht's apartment, perplexed by the man's changing demeanor.

Willknecht drew Harold in and slammed the door, shutting out America. In this sheltered place the German could deny that he was in exile from the Fatherland. Pictures of scenic Germany lined the walls, hiding faded flowered wallpaper. Shelves were crowded with mementoes of trips made long ago, then stuffed into a steamer trunk for the trip to a foreign land. The tired, battered furniture, heavy in an Old World way, contributed to the Teutonic flavor of the flat. In a place of honor was an oil painting of a very large man with long blond hair, dressed in leather, and carrying a spear. A plaque at the bottom labeled the figure 'Arminius the German.' The super led Harold through this shrine of Germandom to the kitchen, a more utilitarian room, where the only note of luxury was a large console radio, tuned to sentimental *lieder*.

"*Herr* Appel, I want you to meet my wife, Helga," the janitor said as a large severe looking woman, her brown hair caught in a bun behind her head, turned from the sink, wiping her work-reddened hands on her dirty apron.

"Well, this is the *Herr* Appel I have heard so much about today," the woman said while coughing consumptively. "And he is from Frankfurt?"

"Yes *Frau* Willknecht," Harold said to the imposing woman. "I am a typesetter, but I could not find work in Germany as the number of newspapers has declined under the *Fuehrer*. Many other parts of the economy are booming under our great leader but my poor specialty is not one of them. I was forced to leave the Fatherland to follow my trade. When I have saved a substantial sum of money I will return."

Willknecht, all rapt attention while Harold spoke, turned to a young woman sitting at the kitchen table, studiously reading a movie magazine. "*Herr* Appel, I would introduce you to my daughter, Christiana. Daughter, I want you to rise and greet our guest properly, as I have taught you."

At her father's urging the girl stood, revealing the full figure of a woman, and gave Harold a small curtsey. Harold was taken aback by her beauty; by her flaxen hair done in braids, her smoldering green eyes, and her oh-so-tight sweater. Had she been dressed in traditional German garb, she could easily have modeled for a German travel poster.

∽

"*Guten tag Herr* Appel," the girl said.

"Please call me Harrold," the reporter stammered, flustered by her beauty.

"OK, I don't care one way or the other." She waved her hand in annoyance.

"Christiana, that is no manner in which to speak to a guest," Willknecht admonished his daughter, but the girl looked anything but penitent as she returned her full attention to her magazine. "Please excuse her, *Herr* Appel. She is turning into an American. I blame myself." The girl continued to sit quietly, all but ignoring the others in the room, so the super turned to a more congenial subject. "Have you seen the latest issue of our Bund newspaper, the *Deutscher Weckruf und Beobachter*?"

"No, I haven't," Harold replied, lifting his eyebrows to feign interest. "I thought the Bund paper was called *The Free American*."

"That is the English version. It is very much shorter. Here is the real paper," the janitor said, handing Harold the tabloid. "I have some extras so you may keep that one. There is an excellent article about the forthcoming Armistice Day parade."

"Georg is going to march. He is a veteran," Helga said proudly. "He was wounded too, at the Argonne."

"It was not much of a hurt, just a flesh wound."

"Now Georg. You can be proud of it. You sacrificed for the Fatherland," the large woman sermonized. "He was shot in the butt, *Herr* Appel, and it's nothing to be ashamed of."

"All right Helga. *Herr* Appel has heard enough of my great wound," a red-faced Willknecht complained to his wife. He then turned to Harold and continued. "There has never been a parade for German veterans of the Great War in New York. We of the *Volksbund* believe that the only objection to our parade will come from the Jews."

Harold wondered in what form the German thought those objections would come. He was about to ask when Helga interrupted with the offer of refreshments.

"Have some cake, *Herr* Appel. Would you like coffee or *schnapps*?

"Thank you, I will have a drink," Harold said. "It's been a long, trying day."

Helga served the cake while her husband poured the liquor. "The best thing that Jew-lover Roosevelt has done," Willknecht exclaimed, "was ending Prohibition. *Schnapps* makes life a little more bearable. Christiana, you can have one small drink, then away with you. The adults want to talk."

The girl quickly finished her drink, gave Harold a cross look, and left the room.

"She is eighteen years old, *Herr* Apple," Helga said after draining her own glass. "Where does the time go? Soon she will finish school then some young man will come and take her away from us." Helga looked at Harold as if he might be a good suitor for the obstinate girl.

"We all grow older *Frau* Willknecht," Harold said to the older woman. "I'm sure when the time comes a proper man will present himself." He turned to Willknecht, eager to change the topic and deflect attention from him being that proper man. "Georg, I'm interested in learning more about the *Ortsgruppe* in Yorkville. I'm anxious to meet some good German men, for the purpose of maintaining my attachment to the Fatherland, and to socialize with the right element."

Willknecht filled Harold's empty glass. "Then I will have to introduce you to my comrades," the janitor said, his face becoming animated. "We meet at the Yorkville Casino on Wednesday for a *gemutlicht* evening, good beer and good conversation. You will join us, no?"

"Harold, if you are interested in meeting some German women we can accommodate you," Helga said in a practiced tone, as if she was a professional matchmaker. "I am sure there are some older members of the *Maedelschaft* who would love to meet a handsome, eligible man from the Fatherland. You are eligible?"

"Oh yes. I am unattached," Harold said with a straight face, feeling both guilty at betraying Sally and relieved that Helga didn't want him for Christiana.

After a few more minutes of conversation Harold excused himself, pleading the lateness of the hour. Walking next door to his sparsely furnished rooms, he congratulated himself on a good start to his under-cover assignment. Willknecht was an excellent contact. The reporter hoped other Bund members would accept him as easily.

As Harold got ready for sleep he thought, *playing a German isn't hard. After all, I know the language.* As he nodded off the reporter remembered some of Willknecht's off-hand comments about Jews. He remembered saying two disgusting words, 'Heil Hitler,' and he woke up. He had said them earlier in Aaron's office but they didn't bother him as when he said them to the super. Those words, his and Willknecht's, kept him up for hours, lying in an unfamiliar room, with strange shadows marching across the ceiling, like ghosts of German soldiers on Yorkville streets.

CHAPTER FOUR

HAROLD BECOMES A STORM TROOPER

'GERMANY VOWS REVENGE on Jews if Envoy Dies,' the headline promised the next day. Harold saw it sooner than most, as he set the type for the story that ran on the front page. *Another threat from Berlin,* he thought as he worked the machine. *The question is will they believe it in London, Washington, and Paris? They should, after all that's gone on in Germany the last few years. I believe it, but who am I? Just a Jew from New York.*

Harold found his old typesetting skills returning. He settled into a routine of typing on the Linotype machine, a keyboard that was different from a normal typewriter. All the most frequently used letters were on the left. His mind wandered as he worked, but after two mistakes, and two rundowns, as typesetters called the corrections, he didn't make any more.

Harold's biceps were aching by the time work was over, the run put to bed. Outside there was a cold drizzle falling. The asphalt glistened under the reflection of the street lights. In between lights pools of blackness ruled. The reporter put his head down and turned up his collar to walk the half block to the subway. He caught a train uptown to Yorkville, trudged up the station's steep concrete steps at 86th and Lexington, and went into a little market to buy supper and call Sally.

He put a nickel into the phone, heard a distant tone, and dialed Sally's number. "Hello Doll. I missed you today."

"Me too, Harold," The girl answered breathlessly. "Just talk to me. Tell me what you would do if we were together."

"Sally! I'm at a public phone," Harold gasped.

"Oh Harold," Sally pouted.

The reporter knew the expression that would be on her face, her eyes scrunched up, her brow knotted, her bright red lips in a tight circle. He loved that look.

"Pam Baker told me about a little game she plays on the phone with her boyfriend. But we can't play if you're in public."

"What about you, Sal? Are your folk's home?"

"I'm all alone Harold. Mom, Dad, and Saul went to a meeting at the synagogue. They'll be home soon. Wait a minute. The meeting is about the Bund; something about a counter demonstration on Friday." Suddenly Sally was more interested in where her parents were than in playing games with her boyfriend.

"Oh no," Harold said. "I hope they're not planning to come to Yorkville."

"I don't know, Harold. I hope not. I'll tell you tomorrow, I guess."

"OK Doll. I'm going to get some words down on paper now, then get into bed and think about you."

"I wish I could be with you," Sally whispered into the phone. "Bye-bye love."

Harold went into the dank night, eager to return to his warm apartment where he could think about Sally and write about the Bund. "I'm doing this for her," he muttered. "Can't let the Nazis get a toehold on this side of the ocean." Turning the corner onto

York Avenue, his coat collar turned up against the slow drizzle, he saw a familiar figure coming out of Willknecht's building. Flattening his body against the wall and hunching his head down into his coat, he hoped to become invisible. He dared another glance up the street. In the dim light of a streetlamp a gigantic figure was hurrying away. From the back he swore it was Finnhandlerr. *He must live in the neighborhood,* the reporter thought, *with all the other Germans, and I'll bet ten bucks he's in the Bund.* Then the big man was gone. Harold turned into his building, went upstairs, shucked off his wet coat, and started to write.

'America's Nazis, the German American Bund, feel that New York is ready for a German Armistice Day parade. This will not be the usual march of doughboys down Fifth Avenue, past crowds waving Old Glory, accompanied by patriotic speeches by politicians. No, this will be a march down York Avenue of the Kaiser's finest, wearing *pickelhaube*, those Prussian spiked helmets. All participants will be recent residents of the United States who fought against our American boys in the late war. The march will not, on this most solemn day, honor the war dead. Rather, it is intended to infuse Yorkville with Nazi attitudes, including anti-Semitism and German superiority.'

Not exactly objective journalism but maybe it'll get by Aaron, knowing how he feels about the Nazis. He slept and dreamt. Barrel-chested men, large-bellied men, brown-uniformed men, their bald heads concealed by *picklehaube*, pursued him around the tables of a *bierhall*. He was caught and forced to drink pitcher after pitcher of bitter German beer. He pissed in his pants. Yellow pee dripped on the floor in the shape of a Star of David. The Germans laughed.

⌀

Cigarette smoke and snatches of boisterous song drifted up the stairwell as Harold and Georg descended into the basement of the old building housing the Yorkville Casino. They had come to a weathered door at street level, knocked twice, were eyed from a high-up peephole, and were admitted down a long stairway.

As they entered the large barroom below, Harold could make out the words sung by many voices, *"Unsere fahnen flatter nuns voran."*

Always their flag, thought Harold. As the music pulsed through his head he felt bitter about the Swastika flag, and what kind of symbol it had become. Why they couldn't find gratitude in making a good living in a country they chose. It made his blood boil.

A full hundred men populated the barroom. Most sat at little tables, but a large group clustered around a piano. These were the singers, providing the promised *gemutlicheit.* Two barmaids rushed around the room, laboring to fill ever empty beer steins. Willknecht, flushed with the cold of the streets, elbowed through the crowded room, exchanging greetings as he went. Harold followed.

"Hello comrades. I bring a friend; a gentleman newly arrived from Frankfurt, who is interested in joining our merry group. Herr Appel is living in a building I supervise."

"Georg, Georg, what are we going to do with you?" said a sad looking, thin faced man wearing a shirt that had once been white and a narrow black tie. "If he is a German citizen he cannot join the *Volksbund.* You know that."

Willknecht looked crestfallen. He turned to Harold as if to explain or apologize, but was interrupted by the stranger, who turned to Harold. *Herr* Appel, I am Rudolf Franz, *Schriftsfuehrer* of *Ortsgruppe* Yorkville. I take minutes at meetings and watch out for our impulsive friend here. Welcome to New York. What is your line of work, if I may ask?

"I am delighted to be here among men of good German spirit, *Herr* Franz. Please call me Harold. As for what I do, I am a typesetter by trade. I could not find work at home and, since I speak English and have no family to hold me back, I decided to come to

New York. It is well known that there is much work in a city with so many newspapers and printing plants. In fact, I recently found a position at the *World Journal*."

"So you work at their printing plant. Do you know our *Ordung Dienst Leiter*, Max Finnhandlerr?"

"Yes, I know *Herr* Finnhandlerr," Harold said mildly as a way to hide his pride at knowing the giant was indeed a Nazi.

"Let me be frank with you Harold," Franz said in a matter-of-fact tone as if he was a bureaucrat rendering a government dictum. "The *Auslandamt*, the Party office in Berlin that deals with Germans living abroad, has forbidden us to have any German citizens as members of the *Volksbund*. During the time when the Fatherland is re-building its industrial might, the *Fuehrer* wishes no conflict with America. Hence, we speak English."

"I was wondering about that," Harold said. "I learned English in gymnasium but many others did not." The reporter in Harold noted that the *Volksbund* took orders from Nazi headquarters in Germany.

"Yes, it is a bother at times, but we all speak English at work so it is not a hardship," Franz said in a more expansive manner. "And we do not leave you out in the cold as far as belonging. You can join one of our auxiliaries without being on the main roster of members. Since you work with Max Finnhandlerr you should join the *Ordung Dienst*, our service order. We have patterned it after the SA at home. Many of the young men here belong and recommend it highly. The training may be harsh, almost military, but the feeling of pride you receive from belonging to a uniformed order is worthwhile."

A chorus of ascent was heard from the half dozen men clustered around Franz. They all pressed forward to introduce themselves to Harold, their prospective new comrade. *I'll never remember them all*, Harold thought despairingly as the names flew. Zollner, Schroeder, Everhardt, and Schmidt were all names he heard but could not attach to faces, handsome young faces of men who liked to don brown uniforms and play at being soldiers of the *Fuehrer*.

"I am thirsty. Bring beer," Willknecht cried to the nearest barmaid, and he and Harold joined the young Nazis in downing mug after mug of bitter German lager.

Talk turned to recent events in the Fatherland. "It is time to eliminate the parasites from Germany," said Franz heatedly. Everhardt and Schmidt and all the rest could not agree more. "If the diplomat dies I predict dire times for all Jews in Germany," the *Schriftsfuehrer* pontificated.

Harold knew that Franz was correct in his assessment of German reaction to the Vom Rath shooting. He had checked the international wire before leaving the newspaper for the day. Although the envoy was holding onto life in a Paris hospital, and his Jewish assailant was in jail, Germans were already attacking Jews. A mob in Mannheim had torched that city's main synagogue. Harold had seen pictures of that building, an architectural monument. Those rioting Germans were barbarians.

At nine o'clock the room quieted. The piano player trilled a Wagnerian fanfare. Three men in brown-shirted uniforms entered the Casino, swaggering down the stairs forcefully, as if they had a God-given right to be on this particular patch of earth. They were led by none other than Max Finnhandlerr, resplendent in brown pants flaring out below his waist, brown shirt drawn tightly across his massive chest, a black belt around his waist and one shoulder, a peaked commander's hat bearing a German eagle insignia on his already large head, and the swastika proudly displayed on his shoulder. The troopers came to attention, the heavy music stopped, and the leader spoke in funeral tones. "With sadness in my heart I must announce the death of an upstanding German man, cut down in his prime solely because he served the *Fuehrer*. We are grief-stricken as we join with all Germans in mourning Ernst Vom

Rath in Paris. The Party appeals to all Germans to remain calm in the face of this senseless Jewish provocation."

"Death to the Jews!" someone cried as shocked silence dissolved into uproar. Finnhandlerr, his chest swelled with pleasure at the results of his oratory, descended into the melee to console his agitated comrades.

Harold was one of the agitated but for opposite reasons. His shoulders shrank as he heard 'death to the Jews.' He wanted to be invisible.

At the front of the crowd, the large man turned, and with commanding presence and stern voice, his speech bursting forth in the staccato rhythm of a storm trooper, announced, "Our march Friday will be dedicated to Third Secretary Vom Rath. Certainly he is a hero to rival the legendary Arminius in the annals of Germandom."

"*Jawohl, jawohl*, to Vom Rath," the crowd shouted.

"A sad day for Germandom, friend Max," Franz said as the big man lowered his bulk onto a rickety wooden chair at the *Schriftsfuehrer's* table.

"Yes it is Rudolf, but we will have our revenge on the Jews," Finnhandlerr promised solemnly. As he looked around the table he spied Harold sitting quietly next to Willknecht. "Harold Appel, what are you doing here?"

"Ha. A lot you know Max," Willknecht laughed, breaking the tense mood so carefully constructed by the uniformed man. "Harold is right under your nose and you don't even see him as German."

Harold spoke quickly, hoping to appease his boss and erstwhile storm troop leader. "I recently moved to Yorkville from New Jersey. I am living in a building supervised by *Herr* Willknecht. I had my heart set on joining the Bund, only now I find that I cannot because I am a German citizen."

Finnhandlerr looked darkly at Harold as if he could not

believe that his job, his livelihood, was being mixed with his true life, his real feelings as a follower of the *Fuehrer*. Then his face lightened. He grew enthusiastic. "Why not?" he asked, of no one in particular. "If you cannot join the parent then you shall join the child. I will bring membership papers to work tomorrow and get measurements for your uniform. Welcome to the Service Order, *Herr* Appel,"

The speed by which he was enlisted in the *Ordung Dienst* stunned Harold. Finnhandlerr was evidently a man of great zeal and passion. That energy was not tempered by reflection, for none of the Germans had solid proof of Harold's Germanness. They took his word for it, showing great trust or great foolishness. As Harold was congratulated by those around the table, a cold shiver overcame him. He was now a Nazi storm trooper.

CHAPTER FIVE

THE FAMILY KNOWS POGROMS

TRUE TO HIS word, Finnhandlerr brought the application at first light. The sun rising cast a dull red pall through the high grimy windows of the printing plant and Harold enrolled as a storm trooper. "We will have the ceremony later, but signing puts you under discipline," the large man said, straightening his recruit's collar with a rough hand.

Rough yet tender, Harold thought, his mind reeling from the contradictory touch of this bear of a man and the devilish light of his surroundings. *He almost yanked me off my feet as he fixed my imaginary uniform then held me as if I was precious to him. I am, but only as a soldier in his Order.*

"You must dress better, Appel," Finnhandlerr lectured. "We demand sharp creases at all times, in uniform or out. Storm troopers represent the Fatherland." The OD leader was caught in an early shaft of sunlight, creating a grotesque shadow on the far wall, an image of Satan rising, crowned with the horns of a swastika.

Feeling dirty from the experience, Harold escaped across the street to the city room during his morning break. He felt the need to talk to real people. "I'm under discipline, Chief," he said to Aaron. "I have to do whatever Finnhandlerr wants."

"Anything, Harold?" Aaron exclaimed. "He's your boss in the pressroom. But anything?"

"Yes chief. Finnhanderr is high up in the Bund. They have something called the *Fuehrer Prinzip*. All Nazis swear fealty to Hitler, he delegates authority, and it comes down the line to me. At least that's the way Finnhandlerr explained it. He's my little *fuehrer*."

The next time Harold found himself free of Finnhandlerr was after work. The OD leader wanted Harold to ride the subway home to Yorkville with him but the reporter demurred, saying he had to buy essentials for his new apartment. Finnhanderr strode up the street, grumbling about the sorry state of new recruits and how Appel would lose his rebelliousness in training.

Harold walked to a pay phone and called Sally.

"Harold, when am I going to see you?"

"I'm coming home Sunday, Sweetie. I need a little normal conversation. You can't imagine what talking with Jew-haters all the time is like. Those Germans, those Nazis, are obsessed with Jews. 'TheYids did this. The Kikes control that.' Jews don't talk about being Jewish all the time. I, for example, talk about everyday things, like how I slept, what I had for lunch, how much I love you."

"That's sweet, Harold. I can talk about that all day." Sally's voice lilted. He recalled her gentle smile and the way she played with a lock of her hair when she was pleased. "But don't they have normal talk too? Don't they live normal lives?" she said.

"I suppose they do with their families. But when the men get together all they talk about is their hatred of, well, me. And I don't like it. It makes my skin crawl."

"Harold, remember why you're in Yorkville," Sally admonished. He knew she was right. He did want to get the story, and please his editor, and maybe win a writing prize. More than that, he wanted to change these people, to destroy their world view, and if he couldn't do that, to destroy them. It was personal for Harold.

"All right Sal, I'll remember. And do you remember you wanted to tell your folks we're getting married? Well, we can do it on Sunday."

"Harold," Sally squealed. "How can I wait till Sunday?"

"Hey Doll, I want to be there too. Now what did your folks say about that meeting the other day?"

"I'm glad you reminded me. My father wants to talk to you. Wait I'll go get him. And Harold, Aunt Annie called last night, she's been trying to reach you all week. I'm going to be late for class. Love you but I've got to go."

Harold stayed on the phone, shivering slightly in the cool evening air, waiting for Israel Schwartz to pick up.

◈

Drab wooden buildings, weathered and worn, were jammed together in a too small place in the middle of the town. But this was not downtown; it was no-where town, where the outcasts of the village lived their lives. To the *goyim* of the village, life in the alleys would have been intolerable. To those who were forced there, who knew no other existence, it was bearable, even uplifting. They lived the life of the spirit. They were led by their rebbe, the Hasidic master of all the Gluskers, Rabbi Dovid Max Shnorer. The *Hasids* of Glusk knew joy beyond physical, they knew the joy of living in G-d's manner.

This was where Israel was born, in 1881, in the *shtetle* of Glusk. It was just a village in Byelorussia, fifty miles south of Minsk on the road to Kiev, but it was so much more to the Gluskers. Life in the Jewish quarter of the village was acceptable for some and tolerable for others, but not impossible for any. They lived for the *Shabbos*, the day when all men could be kings and the

Messiah seemed a little closer to coming. Israel's father was one of the chosen, a *Schechter*, a kosher butcher, a prosperous man by the terms of the *shtetel*, a man who supported his synagogue. He could afford to give his family some of the finer things. This was Israel Schwartz's birthright. But, on the very day he was born, Alexander the Second, the enlightened *Czar* who protected the Jews, died, and suddenly all Jews became beggars, even the ones who could afford silver candlesticks and meat on the *Shabbos* table. In the eyes of Nicholas, the new *Czar*, a Jew was a Jew was a Jew, and the best should have no more than the least. He offered the Jews to the peasants for sport, unleashing waves of pogroms, organized massacres, which crashed down on the Jews as tidal waves of blades and burnings. Life in the ghetto, never easy, became unbearable. In 1894 the *Schechter* decided to protect his oldest son and scraped together the money to send him to the *goldene medina*, the golden land of America.

Rabbi Shnorer gave Israel his blessing on the Saturday before he left. "You will go to this new land, where there are no Russians, to live a decent life, free of fear, and free to follow the commandments of G-d. But remember, Israel, the words of the prophet, 'All Flesh is Grass.' Do not become prideful in your new home. Remember the sufferings of Glusk and how you dealt with them. Then you will certainly be prepared to live a godly life." The thirteen-year-old boy, fresh from his bar mitzvah, certainly intended to follow the instructions of his rebbe to the fullest. A long wagon ride to Poland, a train trip to the port in Germany, weeks spent in steerage on an old ship even through a calm crossing, the loneliness of being away from family and friends, and not hearing Yiddish, changed him.

Israel arrived in New York as a not so innocent lad, and his only talent, that of a *yeshiva bocher*, a young scholar, was not so useful in his new world. He lived with cousins, learned English, and succumbed to the temptations of America. After a short time studying at Talmud Torah, he threw away his skullcap and fringes and enrolled at public school. He had money, the money his father had given him to start a new life in America. He invested in a pushcart and, after school, began buying and selling clothes, junk, candy, small stuff. By the time he was twenty he had enough saved to buy a little candy store in The Bronx. "The yeshiva boy doesn't forget his past. I wanted to follow the 613 Commandments and make my father and Rabbi Shnorer proud," Israel always said. "So on Saturdays I rest from selling Walnettos, jaw breakers, Tootsie Rolls, and study Torah."

"Good evening my boy. How are things in Yorkville?" Israel said over the telephone. "That editor of yours is *meshugenah*, sending a good Jewish boy to join the Nazis. I want to talk to you about them. The other night we went to a meeting at *Mishnah Torah*, that synagogue over on the Grand Concourse. People were there from all over The Bronx. It was about the parade the Nazis are having tomorrow. The meeting was run by a man named Goldwasser, from the Jewish War Veterans. He's organizing a march on Lexington Avenue at the same time as the Nazi march. Saul wants to go and who am I to stop him? In the old country we never stood up to the Cossacks when they came to loot our houses. In America we shouldn't let those monsters have their way. Harold, I know you're going to be there, marching with the Nazis. Watch out for Saul. Don't let him get hurt."

"Izzy, yeah, I'll watch for Saul but I can't be seen with him or talk to him or anything. Remember, I'm a German to these people. I hate Jews." Harold despised the way that must sound to his future father-in-law. How could he refuse to help his soon to be little brother? "Izzy, make sure Saul knows to stay away from me. Better yet, don't let him go."

"I can't stop him, but he knows, Harold. He knows to stay

away from you. He's proud of what you're doing. You be careful too. You're a member of the family."

"Thank you Izzy." Harold was part of the family, yet he had to turn his back on Saul. That was not how family acts. He would call an Irishman a mick to his face, am Italian a dago, or a Jew a kike, but was never serious. They were just shorthand words, spoken in jest. But those Germans, these krauts, were serious. They would kill us all if they could. It was enough to make Harold throw up, as his father did when he was beat up because he was a Jew.

Thoughts of Sam made Harold think of others in the family, of Aunt Annie Appel, who had been trying to reach him, and her husband Frank. He dialed Algonquin 5-5729. The phone rang and rang, giving Harold more time to think about his aunt and uncle, the very ones who introduced him to Sally, the love of his life. Uncle Frank, one of Sam Apple's older brothers, had emigrated from Germany after finishing dental school in Frankfurt. He married Annie Schwartz, youngest sister of Israel, brought to the *goldene medina* as a baby when the *Schechter* finally gave up on life in the old country and moved his whole family from Glusk to New York. Thus the marriage of Harold Apple and Sally Schwartz would be a commonplace; the families were already united, a mish-mash of confusion between Cleveland and New York, Frankfurt and Glusk.

Annie and Frank Appel lived in a ten story apartment on Davidson Avenue in The Bronx. It was a new building with all the modern conveniences, an elevator for people, a dumb-waiter for bundles, an electric Frigidaire, and a gas oven; an appropriate home for a dentist who enjoyed the good things in life. "Teeth are teeth," Frank liked to say. "It doesn't matter if they're German or American. A dentist makes money wherever he is." Money meant the good life in America instead of the constant worry about life or death that Frank had left in Europe.

Where was Uncle Frank when my dad was getting beat up in

school? Harold wondered. *Aren't big brothers supposed to protect little brothers? Maybe he did. Maybe he was off learning about life and teeth. Or maybe he had his own problems with bullies. No one talks much about Germany in my family, not like Sally's family where everything is Glusk, Glusk, Glusk.*

Harold's reverie was broken by the high-pitched shriek of his aunt by marriage, soon to be aunt by two marriages. "Hello. Who is this? Harold? Where have you been? Why haven't you called? I was out in the hall when I heard the telephone. It goes **brinnng**, **brinnng**, just like a fire alarm. Let me catch my breath. Whew. That's better. Harold, your parents are coming. On Saturday. Will we have the honor of seeing you or will you be too busy with that newspaper of yours?"

"They are? Well of course I'll see them." Harold managed to sneak a reply into Aunt Annie's oration. "I'll be there Sunday." *Wow, my folks are coming,* he thought as he hung up the phone. *Why didn't Sally tell me? Maybe she wanted to surprise me. Boy oh boy, will we surprise them when we announce our engagement.*

On his way to the subway Harold stopped to pick up a *World Journal. Oh my, this is horrible.* A story said the Nazis were reacting to the death of the diplomat in Paris with a pogrom to rival any in history. Synagogues were burning in large cities and small. The Nuremberg fire department had itself started the blazes which consumed every Jewish house of worship in that city. Thousands of Jewish-owned businesses had been destroyed. A hundred Jews were dead already and thirty thousand had been thrown into the Dachau and Buchenwald concentration camps. The Nazi propaganda chief, Goebbels, had dubbed the event *Kristallnacht,* the Night of Glass, for the shards that covered streets in Jewish districts throughout Germany.

Leave it to rat-face Goebbels to find a poetic name for this night,

Harold thought. *Krauss would know the story behind these oh so spontaneous riots,* he decided, thinking of his reporter friend in Germany for the first time in days. *But where is Krauss? He's Jewish. He could be dead or in a concentration camp. Or caught in a web of broken glass.* Tears welled in his eyes.

CHAPTER SIX

THE WAR BEGINS ON ARMISTICE DAY

IT WAS THE eleventh day of the eleventh month, twenty years since the Great War had ended. Harold woke in cold darkness from a dream of soldiers marching. Bayonets in place, they had crouched then charged up the stoop of his new building. They reached his floor, burst through his door, and surrounded him in bed. Then, miraculously their rifles turned to tubas and drums and coronets. They began playing. *It's Armistice Day.* The reporter came fully awake in terror, then relief. *Old men reliving past glories, but I'm a modern man. I'll never be a soldier, never go to war. Modern men reason and talk, like Chamberlain at Munich. Then why hasn't anyone bothered to tell Hitler?* His mood turned back to dread. A red glow stole in the window, a reflection of burning German synagogues, carried over the vast ocean ahead of the sun, a reminder of what Hitler could do to modern man.

Finnhandlerr was at the plant, hammering on an old printing press, when Harold arrived for a half day of work. The big man, a thunderhead of a frown upon his face, looked like he was ready to go to war all by himself. "Comrade Harold, we have word of another parade in Yorkville this afternoon, a Jew parade. The police came to Franz last night and told him—nay, ordered him—to make room in front of the Turnhall for the Jews to march by. It turns my stomach. Yes, it makes me sick. The memory of Vom Rath will be desecrated by the very vermin who shot him down." The giant bowed his head in mourning for the diplomat, a man unknown to him yesterday.

"Now I have an assignment for you, an important assignment," Finnhandlerr said, placing his hands on Harold's shoulders. "I want you to be our eyes and ears. You will spy on the start of the Jew march. I need to know how many of them are invading Yorkville."

"Are you sure the Jews will be in Yorkville, *mein herr?* They are cowards. They could go elsewhere."

But Harold was not a spy. He was a double agent able to protect his friends by giving false information.

"Yes, they will be there," Finnhandlerr said with certainty. "The damn Jews are everywhere in New York. And the police protect them. But maybe, just maybe, if we get the right situation... 'It is the spectre of a people's fate—the haunting thought of falsehood and of wrong. The future in a land devoid of song—it is the past that whispers at the gate.'" Finnhandlerr said the doggerel slowly, intensely, meaningfully, as if Harold would automatically understand.

Harold nodded his head as if he agreed, figuring this was probably something that all Germans knew. He turned to his work, setting stories about *Kristallnacht* and listening to his *fuehrer* ranting about the Jews. *Poor, poor giant,* he thought, *longing for a life that never was—and will never be. If he was in Germany he'd be unemployed, on the street, a piece of trash. Or...he would join the ranks of the party, just as he has done here. The Nazis allow him to strut and prance and be important.*

Harold finished setting the early afternoon edition before

noon and went looking for his foreman. The big man was cleaning up the shop floor, heaving boxes of lead type onto shelves. The smell of printer's ink was heavy in the air. The typesetter's eyes watered, a long forgotten reaction to the odor. Finnhandlerr saw this and quickly led him away to a cleaner part of the plant. "I cry too at the stench of our trade," he said. "It is the price we pay for working here. But you are leaving? Good. I will see you soon, in front of the Germania Bookstore as we arranged."

Harold made his way out of the plant, to the clean air of the street. His eyes, swollen by the fumes, cleared slowly. *Finnhandlerr was gentle with me,* he thought. The lout has a soft side. Or maybe he was just being protective of one of his men, one who is doing an important job this afternoon. Suddenly there was a ringing in his ears. *Another effect of the smelly plant? No. I hear trumpets, massed horns, and now tubas among them.* He looked over his shoulder down to Fifth Avenue. *It's another parade. The city is full of them. It's the twentieth anniversary of the end of the Great War. A big deal.*

Harold walked the other way, toward Sixth Avenue, the uptown subway, and a short ride to 78th Street. He climbed from the platform to the sun-washed sidewalk at the corner of Lexington. It was just past noon but the police already had the street blocked to traffic. He headed north on Lexington. Two blocks from the subway he saw a group of men standing in front of a pharmacy. One of them held a large placard proclaiming them members of the Jewish War Veterans. Others held banners: Boycott German Goods, End Nazi Terror. *That's it,* the reporter thought. *That's the entire Jewish parade? Where are the bands, the floats, the veterans in uniform? Where are Saul and his Glusker buddies? They must be late, or maybe, just maybe, Finnhanderr got it wrong. It's not a parade. It's a protest. Maybe it'll be a small protest, much easier for the police to handle, much less chance of violence.* The afternoon sun was getting stronger. Harold unbuttoned his overcoat, turned right on 78th Street, and ran toward York.

Moses had spies, Harold remembered. *When the Jews first got near Canaan Moses sent twelve spies into the land. And ten were killed for reporting the wrong thing.* He stopped for a moment to catch his breath. *The lesson is: report the truth. I have to report what I saw. But who am I reporting to? Not to Moses. I'm reporting to the enemy. So what do I say?*

Harold started moving again, slower now as the crowds on the street grew with marchers and watchers. As he drew near York Avenue he saw the German parade starting to form. Veterans in Prussian uniforms were arranged in precise ranks. There was a marching band in lederhosen and feathered hats, tuning up their trumpets and tubas, with the drummers beating a staccato rhythm. The women wore high waisted, full bodiced dresses with skirts that swept the pavement as they floated along in time to the ragged beat of the drums. *Dirndl* dresses they were called, Harold remembered from some forgotten travelogue. Little girls in frills and aprons and little boys in short pants paraded with their parents up and down the sidewalks, looking for the best place to watch the march.

The wide expanse of York Avenue was adorned with red and white bunting between the shop signs in German and English. It would have been a merry sight were it not for the black swastikas hanging on every building, and the presence of the burly brownshirted *OD* men, pushing and shoving and bracing the parade participants into Germanic order. *This can't be New York,* Harold thought. *It looks like Nuremberg on Party Day.*

While fighting through spectators to reach the appointed meeting with Finnhandlerr at the Germania Bookstore, Harold heard a familiar voice. "Friend Appel, the street is so crowded and we are late," the soldier Willknecht panted. His uniform breeches pulled tight over his ample belly, his tunic stretched to tearing, the campaign hat wearing super pleaded with the reporter. "Please let

Christiana watch the parade with you." And without giving Harold a chance to protest, he was away, trailed by his wife, leaving his sullen, beautiful daughter in Harold's reluctant care.

"I'm going to be moving around," Harold told the girl. "Do you want to stick with me or should I find you a good place to watch?"

"My old man is crazy if he thinks I need a babysitter," Christiana told Harold, shaking her head dismissively. "But I think I'll stick with you. I'm sure it'll be more exciting than watching a dumb old parade." She undid the top three buttons on her tight sweater, shook her long blond hair loose of its ponytail, and linked her arm with Harold's, as if to promenade down the boardwalk at Coney Island.

"OK. Let's go," Harold yelled loudly to be heard over the happy noise of Germans celebrating *Deutschland uber alles* in the heart of New York. He propelled the girl toward the Germania Book Store where he saw Finnhandlerr talking earnestly with two men in storm trooper uniform. One was the morose looking *Schriftsfuehrer*, Rudolf Franz. The other was a large paunchy man with thin brown hair slicked back under his campaign hat. He was talking excitedly, authoritatively, punctuating his words with broad gestures and raising his voice to be heard over the babble of the crowd.

"It's *Bundesfuehrer* Kuhn," Christiana yelled in Harold's ear. "We don't see him so much anymore."

Fritz Kuhn, would-be *fuehrer* of America, was impressive only in his girth. His pale blue eyes were watery and weak, not riveting, as Hitler's were said to be. *Was he a man with a charismatic voice?* Harold wondered. He drew closer, hoping to discern why this man commanded loyalty from thousands.

"In their official statement, the Government announced that the events of yesterday were a spontaneous reaction by the people against the murder of Vom Rath and the excesses of the Jews,"

Kuhn loudly said to Finnhandlerr. Then, as Harold drew even with the OD leader, he lowered his voice to an almost whisper, "I received a telegram from a person high up in the party, saying that *der Fuehrer* turned the storm troopers loose. My source suggested that we do the same. Hitler wants the boys to have a little fun." Kuhn then noticed Harold standing there listening. "Max, who is this man spying on us?" he exclaimed in a shrill voice. "We cannot have spies!"

Finnhandlerr turned and saw Harold standing next to him. "Appel, what are you doing sneaking up on me," he asked putting his hand to his large forehead as if in thought. "Excellent Harold, excellent. *Meine Bundesfuhrer*, this is Harold Appel, a member of the OD. I sent him to spy on the Jews and their parade. If he can sneak up on me then he surely was able to find out what the *yids* are up to."

Harold stepped forward and executed a Nazi salute, arm outstretched to the sky, then bent at the elbow to the forehead. Finnhandlerr beamed while Kuhn looked at the fake Nazi with questioning eyes. "Appel, hmmm, I don't recall an Appel on the membership rolls in Yorkville."

"Comrade Appel is a German citizen," Finnhandlerr replied crisply. "He cannot be on the membership roll. But he is under discipline in the *Ordnung Dienst*. All in all, a perfect spy."

"And he is a good friend of Georg Willknecht," Rudolf Franz, silent until then, interjected. "In fact, here is *Fraulein* Willknecht."

Christiana stepped forward, placing her hand in Harold's, and said sweetly, "Hello Uncle Fritz."

Kuhn appeared flustered by the sudden appearance of the pretty girl. His pale eyes wrinkled as if he was allergic to beauty, a small tic on his lower right jaw line caused his skin to flutter in a regular rhythm, and he abruptly started to stutter. "W-w-why yes, Christiana. I d-d-did not recognize you. You have grown so. G-g-give my best to your father." Then the *Bundesfuehrer* visibly stiffened, as if his spine had become a hard steel rod, and he loomed over Harold. "Appel, is it," he said. "Comrade Appel, what are the Jews doing?"

Harold disengaged his hand from Christiana's and resumed his stiff, respectful posture in front of Kuhn. "*Herr Bundesfuehrer*, I have been to 80th Street and Lexington Avenue where the Jews are supposedly organizing their parade. Lexington is blocked to traffic but there are more police there than Jews. The only sign I saw of a parade was a small group of men carrying signs. There were maybe twenty of them."

Finnhandlerr looked exasperated with this meager intelligence. "Go back," he shouted at Harold. "There must be more activity. That is what we heard."

Kuhn, however, looked satisfied with Harold's report. "Comrade Max," he said, "we vastly outnumber the Jews. I want to emulate our brethren in the Fatherland. Pass the word that if the opportunity presents itself the OD should have a little fun."

Just then a well-creased young storm trooper approached through the crowd on the sidewalk. He was escorting a New York policeman. "*Herr Bundesfuehrer, Herr OD Leiter*," he said deferentially while giving the Nazi salute. "This is Captain Murphy of the Yorkville precinct. He wishes a word with you."

"It looks as if you're ready to commence, gentlemen." Murphy broadly gestured at all the marchers lined up in precise order in the street. "It would be helpful to the department if you could start your parade now. We have many people to supervise in these few blocks today."

"Captain, we would be glad to accommodate the police," Kuhn said decisively. "We march immediately."

As the policeman, his mission complete, turned to leave, Finnhandlerr leaned over Harold, his broad brown-shirted shoulder dwarfing the fake Nazi, and whispered, "Go like the wind, Comrade. Find what the Yids are doing and report back. We are leaving early. We want to be at the Turnhall before them. It's always best to be first on the field of battle."

Taking Christiana by the arm, Harold shoved his way through the parade watchers all the way to the curb on York Avenue. They darted across the street in front of the first unit in the march, a color guard bearing German and American flags and wearing Hessian-style pantaloons and gold jackets. As they reached the far side and began pushing through another audience a band began to play the Horst Wessel Song, the anthem of the Nazi Party.

Harold looked over his shoulder and saw the color guard unfurl the swastika banner as they dipped the two national flags in respect of Nazi power. The Hessians began goose stepping down the avenue. *Do they know what they're marching into?* Harold asked himself, while quickly leading the girl off to find the Jews.

CHAPTER SEVEN

THE PARADES

"I HAVEN'T SEEN Uncle Fritz in a long time," Christiana said, as she and Harold rushed up 80th Street toward Lexington. "He's so busy, by Arminius."

Everyone's related in Yorkville, Harold thought as he ran. *I remember reading something. Who wrote it? Oh yeah, it was by Horace Kallen. He said ethnic differences won't disappear as long as immigrants stick together. That's what Yorkville is all about, keeping the people pure. Wait a minute. Did she say Uncle Fritz?* "Fritz Kuhn is your uncle?" Harold gasped. He was not in shape to keep up with this girl.

"No, not a real uncle," Christiana tossed back over her shoulder as she forged ahead of Harold. "He, Uncle Max, and Daddy used to lift weights at Albrecht's Gym.

"And who's Arminius?" Harold yelled, as he struggled to keep up.

The blond girl stopped in her tracks and Harold nearly ran into her. "Arminius was the Teutonic leader who fought the Romans. He was the first German," she said, her pale blue eyes widening in astonishment. "Harold Appel, are you sure you're German? Everyone knows that."

"Of course I know." Harold felt a blush spreading across his sweating face. *I must be glowing red,* he thought. *How embarrassing.* "I wanted to find out how thorough German education is, here in this forsaken country." He started panting, as much from the work of deceit as the exercise of the run. *I'm trying to fool people. OK, I'm lying. But there are other liars in Yorkville. Kuhn, what a scam he's got going, Fuehrer of America.*

DA DA DUM DA. Turning the corner, the clear notes of a cornet filled Harold's ears. The horn was joined by the THUMPA THUMPA of drums and the heavy notes of a tuba. Harold recognized the Stephen Foster tune. It was one Saul played all the time. Now, a purple-uniformed band was lazily playing as they waited to begin marching. 'Camptown ladies sing this song, doo-dah, doo-dah. Camptown racetrack five miles long, oh, doo-dah-day.' The line repeated in Harold's mind as he approached what looked like a big parade.

An hour ago Lexington Avenue had been empty, even the newsstands at the subway stations had been shuttered. Now big buses were unloading marchers further down the avenue. Soldiers in khaki uniforms and doughboy helmets, marching units, bandsmen with shining instruments, all were milling around. Very clever. Harold recognized some bands and units from this morning. The Jewish veterans had imported most of their marchers from the parade downtown.

Harold started to cross the street when Christiana caught his arm. "I'm tired from running. Can't we rest a minute?"

The sidewalk was becoming crowded with families there to watch the parade as well as the marchers themselves. There was so little room on the sidewalk Harold realized that the girl would lose sight of him if he slipped away. He could hide in plain sight with the parade people still disorganized and standing haphazardly in the street and on the sidewalk. "You rest here Christiana. You can lean against this lamppost. I want to see what's going on across the street."

Harold darted through a line of soldiers waiting for marching orders, past the purple-uniformed band, and straight into a group of men he knew well, all members of the Glusker Young Men's Association, Israel Schwartz's hometown club. *Saul has to be here somewhere*, Harold thought. *Izzy wouldn't let him come all alone.* He hunched his shoulders and glanced furtively around, hoping no one would notice him. *Let's see, there's Sobidor and Kellerman, and there's Moe Drabinsky over by that light pole. And there's Saul, standing behind Drabinsky. Now, how do I get him to notice me without alerting half of Glusk?*

On the street the purple band was standing in place, ready to march. Harold reached out and tapped one of the buglers on his shoulder. "Do you know 'Camptown Races,' my friend?"

"Sure do," said the player. "Doesn't everybody?"

"I guess they do," Harold said, while thinking, *at least Saul does.* "Do me a favor, willya. Play the first six notes, three times over, fast. I'm trying to find a friend and he knows those notes. He'll look for me if he hears them." The notes rang out, clear in the cold air, and Saul looked around, focusing right on Harold. The band started moving away. The reporter threw a "thank you" after the cooperative bugler.

Harold dashed back into the street, past the rear of the band and in front of the marching soldiers. Saul followed him.

"Harold, that's my song," Saul said when he caught the reporter at the opposite curb.

"I know. It got you over here, didn't it? Now listen. I've got a cover story for you to remember. You know my friend Pat O'Rourke? From now on, you're his neighbor. Your name is Solly. You came to the parade with your father. I'm an old neighbor too. If you've got all that, you can come with me."

"Mr. Drabinsky will wonder where I am, Harold. I better go back."

"Saul, there's going to be trouble at 85th Street. You'd better come with me."

"Harold, I've got to go back!"

"Aww right. Aww right. But tell the Gluskers the Nazis are going to start something. If you see me again, remember what I told you about being my neighbor in New Jersey."

Saul ran back into the parade, almost knocking down a marcher in his haste to get back to his friends. Harold turned away from the street, away from the sparse crowd watching the Jewish parade on Lexington, and toward the throngs he knew would be watching the German parade on York Avenue. Who was that boy?" a voice asked over his shoulder. Harold jumped. Christiana had found him.

"An old neighbor. His father is marching with that unit." Harold pointed to a group of Legionnaires. *This damn girl is sharp. She sees everything. I'll have to be very careful around her.* "Come on. We have to catch up with our parade."

They found the Bund parade at E. 84th and York, flowing along, calm and serene. The color guard came strutting along, dressed in red Hessian uniforms, baggy pants and sleeves flapping in the breeze. They held their flags high with the black swastika on a blood-red field in the center, flanked by the German eagle and the Stars and Stripes. Cheers swelled from the crowds filling the sidewalks from building to curb. "*HEIL, HEIL*," they roared. Next came the Yorkville Marching Band, a Bund auxiliary, the silver trim on their black and red uniforms glittering in the sun, swastika armbands rhythmically rising and falling as they banged out the *Fahnenmarsch*, the Flag March, in honor of the crooked cross banner. Following were the veterans, row after row of brown-uniformed, brass-buttoned German soldiers from the Great War, their burnished *picklehaube* reflecting shards of sunlight from golden spikes.

Harold and Christiana threaded their way past many people to reach the curb. "There's my father," the girl called out over the brassy whine of the horns and the THUMPA THUMPA of the brass drums. She hung on the reporter's arm while pointing at a group marching under the banner of the Third Westphalian Grenadiers.

Is this the real Christiana? Harold thought. *Is she a little girl at a parade? Not exactly the way a world-weary femme fatale would act.* "I see him. I see him," he yelled back. "Come on. We have to find Finnhandlerr."

They ran down 84th, away from the crowds. When they reached Lexington the Jewish parade was almost upon them. They ran up Lexington to 85th.

The Turnhall, the center of German life in Yorkville, was on the northeast corner. A line of police blocked access to 85th on the east side of Lexington. Beyond the police were hundreds of uniformed storm troopers in close-packed ranks. Between the police and the OD, Harold caught a glimpse of Finnhandlerr standing on a platform.

Harold and Christiana tried to slip through the police line. They were stopped by a polite young officer. "Sorry sir. We have orders not to let anyone by."

"But we're with them," Harold protested, pointing at the massed storm troopers.

"Officer, won't you let us through," Christiana pleaded, blinking her eyes at the policeman. "That's my Uncle Max standing on the platform."

The police officer was helpless. The appeal of this girl was too powerful. He looked at his companions on each side for help but they were also under Christiana's spell. "All right Miss," the cop whispered. "But don't tell anyone or it'll be my job."

Christiana stood on tiptoe, gave the officer a quick peck on the lips, and slipped by. She pranced down the ranks of storm troopers. Greetings from young Germans followed as Harold trailed behind. *That's the Christiana I know*, he thought appreciatively, *a sexy little trickster.*

"Uncle Max, we're back," called Christiana, leading Harold to the base of the platform. Her cry was shrill, shrill enough to penetrate the hubbub of the parade.

Finnhandlerr heard her. He interrupted a lecture to his troopers, leaned forward, and said to Harold, "I have told the men that we have a much larger parade than the Jews."

"No, OD *Leiter*," Harold yelled up at Finnhandlerr's jackbooted feet. "The Jewish parade has swelled. They now have as many marchers as we do, and they will be here in minutes."

"*Nein.* That cannot be true. I have just told the men that we are much stronger than the Jews and can work our will."

"Uncle Max," Christiana interjected firmly, "there are many people watching our parade and few watching the Jews. Doesn't that make us stronger?"

"*Jawohl* Christiana. You are correct," Finnhandlerr said, relief in his voice as he seized on the girl's words.

The street in front of the Turnhall was filling with marchers. With the outlet of Lexington Avenue blocked by the police, the Germans coming up 85th packed themselves together as the parade moved into the cul-de-sac. Only the disciplined OD prevented the marchers from breaching the thin blue line.

The Jewish parade placidly flowed through the intersection, protected from a roiling brown-shirted sea by a thin blue dike. Competing music from the marches clashed then blended in the afternoon air. On the German reviewing stand someone was trying to make himself heard. Harold nudged Christiana, who stood tight against him, then shouted in her ear. "Who's that on the platform?"

"That's *Ortsgruppenleiter* Stubble," the girl shouted at Harold. "He's going to introduce Uncle Fritz."

The music stopped. A hush fell over the crowd. Even the noise of the Jewish parade, which continued to move slowly past the intersection, seemed muted. Kuhn strode to the podium and started speaking. "Fellow Germans, fearless soldiers of the *Reich*, comrades, ladies, we are here to celebrate the boundless courage of our fighting men. The German soldier did not lose the late war; the politicians lost the peace. But we continue the battle today. We are all soldiers at war against the enemies of the *Vaterland,* America, and Aryans everywhere. Who are these enemies? We need look no further than Lexington Avenue where the Jews, yes the despicable Jews, mock the sanctity of the eleventh day of the eleventh month by claiming that they too are fighters. Jews are cowards, taking what they will by stealth and deception. They claim to be Capitalists. They claim to be Communists. They are neither. The International Jewish Conspiracy seeks world domination by placing Jews in all political movements. Only the Nazi party and the Bund in America, stand in their way. Yesterday in Germany our brothers showed no mercy in dealing with the dirty Jew. Can we in America do any less to fight the Jewish cancer in our midst?"

A guttural cry rose from the throats of the marchers and all who were in earshot of Kuhn. It swelled out over East 85th Street and carried to Lexington, where the Jewish War Veterans were peaceably parading. "Kill the Jews!"

Harold, standing directly in front of Kuhn's platform, turned to look at the crowd of Bundists mashed into the small space of the intersection between police and platform. Out of the corner of his eye he saw rocks rise from the ranks of the storm troopers, arch over the thin police barrier, and fall amidst the Jewish marchers. More missiles were launched, a deadly fusillade of stones falling on Jews, one lethal barrage after another. The blue line dissolved under the weight of the Germans and the storm troopers were amongst the Jews, free to use fists and clubs. Carried along by the surge of bodies, Harold found himself in the middle of Lexington Avenue, face to face with a dazed man, bleeding profusely but still clutching a sign that read 'Glusker Young Men's Association.' Saul was with the Gluskers! Where was Saul? Harold watched in shock as two burly storm troopers converged on the Glusker and, with blood-lust in their eyes, knocked him to the ground and beat him with his sign.

The Jews were fighting back. Jewish War Veterans in uniform moved forward to meet the storm troopers. American Legionnaires, marching with the Jews, came back to face the Nazis. The intersection became a sea of fist-fights. In the midst of the melee several men were on the ground, bleeding from direct hits from storm trooper rocks.

Harold looked for Saul. Had the boy been under the Nazi rocks? Could he be one of those lying broken on the street? The fighting moved away, revealing more bodies on the ground. The reporter saw a flash of red hair. There was Saul, bending over a crumpled figure and crying, "Wake up, Mr. Drabinsky, wake up!"

"Harold, wait for me!" The reported turned. There was Christiana Willknecht, wild-eyed and disheveled, calling his name. Saul Schwartz looked up at the sound and also called—HAROLD! At the same time police poured in from Madison Avenue, hundreds of officers with guns and nightsticks at the ready.

"Come with me Solly," Harold yelled at the redhead. "You can't do anything for him." He pulled the blood-splattered boy away and, with Christiana trailing, dodged through the remnants of the fighting, headed for the safety of his apartment.

CHAPTER EIGHT
KRISTALNACHT IN NEW YORK

"HAROLD, WHY DID you take me away?" Saul yelled. His face was as crimson as his hair.

"Damn it, Solly, you could have gotten hurt. Your father asked me to watch out for you." *Just like Willknecht asked me to watch out for his daughter,* Harold thought. *Apple baby-sitting service here; low rates, riots extra.*

Just then Christiana came panting up the stairs. Harold stood motionless between the Nazi daughter and the Jewish son. "Christiana, this is Solly. Solly, this is Christiana." *They're not babies,* he thought, *turning his head to look first at one then the other. They're as big as I am.* Introductions over, he turned the key to his apartment and went inside, leaving the boy and girl to follow.

Saul came storming after Harold. "I should have stayed with my friends," he yelled. "You had no right."

"Then go back," Harold said in exasperation. "I'm too tired to argue."

"S-Solly," Christiana said hesitantly. "You're all bloody." The girl stood in the doorway staring at Saul's pants, stained scarlet with the blood of Mr. Drabinsky, whose head the boy had cradled on his lap.

Harold stared at Saul too, for the first time seeing the ordeal he had been through, as Nazi rocks rained down on him. His hands, his jacket, his trousers were all blood red. *It's not his blood, is it?* Harold thought suddenly. *What happened back there? I've got to go see.*

"Christiana, I've got to go out. Will you stay here with Solly?"

"Yes, I'll stay with him. Come on Solly, let's clean you up." Christiana pushed the suddenly compliant boy into the apartment looking for the bathroom.

Good, thought Harold. *The girl has some maternal feeling after all. Or maybe it's something more basic. But they'll be all right until I get back.* The reporter pulled his coat back on and hurried out.

᪣

The fight was over when Harold returned to the battleground. All that was left was the detritus of war: broken signs and posters, bloody rocks, and shards of broken glass. A lonely shoe stood guard over a crumpled Glusker banner. You could hear ambulance sirens fading away in the distance.

At the platform in front of the Turnhall, police were loading Nazis into paddy wagons. One of the prisoners threw himself on the rough pavement face first, stretching out his arms to clutch the running board of a police van. An officer stood over him, bending his fingers back one by one to break his grip. The other Nazis, already in the van, jeered. The storm trooper was lifted to his feet. He shook the police off and took a sweeping bow to his fellows. Flashbulbs popped. Harold recognized several news photographers, as well as their subject. It was Werner Everhardt playing to the crowd.

Harold headed east on 85th Street, looking for what was left of the Bund parade. The street was deserted; even the pushcarts that usually lined the sidewalk were absent. *Where is everyone,* the reporter wondered. *There was no fighting down here. Maybe they all ran from the hordes of Jews, come to defile their women.* He gave a sour laugh.

It wasn't until Harold got near York Avenue that signs of life became apparent. On the far side of the street was a small crowd overflowing the sidewalk. Here were the remnants of the Bund parade, men uniformed for the Great War and pig-tailed women in white aprons over petticoated skirts, all in a most jovial mood. In the center of this swirl of *pickelhaube* and *dirndlkleid* were Georg and Helga Willknecht.

"Comrades," Harold called. "Did you see what happened? The OD taught the Jews a lesson." He managed an acceptable acting job, gasping out the awful words as if he'd stepped in the foul stench of Jews by accident.

"Harold, my friend, where have you been? Yes, we saw the great feat of the OD. They sliced through the Jews like a knife through butter."

"Harold, where is Christiana?" Helga asked, wringing her hands. "I saw her with you."

"She is at my flat, Helga," Harold answered the worried mother. "I did not want so precious a person to be sucked into the fighting."

"I told you that we could trust Harold," Willknecht said to his wife. "He is an upstanding German man."

Yes, I am so upstanding that I am playing matchmaker. I saw how that flower of Germandom looked at my future brother-in-law. Maybe my mistake lay in not protecting Saul from Christiana.

"Harold, come with us," the janitor said. "We are going to The Bavaria Inn. Hear me everyone," he said expansively to the group of veterans and their ladies, "I will buy the first round."

The crowd, full-bellied men in tight tunics, and full-breasted women in tight bodices, cheered Willknecht's generosity with a hearty "*Heil.*"

"I will join you later, Georg. I want to tell Christiana where you will be."

But I don't think you're really concerned about your daughter, Georg, Harold thought as he left the Germans. *At least not as concerned as you are about filling your belly with beer.* The reporter started walking away from the group, turned a corner, and began looking for a taxi. In his mind he was already composing the story for tomorrow's paper. A taxi finally answered his hail. He directed the driver to New York Hospital.

A short, fast ride through sparse holiday traffic carried Harold to the emergency room. He paid the driver and rushed inside, pushing through groups of wounded vets. It's like a field hospital in here, he thought as he threaded past doughboys bleeding from gashes on their heads, shoulders, torsos, and arms caused by the barrage of rocks and the cascade of broken glass. Thankfully there were no legs blown off. He recalled the only other time he'd seen this much blood. *It's like the longshoreman in '35, when they were picketing that Hamburg-American Line ship, the **Deutschland** I think it was, and scabs tried to unload it. That was a bloody battle.*

"Damn you bitch, I am not hurt," a redhead, wearing an OD uniform, swore at a nurse closing some gashes on his face.

Well how do you do, Harold thought. *Some Germans got hurt too.*

Another nurse was checking charts at the entrance. She looked puzzled. "Can I help?" Harold offered.

"I've got all these men who are going to be OK but are either unconscious or befuddled. It looks like they all got hit on the head. How am I supposed to identify them for the records?"

"I know most of them," Harold volunteered. He looked around for the German, but didn't see him. They went through the room identifying the injured Gluskers. "This one is Hyman

Shaumlsky of Rodgers Street in The Bronx. The one on the liter over there is Jack Jacobs. He's still breathing, isn't he? Good." *All friends of Sally's father,* the reporter thought. All hurt. *And where the hell is Moe Drabinsky?* His head ached at the thought of not being able to tell Saul what had happened to Moe.

"There's one more in here," the nurse said, motioning to a side room.

Harold looked in. On a slab was a figure covered by a sheet. A doc in a bloody smock stood by the poor guy's head, poking and prodding. "What is he doing to that man?" the reporter asked the nurse.

"Dr. Rangle, this man may be able to identify the body," the nurse said.

Harold stumbled into the room, sick to his stomach. "It's Moe. I know it's Moe," he mumbled. The doc pulled a sheet down to show Harold the face of the cadaver. The reporter stared, alternately horrified and fascinated; horrified because he instantly recognized Drabinsky, identifying him by his most recognizable feature, the heavy five o'clock shadow that covered his jaw, hair that now grew through the waxy pallor of a dead man's face. And fascinated because the brain was displayed, in all of its' convoluted entirety, exposed by a sharp-edged Nazi rock that surgically split the skull and left the organ intact, ready for examination by the prying eyes of Dr. Rangle.

Harold wanted to puke. A man he knew had become a laboratory specimen. *That was Moe,* he thought. *Always poking his nose in where it didn't belong. He didn't have to come to this damn parade. He wasn't a veteran. He could have stayed home in The Bronx, fixed a faucet, and made a little money. Moe the plumber he was, but not anymore. And he dragged Saul down here. That could have been the boy on the slab with his head split open.* "Damn him, damn him," Harold sobbed.

"Sir, do you know him?" the nurse asked. "Can you identify him for the morgue?"

Moe Drabinsky was dead. He had a wife, children, friends, and now he was gone, snatched away not because of anything he had done but because of what he was. The Nazi labeled him *Jude* and killed him with no thought, no remorse, like squishing a roach. *Kristallnacht* continued on American soil.

The police would have to be notified. This was not Germany, where the death of a Jew might be counted but not investigated. But Harold had to maintain anonymity, for the sake of the story. "No," he said. "Horrible how he died." He slipped out of the emergency room and headed for the police station.

Anger set in as Harold walked the six blocks to the precinct house—anger at Moe, anger at the Jewish War Veterans, and finally, anger where it belonged, at the feet of the murderer. But who was the killer?

He learned, when he arrived at the station, nineteen storm troopers had been arrested for inciting to riot. Harold hid in an alcove, watching with pleasure mixed with anger, as officers brusquely booked handcuffed Nazis. As the last three were being led away, Stubble arrived to make bail. *Damn it,* he thought, *they won't have to spend any time in jail.*

After the Nazis had been led away Stubble disappeared into the Captain's office, leaving Harold free to come out of the shadows. "What's going on?" he asked the desk sergeant, flashing his press card.

"Ahh, we picked them *heinies* up for fighting with the Jews," the cop said in a soft Irish burr. "They'll be out in an hour. Seems like inciting to riot ain't a crime in New York anymore."

"How about murder?" Harold asked. "I've just come from the hospital. One of the guys they beat up died."

"Oh, that's too bad, my lad." The policeman picked up the telephone at his right hand and dialed the captain's office, eager to tell of this new development before Stubble walked out with freedom for his Nazis.

Time for me to go, Harold thought, as he slipped out of the precinct house while the desk sergeant was busy. *Don't want to answer any questions from the cops.* He caught a cab right out front and told the driver, "Jaeger's Restaurant."

At the German coffee shop, Harold sat in the back phone booth and dialed. "Sarah. Hello. I'm glad I got you. Saul is with me. There was trouble at the parade so I took him to my apartment. He's going to spend the night with me and I'll bring him home in the morning. Can I talk with Sally?"

Sally came to the phone quickly. "Harold, Mama said there was some kind of trouble. Are you all right?"

"I'm fine. Saul is fine. But I've got some awful news. Moe Drabinsky is dead."

"Moe the Plumber? Dead? I don't believe it." Sally's voice was cracking. Harold knew she was crying.

"He was stoned, Sally, pummeled by rocks, just like in Germany." Harold's voice broke too, but he held back his tears. He had more work to do this evening.

Sally sobbed for long minutes. Moe was a popular figure in Glusker society. "Poor Ida," she finally said. "Does she know?"

"No. I mean, I don't know. I went to the hospital and saw his body but I couldn't tell them I knew him, couldn't identify him. The police would have wanted to ask me questions and I'm on a story." Harold felt badly but it was the truth. He couldn't let the Nazis find out who he was or he might be next on the slab.

"Harold, I have to tell mother. She'll call Ida. I'll talk to you tomorrow. Oh, just a minute. I almost forgot. Your folks are coming in tomorrow morning on the Empire State Express. You have to meet them at nine-thirty at Grand Central."

"Damn it Sally, I forgot they were coming. Sheesh, they

couldn't have picked a worse time. Well, it's not their fault that Moe got murdered."

"Harold, we'll have the whole family here. Can we tell them we're getting married?"

"Yes, we can still make the announcement. Actually, that's a good idea Sally. It will cheer us all up. I'll see you tomorrow sweetie." Harold hung up and, suddenly lost in thought, went to the deli counter and ordered a corned beef sandwich. *I know why I didn't want to tell anyone we're getting married. If no one knew then it would be easier to back out.* He picked up his sandwich and wandered over to a back table, next to the phone booth. *What's different now? Moe died. Death can be sudden, unexpected. I don't want to wait anymore. I want to get on with my life, have a family, before it's too late. I love Sally, I really do. So…no more waiting. I want to leave more to the world than stupid stories. Damn, I've got to write one now, the hardest one yet, about the murder of a friend.*

'The Battle of Yorkville took place this afternoon as the American Nazis destroyed a parade organized by the Jewish War Veterans and murdered one of the Jewish marchers. Broken glass littered Lexington Avenue, just as it did the streets of many German cities yesterday, courtesy of Nazi storm troopers who stoned the veterans then attacked with fists and billy clubs. Morris Drabinsky of The Bronx, marching with the Glusker Young Men's Association, was killed by a blow to his head delivered by a Nazi rock. Nineteen members of the German American Bund, as the Nazi party is called in this country, were arrested for inciting to riot. Murder charges are pending.'

Harold phoned the story in to the city desk then stopped by the deli counter again to get Saul some dinner. Dread coursed through Harold's body as he imagined telling Saul that Moe had died. It was one thing to tell the whole city as a reporter. It was entirely different to have to sit face to face with a loved one and tell them a friend had been killed.

Harold puffed up the stairs to his loft, only to hear furniture creaking, high pitched laughter, and moaning. *I know those noises,* he thought as he fumbled for his keys. *Should I knock or just go in?* He opened the door. On his bed were Saul and Christiana, naked, the boy on top of the girl. Harold rushed by to his tiny kitchen.

✄

After a while Harold emerged from the relative privacy of the kitchen to find Christiana dressed. She was standing by the bed, combing out her long flaxen hair, and looking at Saul with pleasure-glazed eyes. The boy was sitting on the bed, pulling on his blood-stained pants, a goofy grin on his face, which turned redder than his hair when he saw the reporter.

"I'm leaving now Solly," Christiana whispered, bending down to graze the boy with her lips.

He pulled her to his naked chest and they kissed passionately for minutes while Harold watched in growing alarm as the couple showed no signs of stopping. "Oh my," gasped the girl finally, "I must go."

Saul stood up and escorted his new friend to the door. "I'll call you tomorrow, Christiana," he promised.

"Christiana," Harold interrupted the goodbyes, "I'm going to take Solly home tomorrow morning and stay there overnight. Tell your father I'll see him when I get back." The reporter retreated to the kitchen, leaving the teenagers alone.

A few moments later Saul came into the small kitchen and gave Harold a self-satisfied look. "I feel good now but before, when we first got here, I was shell-shocked. I was covered with blood. My coat was bloody, my pants were bloody. And I was alone with her after you left. She had me go in the bathroom and take off my trousers. She tried to get the blood out of my clothes. Her hair was a mess, her clothes were a mess, and she was flushed and breathing hard from the excitement of the afternoon. Suddenly, I wanted her. And she wanted me. Should I feel guilty? Uncle Moe is hurt and I'm thinking about sex. We were in the bathroom. I sat on the toilet while she combed out her hair. And we talked. She's eighteen. Her birthday is September 16th, so she's less than a year older than me. She kept brushing against me. I loved the smell of her. Then she bent down to kiss me." The son of a yeshiva boy smiled at his new *shiksa* memory.

"Was it your first time?" Harold asked.

"Yes. I feel so…exhilarated."

"I'm glad. The first time should be special." But Harold felt dark foreboding in his heart. The next thing he said would destroy any joy Saul felt from his encounter with Christiana. There was no way to soften the blow. "Saul, I followed the ambulance to the hospital. Mr. Drabinsky is dead."

CHAPTER NINE
LIFE GOES ON

HAROLD LOVED GOING to Grand Central Terminal, that great stone edifice Cornelius Vanderbilt had erected for his trains in the heart of the city. It was as much a presence on 42nd Street as the Sphinx was in the desert of Egypt. For Harold, New York was a natural landscape, like the desert. People were part of this landscape. They clustered at pushcarts like antelope at watering holes. They circled cab stands like flocks of birds. They ebbed and flowed down the streets. Whatever they did, their movements were instincts which defined them. At the train station they pushed and shoved, like an elephant stampede.

Harold pondered the crowds. *Do they know what they look like? Do they know what they're doing?* Then his philosophical bent took a dark turn. *Do people instinctively kill other people? People are animals, aren't they? Darwin proved that. Hate killed Moe Drabinsky. Is hate an instinct? Did Darwin know?* Harold suddenly saw the crowds like the tide on the beach, coming in, going out, in even further, obliterating marks of progress, all the while roiling, water battering land. *People are part of nature. Do we rise above nature?* Even the smell of the station seemed to play its role. Steam, metal, gasoline, rubber were artificial but not unnatural. Those scents mixed with those of the animal kingdom—pickles and herring from the pushcarts, sweat from the masses—to make an unforgettable perfume. *Everything is natural? Maybe that's what Darwin proved, that everything from steam engines to Hitler was natural, if you just understood things, saw that they eventually returned to nature. And that's why a swarthy plumber from The Bronx, who never hurt anyone in his life, could die in Hitler's name? But did anyone really care here in this great city with the great train station? It's my job to make them care,* Harold realized. *My words will make them care.*

The Empire State Express was on time. The engine rolled to a stop with an explosion of steam and a final, muted sigh. Redcaps rushed to open the doors of the sleeping cars and well-rested, well-fed people spilled out onto the platform. To Harold they seemed as mechanical as the steel beast that spewed them. They began the march to the concourse, and all the reporter saw was the *pickelhaube* of the German veterans and the Sam Browne belts of the storm troopers. A man in a brown suit reached in his pocket for a cigarette and Harold saw a storm trooper reaching for a rock. He blinked his eyes and the faces of the people, men and women alike, sneered and screamed at him. The screaming, that was different. Yesterday in Yorkville had been silent, watching the rocks rise in slow motion. Here there was noise, hubbub, the sound track of a big city.

"Hurry Harold, the train's here. Hurry."

Who was yelling at him? It was Saul. Harold's dark mood lifted. He would not, could not, forget what had happened on Lexington Avenue, but there was happiness here at the train station. You could hear it, the sound of people going places—the sound of direction. You had to look at people as individuals, not as members of a crowd. They were happy here. They all had someone to meet, somewhere to go.

Harold and Saul found the elder Apples, collected their bags, and headed for the street to hail a cab. He directed the driver to The Bronx even while listening to his mother repeat all the latest gossip.

Ruth Apple was a delicate woman, her silver hair poofed on top of her head like the cap of a mushroom. "Was Harold getting enough to eat?" she cheerfully twittered away. "Look how Saul has grown." She pulled a stick of Juicy Fruit out of her pocketbook and gave it to Saul.

All the while Harold's father, Sam, stayed silent. The cab moved in fits and starts through the Manhattan traffic, but when they reached the Triborough Bridge Sam spoke, his voice thick with sadness. "I've got news from Frankfurt. Uncle Hiram was arrested by the Gestapo, and the store is destroyed, burnt to the ground."

The sack of skin under Sam's left eye was twitching. Harold remembered how it always twitched when there was bad news to report. *Now there is an animal instinct,* he thought. *It was the quiet flutter of skin, like the flutter a deer made while shaking off a fly. But no, it wasn't like that. It was knowledge his father's skin shrank from, the knowledge of Hitler.*

"Dad, we've got to free him," Harold said, mechanically. There was no passion in his words. He had never met Uncle Hiram Appel, a man lost in cloudy perceptions of Frankfurt, a city he had never seen. In those far Germanic reaches he had family who owned a dry goods store. In his youth he had imagined a fairytale store filled with patterned sheets, fluffy towels, apparel from the four corners of the world—an exotic goodness. Now it was ashes. "You never know what's going to happen with the Nazis," the reporter went on. "They're unpredictable." He wondered if he was right. *Maybe they were absolutely predictable. That thought was so frightening he put it out of his mind.*

"Harold's right, Mr. Apple," Saul said bitterly. "You never

know what they're going to do. They killed my father's best friend yesterday." The boy began sobbing.

Ruth reached out a hand to Saul. "There, there, son, tell me all about it. Who was killed?"

"Moe Drabinsky was killed, Ma," Harold broke in. "He was killed by the guys I'm writing about, the Bund. Real pretty, huh? People I know killed Moe the Plumber, who never hurt anyone in his life." People I know killed Moe. The unbidden thought revolved in Harold's mind like a planet around the Sun. *Do I really know them? Do I want to know them?*

"Harold, are you in any danger?"

"No Ma. As long as they don't know I'm Jewish, I'm safe as if I were in your arms."

"Then don't let them find out you're a yid," Sam ordered. "They're too stupid to find out on their own. This *fuehrer* of theirs, what his name, Fritz Kuhn, makes a lot of noise but who listens to him? A few Germans and the newspapers, that's who. We have them in Cleveland, too. The *Plain Dealer* takes them seriously, but everyone else laughs."

"The German Jews laughed at Hitler," Harold said gazing out the window. "But he's not funny now."

A train rattled by on the elevated as the taxi turned onto Jerome Avenue. The driver dodged traffic and el pylons until turning on 186th, going one block before turning again, and stopping in front of a modern ten story apartment building on Davidson. Harold paid the fare, collected the luggage, and watched as his parents hurried into the lobby.

"I'll see you later, I guess," Saul said, as he hunched his shoulders and plowed through the cold November wind to his building around the corner.

Harold watched Saul go out of sight to his own warm apartment, where Sally was. He knew he had to get his folks settled at Aunt Annie's, before he could see her. He recognized it would be grim at the Schwartz apartment. Moe was dead; Saul had held him while he was dying. Life had slipped through Saul's fingers. Now Moe was just a memory, like any other memory. *Like baseball. Like breakfast.* Harold sighed as he picked up the bags and carried them inside.

Aunt Annie was waiting at the door as Harold got off the elevator, drumming her fingers on the door frame. The reporter struggled down the hall with the excessive luggage. "I was cooking this morning, as usual, but somehow my heart wasn't in it," she said as the reporter *schlepped* the bags inside. "I was reading the paper with my first cup of coffee and learning about Moe took the life right out of me. He fixed my faucet just last week. It's horrible, just horrible. Still, Frank will expect dinner when he gets home from the office and we do have company."

Harold wondered what his aunt considered more horrible, Moe dying, the way he died, or the loss of a good plumber. He realized that wasn't fair, to Aunt Annie or the memory of Moe. People in his family had their own problems and, as for Mr. Drabinsky, he would probably think it a compliment to be remembered as a good plumber. "Yes, we do have to eat and my folks are here," the reporter agreed, but he felt glum, as if nothing would make him happy again. And he didn't even know Moe Drabinsky that well. Maybe it was death in general that oppressed him, or death mixed with hate. *Hate wasn't natural,* he decided. *Animals don't hate. Only man hates.*

Aunt Annie had just served the boiled chicken and *kreplach* when Uncle Frank arrived home. He hugged his little brother, slapping his back with the flat of his hand. The two men waltzed through the room like dancing bears, big and shaggy. All of a sudden a thought hit Harold. *They look very German, very much like Willknecht with his family. Burghers* from Frankfurt, safe, solid, showing the appropriate emotion, these men of his family impressed Harold with their sanity.

"I'm happy my parents didn't live to see this *Kristallnacht*," Sam declared to Harold. "My father loved Germany. He wanted his sons to be 100% German. It would have ripped his heart out to be rejected by them."

"The Jewish stores in Frankfurt were so nice," Ruth Apple said. "Jews had a good life." She smiled. "I remember store shelves piled high with goods: dresses, trousers, sheets, towels."

Something was happening in Harold's mind. It was as if he could predict his parents' feelings; first his father dancing to greet his brother, then, his mother's memories of the shops. The little shop he saw in his head, in his dream of Uncle Hiram, was a Santa shop, stuffed with glowing wholesome towels and stacked with sheets covered with flowers: roses, violets and daffodils. It was the shop his ma described. Maybe it was a conversation from his childhood, something he didn't consciously remember. Maybe it was just a coincidence.

The conversation continued. Harold's mother was saying, "I didn't know much about anti-Semitism until I was grown. It was so strange. I got off a bus one day and a young boy yelled 'Sweet Little Nothing.' I turned to see him sneering at me in an ugly way. 'I bet you smell of pansies,' he said. 'Nothing's too good for the rich Jew girl.' I thought he was crazy but he must have had an idea in his head about what was in our shop. The linens, the satins, the six-inch thick quilts stuffed with feathers. My goodness, he must have wanted those feathers. Everything in the world that was soft was locked away in our shop, where he couldn't get it." She shook her head, looking sad.

"I never really had that kind of experience until I was at dental school in Munich," Uncle Frank said while taking his seat at the head of the table and heaping chicken on his plate. "I remember a boy named Gerhard in my dental anatomy class. Every day he sat next to me on the bench that was second from the top, at the back of the auditorium. He always got there before me. When I walked in he would stand up and screech in his high voice, '*Ach-tung! Heir kommt die Jude. Jetzt ist die Zeit, um zu handeln.*' His voice would crack as he said these words of derision, announc-ing my presence as if I was some kind of insect. He would stand and bow to me, whip out a handkerchief, and dust off my seat. The entire class would laugh uproariously. Of course his dusting was even more thorough at the end of class, when I stood up. He would yell, '*Ich muss den Jude-Schmutz reinige,*' I must clean the Jew's dirt. And to top it all off, the professor lowered my grade for disturbing the class."

"Why, Frank, do we have to talk about unpleasantness over lunch?" Aunt Annie shook her head in a no motion, no to death and destruction in her world.

No unpleasantness over lunch indeed, Harold thought. *Nazis exist because people want pleasantness in their lives. So they ignore Nazi bullying. We don't live there, they say, so we don't have to pay them any mind. Many more will die before people notice the Nazis. Moe was only the first.*

"I have to go," he told his family once lunch was over. He needed to go to the one person in the world with whom he could be himself, not a dutiful son, an eager employee, or a good Nazi. He needed to be at peace within and without, to stop the ach-ing. Only with Sally could he find relief. Saying his goodbyes, he slipped out of his uncle's house, traced Saul's steps around the cor-ner, and ran up three flights to pound on Sally's door, his heart pounding fast. He stepped back, leaned over, and put his hands on his knees. "Huff, huff," exploded from his mouth.

Sally answered the door. "Harold, are you all right?" she shouted.

"Yes," he panted, "just not used to running and climbing in the cold air." Harold had to admit that Sally was a welcome sight after all the *dirndl*-dressed women he'd seen yesterday. Cool and crisp in a pale blue shirtwaist, she looked thoroughly up-to-date.

"Harold's here," Sally yelled. She grabbed the reporter by the shoulders and pulled him to her embrace.

As he fell into Sally's arms and their lips met, Harold saw, over the girl's shoulder, Sarah rushing into the foyer, drying her calloused hands on a dish-rag. "Harold, my darling. I could kiss you myself after what you did for Saul." She gave him a hug, reaching around Sally and interrupting the real kiss. "Who knows what could have happened if you hadn't been there. Saul could have ended up like poor Morris. We cried and cried when we heard. Israel and Saul are at synagogue now, praying for him, poor Ida, and the children. It's so sad."

Harold, his girl in his arms, could only say, "I know, but life goes on." *Shit,* the reporter thought. *Listen to me. 'Life goes on.' Is that all I have to say? Life didn't go on for Moe. Did he have to die? Did he die because he liked to take walks, or liked parades, or liked causes? Where was the point where he could have turned back? Maybe he was afraid of the Nazis or maybe he was courageous. Who could know? Did he die because he was Jewish? The Nazis would say yes, because he was Jewish. But there were non-Jews marching in that parade. They were marching with the Jews because they hate Nazis. So why did a Jew have to die?* And Harold, his mind filled with whirling thoughts of life and death and Nazis and anti-Nazis, could not hold his beloved anymore. He slumped backwards so that Sarah and Sally had to hold him up.

"Harold," Sally cried, "what's the matter?"

Harold gasped for breath, then caught himself and straightened. But thoughts of life and death did not leave him. "Life is precious," he said to the women. "Mr. Drabinsky should not have died, but he did."

"You're right Harold, Morris shouldn't have died," Sarah said to him, with a no nonsense tone in her voice, "but he did. We can wrap ourselves up in riddles about the meaning of life and death but there is one truth. Life goes on for the rest of us. You can be sad but don't beat yourself up over Morris, he wouldn't want that. Now Harold, how are your parents? They're coming for dinner, yes?"

"Yes," Harold said, but then he shuddered, as if he did not want to be in the foyer of a normal Bronx apartment with normal people who loved him.

"Harold, what's wrong?"

"We have a funeral to go to, remember," the reporter snapped at the women. "Drabinsky, Moe. Ring a bell? He liked to fix faucets. No one important."

"This isn't necessary, Harold," Sarah said in a calm voice. She shot him a dirty look.

"Of course it isn't necessary," Harold almost shouted, standing there in the foyer where his voice reverberated between the mirror on the closet door and the chandelier vibrating above his head. What was wrong with him? He was out of control. He couldn't stop now.

"Harold, please don't do this," Sally pleaded.

"Like his whole head. When I saw Moe Drabinsky he had no head left."

Sally fled the apartment.

"What I like about being a reporter is how you learn so many things, Sarah," Harold said, bitterness evident in his voice, "like what a man looks like with his skull split open." He stood solid, hands balled into fists, making no move to follow the girl.

"I don't know what's wrong with you, Harold," Sarah said quietly. "If you think no one feels anything except you, you're wrong, but..."

"Life goes on," Harold interrupted.

"It doesn't always go on. There are people with interrupted lives who don't die. Like all those German Jews in concentration camps who are interrupted through no fault of their own. But then there are people right here in New York who have to take responsibility for their own interruption. They'll go on living physically, but in their heads they'll be dead. Are you one of those, Harold? Are you too bitter, too sensitive? I never thought a reporter could be one of the dead ones. Maybe reporters ask too many questions?"

"Ah yes, questions." Harold moved away from Sarah. He paced up the hall of the apartment then back to the foyer. "You don't last in this world if you don't ask questions. But Germans don't like questions. Questions make them feel uncertain."

"And you're a German now. Is that it?" Sarah asked. "You don't ask anymore. Have you become one of the dead, one of those who kill themselves?"

"You mean literally?"

"And figuratively." Sarah folded her work-roughened hands. "Which is only to say quickly or slowly?"

"What is this? What are you getting at?"

"I'm getting at how easy it is to die when Nazis start showing up in your life. Say you're in Germany now. Say you're scared. You don't have to take cyanide. You don't have to go to the medicine chest and watch in the mirror while you swallow capsules. All you have to do is give up and they've won. And Germany is everywhere Harold, at least for Jews."

Harold's eyes narrowed. "You don't believe that, Sarah. Jews are no different from anyone else. And there is no Germany in America. Americans don't assume things. There are no old Bible stories playing like records in our heads."

"A little bit of them has crept into you," Sarah said, placing her hand on Harold's shoulder. "Nazis enjoy hurting others. In a twisted way, you enjoyed hurting Sally. You just turned around and knocked her down without a thought." She shook her head. "You got that from them. You were never like that before."

"Damn it, Sarah," Harold exploded, his voice sounding like steam from a radiator. "Don't you understand that I'm trying to save our necks in Yorkville while you guys are comfortable in The

Bronx?" The reporter started pacing back and forth, one step, two, three, turn around, repeat, in the tiny foyer.

Sarah watched him make three circuits of the room, with a look in her eyes that spoke concern to Harold. Then she spoke softly, so softly that he asked her to repeat herself.

"Do you love Sally?" she repeated, after a pause.

"Yes." Another explosion came from his lips.

"Then go after her. Apologize."

᪥

Sarah was right about Sally, Harold had hurt her. His excuse was that he needed time, more time than his deadline offered, to recover the memory of love. The safety he had hoped to find in Sally's arms was an illusion. He had to find safety in his own mind before he could love again. But talking to Sarah had opened some doors for him. He knew where Sally had gone when she ran out of her house. She went up the street to his tiny apartment. She carried the key in a gold locket around her neck, a locket he had given her. He rushed out to the cold street.

᪥

Sally was standing in Harold's living room, looking out the window at the air shaft. She saw her reflection alone and then, the two of them, together, then apart, then together again, as the reporter quietly opened the door and stole in behind her. She forgave him, of course. "I understand your feelings Harold, really I do. But our families are not callous. They care about Mr. Drabinsky and everyone else who's been hurt by the Nazis. But they're not like you."

"Like what?"

"They're not courageous," Sally said as she embraced the reporter, squeezing him like she didn't want to ever let go. "Our families aren't brave like you. They're everyday people who just want to get on with life. I'm like that too. You're the only Nazi-fighter we've got."

"But what's courageous about telling disgusting stories of people with bashed-in heads?"

"If it's the truth you have to tell it," Sally said, holding Harold's face in her hands. "It isn't just one story. People don't want to know about Nazis. Your job is to pull their heads out of the sand."

That sounded right, and it was just what Harold needed to hear. Sally looked composed now, not at all upset as she'd been minutes ago when she had run out of her apartment. If she could regain her nerve then he could too. "Thank you, Doll," he whispered in her ear as he embraced her, this mere slip of a girl who could so screw his head back on when he was in danger of losing it. They left the small apartment hand in hand and walked the block to the Schwartz house with a light step.

When they arrived Israel and Saul were preparing *Havdalah*, the ceremony for the end of *Shabbos*. Then Aunt Annie and Uncle Frank walked in, with Harold's parents in tow. Everyone sniffed the spices and watched the tapers burn, signaling the end of the day of rest. Harold had never done *Havdalah* before meeting the Schwartz clan. Now he was a pro. He called everyone into a circle around Saul, who was holding the braided candle, and raised his hands to feel the heat. That was what it was all about to Harold—the circle. The circle was the story that continued without end. The circle surrounded the light, not letting it escape until the proper time. The circle protected the Jews from lines. Harold imagined Uncle Hiram standing in an endless line at the entrance to a German camp. No circle there.

When *Havdalah* was over dinner was served. First Sarah and Sally brought out jellied fish. Then they served flank steak with horseradish, potato *kugel*, and green bean and onion casserole. Dinner conversation was carried on by the women. The men were busy eating and drinking, filling up and putting out the fire, then stoking it again with more horseradish on the meat.

Aunt Annie waxed poetic about the Christmas lights downtown. She could be counted on to talk about them every year. "They have Santa in a white tuxedo this year and satin angels with halos made of tiny candles. It's a fairyland, a real fairyland. We have to go see them, Ruth, while you're here."

What's with them? Harold thought. *This is an odd lot of Jews, what the cat dragged in from a Europe that is a rubbish heap looking for torches. Here we are in this golly by jingo gee goyland, with salvation Santas hustling dimes on the corner of everywhere and nowhere, and there go the Jews by the goyland windows, where little white angels with renaissance curls swoon over dolls and donkeys and virgins in haystacks. Oh, it's a fairyland, all right. Let's not miss the lights of the Christ child. They've always been good for the Jews.* Listening to his aunt prattle on about lights and such nonsense, while eating such a solid middle-class, Jewish meal made Harold angry all over again, as he was before Sally had calmed him down. He shook his head, clearing his cobwebs, or maybe just rearranging them.

"Harold, what is it?" Sally looked at him with renewed concern.

Harold was certain his mood swings were driving her crazy. "This is America," he said. "The promise of America is that lights are just lights, decoration. Jews don't have to worship at sawed off pine trees stuck in pots and covered with lights.

"Harold, Annie was just talking about the Christmas lights," Ruth pointed out. "She wasn't going to become a Christian. But I want to hear about your job, Sally. Is it very hard work? Do you enjoy it? My son told me you're going to art school at night."

"Well you know, I'm a bookkeeper now, but I'd rather be a designer. That's why I'm going to art school. But who knows? I might just quit my job after Harold and I get married in March."

It was out. They were getting married. Shouts of joy and hearty *mazel tovs* resounded across the dining room. Harold felt like a fool. He and Sally had agreed to announce their marriage this very night and he had forgotten all about it. He was so wrapped up in Moe's death and the Nazi mess, so self-absorbed in his own troubles that he had blown it. Leave it to level-headed Sally to bail him out, again. Of course he wanted to marry Sally. He would be lost without her.

Dinner was forgotten. Israel brought out his best *schnapps* and toasts were made. "May you have health and happiness for a hundred and twenty years," the father of the bride said.

The dental uncle said, "May you have whatever you want from life."

And Harold's father wished that the happy couple make him lots of grandchildren.

Harold heard the wishes and came up with some of his own. *May all of us be here at this time next year. May Finnhandlerr not pull my pants down and find out I'm Jewish. May nobody else I know wind up without a head ala Moe Drabinsky.*

Harold arrived at the Schwartz's house at nine Sunday morning. Israel and Saul had already left for *shul,* and Sally and her mother were still dressing for the funeral. They emerged in black, like crows. The funeral would be populated by black birds, fat ones, and thin ones, middle aged ones and young ones, all flying in ever smaller circles, eyeing Moe's body for the carrion it was. He helped Sarah on with her coat and they walked slowly toward Bet Tikvah of The Bronx, the Glusker *shul.*

Again Harold had the odd illusion of natural landscape as they walked the few blocks in the cold morning air. This time it was not as a sandy desert. The Bronx was a series of canyons, like mud flats cracked open by months of drought. Children playing on the stoops looked like old sepia-toned photographs. But they were happy, not grim-faced as he was. He guessed that the canyon landscape did not revolve around funerals. The background noise was peculiar to the dry New York landscape, whether sandy or mountainous. It was the low growl of the elevated going by, punctuated by barking dogs and car doors being thwacked shut. Gershwin heard it as music but strangers to the city could not sleep with the windows open in their hotel rooms. It was normal to New York, and normal was what Harold craved as he walked through the strange streets toward the finale of the plumber's life.

The *shul* was a nondescript storefront on Jerome Avenue, in the shadow of the el. Inside was a large room, with partitions to separate the men and the women. "I'll see you after the service," Sally whispered as she disappeared behind the wall separating the sexes. Women were not equal to men in the Glusker world.

Harold stood in the back on the men's side of the semi-darkened room. Sunlight filtered through stained glass windows on the street side. It bathed the coffin in red and blue tones. Behind the closed pine box was the dim bulk of the Ark of the Torah, fronted with blue velvet curtains, containing the scroll, the center, the law. Written in gold letters, in both Hebrew and English, above the blue curtain, and illuminated by a light bulb that was never supposed to go out, were the words 'Rejoice in the Torah.'

Harold saw Saul and Israel in the second row of folding chairs, where they'd saved him a seat. He was behind Howard Drabinsky, Moe's only son. The reporter squeezed in past Izzy and leaned over to say something comforting but Howard wasn't listening. His eyes, behind bifocals, were closed. His black hat was pushed back. He grasped his forehead with both hands and rocked back and forth. Tears stained the torn lapel of his black suit.

Harold looked to the left, towards the women's section. In the front row, the only row visible, he saw the widow Drabinsky and her daughter, both veiled and dressed in black. Blue light from the windows found the two, turning them ghostly. The cantor's voice rang out: "*Yit-ga-dal v'yit-ka-dash shmei rabba,*" the words of the prayer for the dead. "Magnified and sanctified is the glory of G-d."

For the first time since Moe had died, Harold cried.

The Glusker rabbi, Moishe Kabakoff, entered as the Cantor was finishing. He was a pale man, made paler by his black clothes, black wide brimmed hat, coat of black satin reaching to his knees and belted with black velvet. He strode to the front of the room, stood beside the pine box, and repeated the prayer. He continued. "Grant perfect rest beneath the sheltering wings of thy presence. Lord of Mercy, bring Morris under the cover of thy wings."

An image of Moe the Plumber catapulted into space to plunge the stars flashed through Harold's mind. *At least he has a mission, to bring good plumbing to the galaxy.*

At the mention of Moe's name sharp cries came from the women's section. Harold turned to see the dead man's daughter beating her fists on her mother's shoulder.

"My friends," the rabbi began the eulogy, "we have come today to celebrate the life of a man who, if he were here, would be embarrassed by all the attention. Morris Drabinsky was a modest man, a man who exemplified the spirit of *tsadakah*, of giving. He gave of himself in so many ways. He was president of the *shul* when I became your rabbi. I owe my job to Morris because he begged the board to hire a rabbi educated in this country. He was proud to be an American and a Jew. But he was also proud of his origins in Glusk. And he was always humble before G-d."

Yeah, yeah, Harold thought. *It's easy to be from America and Glusk. He left his heart in Russia but his brains are smeared all over Lexington Avenue. The salient fact about Moe Drabinsky is not his life. What matters is how he died.*

CHAPTER TEN

JEWS MOURN, NAZIS REJOICE

SIX GLUSKER PALLBEARERS carried the coffin out of the *shul*. As Harold watched Moe leaving, he thought about how Jews carry their Holy Land with them, wherever they go. A gleaming black LaSalle hearse stood outside the synagogue, waiting to take the plumber on his last ride. "That's gotta be the most elegant car Moe ever rode in, and look at the size of the procession," the reporter exclaimed as he and Sally exited the synagogue. The police had blocked off part of Jerome Avenue for cars making the long ride to the cemetery in Yonkers to line up behind the hearse.

"Do you want to go to the cemetery?" Sally asked.

"No, I'd rather spend time with you."

The family slowly walked the blocks to Aunt Annie's apartment. As they passed a newsstand Harold stopped to buy a *World Journal*. The headline on the front page read, 'Nazis demand billion from Jews.'

Hitler is a fussy old woman, Harold thought as he scanned the article. *He wants to know who will clean up the broken glass. Never mind that he broke it.* The reporter read on. Insurance claims by

Jews were *verboten*. Jews who had been arrested were put up for sale, ransomed to their families for a set price. *Goering wants one billion marks from the Jews. So no matter what the Nazis say about racial purity—it all comes down to money. Where are the German Jews keeping all their money anyway, in pillow cases from Hiram's store? The Nazis made them poor already. I wonder what happens to Jews whose families have nothing. Are they sold to the highest bidder?*

All sense left Harold. He was in another landscape, a desert this time, and he was surrounded by barbed wire. Thousands of people were with him, on their knees, hands in the air, all screaming, imploring, beseeching. But he couldn't hear any of it because he was screaming too, wailing for something. Suddenly, all was still, the desert outside the wire disappeared, leaving nothingness. "Help me," exhaled Harold.

"Let me see that paper," a voice said. It was his father, bringing Harold back to Jerome Avenue.

Harold handed the newspaper over. The helplessness that surrounded the reporter receded. The old familiar landscape returned, The Bronx, USA. No Nazis here. Just Germans playing Hitler's game. But wait, tell that to the plumber.

Sam took the paper and scanned the article. "So they want money for Hiram. Money we got. Money for brothers we definitely got. Let's go home and call Western Union."

The cable Sam sent to his sister-in-law in Frankfurt read: 'Will raise ransom for Hiram. How much to get entire family out of Germany?'

"Harold, do you know how hard it is to get a visa?" Sam asked.

"There are quotas, Dad. But we'll work something out." We had better, Harold thought. *Here I am, sitting on Aunt Annie's overstuffed sofa while my uncle is in a camp that's worse than the roughest jail in New York.* He closed his eyes and for an instant was back in the desert, surrounded by soundless screaming. He opened his eyes and saw Sally, warm comfortable Sally. Nothing bad could happen while she was here.

"Mr. Apple, maybe I can help," Sally volunteered. "One of my friends in figure drawing class, Rose Nathanson, is married to an immigration lawyer. He worked out a way to get my friend Sadie's mother from Hamburg to New York. He'll do the same for your family."

"Lunch is ready children," Ruth called from the kitchen. Everyone went into the dining room, pulled in by the smell of warm bagels slathered with butter and strawberry jam.

Uncle Frank arrived home from the cemetery as the family was finishing their meal. "Harold, are you and Sally going to visit Ida?" he asked. "Wait a few hours before you go over. She said she and the kids want to be alone before people start coming for *shiva*."

A few hours with nothing to do was wonderful. As long as Harold didn't obsess about all the damage the Nazis have done. Just a few miles from here, in that little park across from the Casino, storm troopers were practicing their goosestep. Small boys were watching them, imitating their quick march, and wishing they were older so they could fight Jews. Before Sally and Harold could have a future they had to change the minds of those boys. Damn. Damn, damn. "Let's go for a walk doll," he said to his fiancée, interlacing his fingers with hers. "It's a nice afternoon." Being with Sally was the best medicine he knew.

It was almost warm outside, with scraps of clouds scudding across a bright sky. Harold and Sally strolled leisurely through the neighborhood: he put all notions of Nazis out of his head while she filled the void with talk of weddings and family and familiarities. They stopped at a small park, took seats on a bench beneath a bare-branched oak, and smooched a little bit. Harold looked up and saw an old *babushka* smiling at them from her stoop across 187th Street. *Yes grandma*, he thought, *we're kissing in public. It's natural. We're part of the landscape.*

They returned to Sally's house. Harold approached Saul. "How are you feeling? What was it like at the cemetery?"

"I'm all right," Saul said, "but Howard isn't. He blames himself for his father's death. He kept saying that he should have been there instead of me. He insists that he would have shielded his old man. I told him that no one could have done anything. There were too many rocks. He could be lying in the cold ground right now."

"Why wasn't he at the parade?"

"He goes to university. NYU didn't have a holiday on Armistice Day. He had classes."

Class, Harold thought. *Moe would insist his son go to class. Too bad Saul's high school had a holiday. I wish he hadn't been there.* "Saul, do you realize the cops are going to want to talk to you, at least if they're serious about investigating Moe's death as a murder?"

"It was a murder, Harold."

"I know it was. That's why you're going to be interviewed. And I want you to do something for me."

"What?"

"Don't tell them I was there. Don't say anything about me or going to my apartment."

"You want me to lie?"

"Yes, for chrissakes. I think the Nazis have a plant in the Yorkville precinct. If they find out that I helped a Jew, then I'm finished and I might end up dead."

"But, what about Christiana?"

"She doesn't know you're Jewish."

"Yeah, but she saw I'm circumcised."

"A lot of boys are circumcised, Saul. Remember, Christiana thinks you're Solly O'Rourke from New Jersey."

At three o'clock the family left for the short walk to Crescent Avenue. The Drabinskys lived on the first floor of a three story building, with their entrance off a small parking lot, where Morris kept his panel truck. The picture on the side of the little truck was a caricature of The Plumber himself with his prominent five o'clock shadow and a broad grin saying, 'Call Moe to Clean Up.' Harold wondered how much longer the dead man would be allowed to greet the street. Someone should have the forlorn truck repainted or removed.

The family entered the open door of the mourning house. Sarah took a casserole to the kitchen while everybody else went into the parlor where the Drabinskys were sitting *shiva*. Little light seeped into the darkened room. Israel went instinctively to Ida, who was perched on the edge of an overstuffed chair, like a sparrow on a ledge. They talked in hushed, reverent tones before embracing. Sally went to the daughter, Cynthia, who was surrounded by girlfriends. Saul went to Howard, who was standing stiffly, alone by the fireplace. The two boys were speaking when Howard smashed his fist on the mantelpiece, knocking Morris's bowling trophies to the floor.

"Damn you, damn you, damn you, Saul!" screamed the plumber's son. "You were there. Why didn't you do something?"

"I was there," sobbed Saul. "I was next to your father. One instant we were walking down Lexington Avenue, surrounded by Gluskers, then rocks were flying everywhere and I was the only one left standing. Your father was on the ground. Stones, big ones the size of baseballs, hit the pavement all around us. I fell on your father to protect him, but it was too late. He was already dead."

Howard started keening, a horrible high-pitched howl. "Eeeyow! Eeeyow! Eeeyow!" Saul grabbed his friend's shoulders to stop him from toppling over and with the help of several young men, they half-guided, half-carried the boy up the stairs to his bedroom. One of the women brought aspirin, another cold compresses, and Saul sat down next to Howard's bed to see his friend through the ordeal.

Harold was witness to Howard's breakdown but not part of it. He stood, aghast, near the door to the parlor along with several other friends. "It seems that Morris was not very responsible, financially speaking," the man standing next to Harold whispered.

"Are you speaking ill of the deceased, Lev Sobidor?" Harold hissed back.

"Come, Mr. Apple. I'll tell you all about Drabinsky's problems," Levi Sobidor said as he drew Harold out to the entrance foyer. "You know I'm head of the Young Men's Association. Hell, I'm practically the mayor of Glusk. Everyone brings me their problems."

"So what kind of problems could Morris have had?" The diminutive, balding Sobidor, unprepossessing as he looked, could have some information. He was an accountant in real life and did the Drabinsky's taxes. Harold's reporting instinct was piqued.

"Well, a plumber should be able to make a good living, even in these troubled times, but Morris couldn't. He was practically giving away his work."

No wonder Aunt Annie loved him, Harold thought. She got free work, even though she could afford to pay. But there's nothing illegal about doing free plumbing.

"Ida knew he wasn't charging enough," Sobidor went on. "And they argued. Howard didn't want to be a plumber. He wanted to go to school. So they fought. And worst of all, Morris's life insurance was cancelled last year because he couldn't make the payments."

So Moe the Plumber was a good man but a rotten business-man. Nothing unusual about that. If it had been the other way around, if he'd been a sharp businessman and a rotten person, there might have been a story. "What's going to happen to Ida and the kids?" Harold asked Sobidor.

"Cynthia has a job," Sobidor admitted. "So they have that income. The best outcome would be for Howard to quit school and take over the plumbing business. But he doesn't want to do that. He may have to, however, because Morris was paying his tuition. In any event, Morris was a member in good standing of the Young Men's Association, so we paid for his funeral."

It was time for Harold to get back to life on the outside, where Nazis plotted to kill Jews and reporters plotted to expose Nazis. Before he left he wanted to console the widow. He moved over to the group in front of Ida and when his turn came mumbled, "Morris was a good man." Ida didn't know who said the words but it made Harold feel better to have said them. He looked for Sally, gave her a good-bye kiss, and slipped back to his life as a German.

❧

Now how the hell am I going to do this, Harold wondered as he returned to the streets of Yorkville. *I've got to face all these Bund people and offer up a little cheer, a little self-satisfaction, because a Jew is dead. Hooray.* He gave a "guten tag" to the waitress, a nod to the busboy, and settled into his usual booth, in back near the phone. Then, as Harold was pondering the sameness in physiology and differences in psychology between Nazis and Jews, who should plop himself down in the back booth but Max Finnhandler, the last person in the world the reporter wanted to see after Moe's funeral.

"Harold, we will share a meal, bratwurst and sauerkraut, *ja,* and I will tell you of goings on here while you were visiting friends in New Jersey. *Fraulein* Willknecht told me where you were. You should not leave without notifying me. You are under discipline, *ja,* but I will overlook your transgression this time."

Beads of sweat appeared on the reporter's forehead even before the spicy German sausage arrived from the kitchen. What had Christiana said to the big man? Harold changed the subject quickly. "Was I not right about the Jew parade, Max? It was a big parade." *How easily I slip back into the role.*

"*Jawohl* Harold, it was a big parade. But you told me too late. What had been set in motion could not be stopped. Nor should it have been. The Bund proved itself to Berlin that day."

"What do you mean, it could not be stopped?"

"I ordered the OD to break through the police line and disperse the Jews. If I had known how many there were, I might have not issued the order."

"But the stoning…"

"Oh, that was entirely in order. The Jews came to our territory. They needed to be taught a lesson. Where were you while all this was happening?"

"I was in front of the reviewing stand when the OD burst through the police and ended the Jew parade." *It's all so matter of fact with Finnhandlerr,* Harold thought. "I read in the paper that a Jew died and some of our boys were arrested. What is going to happen now?"

"Two dozen of our men were arrested, charged with incitement to riot, and released on bail. But some old Jew died, as you said, so there may be a charge of murder. The grand jury meets tomorrow. That is the body that declares a crime in this forsaken country. Word is out that the police have an eyewitness but we have no idea who it could be. So we wait."

The food came. Finnhandlerr, with a healthy appetite, shoveled the food in fast. Harold, with no appetite, cut his sausage into tiny pieces and hid them among the cabbage. The Nazi and imposter finished, with the giant not noticing how little Harold had eaten. They left the restaurant together. Harold could not shake the OD leader.

"I am on my way to see *Herr* Willknecht," Finnhandler said placing his hand on the reporter's shoulder. "You will join me." Harold knew this wasn't a request but an order from his superior.

At the Willknecht apartment Helga answered the door. "Georg and Christiana are listening to *lieder* on the radio," she said as she ushered them into the kitchen, which was filled with the smell of fresh bread. "They will be pleased to see you. And Harold, thank you for watching over Christiana at the march. She told us how you hustled her off to your flat when danger threatened."

The irony that both a German mom and a Jewish mom had thanked him for protecting their child during the same event wasn't lost on Harold. He realized that at the end of the day, all mothers are alike.

"Max, Harold, how good to see you," Willknecht gushed as Helga ushered the two men into the warm kitchen. "Our daughter told us how quickly you acted on Friday. Let us have a *schnapps* to celebrate our deliverance from the Jews."

"I'm sorry to decline your kind offer, Georg. I am too weary for drink tonight." Escape from the joviality of Willknecht and Finnhandlerr, flight from their anti-Semitic innuendoes, was the only thing Harold wished to contemplate at the moment. The grief of the Drabinsky family was too fresh in his mind. The reporter didn't trust himself to maintain composure in the face of the Germans. "I only stopped to inform you that I have returned from New Jersey."

"I'm glad you did Harold. There are things I have to tell you. We are having a general membership meeting Friday at the Yorkville Casino. You will be there."

"And Harold," Finnhandlerr chimed in, "I am lifting weights on Wednesday after work, at Albrecht's Gym. You will join me."

Christiana, slouched at the kitchen table with a movie magazine in front of her face, peered out at her father and his authoritarian friend thwarting Harold's attempt to leave. "*Vater*, poor Harold looks so tired. Let me walk him to his door."

"Yes Daughter," Willknecht said gruffly. "*Herr* Appel should rest. He has much to do tomorrow." And the building super turned to Finnhandlerr, releasing Harold from his attention.

Accepting his dismissal, Harold rose, and with a quick goodbye to Helga, exited the apartment, went around the corner, and up the stairs to his flat, followed at every step by Christiana. "Come in," he ordered the girl as he fumbled with his keys. "I have to talk with you."

"Yes Harold, I've been waiting all weekend to talk to you.

How well do you know Solly?" Christiana followed the reporter into his sparsely furnished apartment.

Alarm bells went off in Harold's head. Had Saul slipped up? Had he revealed something? "I know him well Christiana. I lived next door to him before I was lucky enough to move here."

Before Harold could shrug out of his overcoat, before he could sit down, Christiana started talking. Her words came in a torrent. "I love boys. I love doing things with boys. To be frank, I love sex," the girl confessed. Her face turned bright red, either from excitement or embarrassment. "I had sex with Solly and it was great. But Harold, he isn't like other boys I've been with. He's circumcised. Is he Jewish? I don't care if he is. He was good in bed."

The German daughter was confessing to be fast and loose. But why would she confess to Harold? Was it because they were near the same age? And what should the reporter say to her while maintaining his cover? "No Christiana, no. Solly is not Jewish. He's Irish. I know his family. He was born in this country. I've heard that babies born here are circumcised in the hospital as a matter of course. Have you never been with an American-born boy?"

Christiana's pretty face grew contemplative, as if she were considering her many liaisons. How many could there have been in an eighteen-year-old life? "Harold, Solly is the first boy I've been with who wasn't German."

Saul had slipped, slipped his pants off and revealed his circumcision, but it wasn't fatal, not with Christiana's love of boys. Circumcision could be fatal, though, to Harold. He might be expected to shower with the Germans on Wednesday, when he was ordered to the gym with Finnhandlerr, for he as with all Jewish men, lacked a foreskin.

"Solly was the best I've ever been with." Christiana continued. "I want to see him again."

"Girl, this is not something I want to know. Where is your German upbringing? What would your father say?"

"I have shocked you Harold. I thought that you, being not much older, would understand. My parents don't. I can't talk to them at all. Do you know I can't even listen to the music I like? No swing, no jazz, just those damn *lieder*. My mother doesn't like me because I'm young and pretty, and I'm just in the way to my father. He ignores me or he yells at me. I hate living there. I'm moving out as soon as I finish high school and get a job."

"Your parents worry about you, Christiana."

"Yeah, worry as in 'Is she doing the proper German thing?'" The girl rolled her eyes. "They don't care about me, about how I feel. It's German this, German that, and all for the *Vaterland*. Hey, you probably take this Bund stuff seriously too. Why am I wasting my time talking to you?"

"Christiana," Harold said, leaning forward to make himself more convincing, "it is deadly serious business protecting our families from those who would destroy us."

"Ohhh! I should have known better than to trust you. You're another damn Nazi! My life is so full of them!" The girl threw up her arms, turned, and stormed out, slamming Harold's door behind her. The whole building vibrated as she stomped down the stairs.

The teakettle whistled. Harold couldn't prevent a grin from stealing across his face as he poured the hot water. Christiana hated Nazis. Something had immunized her. Willknecht had trouble in his own family.

Harold still had to write a story about Morris Drabinsky's funeral. He sat down in front of his typewriter and sipped his tea. 'Man killed by Nazi rocks in Yorkville buried in Westchester yesterday,' he typed. *It's journalism,* the reporter thought. *I can't let my feelings influence the reporting. But I feel the same way as Christiana; my life is too full of those damned Nazis.*

CHAPTER ELEVEN

LIFTING WEIGHTS

THE CITY-ROOM WAS quiet at five in the morning; the only sounds were the steady clack-clack of Pat O'Rourke's typewriter and the chatter of the international teletype bringing news from Europe, where it was already midday. O'Rourke sat in his shirtsleeves, surrounded by a pool of light in the otherwise darkened room. "Go away, unless you have coffee," he called out.

"No coffee," Harold replied as he made his way through the jumble of desks he knew so well. "Just curiosity. What are you doing here at this ungodly hour?"

"Working. I've been working all night. Another showgirl was murdered."

"How was she killed?" Harold rummaged through his desk drawer while awaiting the answer.

"A bum found her body, naked, in an alley off 42nd Street near Eighth Avenue around eleven o'clock last night. She had a stocking wrapped around her neck, just like the other two this month. Some nut must have it in for showgirls. She had a part in Cohen's new play and now she's dead. I saw the body before they took it to the morgue. She was a real pretty one." O'Rourke's voice was flat, devoid of its usual Irish lilt. "What are you doing here Harold? Shouldn't you be at the printing plant?"

"Yeah. But I've gotta leave this story on Aaron's desk," Harold said as he clipped the pages together. A quick step took him across the aisle to where O'Rourke slumped dejectedly over his typewriter. He punched his friend on the shoulder. "Why the long face? We don't make the news. We just report it. Ohhh, I get it. She was real pretty, huh?"

"Yeah, she was pretty. So what? She's dead. What's the matter with you? Are you happy another pretty girl got killed? Maybe Aaron should put you on the Showgirl Murders instead of the Nazis."

As if on cue Aaron appeared. "Morning gentlemen. What's news?"

"Another girl got killed last night," O'Rourke said flatly.

"Do you have the story?" the boss asked.

"Yeah, I got it." O'Rourke pointed at his typewriter.

"And what about you, Apple? What do you have?"

"Chief, I've gotta go print this rag you call a newspaper. I just wanted to leave this small contribution to its exalted pages."

"Apple, you don't bother me with your high and mighty act. Your piece on the parades in Yorkville was good. Stories like that get us readers. Keep them coming. Are you having any problems I can help you with?"

Harold loved praise from his boss. His quick smile showed his pleasure and then the smile disappeared as he grew serious. "A grand jury will be looking into murder charges, chief. I could use some help with that. Also there will be the police investigation. I can't handle that while I'm undercover. Why don't you put O'Rourke on it? We work well together."

"Well Patrick? Would you like to work with Apple?"

O'Rourke perked up. "Anything would be better than these showgirl murders."

"I'll put Cassanova on the murder story," Aaron said. "He likes to write about the fruits and nuts in this town."

"Yeah, I do need a change." O'Rourke sighed while he stretched out in front of his typewriter. "And I do like working with Apple, even if he infuriates me sometimes."

"OK, you deadbeats can work together," Aaron said. "But I want stories, not hot air."

"That's great," Harold said. He was half out the door. "Oh yeah. I almost forgot. I'm getting married when this Nazi stuff is over."

"Does your girl know that?" Aaron yelled as the door slammed shut behind the reporter.

At least Harold didn't have to put up with interruptions from Finnhandlerr. The OD leader was busy with a repair of one of the auxiliary presses, the one used to print the Sunday supplement. *He can repair machinery,* Harold thought as he wrestled with the big linotype keyboard, *but he can't fix his own head. The guys in Yorkville don't think like anyone else. So much German stuff, not enough American.*

Just before quitting time Scudari called Harold into his office. "Mr. O'Rourke is waiting for you in the lobby."

"God damn it. What's he doing here?" Harold muttered under his breath as he collected his coat and ran off the plant floor. He saw Finnhandlerr out of the corner of his eye as he exited. The big man was sitting in the middle of a pile of machinery, looking bewildered. *Germans can't do everything, you asshole,* the reporter thought. *I hope Scudari fires you for messing up his machine.* Harold kept moving, trotting through the lobby and motioning to O'Rourke, who was leaning against a wall with a butt in his mouth, to follow him. He hurried down the street.

"What the hell is your hurry?" O'Rourke panted as he caught up to Harold inside of Bernie's, the bar where reporters hung out.

"You dummy," Harold yelled at his friend. "I told you that a Nazi works at the printing plant. If he sees me with you it would raise all kinds of questions in his mind. Hell, my life could even be in danger." He slid into a booth and huddled by the wall, out of sight of anyone coming into the seedy saloon.

Bernie, the barkeep, came over to see what the reporters were drinking. "Two whiskies, straight up," O'Rourke ordered.

The warmth of the whiskey streaming slowly down his gullet calmed Harold enough to talk with his friend about his plans. "Yeah Pat, Sally and I are getting hitched when this Nazi story is finished."

"Good luck, old man. You won't catch me following your example."

Still, the news called for another round of drinks, a toast to Sally, more liquor, a toast to marriage, and a beer chaser. The two friends staggered out of Bernie's hours later, looking for a hot meal to sop up all the alcohol sloshing around in their bellies. A few blocks walk brought them to The Delmonico Grill, their favorite steakhouse. Inside O'Rourke doffed his fine camel-hair coat while Harold took off his second-hand overcoat.

"I'm not dressed for this place," Harold whispered to his friend.

"No one cares how you're dressed, Buddy. I look good enough for both of us. Why would anyone look at the Hanukah menorah when they can look at the magnificent Christmas tree?" O'Rourke pointed at the angel-clad fir by the door of the restaurant as they walked to their favorite table.

While waiting for their steaks, Harold and O'Rourke fell into their normal debate on the merits of each other's religion. Which was better, Catholicism or Judaism? O'Rourke was fallen away, but he argued with the tenacity of a Jesuit. Harold knew the arguments were never serious to his friend. The Irishman just liked to argue. But their discussions meant something to Harold. He wasn't the most religious guy, but being Jewish meant something to him.

"Your tree is good for one lousy day. Our candles shine for a week and a day," Harold huffed at O'Rourke, a sure sign that he was into the argument. He saw that landscape again, the one with barbed wire and the Jews lined up behind it. "Fire trumps trees, Pat. They're both natural parts of the world grafted onto our religions but you have to agree, fire is more powerful. I know what the Nazis believe. I'm an expert in Nazi ideology. I've had a crash course. They believe in blood, another part of nature. Blood puts out fire. That's blood shed today, not 2,000 or 5,000 years ago by some made-up Jesus or fake Moses."

Race, blood, and soil are Nazi dogma, Harold thought as he cut into his bloody porterhouse. *They believe in blood and race like it was the word of God through Hitler. Now there's something to chew on.* He took a bite of meat. *Party dogma as religion. Hitler as Pope. All rare meat to the Nazis, just like this steak.*

"Harold you're crazy if you believe any of that Nazi crud," O'Rourke said, his voice shrill. "You're just trying to get my goat."

What happened? Something I said hit a nerve with Pat and he stopped arguing.

"Tomorrow morning I'll go to the Criminal Court and find out what charges the storm troopers are up against," O'Rourke continued. "If you want to believe in something, believe in American justice. The Nazis killed; the Nazis will be punished."

"I want to believe in justice, Pat. But who writes the rules? At work I listen to Finnhandlerr. I go home and listen to Willknecht and all the rest. A Jewish life isn't worth a plug nickel to those guys. So say a Nazi gets punished in an American court. And only one will, because only one guy is dead. It won't make any difference to the Nazis. We'll be making a martyr." *The gospel according to Hitler,* Harold thought. *Kill a Jew and go to heaven.*

❧

The street lamps came on but their glow did nothing to dispel the dread Harold felt for the evening of activity Finnhandlerr had planned for him.

"You will enjoy our little exercise session, comrade. It's always good to build the body for *Vaterland und volk*. Hitler himself directs us to be strong." Finnhandlerr was going on with his usual Nazi blather as he and Harold walked down a shabby street near the East River.

They arrived at an old warehouse and climbed to the second floor. The wafting odor of stale sweat permeated Harold's nostrils. Renewed concern over keeping his cover had his senses on high alert. His experience with weightlifting, which seemed to be the German national sport, was less than none. He sensed an evening of embarrassment over his average muscles, only to be topped off with horror if the *ubermenschen* discover his circumcision.

At the top of the stairs Finnhandlerr pushed open the door to a very large room filled with benches, racks of dumbbells, and large perspiring Germans. Three walls of the room were glass, large windows through which the streetlights shone weakly and reflections off the river danced with the waves. But what struck Harold the most was the filmy distortions of the contents of the room on the inside of the windows, like fun-house mirrors making the weight-lifters hugely fat or vanishingly skinny. Finnhandlerr didn't seem to notice the surreal images surrounding him as he said, "Welcome to Albrecht's Gym Harold. You will have good times here."

Like looking at life through a Nazi prism, Harold thought.

Benches littered the scarred wooden floor of the gym. Weights were arrayed around the perimeter of the room. In front of the one wall without windows ran a long counter. A tall man, his well-muscled torso calling out 'youngster' in contradiction to his graying hair and worn face, stood behind the counter, handing out towels and greetings in German to all who ventured into his sweaty realm.

"That is Hans Albrecht, the owner," whispered Finnhandlerr into Harold's ear as they passed the counter. "The old man is still fit. He can out-lift half the OD."

The two men entered the locker room and Finnhandlerr was immediately the center of attention, mobbed by his acolytes of the OD, in various states of dress and undress. "I'm going to out-lift everyone in the City Contest," roared the big man. "Even that damned Jew who beat me last year. I am ready to counter his trickery now."

Harold hung back, relieved that no one seemed to be paying him any mind. He had dreaded being in the locker room where his circumcised state might become public knowledge when he changed clothes. But everyone was crowded around the big man; no one noticed Harold quickly slipping from street pants to flannel shorts. *Halfway there. Now if I can avoid showering.* The reporter glanced around the locker room one more time. *Whoa, that guy over there is looking right at me. I don't like his eyes. They're shifty, as if he'd throw me, or anyone, under the bus. What's his name? I know I've met him. Oh yeah, it's Everhardt, Werner Everhardt. I met him at the Casino the other night. Was he looking at me? What did he see? I was only exposed for an instant.* Everhardt's eyes locked with Harold's. He turned towards the OD leader as if to say, 'I've got you, Jew.' Chills went up and down Harold's body even though the locker room was warm.

Men in flannel shorts and grey sweatshirts bearing the double lightning bolt insignia of the OD filed out of the locker room. The main gym was colder, with frost appearing on some of the big windows. Harold shivered as he looked around for something to do, some weight he could lift without embarrassing himself. He pivoted in place, looking for some kind of exercise a neophyte could do, and cracked his shins on a rack of low-lying dumbbells.

Finnhanderr turned at Harold's cry of pain. "Apple, haven't you been in a gym before? Stay with me."

Harold got red in the face. *The big Kraut didn't have to rebuke me. I'm his equal here, aren't I? I'm not on OD duty. But maybe I'm always on duty. I think that's the way it is with the Nazis, duty above all, duty to the leader. If they knew I was really a Jew, a dirty kike, their duty would be to kill me. I'm walking on dangerous ground here.* Harold grimaced and joined the Germans around a man lying prone on an exercise bench, preparing to lift an outrageous amount of weight.

It was Everhardt, the guy with the untrustworthy eyes, which were now staring up at a big pile of plates on either end of a steel bar, held above his chest on a rickety stand. He reached for the bar and lifted, his shifty eyes almost popping out of his head with the effort. His neck arched and the tendons on the back stood out as he held the weight; one second, two, three, five, ten seconds, straight up above his head, until he finally bent his arms and puffing mightily, slammed the barbell back into the safety of the stand. Two of his comrades, one on either side, caught the weight as it bounced and lowered it to a resting place. Everhardt rested also, but his breath was ragged and sweat soaked his shirt.

"We set a record every time we come to the gym," Finnhandlerr said to the group gathered around the lifter. "A personal record. Our hero, of course, is Josef Manger, who won the heavyweight title in the 1936 Berlin Olympics. Germany tied with Egypt for the most weightlifting medals in Berlin. Everhardt here never lifted 300 pounds before, so even if it does not seem like much to you," and he looked at the biggest guys in the crowd, the ones who caught the rebounding barbell, "it is an accomplishment for him. National Socialism teaches us to build our bodies for the good of the state. If we are strong in body we will be strong in battle." The men nodded and reached to applaud the still panting Nazi, clapping him on the shoulders, shaking his hand, and punching his quivering legs. Harold joined in, slapping the happy man on the back as he sat up. But the OD Leader was not finished. "One year ago Everhardt came to the gym, soft in body and spirit. He had quit school and had no job. I made him join the OD. Now he has finished high school and has a job. He is the New German Man."

So the Storm Troopers are social workers, in the business of saving souls, Harold reflected. *I bet they only save German souls.* He had to clench his throat to stop the bile from spewing out.

The New German Man basked in the appreciation of his fellows for long minutes before resuming the prone position. He called for the barbell to be restored to the stand and weights added. Theatrically huffing and puffing, he grabbed the bar, his biceps bulging with the strain. He lifted the bar, bent his arms outward, and dropped the weight to his chest. Long seconds passed; everyone was quiet. The big man standing behind, the spotter, reached for the bar, as if to relieve Everhardt of his burden. The red-faced weightlifter hoarsely called him off. With eyes popping and all the muscles in his body extruding, Everhardt heaved the barbell straight up. His elbows locked and an explosive groan escaped his lips. The weight wobbled in mid-air. Spotters leaped to grasp the bar. The young OD man popped up, a triumphant grin staining his sweat-streaked face.

"Good," Finnhandlerr said curtly. "Next time you will do repetitions." The OD Leader turned quickly and moved away. The group surrounding Everhardt dissolved, leaving only Harold hovering over the man.

"Hail Werner. That was an impressive performance," Harold said.

"You know my name, *Herr Appel.* Well, I make no effort to hide either my name or my deeds. You, on the other hand, have something to hide. I saw you in the locker room. You are right to conceal that miserable excuse for a *schwanz.* Go on hiding

Appelstein. I won't tell on you—yet. Remember my name. I have uses for you."

Everhardt's words hit Harold like a hard slap on the face followed by a punch to the belly. He started to double up in fear of what this miserable young Nazi could do to him. He saw larger than life Germans, wavering reflections in the big windows, become real, jumping down and surrounding him, pulling down his pants, exposing his lack of a foreskin. *Germans have foreskins, Jews don't.* The cry rang in his ears. *Foreskin! Foreskin! Chopped off at twice four days.* Nazis swirled about him, laughing, pointing at his circumcision. *He doesn't have a cock!*

"Appel, what is the matter with you? Are you sick?" It was Finnhandlerr. The OD Leader had snuck up behind Harold while he was bending over.

Harold popped back up at the sound of Finnhandlerr's voice. "No. No. I had a pain in my stomach because I was contemplating lifting as much weight as *Herr* Everhardt. Someday I will. Someday."

"No more thinking. We demand action in the OD." Finnhandlerr set to work on the dumbbells, lofting a sixty-five pound weight in each hand, lifting from his side to his chest in an alternating rhythm.

Harold, head still whirling from his encounter with Everhardt, eyed the sixty-five pound weights, and then decided on a more modest twenty pound pair. Up and down, he imitated Finnhandlerr's movements, building a sheen of sweat with each curl. The repetitive movements calmed him. He saw nothing in the windows but what was really there: the reflections of a bunch of sweaty Germans, and one lone Jew, lifting weights. Despite his leader's order, Harold thought while he lifted. *What did Everhardt see? I was careful to shield myself and I wasn't exposed for more than seconds. Was he guessing? What reason would he have to guess at anything? I barely know the guy. Still, there are his eyes. Shifty. He looks like he enjoys having power.*

After warming up with the dumbbells the men did some stretching. Finnhandlerr then built his weight, three fifty pound plates on either side of a fifteen pound bar. "Starting from a standing position, I will kneel with my knees, and grasp the underside of the bar," the big man explained to Harold and the crowd of onlookers who gathered to see him work. "Then, in one move, I will rotate my arms, bring the weight to my chest, and stand up. That is called 'the clean.' From there I will flex my knees once and 'jerk' the bar over my head. The move is called the 'clean and jerk.' I will do ten repetitions. My record for this move is three hundred ninety-five pounds, so you can see I am taking it easy on myself to begin with."

Harold watched in wonder as Finnhandlerr repeated the exercise time after time with ease. As the big man lowered the bar to the scarred wooden floor for the last time, he pointed at the smaller man and said mockingly, "Let us see what you can do, Appel."

Harold did not want to embarrass himself by trying to lift too light a load but it would be awful to attempt too much and fail. "I need your advice Max. Do you think two hundred pounds is too much for a beginner like me to lift?" Two hundred was probably too much. Harold hoped Finnhandlerr would have pity on him.

Finnhandlerr looked at Harold with a practiced eye. The reporter felt like his body was being dissected in public. "You do not have much muscle, Harold. Start with a hundred. We will build you up." The OD men still in earshot tittered, until Finnhandlerr stopped their laughter with cold words. "*Herr* Appel is willing to work to improve himself, just like *Herr* Everhardt. Are you?"

Harold quickly prepared his bar, grateful for the support. He imitated the big man's moves and lifted the bar to his chest. He braced himself for the next move and lifted. To his amazement it was easy. He stood waving the hundred pound weight over his head like a victory flag.

Harold completed ten repetitions, did twenty sit-ups and a

dozen pushups, enough for his biceps and abdominal muscles to hurt. But it was a good hurt, the hurt of accomplishment.

Finnhandlerr wandered over. "Good Harold, you will make yourself strong for the Reich. Someday you will return and be strong enough to fight for the Fatherland."

NOOO, Harold cried in his head. *I don't want to hurt for Hitler. I want to hurt for Harold.* Still, he managed a grin though a grimace, and Finnhanderr seemed satisfied that his protégé was building his body for National Socialism. As soon as the big man turned to harassing another trooper the reporter dropped to a bench, hoping to catch his breath.

From his solitary seat, sheltered by racks of weights, Harold had a good view of goings on in the gym, without being visible himself. There was some kind of commotion going on at the center of the front counter, where the oldster who ran the place was tacking a red, black, and white poster to a pillar. "When is it Allie?" Cries rose from the crowd around the still fit man.

"December 17th is the date, Comrades. There is still time to train, but one must be serious. Competition will be fierce. Lifters will be there from clubs all over the city."

Harold rose from his seat of pain and went to see what all the excitement was about. The poster read INTERBOROUGH WEIGHT LIFTING CHAMPIONSHIP in large red letters, weight classes from flyweight to heavyweight. "This is what I have been waiting for all year," Finnhandlerr rumbled from a spot directly in front of the crowd. "Last year I was cheated out of the trophy by a Jew, who claimed my final and best lift was illegal. Now I shall have revenge." The big man's words seemed as blood red to Harold as the letters on the poster, streaming from his mouth to circle the room.

I've got to get out of here. The words ran through Harold's head.

The reporter slipped into the changing room while everyone's attention was focused on Finnhandlerr, quickly gathered his stuff, and rushed down the stairs to the cold, dark street without even pulling on his pants or coat. "No one saw me," he said to himself hopefully as he left the building and hurried up York Avenue, shivering from the cold and the bloody hate he left behind. He was in New York City, yet he felt like he was in Germany, planning the next move in the minuet of his masquerade, the choreography continually growing more complex. Avoiding a public shower where his shaved penis would be exposed was a small, if necessary, move. But the big problem lay within him. How to act like a Nazi, share their single-minded rage, participate in their fervent Jew-baiting, and remain a good person. *I'm a reporter, not an actor. Am I in over my head? And now I have Everhardt to complicate it all.* The few people passing him on the street all had collars upturned against the chill night air. Harold stopped to shrug into his overcoat then, still in shorts and carrying his pants, headed up 86th Street toward Jaeger's.

At the restaurant Harold went to the phone booth and put on his pants. *Just like Superman.* He dialed his partner. It was half past seven, too late for O'Rourke, recently reprieved from the night shift, to still be at the office and too early for him to be out carousing.

O'Rourke's mother answered. "Hullo, my boy, how be ye?" she said in her almost unintelligible Irish brogue. "I'll git Pat."

A short wait and O'Rourke came to the phone. "Pat, what did you find out? Is the grand jury returning an indictment?"

"I earned my pay today, Harold. I talked to everyone I could find at the Criminal Courts Building. No one knew nothing. They've really got a lid on this one. Finally, about five in the afternoon, right before quitting time, I found one old broad I could charm. It was the chief clerk of Superior Court, Sarah Thaler. She knew all about the Nazis, and was positive two of them would be charged on Wednesday. Then I went uptown to the Yorkville precinct house and looked for a talkative desk sergeant I know.

He told me homicide has two eyewitnesses who can make positive identification on the rats who threw the stones."

"That's awfully fast work Pat. Someone must want to lock this up pretty bad." *Someone besides me.* "Hell Pat, I was there and I couldn't tell you who flung those stones."

"Maybe the witnesses weren't on the ground," O'Rourke crowed. "The sergeant said detectives went door-to-door in the building across the street from the Turnhall to find people who were watching out their window."

The police had acted quickly. They had been officially notified of the death of Drabinsky shortly after Harold had left the precinct house Friday evening. That gave them all day Saturday and Sunday to find their witnesses, develop the case, and present it to the grand jury Monday morning. The case must be air-tight if indictments would be handed down in two days. Also, someone up the line, maybe in the prosecutor's office or city hall, had made the connection with *Kristallnacht* and decided that the killer of a Jew would not go unpunished in New York City. Harold wondered who in government had made the leap: Mayor LaGuardia had clashed with the Bund, several Congressional committees were investigating fascist activity, and District Attorney Tom Dewey was a smart guy with a political nose. *Yeah, it's Dewey, all right,* the reporter concluded. *The case fits with his ambition. But I don't care if Tom Dewey wants to be governor. He's doing the right thing.*

Harold hung up on Pat, dug another nickel from his pocket, and dialed Sally.

"She's not at home," her father said. "She and Saul are over at the Drabinskys. But Harold, the police called. They want to talk to Saul tomorrow. Levi Sobidor gave them his name."

"I thought they would. The police are doing a complete investigation. Don't worry, Izzy. He knows what to say. And would you please tell Sally I'll talk to her tomorrow. Oh yeah, have you seen my parents? I've been so busy I haven't called them."

"You haven't even bothered to call your parents? They're not in Cleveland; they're in New York. No long distance. So pick up the phone and call." Izzy suddenly left his aggrieved parent lecture voice. "I'm glad you talked to Saul about the police. I didn't know whether to be worried or not. In Russia if the police called you in, sometimes you never came back."

"You're not in Russia anymore. Goodbye Izzy." Harold slipped out of the phone booth and found an empty table, all the while thinking of the police and Saul. He had no choice but to trust the redhead to tell the truth but not the whole truth. The masquerade was in Saul's hands, and Everhardt's hands, and who else. It was so complicated. *I'm just going to plow ahead until it falls apart, then, if I'm lucky, I'll get out in one piece. Sally won't be happy if she finds out how shaky I am.* A morbid thought ran through Harold's head. *I hope Aaron doesn't have to pick up my body at the morgue.*

There was an early edition of the *World Journal* on the table. The headline screamed 'German Army marches into Austria.' The talkative old crone was there again. Harold ordered the Tuesday special, sausages and boiled potatoes, a rather bland meal. The spice was in the waitress's talk. "If Roosevelt does not like what we do in Germany, that's too bad. He cannot tell Hitler what to do. I come from Austria. It was we who cried out for *Anschluss* and Hitler obliged. President Rosenfeld should mind his own business. We don't tell him how to solve his nigger problem. He should stop meddling in our business."

Harold took an angry bite of sausage. *The problem is, you old crone, you're not in the Vaterland. You're in America. And you have to live by our rules.*

Chapter Twelve

TO MARRY THE BUND

G OOD GOD, FINNHANDLERR *tells some awful jokes,* Harold thought as he left the printing plant at the end of the day. *Why do Jews get circumcised? Because they always like to get half off.* The reporter crossed the busy street, dodged a big red truck rumbling to its delivery of raw newsprint at the loading dock around the corner, and found the safety of the World Journal lobby on the other side. He climbed the stairs to the city room. Printers didn't hang out in the lobby of the main building, just like news staff did not frequent the printing plant, which was an industrial building, smelling of ink and oil, unfit for the tender sensibilities of reporters. He stood at the door and looked around. No O'Rourke. Where could he be? But there was Aaron, ready to pounce on any reporter who did not look busy.

"Apple, come see the story your partner wrote," the editor called from across the room.

"This is a great story, chief." Harold handed back the galleys destined for the early morning edition. "Pat even got the names of the guys they're indicting. How'd he do that?" His fingers, smudged with ink from the galleys, tap-danced across his forehead. "The Thaler woman, the court clerk, I bet that's how he got the names. And Everhardt is named. I know that rat. He's one of the dangerous ones. He may have seen me changing in the locker room the other day. *Achtung*, that's why he didn't turn me in for having a sliced-up *schwanz*. He knew he was being investigated for murder and figured he needed an angle. I'm his ace in the hole. Well, he won't fry. It's only second degree. I guess the grand jury doesn't understand how bloodthirsty the Bund really is." The reporter cradled his forehead in his hands, lost in thought.

"Harold, now you look like a proper printer," Aaron laughed. "You've got ink all over your face."

Soaping his hands in the newspaper's washroom, Harold thought about why the rap was only murder two. He dashed water on his face, trying to erase the brand of the printer, and wondered what he could do to make New York see the evil in the Bund.

❧

The reporter took a long walk to Sally's office at West 22nd and Eighth Avenue, automatically cutting through the throngs of people on the sidewalks and the traffic in the streets. He was thinking about the parades, Moe's death by stone, and what he could do to bring down the Nazis. *I'm not an impartial reporter this time. I'm a Jew.*

Sally's office sat in the heart of the garment district. Evidence of the dress biz lay all around. Set-up boys were pushing carts filled with garment pieces across sidewalks, over cracked pavement, between work rooms on opposite sides of the street. Well-dressed salesmen were strutting down the middle of the sidewalks while mousy secretaries and machine operators scurried along the edges from paycheck to paycheck. And what did they all have in common? They were all Jewish. Well mostly. The workers were immigrants; Slavs, Poles, Russkies, Italians, as well as Jews. But Jews ruled the rag trade; the sharp-eyed, well-dressed men, all were Jewish, clothing America, and much of the world for that matter.

It was quitting time all around him. Harold looked at the sewing machine operators streaming onto the sidewalks. *One of them probably put your brown flannel uniform together, Finnhandlerr. The stripe down the pants might have been sewn on by Jews. And certainly a Jew sold you your Nazi suit. I hope he made lots of money on it.*

Sally's firm, Fancy Frocks, took up the top three floors of a five-story building. Harold entered a large freight elevator, half filled with empty dress trucks—closets on wheels, actually. The clock was balanced on five as the cage crawled up to the third floor, the clamshell doors rose and fell synchronously, a bell dinged, and the sole occupant of the elevator was trampled by the workers anxious to leave the dreary cut and sew, press and fold, of their lives. As the reporter fell into the dress trucks in the back of the elevator, Sally materialized to pull him to his feet and into her arms. The employees of Fancy Frocks took a moment in their rush to the street to applaud the newly engaged couple.

"You're a stitch in time, Doll." The elevator opened on the ground floor, the crowd flowed into the lobby and onto the street, and Harold held Sally in an embrace that turned into a long delayed kiss. "Let's go to Angelo's," he said after they caught their breath.

The couple walked up the block and around the corner to Angelo's Roman Garden, a small café and a favorite of Sally's. They settled into the last of a row of tables, furthest from the entrance, set against the wall of a narrow room. On one side were pictures of noble Romans, from Julius Caesar to Benito Mussolini. The other long wall was mirrored, reflecting candles stuck in wine bottles and red and white checkered tablecloths. Harold put his elbows on the table, cupped his chin in his folded hands, and gazed around the flickering flame at the gentle face of his beloved. What he saw was a small, delicate nose, perched above a rosebud pout of a mouth, and two delicate arching brows over deep brown eyes he could lose himself in. What he didn't see was the hook-nosed hag or heavy-browed harridan of the Jewess in Nazi magazines. A certain peace descended over the reporter, knowing he did not have to act the hard-edged German. He could sit without hatred in his heart for the next couple of hours. Still, the thought that he could picture propaganda images in his head while looking at his girl troubled him.

Harold reached for Sally's small hand, to which she returned a radiant smile. With his other hand he dipped into his pants pocket and withdrew something he'd been carrying all day, a tiny box. Her eyes widened as he fumbled it open, held up a ring for her inspection, and placed it on her finger. The diamond caught the candlelight in the darkened room, absorbing it for an instant, and reflecting it back in a sparkling dance. The mirrors magnified the glow, spreading it down the long room as Sally waved her hand above her head, spreading the light in a cascading rhythm. She reached across the table and drew Harold's lips to hers. They continued the elevator kiss, until Sally sensed the waiter standing next to her. "Oh Carlo, look what Harold gave me." And she held up her hand again to display her prize.

"Congratulations *Senorita*," the young waiter said, his dark eyes sparkling from the brightness of the diamond. "May you have a long life and much happiness. Some *vino* to celebrate?"

"They love you here Doll," Harold said as Carlo returned with a bottle of good wine, not some cheap *chianti*. *This is a part of Sally I don't know. What does she do during the day, at work? Does she have lots of friends? She's on a first name basis with this guy.* He looked at the waiter, who was pouring the wine with a flourish. Slicked back hair, a thin waxed mustache, Latin good looks. *Should I be jealous? How well do I know anyone, even myself? I'm thinking things now I wouldn't have considered a few weeks ago. Like that guy I saw outside Sally's building, the one with the huge honker that rivaled Durante's. I thought to myself, 'Now there goes a Yid.'* The good feeling he had felt watching Sally enjoy the ring was gone, replaced by fear, fear of others, fear of himself.

Sally was talking, he realized. Her words were going over, around, but not into, his head. "…and last year I did some artwork for the restaurant, for one of their newspaper ads. It was really nothing, didn't pay much at all. But I got to know the people here."

"I didn't know that Doll." Harold smiled vacantly at his girl. *Hoo boy*, he thought, *I have to get a hold of myself, get the old happy-go-lucky Harold back, or I'm going to have all kinds of problems.*

They sipped their wine and Sally said, "Saul's been acting crazy since Friday."

"You mean because Moe died?"

"No, that's not it. He met some girl at the parade."

Harold was relieved. It wasn't all about him. Some of his fear started to dissipate. "Yes he did. He met Georg Willknecht's daughter. I've told you about him, the super of my building and a big Nazi. Christiana's a nice girl, not at all like her father. She and I were together when I ran into Saul because Georg had asked me to watch her, make sure she didn't get into trouble. He and his wife can't handle her. She doesn't like all the Nazi stuff."

"That's good. She's not a pushover, but she is still German."

"Yeah, so what?"

"She's a *shiksa*. Don't tell Father. He wouldn't like Saul being with a non-Jew."

So we get hatred from both sides. Well I can't stop Christiana from seeing Saul. She's headstrong. She'll do what she wants. But I can do what Sally wants. "OK, I won't tell your father."

❧

Loud, boisterous singing greeted Harold as he descended the stairs to *Das Bierhaus* at the Yorkville Casino. He had hopped a subway and come straight to the beer hall after dropping Sally off at her figure drawing class near Washington Square. The crowd in the basement, immersed in camaraderie and beer, raised their voices in German song, repeating one line over and over again, *Der soldat marsch...marsch...marsch*. Harold was chilled by the power, the vehemence, in their voices. Two men in brown storm trooper garb stood in front of him, blocking the way. The singing suddenly stopped and the two goose-stepped, a straight-legged quickstep that was the signature of the Nazi party, into the barroom. Their right arms were held high in the Hitler salute. Tumultuous applause engulfed the room. The German American Bund was cheering for Werner Everhardt and his fellow accused murderer, Klaus Groening.

Harold entered the bar unnoticed. All eyes were on the two heroes standing at attention at the center of the room. Barmaids scurried about distributing flagons of dark German beer. When all had their brew, mugs were raised and Max Finnhandlerr offered a toast. "We salute two sons of Germany, two soldiers who dared to confront our enemy. We drink to Werner and Klaus. Heil Hitler."

A manic energy filled the room. The magic words were repeated over and over. "Heil Hitler! Heil Hitler! Heil Hitler!"

Harold pushed through the milling men, to where Willknecht was sitting at a small table with Reinhold Stubble. "Have you heard the news, my friend?" the super called out. He sounded agitated. "Two of our finest youths have been accused of murder. Poor Werner and Klaus. All this fuss over the death of a Jew."

"Georg, according to the newspaper he was an important man. I'm not surprised that the Jews are making trouble for us. They have power here. But I have one question. How did the police know who to accuse? Everything happened so fast that afternoon."

"They claim to have witnesses, eyewitnesses who will identify our boys."

"How can that be?" Harold feigned surprise. *Poor Nazis, they have blinders on, they don't look up even when hurling stones.*

"Everhardt and Groening are scapegoats," interjected Reinhold

Stubble. "But we will find out more tomorrow. There is a hearing in the morning."

"It is sad there has to be a hearing," Willknecht said angrily. "We did nothing wrong. The Jews came to us."

"If we were in Germany there would be no uproar over the death of a Jew," Stubble said. "It is only in America and only because the Jews have power here. Look at all the newspapers they control. But rest assured, Georg, an action against a member of the Hebrew race is not a bad thing."

A large shadow fell across the small table. Finnhandlerr had arrived. "Kergan says not to worry. We'll get the boys out of this." The OD leader turned to Harold. "Kergan is our Irish lawyer, a real weasel with words. He always keeps us out of trouble."

Kergan? Harold shook his head. *I know that name. O'Rourke talked about a shyster in New Jersey who worked for the Bund. Must be the same one. Lawyers, they'll work for anyone if the money is right.*

∽

Look at me, Harold thought. *I'm dressed for a funeral.* He raised his hand to knock on Willknecht's door. He needed to get his suit cleaned after they buried Moe because it smelled like death. *Now it smells fresh, but that new cleaner used too much starch. That's what I get for taking it to a German cleaner, too much stiffness. But I've got to be well dressed. It's not every night I get sworn in as a storm trooper.* He knocked on the door in front of him. "*Gut abend,* Helga." He handed her a bottle of whiskey. "Some *schnapps* to heat a cold evening."

Helga took the bottle and led Harold into the warm kitchen where Georg poured the whiskey, neat, into shot glasses. "A toast," Willknecht said, raising his glass to Harold, "to the newest member of our Corps. And to Germandom, may we never forget, even though we live in this bastard country. And to Adolf Hitler, of course."

Harold drank, not to honor the *Fuehrer*, but because he wanted the heated glow the whiskey would bring. *Enough of this stuff, and I won't even know when we go to the meeting.*

Christiana, sitting at the kitchen table, downed the small shot of whiskey her father had allowed her. "It's not a bastard country. It's a wonderful country. I'm proud to be an American."

"Daughter, you are embarrassing me in front of our guest." Willknecht's neck turned red as his face began to flush.

Harold felt he had to say something to lower the tension in the room, and Willknecht's blood pressure at the same time. "Christiana, are you not proud of being a German also?"

"Well, I guess so." The girl was hesitant, as if she had not thought of being prideful in those terms.

"I did not grow up here, of course," Harold said. "So my identity revolves around my Germanness. But I can see how one would identify with the place you spent most of your life. I can also see how you think this is a wonderful country. One can do a lot here to better oneself. I myself came here to make money, something that is not possible in Germany, thanks to the selfishness of the British and French. But you should be proud of being German as well as American."

Helga served dinner. She looked at Harold with what the reporter thought was gratitude. *Probably an old argument,* Harold thought. *Christiana is rebelling against her parents and the biggest thing to rebel against is Germany. I was rebellious too when I was her age, which was not that long ago. Now let's see what I can do for her parents.*

"Georg, I was too small to know what was happening at the end of the War. What was it like? And what was Germany like after the War?"

"After long years of fighting, long years of living in the mud of the trenches, Harold, I was wounded a month before the end. I came home from France to find everything changed in my village.

There had not been any fighting in Windecken but then the government of the Kaiser fell and there was chaos. Before the War the Jews had owned some of the stores. When I got home they owned everything. My mother had died in 1917 and her house was sold to a Jew. I tried to find a job but there was nothing. I decided to go to Frankfurt. Once there I joined the *Freikorps Seibert* and fought the Communists and the Socialists of Weimar. But there was little money to be made in the militia, so I decided to come to America, where everyone knew the streets were paved with gold. I did not find gold but was able to make a living. So I sent for my wife and baby and made my life here. Christiana is of a different generation. She will never understand the way Germany was after the War, no matter how many times I tell her. But Harold, do not believe anyone who tells you the War was glamorous. It was hard and dirty and I do not like to talk about it."

Good gravy, I opened a can of worms. But at least I got Georg calmed down. Harold took another bite of sauerkraut. *Now let's find out what I want to know.* "Georg, what happened at the hearing yesterday?" *I know what happened. Let's see if the Nazi version is close to reality.*

"What we expected Harold," Willknecht replied in a monotone, as if he resented Harold for drawing him into talk of the war. "Bond was set at ten thousand dollars for each man. Too high but we paid it. And a trial date was set for January. District Attorney Dewey was there. He wants to make a reputation on the back of the Bund."

Helga poured coffee for Harold and her husband, then she and Christiana cleared the table. *Georg knows about New York politics,* the reporter thought as he sipped the bitter brew. *O'Rourke said the same thing about Dewey. He's supposed to be a straight and true reform Republican, but he knows a political case when he sees one. Maybe he'll get the charges changed to murder one.* "Wasn't Dewey involved when Fritz Kuhn was dragged into court last year?" Harold asked.

"Yes, he tried to get the *Bundesfuhrer* on a corruption charge but there was no real evidence." Willknecht's voice rose. "No true Bund member would testify against the leader."

It was time to go—time to become a Nazi storm trooper. They all donned coats and hats for the short walk to the Casino. Christiana, taking Harold's arm as they walked out the door, began singing, "I'm dreaming of a white Christmas…," as they hit the snow-dusted street. "Just like the ones I used to know…"

White Christmas, a strange song for the daughter of a Nazi to sing. Harold glided with the music. *Everyone knows it was written by a Jew. Well, at least everyone in The Bronx knows.*

The wooden platform in front of the Yorkville Casino had been taken down. There were no formations going by in front, just a few pedestrians minding their business or walking to the meeting. Still, this was the place where Moe had taken his last breath. Harold had a foreboding about this intersection. Nothing good would ever happen here in this forlorn landscape.

The ballroom on the first floor of the Casino was arranged for a meeting, with rows of folding chairs set up before the stage. A large Bund banner, bearing the gold AV symbol of the *Amerikadeutscher Volksbund* rising out of a swastika sun, was suspended from the ceiling above a small podium in the center of the platform. On the other three walls of the room alternating swastika and American flags hung limply. The harsh red field of the Nazi banner overwhelmed the softer, somehow gentler red, white, and blue. Even the red drapes covering two large windows were decorated in a black swastika motif. *What a fine habitat for homo nazium*, Harold thought. *A new race lives here.*

A grainy photo of *Der Fuerhrer*, dressed in civilian clothing and looking bored as only Hitler could look, shaking hands with an obviously awestruck Fritz Kuhn, decked out in full OD regalia, hung off to one side. *That picture is everywhere*, Harold thought. It

had been snapped during Kuhn's visit to the Berlin Olympics in
'36, the only one in existence of Hitler and Kuhn together.

Harold paused at the entrance. "You wait here," Willknecht
said. "You are part of the show." And he continued on with his
family to find seats in the orderly rows.

At that moment Harold found himself in the clutches of a
giant, the *OD Leiter* Max Finnhandlerr, in full uniform, including
a peaked cap which made him look a foot taller than his already
imposing stature. "Tonight you will be joining a noble order,
Comrade Harold. Here is your uniform." He handed the reporter
a bulky package. "Comrade Langbart will show you where to
change." He pointed to a blond storm trooper, the perfect Nordic
specimen, standing by the door.

Harold followed Langbart down a dark corridor and up
a creaky flight of stairs. At the top, dull light struggled through
a glazed window. The storm trooper pulled a key from his back
pocket and unlocked a heavy door. It could have been any office,
with three wooden desks littered with the debris of business—
invoices, forms, correspondence—and two metal filing cabinets.
Except it wasn't any office. It was the headquarters of the Bund,
evidenced by the framed picture of Hitler and Kuhn, flanked by
swastika banners. A large couch sat underneath the picture. His
escort gestured at Harold to sit.

"I vill vait outside. If you need help with the uniform open
the door."

Opportunity knocks but once, thought Harold as he turned
at the clunk of the closing door to the closest desk. A battered
lamp threw enough light for him to see the papers scattered there
were all routine: requests for Nazi paraphernalia, rent receipts,
beer invoices, and so on. What am I looking for? He turned to
one of the filing cabinets and began rifling through folders. *Ahh,
here's some meaty stuff: papers about last year's court case, correspondence with the lawyer, letters from Berlin.* He swiped a few of the

last, folded them four times and pushed them deep in his pocket. Damn, no plans to blow up the customhouse. He heard a rustling in the hall. Time to change. He tore into the package containing his new uniform. He skinned out of his suit and twisted into his brown pants with the black stripe up the side. The door opened and the blond storm trooper waltzed into the office.

"Take your time. They won't need us for a short while." Langbart settled into the sofa right next to Harold and his pile of clothing. "Finish dressing and I vill show you how to put on your belt. It can be tricky."

Harold threw his shirt on and quickly tied his tie. He did not want to be half naked with this preening example of Nazi virtue so close on the couch. *I've heard that there are fancy men in the Party leadership in Germany. It's never talked about openly because it doesn't fit in with the ubermenschen thing but it's a dirty little secret that's not so secret.* He slapped his shoes on and was ready for the belt. Langbart was right. He didn't know how to put it on.

Harold stood and clasped the belt around his waist but a part of it, destined for his shoulder, hung off his waist. "Comrade, I do not know how to do this."

Langbart stood and reached both arms around Harold. He did something to fasten the belt securely in the back then drew the other half across Harold's right shoulder and fastened it at his waist on the left side. The storm trooper's movements were practiced, sure, and intimate, and left Harold feeling violated, as if this belt contraption the Nazis wore was sapping his will to be free, a man, and a Jew. Harold shivered. Langbart reached into the bottom of the package and drew out a crooked cross armband in red and white and black and slipped it on Harold's right arm. The swastika said to the world, 'Here is a Nazi.'

Fully dressed, campaign hat upon his head, belted and swastikaed, Harold had no desire to stay in the dark office, no matter the comfort of the seat. If the company had been different he might not have minded, if it was someone like Willknecht with whom he could talk, gently mock, or laugh with, but no, it was this strange blond god who made him uneasy. But what about those letters he had stuffed in his pockets? If the Bund discovered he was robbing them, for whatever reason, his life would be over. "Comrade Langbart, where can I hang my good suit? It is newly pressed."

"Here is a closet, Comrade Appel. I must lock the office when we leave so you will have to find me later to retrieve your clothing." The reporter hung his suit and the two men, brothers in dress if not intent, went back down the creaky stairs and the darkened corridor to find the hall where Harold would dedicate his life to Hitler and the Bund.

It's nothing more than a fraternity initiation, Harold told himself, almost wanting to believe. *Just like ZBT in college.* But it wasn't a frat, it was something far more serious, it was life and death. The reporter felt more excited than nervous, his journalistic muscles were flexing, and he was already writing the story, 'How I Became a Stormtrooper.'

Reinhold Stubble was presiding over the meeting when Harold and his new friend entered the room. Langbart took a place in line with other uniformed OD off to the side while Harold wondered if he should join them. His problem was solved by Finnhandlerr, who pounced before the door could shut on Harold's backside.

"You will guard the door, Comrade Harold. Soon it will be time to induct you into the Order." The head storm trooper braced Harold into the proper posture, a military attention identical to all the other brown-shirts in the room.

Stubble, in the front, was calling for committee reports but the acoustics in the hall were bad and Harold, in the back, could only hear half of what he said. A man named Duckwaller was reporting on activities at Camp Nordland, the Bund camp in New Jersey. Harold's ears pricked up. He wanted to hear this. O'Rourke had told him of strange goings-on at the Bund camp. Northern New

Jersey was abuzz with rumors of noisy midnight rallies and big bonfires, uniformed men drilling, and weapons being cleaned and stored in preparation for *Der Tag*. There had been stories about Nordland in the *Newark Ledger*. Aaron wanted those stories in the *World-Journal*. But what was that man Ducksalot saying? Something about a Sports Day at Nordland. When? Harold wanted to move up so he could hear, but he didn't dare leave his post at the back of the room. End of November. *Was that what the Duckman said? It could be cold in the country in November. What kind of sports could you play in the cold?*

The meeting went on. A Christmas festival was being planned for the second week of December. The Bund's activities seemed normal to Harold. Where were the feared Nazis of New York whose anti-everythingism worried even the Congress of the United States? Harold's attention began to wander.

Suddenly the boring business was over. Stubble, still at the podium, paused for dramatic effect, and announced in a loud, clear voice, "The two heroes of the Battle of Yorkville will stand forward."

Werner Everhardt and Klaus Groening goose-stepped their way to the front, joining Stubble on the platform. Wild cheering filled the room. The two troopers swelled with the applause, their brown-shirt buttons threatening to fly off their proud chests. Groening's face grew crimson, the same shade as his hair. Right arms everywhere flew up in the Nazi salute and the clapping changed to a rhythmic chant, "Heil Hitler, Heil Hitler."

There was power in that chant; two words, repeated over and over to a crescendo, until the ear no longer heard distinct syllables, just the HE's and the HI's. *And why is Everhardt staring right at me?* Harold thought. He flinched at the perceived gaze as the aural assault left him defenseless.

Then it was over. Stubble stood before the crowd appealing for money, for legal defense, he said. Harold felt shaken by the whole thing, glad he wasn't at the front where he would have been exposed as a fraud. He braced himself to attention, assuming what he thought was a proper posture, while in front of him the Germans gave and gave, so the lawyers could eat.

It is time, Comrade Harold." Finnhandlerr appeared beside the reporter. "*Ein, zwei, drei, marsch.*"

Harold gave a little jump, unnoticeable really, except to him. *Now I dedicate my life and soul to Hitler.* Grim-faced, he followed his leader down the aisle. Surrounded by arms out-stretched in the Hitler salute, deafened by the Hitler chant, the new Hitler acolyte marched to his fate. The lights dimmed and a spotlight somehow highlighted goose-stepping storm troopers on the big AV banner. Harold reached the platform and turned. The spotlight was in his eyes. Finnhandlerr, next to him again, gently, almost reverentially, removed his swastika armband, folded it in two, and held it out toward Harold.

"Place your left hand on the swastika Comrade Appel, raise your right arm straight up, palm out, and repeat after me. I pledge to devote my life…"

"I pledge to devote my life…," Harold repeated, his voice starting to crack.

"…to the cause of the *Fuehrer*, Adolf Hitler."

"…to the cause of the *Fuehrer*, Adolf Hitler." Harold's voice cracked. He squeaked out the name but was drowned out by the endless, recurring chant.

"HEIL HITLER, HITLER, HITLER…"

When the din died down Finnhandler continued the oath. "I will accept orders only from his designated representatives in the *Ordung Dienst* of the *Amerikadeutscher Volksbund.* In executing this oath I totally accept the leadership principle embodied in the creed of the National Socialist Party. I will follow in the path of the *Fuehrer* always." The hall was hushed as Harold swore the oath and gave the Hitler salute to Finnhandlerr. The storm troopers began to sing, and were soon joined by everyone in the room.

'Up, up for battle, we are born to battle, for the German Fatherland. Sworn to Adolf Hitler, we extend our hand. Firm stands a man, like an oak, braving every storm. On the morrow we will be a corpse, and to Adolf Hitler we extend a hand. Up for battle, all you brown battalions, the World War's departed, all of those two millions, are forcing us to battle.'

CHAPTER THIRTEEN

THANKSGIVING IN AMERICA

"WHY WILL YOU not join us for Thanksgiving dinner, Harold?"

A mug of coffee warmed the reporter's hands while a cold wind whistled outside Willknecht's apartment. "I cannot join you because my friends in New Jersey already asked, and I accepted," Harold replied. "I do not understand the significance of this strange holiday, Georg. Have you become so acclimated to America that you wish to remember the survival of Englishmen, or was it Dutchmen? Better to remember the heroic actions of our *Fuehrer* in November 1923 than some English eating a meal with savages three hundred years ago."

"You are correct, Harold," Willknecht said with a note of regret. "Still, we celebrate just like everyone else around us. When you have been here longer you will see what kind of hold this strange, strange country has over those who spend time here."

Is Willknecht admitting affection for America? Harold wondered. *If so, that is the first non-Nazi thought I've heard expressed by these ubermenschen.*

Christiana appeared and gave him a hug. "Congratulations

on your induction into the OD, Harold," she said as she pressed something into the fold of his coat, something she obviously did not want her father to see.

Once outside Harold looked at what the girl had given him. It was a sealed purple envelope, addressed to 'My Darling Solly' in a flowery hand. It smelled faintly of lavender. *Willknecht has secret dreams of pumpkin pie and his daughter loves a Jew.* He looked up. Everything seemed normal—apartment houses with lights at every window; cars going by, Hudsons and Packards and Fords; but no, it wasn't a normal cityscape. Harold saw the lights going up into the sky as giant searchlights at Nuremberg rallies. He heard the backfire of a car as thousands of voices cheering as one, *'HEIL HITLER, HEIL HITLER.' Who was crazy, Willknecht or him?*

Thanksgiving is a triumph of appetite over ideology, Harold thought as he rode the el above Jerome Avenue. *It's probably the only time of the year that Nazis and Jews have the same thing on their minds, not to mention on their plates.* The regular motion of the elevated train, swaying gently as it went deeper into The Bronx, set up a staccato rhythm in Harold's head. Left and right, side to side, always forward until the next clanking station stop. The movement and the noise translated into a sub-vocal refrain: 'I'm a Nazi...I kill Jews...I'm a Nazi...I kill...' The train stopped with a jerk. *193rd Street. Almost there, just two more stops. I wonder what Finnhandlerr and all the rest are doing now. Eating dinner? Maybe? More likely they're hatching some wild scheme to win the Interborough. Why? Why do they hate us so?* He reached in his pocket and pulled out a dog-eared pamphlet. He looked at the title, *The Protocols of the Learned Elders of Zion. Is this why they hate us so much?* The train stopped again. *I'm a Nazi. I kill..,* Harold thought as he climbed from the almost empty car. As he walked down the steps of the elevated station to the safety of Jerome Avenue the refrain receded to be replaced by the normal noise of the street, honking horns and raised voices. The cold wind, which had swayed the train and set up the Nazi chorus in his brain, cut into him now and he hurried away, thoughts of Nazis banished.

Sally's street was quieter and warmer. The buildings broke the force of the wind, and the sun, when it came out from behind the scudding clouds, warmed the air. *It might be a nice day after all,* Harold thought. In front of Sally's house four boys were playing stick ball, their excited cries echoing up the street. *It's a normal day in a normal city with normal people going about their normal business. Normal Jews.* Thoughts of Nazis flooded back into the reporter's mind, or thoughts of how Nazis saw Jews. *I've been reading the Learned Elders too much. It's all about a Jewish plot to take over the world. But if there is a Jewish plot, why didn't anyone tell me?* He rushed into the lobby, decided the elevator was too slow, and vaulted up the stairs to his girlfriend's apartment.

The sharp notes of a trumpet solo greeted Harold as he knocked at the door. He knocked louder and was rewarded when the blaring stopped and Saul, horn in hand, threw it open. "Harold's here," he shouted over his shoulder, then asked, "How's Christiana?"

Harold reached in his pocket, found the lavender envelope, and handed it to the good-looking boy while asking, "Where's Sally?"

"She's in the kitchen," Saul answered, trying his best to juggle his horn and the letter. The trumpet found the floor, forgotten, as the boy fumbled with the envelope. Harold brushed past, obviously also forgotten.

Sally was at the counter, her back to Harold, up to her elbows in turkey stuffing. The reporter snuck up behind her and nuzzled her neck. "I hope you took your ring off. Diamonds don't go well with turkey." *Diamonds, hardest substance known to man,* he thought, *certainly don't go with turkey, a soft, stupid bird. Yet turkeys would have been the symbol of America if Ben Franklin had had his way. Diamonds are like Nazis, cutting through all the soft sentimentality of man.* Suddenly Harold jumped, releasing his gentle hold on his beloved's shoulders and fell back. *Why, why, why,* went through his mind, *am I thinking of Nazis at a time like this, when I should be happy to be away from them?* He sagged at his knees. *Why am I thinking like a Nazi?*

Sally turned when Harold backed away, grabbed a dish cloth, and wiped the bread cubes and vegetables off her hands. She didn't catch Harold's stumble but saw the pain in his eyes. "What's the matter, Harold? Yes, I took my ring off." She patted the pocket of her apron to show him where it was. "I'm so glad to see you." She reached up and drew him to her, wrapped her arms around him, and began a long kiss.

"I made her take the ring off," Sarah said, interrupting the reunion.

Harold jumped, startled to hear Sally's mother. Only having eyes for Sally, only wanting to seek her comfort, he had missed seeing the older woman when he entered the kitchen. "Such a beautiful ring." Sarah was standing at the sink chopping vegetables, her back to the couple, but Harold knew that a broad smile was spreading over her face. "I told her never to take it off except when she's working in the kitchen. Twenty-seven years I've had my ring and I always take it off when I'm in the kitchen."

Sarah's interruption broke Harold's mood. He left the two women chattering about rings, and went looking for Saul. He found the redhead sprawled on his bed, reading Christiana's scented letter.

"Harold, Christiana wants to see me! She's inviting me to the country on Sunday."

Before Harold could respond Sally showed up at Saul's open door. "So what are you boys plotting now?" she asked in a low, conspiratorial voice.

"Nothing Sis, nothing," Saul replied, his big ears flushing as red as his hair.

"Saul, don't hide Christiana from your sister." Harold's voice went up a notch. "She knows you met a German girl at the parade. I told her."

Sally spoke to her brother in a low but intense voice. Harold had to lean forward to hear her. "I want you to see Jewish girls only, but as long as you're seeing this *German*," she spat out the word, "don't let Father find out." She shuddered at the thought of her father finding out his only son was seeing a *shiksa*.

"Maybe this isn't such a good idea, Saul," Harold said, knowing what the boy's response would be.

"Harolddd," Saul wailed. Then, in a determined voice, "I want to see Christy."

I'm tickled that Willknecht's daughter wants to see a Jew, Harold thought. *I wonder how she'd feel if she knew Saul was Jewish. Probably the same. Christiana's an independent girl. Still, if it upsets Sally's parents...* "Let's think about it," he said as he and Sally left the room, closing the door on a very stubborn Saul.

In the hallway outside the bedrooms, Sally's mother had rearranged a grouping of family photos, leaving a place of honor for her daughter's wedding portrait. Now Harold imagined that picture: the bride in white gowned splendor; the groom, stiff in starched brown shirt, proudly wearing a swastika armband on his shoulder. In the background stands the brother of the bride, arm raised high in the Hitler salute. The reporter shuddered as he passed.

"I made a big mistake, Sally, letting Saul and Christiana get together."

"Harold, it wasn't your fault," Sally said. "You remember what it was like when you were in high school. Saul's not going to listen to you."

She wouldn't blame me if Saul heiled Hitler all the way to Nuremberg, Harold thought. *Then he could dance with Goering's wife while the orchestra played Wagner. I'm completely innocent to this wonderful girl. Then why do I feel so guilty about what I'm doing in Yorkville?*

The couple was in the foyer of the apartment, about to take a left into the living room, where heavy drapes blocked whatever daylight came from the few breaks in an overcast sky. A key scraped in the lock and the door flew open. "Happy Thanksgiving, everybody," shouted Izzy. He shrugged out of his overcoat and handed it, along with a big box of fancy chocolates full of raisins and crèmes and nuts, to a startled Sally.

"How was work today, Daddy?" Sally deposited the candy on a nearby chair while putting the coat in the closet. She finally picked up the candy, un-wrapped the lustrous paper surrounding one of the treasures, and daintily placed a milk-chocolate covered cashew in her mouth before passing the box to Harold.

"Everyone wants to buy candy on Thanksgiving. I'm not a big store like Krum's but I do okay. Thank God for Christian holidays," Izzy said devoutly.

"Thanksgiving isn't Christian," Harold protested to his future father-in-law. "It's the American Succoth."

"OK, it's an American holiday. But I thank God anyway."

Sally and Harold left Israel to clean up after a hard morning selling sweets, and joined Sarah in the kitchen to listen to the radio broadcast of Macy's Thanksgiving parade. Amid the vibrant bands playing popular music and the familiar voices of the celebrities—Eddie Cantor, Mayor LaGuardia, and little Shirley Temple among them—describing grand floats and giant balloons, Harold suddenly had visions of the last parade he had seen.

Massed swastika pennants flowed down the street and swept over the sweet soprano voices bursting forth from the Philco. Drums and trumpets and harsh voices bellowed *Deutschland Uber Alles.* There was no peace and happiness in Harold's vision, no joy to the world, no buying your Christmas presents at Macy's, just the obsession with Nazis in his mind.

The reporter shook his head, blinked his eyes, and willed the spiked helmets, brown shirts, and high bodice *dirndl* dresses to disappear, replacing them with Sally's pretty face.

"Harold, your family should be here soon." Sarah's words pulled Harold out of his Yorkville nightmare. "And I invited the Drabinskys, but only Ida and Cynthia are coming. Howard won't leave the house, not even to go to class. I know it hasn't been that long but there is something unhealthy about mourning so deeply. Ida is worried about him."

Four Schwartzes, five members of Harold's clan, and two leftover Drabinskys sat down for Thanksgiving dinner. Israel gave a blessing and they ate at once, unlike Jewish holidays where the meal was preceded by prayers and rituals and more prayers. Still, dinner was as substantial as Rosh Hashanah or Passover. There was turkey and stuffing, cranberry sauce, baked yams, green beans, and later, much later, when the rules of *kashrut* allowed, pumpkin pie with whipped cream. It was a traditional meal but the conversation was decidedly non-traditional.

"I've been to see Nathanson, the immigration lawyer," Frank Apple said. "We're exploring ways to extricate the family from Germany. But the problem isn't in Germany. With enough money, Hitler will give any Jew an exit-permit. No, the problem is here, in Washington. Congress is anti-immigrant, and most of the people in the State Department are downright anti-Semitic. Still Nathanson is optimistic. He told me that with three of the five brothers already American citizens, getting the other two in should be a snap." He cleared his throat with a loud 'har-rump,' and settled back in his chair like it was Passover.

"Did he give you any idea of how long it would take?" Sally asked.

"He said that, because of *Kristallnacht*, the whole process might be speeded up. But we have a lot of people in Germany, my two brothers and their wives with seven children between them.

Nathan's oldest, Manfred, is married and has a baby. We're gathering information on all of them so Nathanson can file visa applications in Washington. He also wants them to apply at the American consulate in Frankfurt. Try everything, he says. Something is bound to work."

"Thank goodness we don't have anyone in Germany," Ida Drabinsky said. "They're all in Russia. My oldest brother moved to Kiev ten years ago. Everyone else is still in Glusk."

Ahh Glusk, the mythical homeland. I wonder why Ida's brother moved to the big city from that land of milk and honey.

"He couldn't make a living in Glusk," Ida said as if reading Harold's mind. "He wanted to come here but the Communists would only let him go to Kiev."

"I remember Yankel," Israel said. "I hope he's doing well, *baruch Ha'shem*. No place in that land is a bargain, Kiev, or Minsk or even Glusk. It was hard for the Jews under the czars but it's even harder under the communists. At least the czar let us live like Jews. The Reds don't even give us that. We're better off here." He gave the table a thumbs-up with his right hand.

"Tell that to my father, Mr. Schwartz," Cynthia Drabinsky said, her voice as black as the mourning dress she wore. "Jews aren't safe, even in New York. Only when we have a state in Palestine will we be safe."

"Well, I'm thankful to be an American," Ruth said. "Sure, we've got problems here, but nothing like Europe."

The older women went into the kitchen to get dessert. Cynthia, still fuming, whispered to her friend Sally.

Harold stayed silent, thinking. *Those are my supposed friends who killed her father. We've got Nazi problems here, in New York, just like in Europe. I've got a Nazi problem.*

Sarah emerged from the kitchen bearing a steaming pot of fresh coffee. Ruth followed with a large pumpkin pie, top glistening with moisture. Aunt Annie brought up the rear with a bowl of homemade whipped cream. Harold salivated at the sight of his mother's pie, a recipe she held closely guarded. All thought of Nazis vanished from his mind.

"This pie is famous in Cleveland," Harold said. "All the neighbors used to crowd in our kitchen when Ma made one, anxious for a piece."

"Flattery won't get you anywhere Harold," Ruth said. "You still only get one piece."

"Aww, Ma."

While the women bustled about cutting the pie and pouring the coffee, Saul changed the subject of the conversation, not very far, but a change nonetheless. "Did anyone hear what Father Coughlin said on the radio the other night? He said that *Kristallnacht* was all the fault of the Jews and we should pay for it. He was talking about money, of course. He thinks Jews have all the money in the world."

"Ayyy, that Coughlin, he's completely nuts," Israel said. "The trouble is the *goyyim* listen to him. You know Mrs. Kelly, who lives upstairs from the store, the one with the six-year-old twins? She won't let the boys come in anymore to get lollipops. She pulled me aside and said that Father Nonsense-for-Brains warned on the radio about Jews poisoning Christian children. Then she said, 'I don't believe you would do something like that, but one can't be too careful these days.' Looney, that's what he is."

"Those Kelly boys are sooo cute. No one would hurt them," Sally said. "That priest should be banned from the radio."

"But what about freedom of speech?" Harold griped. A need to stand up for The Bill of Rights rushed through him. "Even if I don't like what you say, I'll defend *to the death* your right to say it."

"To the death?" Ruth asked. "You would defend our enemies with your life?"

"If the Government asked me to fight, I would. I would fight for all our freedoms, including the right to read this." He pulled the slim, paperbound copy of *The Protocols of the Elders of Zion* from his back pocket. "I picked this up at a bookstore in Yorkville the other day."

Israel snatched the pamphlet from Harold's hand. "I know this book," he said. "It was written in Russian, many years ago." He glanced through the pages. "It's all here, every hateful word, and in English." Izzy passed the booklet to Saul.

The red-head paged through it. "This is awful! We've got to do something!"

"If there was a Society of Learned Elders, Saul, don't you think they'd do something to suppress it?" Harold said, throwing his hands in the air. "But there's no help for it, so we have to rely on the good sense of people to reject it. And ninety-five percent of Americans do reject it."

"Should be one hundred percent," Saul said quietly.

"There's no accounting for crazy people," Harold said. *Listen to me,* he thought, *I'm accepting crazies, Jew haters, and all those good Germans out there. And yesterday, when I was with them, I thought the Nazis made sense. Race, blood, and all that stuff. I must be going crazy myself.* He ate his pumpkin pie while listening to the outrage around the table caused by his devotion to free speech and defense of the *Protocols*. *I didn't mean to upset my family but I've got to talk about this stuff with someone who understands what I'm going through.* He pushed his chair back from the holiday table. "Pardon me, folks. I've got to make a business call, about a story."

The reporter hurried to the back bedroom, Sally's parents' room, to use the phone, thankful they no longer had a party line nosey neighbors could listen in on. He dialed O'Rourke's number.

"Pat, you've gotta help me," Harold blurted out as his friend answered the phone on the third ring. "I'm getting in too deep!"

"Whoa, pull up there partner." Pat slid his smooth tongue around the alarm in Harold's voice. "Whataya mean by too deep?"

"I mean, those people in Yorkville, they're not Nazis anymore.

They're friends! What am I gonna do? Willknecht's daughter thinks she's in love with Sally's brother. She even invited Saul to come to that Bund camp in New Jersey on Sunday."

There was silence for a few seconds on the trunk line to New Jersey, broken only by faint hissing and popping, then by Pat's loud laughter. "You're not gonna be a Nazi, my friend, not in this or any other lifetime. And Saul's not going to fall for one of them, either. It's my bet that the girl's not a Nazi, that the camp is just somewhere she likes to go to get away from the city. Didn't you have somewhere like that when you were growing up? Or don't they like to get away from Cleveland? Anyway, you and Saul can spend Saturday night at my house, then go up to that camp Sunday morning. And Harold, I think I can set up a meeting with Tom Kergan, the guy I told you about, the one whose father is the Bund lawyer."

Harold's anxiety calmed as the two friends said their goodbyes. He knew Pat was right. Christiana wasn't a Nazi, and Nordland was just somewhere she and her parents went to get away. Saul peeked into the back bedroom. "Harold, here you are."

The reporter looked up at the lanky red-head, shuffling his feet on the hardwood floor. Harold wondered if Saul was as grown up as he was tall. How he handled himself during the weekend would tell all. "Saul, I want us to go over to Jersey City Saturday, spend the night at O'Rourke's, then go to Nordland Sunday. Are those plans all right with you?"

"Sure. I'll spend the night at your friend's house. Will I meet his brother?"

"Yeah, you'll meet Frankie. Hey, maybe he can give you a few pointers. After all, you've got to act like a kid from New Jersey on Sunday."

"Aw, c'mon Harold. I'll fool all those Bund chowder heads."

"It's not so easy Saul. The last time you ran into those 'chowder heads' they killed Mr. Drabinsky. And you've got to fool Christiana, too, which is something you might not be happy doing."

Saul thought about that for a minute. "You're right Harold. I won't be happy lying to Christy. I have to, don't I?"

"You sure do, for you, for me, for everyone. And Saul, I want you to tell your parents about Christiana."

"What! No! They won't like it at all."

Harold looked at the scowl on Saul's normally placid face. *He's acting like a little brat refusing to eat his oatmeal.*

Saul glared back and his defiance collapsed. "All right. I'll tell them. But I'll tell them I'm not marrying her."

When Harold and Saul came out of the bedroom everyone was getting ready to go home. Ruth hugged her son. "Don't be such a stranger. You can write once in a while."

"Ma, that's too much like work. Please don't ask me to write," Harold laughed. He knew that his mother would open her mailbox every day, hoping against hope for a letter. "Next time you'll come for the wedding?"

"For my son, of course I'll come for the wedding."

Harold turned to his father. "Pa, it was really great to see you. I wish we'd had more time to spend together."

"Harold, you've got your own life to lead, your own job to do. Give it to those Bund boys good. I'm proud of you." Father and son shook hands and fell into an embrace.

"Bye Pa. See you in a few months, after I've broken the Bund." Harold turned away, a solitary figure in the midst of his family. *Yeah Pa, you'll be proud of me after I bust the Bund. The question is, 'Will I be proud of me?'*

Harold, wait! I'll walk you home," Sally cried over the hubbub of her family. In the block and a half to the reporter's old apartment, where he had not been in, it seemed, ages, Sally managed to get to the heart of Harold's problem. "Were you embarrassed when your father hugged you?"

"No Sally. No, no, no. I wasn't embarrassed. Surprised is more like it, or even shocked. My father just doesn't do that. I don't remember him ever hugging me." Harold fumbled for his keys and unlocked the now unfamiliar door. "But it was what he said in my ear that really shocked me. He said he's proud of me. Proud! My father has always withheld his approval, then I withhold my affection, and it just goes around and around. Even last week, when I met him at the train, he mocked my assignment. Said that all the time I'm spending with Nazis wouldn't come to anything, as if my outrage doesn't matter. I'm not a good enough writer to convey my feelings. That's why I was stunned by what he said."

"But you're fighting Nazis when they're after your family. That impressed him," Sally said kissing Harold on the cheek. "Your determination, your courage, your conviction – it impresses all of us."

CHAPTER FOURTEEN

NEW JERSEY

ELEVEN O'CLOCK SATURDAY morning, a chilly drizzle was dripping on the windows of the 23rd Street Ferry Terminal, obscuring the view of the choppy grey waters of the Hudson. Harold sat on a stiff-backed wooden bench where he could see the entrance to the big shed of a room which people passed through on their commute to work in the city or home to New Jersey. He was waiting for Saul to join him for their expedition to O'Rourke's house and their undercover visit to Camp Nordland. Harold's legs ached and the cold, clammy air of the waiting room didn't help. The muscle memory of hours spent practicing the goosestep yesterday, marching hundreds of times around the perimeter of the ballroom at the Yorkville Casino, hurt too much. Harold, and thirty or so comrades of the OD, had been abused by Finnhandlerr with the *fuhrerprinzip,* the hallmark of obedience for all Nazis.

Harold thumbed through the early edition of the *World Journal* while waiting, rereading the story he'd written for the paper. 'The German way of marching, the goosestep, has come to New York, as Bund storm troopers from all over the metropolitan area practice their unique way of strutting three times a week, preparing for the day when they can openly march down Fifth Avenue, to what end we do not know. What we do know is that the storm troopers practice at their camp in Northern New Jersey and various halls throughout the five boroughs. Are they practicing in uniform? Yes. Are they armed? We do not know. The question is: Is this a military force secretly in our midst? Only time will tell.'

Just then Saul burst through the entrance to the terminal, only minutes to spare before the next boat was scheduled to leave. "You're late," Harold said, standing up and grabbing his bag.

"I know. I'm sorry. But the ferries run all day. Sally insisted I go to the bakery and get some pastry for Mrs. O'Rourke." Saul held up a small white cake box. "They're fancy cookies and *rugelach.*"

"Good thinking on Sally's part. Now, let's hurry." Harold rushed Saul to the other end of the room, where they saw another boat pulling into the slip. The boat ride across the Hudson gave Harold time to calm down. He played tour guide to Saul, who had never been on this ferry before. From the New Jersey terminal to O'Rourke's house on Monroe Street was a familiar streetcar ride, giving time for the ache in Harold's legs to subside. They got off the trolley in a neighborhood of aging frame houses, set close together with tiny yards shadowed by high gabled roofs. They stepped around a forgotten hopscotch game chalked on the sidewalk, now dissolving from ordered squares to abstract shapes as the rain puddled the pavement. Further down the street a gang of boys was watching one of their number doing bicycle tricks on the slick street. The rider was spinning in a tight circle in front of O'Rourke's house, avoiding puddles and keeping his hands on his hips, thumbs hooked into his belt loops. *The kid is good. Just like me, keeping his balance, avoiding the potholes.*

Harold and Saul climbed the steps to the porch of a freshly painted white house. The door was a welcoming Irish green. The reporter pressed the doorbell. 'Da DA da DA da DA DA,' the first notes of **When Irish Eyes are Smiling** washed over them. "Mr. Apple," a thin, reedy voice said from the street, "no one's home yet."

It was the daredevil rider, a small boy, just dismounting from his old bike. "Hey Frankie, is it really you?" Harold said. "You're good on that bike. Saul, it's O'Rourke's brother."

Frankie dropped his bike at the bottom of the steps and climbed up to open the door. "See ya later guys," he called out to his companions. "Pat's not home," he said to Harold. "He went to see an old friend. Said he'd be home soon. My dad and sister are working at the bar, and my ma went to the market. You must be Saul." Frankie stuck out his hand at the redhead. "Pat said I've got to work with you tonight, teach you how to be a Jersey boy. Come on in guys. Oh Harold, Pat left something for you to read. It's on top of the piano. Saul, you wanna try my bike?"

"Sure, Frankie," Saul yelled out. He dropped his overnight bag and ran down the steps. Soon he was pedaling down the street, while Frankie ran behind, his shirttails flapping in the wind.

Harold went into the house. In the living room sat a grand piano, bathed in a dull crimson glow from a big window mostly covered with red brocaded drapes. On the far side of the living room was a fireplace topped with an oil painting of Jesus with his arms outspread. Jesus's eyes followed Harold as he walked to the piano, clicked on a reading lamp atop the big instrument, and looked at the surprise Pat had left him. In an accordion folder were onion skin copies of court documents: grand jury transcripts, indictments of the two Nazis, and even correspondence between District Attorney Dewey and Mayor LaGuardia. Harold marveled at the treasure trove O'Rourke had managed to put his hands on. Harold sifted through the correspondence. On November 12th the District Attorney had informed the Mayor that '...as per standing orders regarding any disturbances involving the German American Bund or its members,' that several Bundists had been arrested for rioting on Armistice Day. *Dry stuff,* he thought, *gotta spice it up for the paper.* Dewey went on to say that the Grand Jury was considering murder charges against the rioters. 'We can make the charges stick because we have two good witnesses.'

While Harold was wondering who the witnesses could be, O'Rourke entered the parlor. "Hello pardner," he said in a western drawl. "I see you found my gold nuggets." He sprawled in a big easy chair right next to the piano, "Well, whadaya think?"

"I'm amazed you can get stuff like this, Pat. Who the hell is your source?"

"It pays to cultivate secretaries." O'Rourke grinned at Harold. "They know as much as their bosses, sometimes more." The raffish reporter looked around the room. "Hey, where's Saul? I thought you were bringing him for some lessons on how to be a Jersey boy."

"He's outside with your brother. I guess he's learning already." Harold turned serious. "I didn't know LaGuardia had standing orders to be kept informed of Bund monkey business. We can use that."

"Yes we can. But I've got something even bigger. I've talked about my old friend, Tom Kergan, whose father is the Bund lawyer."

"Yeah."

"Two months ago he up and married the daughter of one of his father's clients."

"The only daughter I know is Christiana Willknecht, and she and Saul seem to be having an affair."

"Well, that's news, but I don't think you want it in the paper," O'Rourke laughed. ""No, Kergan's bride is the former Regina Stubble, the daughter of some high muckety-muck in the Yorkville Bund."

"If Kergan is married to the *Bundeslieter's* daughter then he won't cooperate with us," Harold sighed, a crestfallen look on his face.

"Don't be so sure," O'Rourke said. "I just spent an hour with

Tom, talking about old times. He's not happy with his new wife. Regina's a real Nazi, and crazy to boot, while old Tom's an easygoing sort of fellow. At St. Pete's he was more interested in partying than politics. Well, I put on the old charm and got us a dinner invite. You can judge for yourself whether the Kergans will add anything to our story."

The front door clattered open and a high voice rang out. "Paddy, come and help your ma with the groceries."

Laying aside the court documents, the two partners got up to help. Margaret O'Rourke, a large woman with carrot colored hair and a red face, was shucking off her heavy coat and putting on a white apron which had been hanging from the door knob.

"Faith, here is Mr. Apple and me looking like this." She brushed her wind-blown hair back with work-roughened fingers. "Where is Frankie? He can bring the groceries in. Guests in our house shouldn't have to work."

"Frankie's off with Saul, Harold's soon-to-be brother-in-law," said Pat. The two reporters soon staggered into the kitchen under an impossible burden of packages, which Mrs. O'Rourke had dragged two blocks down the street from the market in her old two-wheel wire shopping cart. "Don't be cross with Frankie, Ma. He waited here for Harold and Saul, just like I asked him to."

"I hope that boy is home for lunch." The lady of the house turned to Harold. "Paddy told us about your engagement, Mr. Apple. All the best to you and your bride."

"Why thank you, Mrs. O'Rourke. We hope you can come to the wedding."

Frankie and Saul returned just then, looking winded but happy. Mrs. O'Rourke served them all a fine lunch of corned beef and cabbage with pickles and boiled potatoes, after which the two boys went off to Frankie's room to rehearse Saul for his role.

Harold felt like napping after the big lunch but Pat wanted to take a stroll to his father's tavern. The Manhattan Avenue Bar &

Grill was a dimly lit room with white Formica table tops bright like shiny puddles on the dark linoleum floor. Along the back wall ran a bar guarded by twenty or so barstools. The wall itself was mirrored, reflecting liquor bottles four deep on stepped shelves. *A comfortable place,* thought Harold.

A dozen people were gathered at the bar, passionately arguing about something or other, when the reporters walked in. "Hague is getting in bed with those damn Germans," an old man protested. "He gives the Hitler Bund police protection."

"So what's wrong with that, Roy?" replied a younger man. "Someone could get hurt if cops weren't there."

"Hell Johnny, the cops aren't there to protect people," Roy exclaimed. "They go to protect Nazis."

"Hague thinks the Nazis are going to fight the English," Henry O'Rourke said. "That makes Hitler royalty in his eyes."

"Mayor Hague is right, sure as my name is Liam Reilly," said another man with a hint of the Emerald Isle in his voice. "Germany will take Poland and England will declare war, mark my words. Now, I'm no friend of the English. Too many in my family suffered at their hands. But someone has to stop those crazy Nazis. It may as well be the damned tea-drinkers."

"Remember how, in '34, Mayor Eastmead, over in Union City, wouldn't let the Nazis hold their meetings in Swabian Hall?" Roy asked. "He sent the cops in there to bust some Nazi heads. That's the way to handle Nazis. Come to think of it, it was right after that the Nazis started meeting at the German Club, where they should have been all along. And that's when our lovely mayor started giving them police protection. He even goes to their meetings, I hear. Sits up on the speaker's platform, like a fat sausage. I haven't voted for the bastard since."

"Don't make no difference Roy," Liam Reilly said. "He wins anyway."

"What do you think of our exalted mayor, Mr. Apple?" the

elder O'Rourke asked Harold, who had been sitting quietly at the bar, taking in the New Jersey political talk.

"He knows how to win elections, Mr. O'Rourke. How long has he been in office? Since 1917? His machine is arguably better than Tammany, at least at winning," Harold admired how the elder O'Rourke unobtrusively directed the talk.

Harold and Pat stayed for hours, nursing their beers and soaking up all the politics. "Pat, did you spend much time down here when you were growing up?" the reporter asked his partner after listening to men arguing about politics. *I bet that's where Pat gets his easy way with people, from all the talk at the bar.*

At dinnertime Harold and Pat left the men arguing about Roosevelt and whoever was going to run against him—Dewey or Willkie—and sauntered out.

Hands in their pockets, they walked through the early evening darkness to Kergan's house at the corner of Baker Street and Newark Avenue. They climbed the outside stairs of the two-family home and Pat knocked on the solid oak door, which immediately opened a slit. A high-pitched voice yelped, "Who *Komen*?"

O'Rourke jumped back at the unexpected shriek, tumbling into Harold and almost knocking him down the long flight. "Mr. O'Rourke and Mr. Apple," Pat nervously replied in a high voice himself. "Tom invited us for dinner."

The door slammed shut. There was a rattle of chains, bolts flew, and the heavy door slowly opened to admit Harold and Pat to a shrine of Nazism. The first thing one saw, sitting on a low coffee table, was a large lacquered swastika, painted in the center, where the four arms met, with a noble eagle clutching lightning bolts in its talons. The walls were decorated with portraits of Hitler, Goering, Goebbels, and that ubiquitous shot of a stiffly uniformed Kuhn saluting a bored-looking Hitler. The sofa was upholstered in a black and red swastika pattern. *Where on earth do they get that material?* Harold wondered. *It's the same as the drapes at the Yorkville Casino.*

Off to the side, was the most decorative object in the room—to Harold's eyes. Mrs. Kergan, the mistress of the house, was standing with her gaze down, staring past her high bodice and her long white apron, at the floor, where the abstract design of a new Persian carpet had her full attention.

"Hello Regina, you lovely thing," O'Rourke said, trying to charm the woman.

She is lovely, with that pile of strawberry blond hair, braided and whirled atop her head, thought Harold. *But Irish charm is not going to win this Nazi wife. Poor Mr. Kergan, he can't provide what his wife needs, a proper German home. Maybe I can help him out.*

Harold returned his full attention to his fellow reporter, who was handing Regina a large bottle of whiskey, liberated from his father's storeroom.

"This is for your handsome husband, my dear. And let me present my friend Harold Appel, now of Yorkville but formerly of New Jersey, and originally from Frankfurt."

Harold bowed to the young woman. "*Frau* Kergan, I know your *vater*, the *Bundesleiter*, a fine man and a powerful leader of our people. I can see, just from looking at your home, that you embrace his *weltanschauung*."

Tom Kergan entered the room in time to hear Harold say that his wife's world view was the same as her father's. Storm clouds roiled the face of the handsome young lawyer at the mention of his wife's Nazi father. *Why? Maybe there was a row between the families or maybe Tom had a general dislike of Nazis.* Tom's dad had represented the Bund for many years but familiarity did not necessarily breed respect. Harold noted Tom's scowl and filed it for future reference.

"Make yourselves at home gentlemen." Tom Kergan's displeasure with Harold's words was fleeting. He took the bottle of whiskey from his inanimate wife, examined, it and said, "A fine gift Pat. Let's open it now."

Kergan poured the drinks while Regina went back to the kitchen. O'Rourke sat down in front of the wooden swastika. He looked at it and said to his friend, "Tom, why do you have this awful thing in the middle of your living room?"

"Sweet Mary, Mother of God, it is awful." Kergan looked at Harold apologetically. "No offense, Mr. Appel, but my wife goes a bit overboard in displaying her enthusiasms. And I can't say no to her. She snuggles up to me, rubs her cheek against my shoulder, and I'll do anything she wants."

"She is gorgeous," O'Rourke said enviously.

"Yes Pat and you like good-looking women just as much as me. But I've learned that you need more than beauty in a wife. I wish I'd realized that before." Kergan looked wistful as the lady in question appeared.

"Mein herren, dinner is ready," Regina announced. *"Herr* Appel, you will sit next to me. It is so seldom that I have a good German man to talk with." With that she led the men to the dining room.

So she can talk after all, Harold thought, then an idea occurred to him. "Now that is a shame, *Frau* Kergan. No German should be denied the company of the *volk.* You and your husband should accompany me tomorrow to Camp Nordland. Many Germans will be there. Why, even your father will be there."

"Oh, I have not been to Nordland in ever so long. Can we go Tom? Can we? Please," Regina pleaded with her husband.

"I'm sorry, my beautiful girl, but I have to work tomorrow." Kergan did not look sorry, in fact a touch of glee showed in his voice. "I have to go to the city to take a deposition about a Bund case."

The light went out of Regina's eyes. She looked down at the floor and said dully, "Yes my husband."

"Who are you going to talk with tomorrow, Tom?" O'Rourke said in a casual manner.

"Oh no, Pat. You're not weaseling information out of me that easily. I know the *World Journal* is covering the very case I'm working on."

That's just the hint Pat needs, Harold thought. *I wonder if Kergan gave it to him intentionally or not.* The reporter watched the byplay between the old college chums, the way they traded friendly barbs over the roles of lawyer and journalist, and decided that Kergan meant for O'Rourke to know what Bund case he was working on.

Regina served the meal, sausage and spaetzle in brown gravy. *Right off Jaeger's menu,* Harold thought. They washed it down with a dark Bavarian beer. After eating, he looked at the woman, list-lessly clearing the dishes, and had an inspiration.

"*Herr* Kergan, would you permit me to escort your wife to Camp Nordland tomorrow? She can enjoy a day of sport and German company, and I will return her safe and sound in the evening."

Regina was beside herself with joy. "Oh please say yes, Tom. You can do your work and I won't be alone in the house."

Kergan didn't take long to decide. "Why not?" he said to Harold then looked up at his wife, who almost dropped a serving dish, she was so happy. "It may be just the thing you need, getting away for a day and seeing your old friends."

The mood of the evening lightened. Kergan brought out the bottle again and the men retired with their drinks to the living room. Harold could hear Regina singing *lieder* as she moved around the house, putting things away.

"Where on earth did you meet Regina Tom?" O'Rourke asked his old friend.

"It was this way, Pat. I was with my dad, in Yorkville, about a year ago. I'd just started in his firm and was going out with him for the first time. He had to take a deposition from one of his clients, Fritz Kuhn. Of course you know who he is."

"Yes," O'Rourke said in a flat voice. "Appel, here, has met him."

"That's right, Mr. Appel, You do live in Yorkville," Kergan said. "In any event, we came to this apartment on 77th Street. I didn't know whose apartment it was but Kuhn was holding court before a bunch of men in the parlor. We were going to go in another room to question him. I was supposed to write everything down, like a court reporter, when this incredibly beautiful woman walked in, sat down and crossed her legs. She was wearing a tight purple dress that came down below her knees, but she had to hitch it up when she crossed her legs. I dropped my pen and pad, dropped to all fours to retrieve them, but didn't drop my eyes from those perfect legs and the patch of thigh she was showing. My father was embarrassed and Kuhn was furious, but I kept on looking. It was Regina of course. We were in her father's apartment."

"Regina is certainly one of the most beautiful women I've ever seen," O'Rourke said. "And you know me. I've seen a lot of women in my life. But answer me this, Tom." O'Rourke lowered his voice so that Harold had to lean forward to hear. "Why aren't you happy?"

"The trouble became apparent to me soon after we were married," Kergan said. "And I speak openly about this, Mr. Appel, because it seems that everyone in Yorkville knew about Regina. I was so blinded by her beauty that I ignored the evidence right in front of my eyes, a bad thing for any lawyer to do. She can be very personable, even agreeable, at times, especially when she gets her way. But most of the time she is a petulant, spoiled child. She wants all my attention and then wants me to leave her alone. And when she has one of her spells she is mean, oh so very mean. She has a mouth like a fishmonger. It shocked me that a woman knew such foul language.

Harold could hear Regina washing the dishes in the kitchen.

The water was running and she was singing in German. It all sounded so normal.

"Hell Tom, you can make her change now that she's away from her family and all that Nazi stuff she got in Yorkville." O'Rourke was mad at his friend.

"No, Pat, you don't understand. She's got something wrong in her head. I finally got it out of her father. She's been in Bellevue three times in the last several years. There's even a name for it. The docs call it schizophrenia. When she's good, she's very, very good, and when she's bad, I'm miserable."

"I don't know about what doctors say," Harold interjected. "Mrs. Kergan seems normal to me. A little high-strung, maybe, but women are like that. I'm sure she'll relax tomorrow among her German friends. *Oh God, Sally would kill me if she heard me talking like that. But I do know about schizophrenia. I wrote a story about Bellevue a year ago. Maybe there's something I can use if I write about Regina.*

The sounds from the kitchen ceased and Regina, bearing cups and saucers and a steaming pot of coffee, joined the three men in the parlor. The conversation turned to lighter topics. The young wife was charming, regaling the men with stories about growing up in Yorkville, the daughter of a self-important German man. Any doubts Harold might have had, after hearing Kergan's woeful description of his wife, were put to rest. Regina's beauty was so great that all sense abandoned Harold. His lustful dreams that night were of her.

CHAPTER FIFTEEN

TROUBLE AT NORDLAND

HAROLD LABORED THROUGH layers, searching for a solid surface. Finally he twisted out of the big four-poster in the O'Rourke's guest room, awake but shivering outside the warmth of the down comforter. *Jeez, what a dream,* he thought groggily. He sat with his head in his hands on the edge of the bed, his flannel pajamas moist from the heat of the blankets, and willed himself to remember. *Regina, dancing toward me in the moonlit woods, wearing a transparent gown, singing. What was she singing? A German song. A love song.* **Liebschen, mein liebschen...** *I see every dimple on her body. She has a soft downy sheen on her arms and legs, a golden sheen. Her hair is the same color. She gets closer and closer. She stops. She stands at attention. She raises her right arm.* **Seig Heil...Seig Heil.** *And the look in her eyes. Devotion. Love.*

It was dark and silent in the house, the only light a glimmer of pre-dawn sneaking around the drawn drapes. Harold padded in his stocking feet through the shadows to Pat's brother's room, where Saul was curled up on a small roll-away bed, shoved right next to Frankie's bigger bed. The red-head's ears were the only sign of life above the blanket. "Wake up," the reporter whispered, shaking the boy. "It's six-thirty and we've got a train to catch."

O'Rourke drove them to the Hoboken station of the Lackawanna Railroad, stopping on the way at the corner of Baker and Newton to pick up Regina. "*Guten morgan, Herr* Appel. I'm ready to go to Nordland. Oh, the memories!" As she climbed into the car Harold caught a tantalizing glimpse of the young wife's thigh.

At the depot the three Nazi pilgrims boarded the eight o'clock local, destination—Andover, New Jersey—home of the Hercules Munitions plant. *It was clever of the Bund to put their camp there, right next to one of the largest ammunition factories on the East Coast. They can keep track of production while taking in the country air.*

Harold, Saul, and Regina lurched through the swaying train, looking for the group from Yorkville. They found them in the last car. The men were around the perimeter, some looking out the windows, some sleeping. The women were in a tight knit group in the center of the car. A few children played in the aisle.

Helga Willknecht's eyes widened in shock as she spied the trio. *Oh my God,* the reporter thought, *it's as if Helga has seen a ghost.* As they moved into the car, Harold saw Frau Willknecht's eyes were not focused on him but were boring into Frau Kergan's innocent face. *What did Regina do?* He noticed the same look on other faces. *Do they hate her? Are they afraid of her?*

Helga approached Regina warily. "Gina, I'm overwhelmed. None of us has seen you since your wedding."

Why is Helga surprised? Harold wondered. *Regina is one of their own. There must be something here I'm not getting. Why do all these women look so shocked?*

Helga gestured to Regina to come sit by her, at the center of the Nazi coven.

Only Christiana Willknecht did not stay with the women. She spied Saul in Harold's little band and jumped to her feet. Her mother did not even notice the girl leading the boy to a pair of vacant seats at the far end of the railroad car.

Harold, abandoned by his small party, reeled down the aisle to where Georg Willknecht was sitting, gazing out the window at dawn lighting up the New Jersey landscape. "I see you picked up a stray along the way," Willknecht said. "Where on earth did you find Regina Stubble?"

"It was coincidence, Comrade Georg. The friend I was visiting knows Herr Kergan from college. We had dinner together last night. When Regina commented that she had not been in German company since her wedding, I asked her to join me for a day of sport with her brethren."

"It is only for one day, thank the *Fuehrer*. It will be all right. I will calm Reinhold when he sees her," Willknecht said. He rolled his eyes heavenward. "I thought we had rid ourselves of her, but some problems never go away. I do not blame you, Harold. How could you know?"

"Know what, Georg?"

"That Regina Stubble is crazy."

"No. Crazy? She does not seem crazy. I think she is charming," Harold said quietly, so as not to be heard by the other passengers.

"That is what the Kergan fellow thought also." Willknecht made no attempt to lower his voice. He laughed out loud as he told Harold of a smitten Tom Kergan falling all over himself to impress Regina's father, when all Stubble wanted was to get rid of his daughter. "Tell me this Harold. Did her husband seem to be in love or did he seem weary of her?"

"Now that you mention it," Harold tapped his fingers against his jaw, pretending to be lost in thought, "when I invited the husband and wife he said 'no' instantly and emphatically, but was very quick to agree when I suggested that Regina could go without him."

"Exactly! Regina is a burden to all who know her. If you let her, she will attach herself to you, like a leech. Let me give you some advice, friend Harold. After today, disappear from her life."

That is good advice, Harold thought. *Can't take it though. This is a game I'm playing and Regina is a piece on the board. I have to see how it works out.*

After an hour or so the train pulled into the tiny Andover depot, right at the edge of the village itself. The tracks branched at the station and the German group set out for a walk along a gravel road that paralleled the branch line. They walked for a mile, past fields of dry yellow stalks, past the fenced entrance to the arms plant, where the railroad spur ended at loading docks easily visible to any passerby. A plume of white smoke rose from one of the factory smokestacks but the docks were devoid of freight cars. *It's Sunday,* Harold thought. *No work today. But a spy with binoculars would like this walk during the week.* A dozen members of the *volk* sang a marching song. *No binoculars in this group. Just a bunch of harmless Germans out for an autumn hike, in a natural landscape.* The reporter laughed out loud.

"Why did you laugh, Harold?" Willknecht asked. "Did you think of a joke?"

"No George." Harold said. "I am happy, happy to be outside, in the country, on such a bright morning." *And I'm happy to be part of such a fine group of non-spies.* But most of all, he was happy to know that the master race had problems with crazy people, the same as anybody else.

Morning sunlight filtered through a forest of leafless trees. The Germans marched on. The trees changed to scraggly pines. The Germans marched on. Suddenly, the poorly-marked road ended at a sturdy fence topped with barbed wire. Beyond rose a low, barren hill topped with a barn-like structure. A sign over a gate in the fence proclaimed, **CAMP NORDLAND**, and in small bold letters: **No trespassers, communists, or Jew-lovers**. *They don't say anything about Jews,* Harold mused. *Guess I'm welcome.*

Far, faint drumbeats, felt rather than heard, greeted the group as they hiked up the dirt driveway to the top of the hill. Then the clear notes of a trumpet rang out, calling the faithful to sport, to purify German minds and dedicate German bodies to the *Fuehrer. I'll dedicate part of my body, all right, the part I sit on.*

Regina hung back as the Yorkville party entered the barn. *Does she think she is no longer one of them?* Harold wondered as the woman picked at a thread on her glove. *Because I think she's as Nazi as any of them.* "Come!" he ordered Regina. "What is the matter with you?"

Regina looked distraught. Her brow furrowed, her eyes swelled, and tears rolled down her rosy cheeks. "My *Vater* is an awful man," she sobbed, muffling her cry in the sleeve of her coat. "I am afraid to go near him. He will hurt me for sure."

"Your father is a fine man, a leader. Come Regina." Harold coaxed the woman up the hill and into the barn while the rest of the Yorkville party streamed by, shouting greetings to old friends as they entered the farm building that was now a German retreat. An animal smell still lingered in the structure. *It used to house goats and pigs. Now it houses Nazis. The pigs and cows were better neighbors.* Two long, low additions ran the length of the building on either side, giving the barn the feel of a country cathedral, high space in the middle flanked by low naves, all in weathered wood painted a dull red. The big windows along with bare bulbs hanging from the roof illuminated the smiling faces of the *volk.* Harold admired the carpentry of a small stage that had been erected in the center of the room, while inhaling the rich smell of *bratwurst* cooked in beer steaming from a hot table tucked into a corner. Small tables were scattered around, where cows had once been milked. *A fitting place for Nazis, a barn,* the reporter ruminated.

Inside the barn the Nazis were busy. About a dozen women were decorating, climbing on furniture to hang black and red streamers from the ceiling, alternating small cloth American flags with black swastikas between the streamers. Musicians were tuning their instruments off to one side. Discordant notes from fiddle, trumpet, drums, and accordion filled the room, leaving little room for thought. Harold suddenly noticed a file of uniformed storm troopers enter, laboring under weights and benches, carrying everything for a competition. *Of course,* the reporter thought, through the attempts of the band at harmony, *trials to determine the best-of-the-best for the Interborough.*

Harold still stood by the entrance to the barn, urging Regina to enter and greet her friends. "*Komen, Frau* Kergan, inside is true German spirit." He pulled at the young wife's arm and was surprised by the muscle tension he felt through the heavy sweater the woman wore.

Harold felt a touch on his shoulder. It was light, but he felt strength in those fingers. He turned to find himself face to face with Helga Willknecht. "You will want to join the other men. *Frau* Kergan has old friends here. We will watch over her." Harold released Regina's arm and watched Helga lead her into the crowded room. He noticed that the girl's eyes seemed full of fear.

Harold joined the men by the stage. "Comrades, put on your uniforms," Finnhandlerr said greeting the new arrivals. "You will be needed to maintain order."

The storm troopers hurried toward the rear door of the barn. Harold followed his fellows when, much to his surprise, Saul appeared by his side. "Christy wants to show me the camp," he said, his eyes bright with pleasure.

"Go ahead, but try not to talk with anyone else," Harold cautioned the boy. "And stay away from me. I'm going to be a storm trooper for a while."

Saul scampered away and Harold headed for the back door, following the last of the troopers. On this side of the barn was a small parking lot, almost empty now but soon to be filled with dozens of cars and trucks bearing New York plates. At the end of the dirt lot Harold saw the storm troopers disappearing down a path that led into the bare-limbed woods. He ran to the trees then slogged through a sea of fallen ocher and yellow leaves, oak and maple and ash, until he reached a small bungalow set among the trees.

Harold already wore his uniform pants. *It'll be a hot day in hell before I drop my trousers with Nazis around again.* He entered the cabin, full of men changing from holiday clothes to Nazi glory. He pulled off his shirt and took the brown garment from his small overnight bag. *Ah good, it's still got a fresh looking crease. I wouldn't want to be wrinkled.* He slipped it on, followed by his armband, mindful of the crooked cross it bore. The reporter sat down next to Willknecht to adjust his boots. "So this is Nordland," he said to the super. "It must be beautiful in the summer."

"Yes, it reminds me of home, the country around Windecken," Willknecht said while pinning his wartime decorations to his brown shirt. "The trees, the bushes, the hills, they are all the same."

I wonder which one of those pins commemorates you're getting shot in the ass, Harold thought, but he said, "I have heard you talk of Windecken. Where is it?"

"Windecken is an hour from Frankfurt. It was so beautiful before the War."

As they talked Harold and Georg walked back to the barn. In the short time they'd been gone, cars had filled up the parking lot, and streams of German merrymakers were flowing into the ramshackle building. Finnhandlerr was pacing up and down by the entrance, looking agitated. "Georg," he said. "We don't have enough men to do all that needs to be done." And brusquely, "Harold, take your post by the east door."

Harold headed to his assigned place, fixed a stern look upon his face, and stood at attention. He did not want to be reported for laxness. The Germans all around him were in good spirits. *I feel their gemutlicheit,* he thought. *It's like a bar mitzvah. Yeah, these guys are celebrating their 13th year in America. Of course they don't understand the symbolism. Why should they?*

But there was no good cheer in one place in the big room. Harold saw Regina Kergan sitting at a table not far from him. She was stone-faced, looking neither to the right or left, ignoring the hubbub and gay chatter that surrounded her. *She looks so lost, here, amongst all her old friends.*

Reinhold Stubble entered the room through the very door Harold was guarding and strode past him in an instant. *Good, I don't have to tell him his crazy daughter is here. Let him find out for himself. I hope I'm here to see his face. Still, I feel responsible for Regina. She came with me and she'll leave with me. And she is so pretty…*

An insistent clanging rang out across the room. Finnhandlerr was on the pine-board stage tolling a large brass bell. "Welcome to Sports Day, comrades," he boomed. "We have gathered, in the name of the *Fuehrer*, to further the ideals of The Party. Strength Through Joy is the thought for today. Joyous hearts in strong bodies are weapons of the *volk*. Sport calls all Germandom to arms. I present you *Ortsgruppenleiter* Stubble to open Sports Day 1938."

Stubble climbed up on the stage. "Comrades," he began in a stern authoritative voice, so unlike his usual mild tone, "the *Fuehrer* says sports are a tool, a means to an end. Sports will unify the *volk* into one master race."

The crowd cheered, *seig heil, seig heil."* The old barn shook. The door behind Harold flew open. He ducked to one side as the mass of Germans moved past him, into the cold November air. "*Seig, seig heil,"* they yelled ecstatically as they flooded the field for the outdoor competition.

The uniformed storm trooper detachment took positions on either side of a wide cinder path running downhill from the barn to the edge of the woods. The crowd gathered behind them, waiting for the starter's gun. Eight young men in white shorts, sleeveless shirts, and sneakers strode through the tall grass at the side of the makeshift track. The bright sun, approaching its highest point of the day, had not warmed the spot where Harold stood guarding the foot of the track. *It's cold. Strength Through Joy must mean freezing your ass off.*

Finnhandlerr announced that the race, a one hundred meter dash, was to be run in two heats, with the winners facing off in the finals. The first four contestants knelt in their starting positions, their course marked out in white chalk. Willknecht stood behind them, a pistol raised in the air. He fired and the race was on.

"Comrade Appel." Harold jumped. It was Finnhandlerr, coming up behind him. "Make a circuit of the cabins. Make sure there is nothing unusual going on. The longer races will be run there." The big man strode off to other duties and Harold trotted past the cheering crowd toward the woods. As he crunched along the gravel path past the first of the bungalows, he thought, *just the normal Nazi paranoia. What could possibly be going on way out here in the country?* He picked up the pace and ran toward the last of the bungalows, where he had changed into his thin uniform shirt, and foolishly left his coat. *At least I'm going to be warmer.*

At that moment Christiana and Saul were becoming reacquainted with each other's bodies. The girl led the young man deep into the woods, past the last cottage, over rolling hills, to the shore of a lake. There, nestled at the bottom of a big bare-branched tree, a short way from the grey lake waters, sat an open-sided lean-to, its wooden roof invisible beneath a layer of faded red and yellow oak leaves, spilling out all around the small structure so it looked like a natural nook snug in the loamy ground. The girl found a ratty old blanket stuffed between two loose boards in the back of the shed. She spread it on the dirt floor and pulled Saul down on top of her. Their lips were joined, their bodies intertwined, as they rolled over to the crunching of dry leaves and the sound of water lapping against the shore. They moved slowly at first, in contrast to their first time when Saul, traumatized by Nazi violence, was led quickly by Christiana into the act of love. This time the red-head took the lead, kissing the blond girl on her lips, ears, and hair. He undressed her, easing her skirt over her legs and removing her white underpants. He knelt between her outstretched legs, almost like a sprinter preparing for a race. She gasped as the cold air touched her body, then gasped again as the boy touched her and filled her. They buffeted each other, back and forth, until climax, then they settled into a companionable embrace while they listened to the honking of geese far above the lake.

Harold returned to the barn after a quick circuit of the remaining bungalows. He noticed that most of the people watching the races had left for the inside. The second heat was over and the two shivering winners were preparing to run their final race. Harold didn't wait to see a winner. He entered the barn and found Regina in the same place he'd left her, yelling at scores of people in the barn. "How dare they drag me here and then abandon me? I have been sitting here all morning. All alone. Not one of these *schweinhundt* has talked to me. I am so miserable." She started crying, loud rasping sobs that startled everyone around her. The crowd watching drew away several steps.

"B-b-but Regina, y-y-you wanted to come," Harold stuttered. "You begged your husband. 'Let me go,' you said. 'I want to see my old friends,' you said. I never promised to stay with you. I have duties as a member of the *OD*."

I wouldn't stay with her even if I could, Harold thought. *Georg is right, she is crazy. Such a shame. She's so beautiful. What's the matter with these people?* He looked around at their audience. *Some of them must know her. Why don't they talk to her?*

The crowd parted to let someone through. It was Stubble. He stood over his daughter as if to isolate her. People, seeing the *Bundesleiter* arrive, started to drift away.

"Regina, what are you doing here? Come with me." And the father led the suddenly docile daughter away before Harold could close his gaping mouth.

Willknecht approached the shaken reporter. "I told you she was crazy. Poor Reinhold has been living with this for years. He was so relieved when young Kergan announced his intention to marry Regina. 'Let her be some other man's problem,' Reinhold said."

"She did not act like this last night," Harold said. "You should see her house. Hitler himself could have decorated it. The walls almost speak German. She misses being with the *volk* so much, I thought, so I asked her to join us today. She was happy. I do not understand how she could change like this. It is unnatural."

Regina came storming across the room, Stubble trailing in her turbulent wake. "Leave me alone, you bastard," she cried out. "You are not a *vater*. You are the devil!" She fled the barn.

"Let her go, Reinhold," Willknecht said, grasping Stubble's arm. "Let her go. You know there is nothing to be done when she is like this. Let her calm down. She will be back." He led the weary father to a table, the same table Regina had been sitting at when the blowup began.

Helga came up to Harold as her husband led Stubble away. "This has been happening for many years, Harold, ever since Gina's mother died. Reinhold has taken the girl to doctors, but they cannot find a physical cause. It has to be in her head. Sit down and have a beer and I will tell you the story."

They found a secluded table near the back of the barn. Helga propped her elbows up on the thick pine wood and began speaking. "It was in 1927. Reinhold and his wife, Braunwin, were living in Berlin. Regina was nine. Reinhold was a clerk in the Foreign Office, and happy to have a job. Work was hard to come by in those days."

"Hitler was coming to Berlin to address a party meeting at Pharos Hall on the Unter den Linden." Helga took a sip of her beer. "Hitler had not been in Berlin for a year at the time. He was banned by the city government, thought to be a rabble-rouser. But he came anyway. Braunwin pleaded with her husband to see him. Reinhold begged three tickets from friends in the Party. Their seats were at the center of the auditorium with a clear view of the stage. The lights dimmed. Spotlights beamed down from the rafters, focusing on ranks of brown-uniformed SA. Cries of 'Heil Hitler' boomed throughout the hall as the leader entered. There was thunderous applause, then silence. Hitler spoke. He denounced the Jews and the Communists who ran the Berlin government. He railed against unemployment. Then he announced that a large crowd was outside the hall, demonstrating against him. At the call to arms, hundreds of storm troopers marched to the exits, bent on punishing their enemies."

Helga paused to wipe tears from her eyes. "In the crowd Reinhold was separated from his family. Regina clung to Braunwin's hand until they reached the street, where a Jewish hooligan, black beard underlining a huge pockmarked nose, threw them on the sidewalk and started kicking them. Four other Jewish brutes soon joined in. The young mother managed to cover her daughter, taking all the blows. The father found them like that, dead mother over terrified child."

"Reinhold was devastated," Helga continued. "But he had a nine-year-old daughter to care for, so he hid his grief as well he could, and made arrangements to leave Berlin. Regina never recovered from the trauma. She blamed her father, of course. She has been depressed, she has been angry, but she has never been the sweet little girl she once was. That is not to say that she is in one of her moods all the time. She can be mild at times, almost normal. Young Kergan certainly thought so. But she always returns to the anger."

What a story! Harold thought. *Regina sees Hitler and is attacked by Jewish thugs. It's wonderful propaganda. I don't believe a word of it!* He shivered.

A shrill sound washed over the Bund barn. All conversation stopped. It was Finnhandlerr, up on the stage, a big brass whistle in his mouth. He tooted twice more and in a loud voice, said, "All weightlifters—it is time to compete." The OD leader was in his element; this was his sport. He controlled the lineup of contestants, from prancing lightweights to lumbering heavyweights. He decided who would lift first and who would have to wait. Twenty contestants were at Finnhandlerr's mercy.

✍

At that moment Saul and Christiana were on the path back to the barn. Walking slowly, arm in arm, they approached the furthest of the cottages.

"Hilf mir! Help!" A muffled scream came from that direction.

"Who could that be?" Christiana asked. She drew closer to Saul.

"It's a woman's voice," Saul said. They heard a smashing sound from the Bund cottages. "And that sounds like breaking glass."

There was a flash of red through the trees. The screaming voice grew louder, coming toward them. Saul pushed Christiana off the path and down behind a fallen log. He fell flat beside her. A big man broke out of the forest, a squalling sack over his shoulder. Saul looked up through the undergrowth and saw Regina, her body stuffed into a canvas sack, carried on the big man's back like a load of kindling. Her face was contorted into a frightened mask but she was still pounding on her abductor's red plaid clad shoulders with balled fists, all the while bucking and kicking with her captured legs. Saul was close enough to see the cold sweat dripping from the man's face. His eyes, tucked under the brim of a faded red hunting cap, were dilated into a mask of their own. Saul remembered that later, along with the bright red tooth marks on the man's neck and the blood dripping from the corner of Regina's mouth as she screamed and screamed.

A small man charged from the woods. "Sheriff, wait up," he panted. "Damn her, she gave me a bloody nose."

"Serves you right," the big man called 'Sheriff' huffed while grimacing in pain. "You got too close to the bitch. Now, come on. Help me get her to the car. We'll tie her up good. Then I want to get back to the others. We've still got some work to do. OW! She bit me again." He dropped Regina on the hard ground and shoved her head all the way into the sack. "Come on. Lift her feet."

Saul slid closer to Christiana. "They haven't seen us," he whispered. "Can you circle around, get back to the barn, and sound the alarm? I'll follow them and free Regina if I have the chance."

"Yes, I'll tell the OD," hissed Christiana.

For a few minutes Saul stayed where he was, watching Christiana work her way through the trees, until he was sure she was out of sight. *What have I gotten into? I've got to follow Mrs. Kergan. Harold would want me to.*

The big man carrying Regina resumed his trek through the trees. His puny companion followed. Behind them came Saul.

It wasn't hard to track the trio. Saul followed the muffled screams of Regina inside her sack, the loud panting of the big man on the narrow path, and the sounds of the small man scrambling through the underbrush. After a while they emerged at a clearing, where a half a dozen old cars were parked along with one new black pickup. A dirt road led off into the trees. Saul crouched down behind a big rock, out of sight.

The man called Sheriff dumped Regina out of her sack and

held her tight while his small companion tied her legs to a stout tree trunk with some rough rope pulled out of the pick-up. He then tied her arms crossed behind her to the same trunk. But Regina drew fresh blood from the big man, biting his wrists and hands until he managed to pull an old rag from his pocket and stuff it in her mouth. Blood stained his red plaid hunting jacket in odd patterns. The young wife hung limply from the tree. Her clothes were torn and one breast was exposed. But she had punished the men. From his hiding place Saul could see blood seeping out between Sheriff's fingers as he held his neck. The small man's nose was gushing a vivid red stream, staining the ground he was standing on and the shoes he was standing in.

Saul stayed out of sight, listening to the hurried conversation in the clearing. "Butler, there wasn't supposed to be anyone here today," the big man cried, as his companion tried to staunch the blood flowing from his nose. "Now what are we going to do? We've kidnapped the bitch."

"She's wild," Butler shrilled. Regina spat in his face. "Slut!" he cried, and slapped her. "Naw, we didn't kidnap her. We arrested her."

"I'm going back to see how the others are doing. Ow, she bit me good!" the big man moaned as he lumbered off toward the Bund camp.

Butler stared at Regina while the gushing from his nose slowed to a trickle,. *He said they arrested her,* thought Saul. *That means Sheriff really is a sheriff, but he's acting like a criminal. I wish Harold was here to tell me what to do.* Suddenly, Butler stepped forward and pinched Regina's exposed breast. The girl screamed. Saul leapt out of his hiding place and slugged Butler on the side of his head. The small man collapsed to the ground, out cold.

◆

Christiana reached the barn while Saul was still hiding behind the big rock at the edge of the clearing. The Germans were crowded around the stage watching the weightlifting competition. The reporter spied the out-of-breath girl as soon as she slipped in the door. "Christiana, where is Solly?" *What's going on? Has Saul been chasing her around the woods?*

"Harold, some men took Regina from the woods beyond the cottages! Solly went after them!" Christiana sagged in the doorway.

Harold quickly rose out of his chair, but bumped heads with Helga. He just as quickly sat down, dazed for an instant, while Helga rushed to her daughter. *I've got to get Finnhandlerr. He'll know what to do.*

At that moment the storm trooper leader was lifting a bar loaded with 400 pounds, a winning lift in the heavyweight division. Thunderous applause washed over the barn as Finnhandler lowered the bar to the ground. The big man was mobbed by his followers, both in brown uniform and white competitor's garb. *Oh no! I'll never reach him now. Not in this crowd.*

Harold looked desperately around the barn, trying to find someone to help who wasn't celebrating with Finnhandlerr. He spied Willknecht approaching Helga. "Georg," he cried, "Regina has been abducted. Christiana just now told me."

"What!" Willknecht gasped. He grabbed his daughter by the shoulders as if to shake her but his wife restrained him with a touch.

"Georg," Helga said calmly, "Find out what happened and send some men to help. Harold, find someone to help, then run back to find Regina."

The reporter turned for the back door and came face to face with Everhardt, still dressed in white shorts, who had been listening to what Helga had said. "Werner," Harold said, "we have an emergency in the woods. Come with me."

Harold dashed out of the barn, followed by Everhardt. They went quickly down the path where the races had been run and into the woods where the Bund bungalows sat under the trees. The first cottage they saw had all its windows broken out and big men in rough clothing running out the door. The last man, wearing red plaid and holding an iron bar, raised his free hand to shade his eyes from the sunlight filtering through the bare branches. Harold, in his OD uniform, and Everhardt, in shorts, charged at him, yelling in German, *schwein, schwein*. The real OD man added the curse, *Juden, Juden* to his tirade. He picked up some sharp-edged stones from the gravel path and began flinging them at the retreating invaders. The reporter, yelling like a banshee, took the iron bar away from the startled man wielding the weapon and began beating him about the head and shoulders with it, until he managed to flee.

Harold and Everhardt chased the invaders through sparse forest, past smashed bungalows, to the clearing by the side of the road. At the edge of the clearing, however, the two OD men held back. "There are too many of them," Harold panted, while bending over with his hands on his knees. "We have to wait for reinforcements."

The invaders wasted no time getting in their cars and fleeing. The black pick-up was the last to leave. Everhardt stepped out of the cover of the trees and launched a baseball-sized rock after the truck. And he hit it, shattering the rear window. The vehicle swerved, righted itself on the dirt road, and accelerated out of sight. *What an arm,* Harold thought. *Just like Sid Luckman at Columbia. Dewey was right to nail him for Mo's death.*

The other Bundists arrived in time to see a cloud of dust kicked up by the fleeing cars. They knew what had happened in the clearing because they were led there by Saul and Regina, who had fled through the woods and met Finnhandler, the Willknecht family, Stubble, and the others as they burst out of the barn in pursuit of the invaders. Regina, rescued from captivity and modestly holding her torn dress together, was the center of attention. She was anointed a hero, willing to sacrifice all for *volk und Fuehrer.*

"No dirty Jew will ever break my spirit," Regina bravely declared, letting her torn dress fall open to reveal her violated body. There was applause all around. Even *Ortsgruppleiter* Stubble beamed approval of his wayward daughter.

Solly was a hero. Harold was a hero. Everhardt was a hero too, telling and retelling the story of the chase and his mighty heave. Christiana was a heroine and no one even questioned what she had been doing alone with Saul all afternoon. But the attention of the Germans was really on Regina, the victim and the victor. So no one noticed Harold, the reporter, unobtrusively searching the clearing for evidence of what had happened there. Half hidden under a bush, he saw a flash of brown. Bending down, he picked up a well-worn wallet and slipped it into his pocket.

The Germans were appalled by the damage to their holiday cottages. Broken glass was everywhere. *Kristallnacht in New Jersey, only it happened to Germans,* Harold thought.

"This should be reported immediately," Reinhold Stubble declared, his voice rising to a shriek. "Max...Max...Max," he called, until he regained his normal voice. "Please go to the county seat, see the sheriff, and tell him what happened. Tell him Jews did this. Take Appel and Everhardt with you." He was yelling again. "They saw the pigs!"

You can dish it out but you can't take it, Stubble, Harold thought. *Your boy Everhardt killed a friend of mine the other day. Killed him! And now you're whining about broken glass.* "Why do you not report the damage by telephone," he asked Finnhandler as they drove off.

"Sheriff Acton is not a friend of the Bund," Finnhandlerr said, resignation in his hoarse voice. He was still wearing the wet sweat shirt he had worn for the competition and the cold air of the woods was giving him fits, and a cough. "We have dealt with the sheriff before. We have been vandalized before. He ignores our phone calls. Hence we go in person, to show him we are men of substance, who must be dealt with."

"You must have known there would be trouble. You looked worried earlier."

"We always have trouble when we come to Nordland," complained Everhardt from the back seat. "There is a black cloud hanging over this place."

"We have had vandalism before," Finnhandlerr said. He was driving very carefully on the country road that led from the German camp to the county seat called Newton. "Hitler himself was not welcomed in much of Germany for years and years. When we have disputes with the local farmers I remind myself of that fact. Eventually, they will see the rightness of the Nazi cause. Never before," his voice rose to the level Harold expected from a giant in distress, "have we had anyone, much less a beautiful woman, abducted and held prisoner, and that is the reason we are going to Newton, to stop those Jews in their tracks. Harold, take off your armband. I don't want to give the sheriff any more reasons to hate us." Harold did as he was told.

They rode in silence the rest of the way to Newton. Harold was lost in his thoughts. *What were the motives of the intruders? Could they have been in the pay of Jews? Or maybe they were just locals who didn't like Nazis. O'Rourke could sniff around Newton. Maybe there's a story to be gleaned from that wallet I found.*

Once in Newton, they passed faded frame houses and blocks of failed stores. In the center of downtown was the courthouse, a temple in the Greek revival style, impressive but badly in need of a new coat of whitewash. Finnhandlerr slid into a parking space right in front, his new sedan looking out of place among the decrepit Model T's and old pick-ups lining the street. "This town should be prosperous, with that big arms plant in the county, but it is not, and I do not know why," the large man said as he got out of the car and pointed to the building in front of him. "The sheriff's office is here."

Finnhandlerr led the way to heavy double doors, bright with a fresh coat of brown paint, beyond which was a long corridor lined with benches. Locals, mostly in faded jeans and flannel shirts, lounged around, warming themselves with coffee in paper cups. At the end of the hall another door, fitted with frosted glass, announced in flaked gold lettering: *Sheriff James T. Acton, Sussex County, New Jersey.* On the next line, smaller letters read: *Hours 9-5, Monday-Saturday. All others times, ring bell.* Everhardt rang the bell. A small balding man, with hard, steel-grey eyes and a lump on top of his noggin, opened the door. "Hello Butler," Finnhandlerr said in a loud German-tinged voice, "Ve vant to see Sheriff Acton now."

Butler tried to shut the door but Finnhandlerr pushed his way through. Harold peered around the big storm trooper to see an equally big man sitting with his booted feet atop a cluttered desk. A bloody bandage peeked out from the collar of his flannel shirt, upon which hung the tarnished star of the sheriff's office. His wrists, poking out of plaid sleeves, were painted the pale red of mercurochrome.

"Why Sheriff, you are hurt," Finnhandlerr said, his voice, full of false solicitude, mocking the injuries of the other man. "What could have happened to you?"

"I fell down the stairs, if it's any business of yours," Sheriff Acton said curtly. "What are you doing here? More trouble at the camp?" He sounded weary of any news about Nazis.

"Vandalism, Sheriff. Vandalism." Finnhandlerr was forthright. "All the windows were broken in eight cottages."

"You've had vandalism before, Finnhandlerr," drawled the Sheriff. "And we've never caught anyone. There's no evidence."

"This time was different. We were there when it happened. These two men chased the vandals." Finnhandlerr clasped Harold and Everhardt around the shoulders and drew them forward. "And another thing Sheriff. A woman was abducted, taken away, tied up, and assaulted. The daughter of our leader, Sheriff. Do you understand what this means? German honor has been violated!"

The office was quiet. The hard face of the sheriff was unreadable, but the deputy's eyes held undeniable guilt. Finally Acton spoke. "That's a very serious charge, Finnhandlerr. I'll come out first thing tomorrow morning to see the damages and look for evidence. Have the woman and any witnesses available to be interviewed."

"We cannot hold the woman overnight!" Finnhandlerr exploded. "She has been through an ordeal and wants to return to her husband. But these two men," the OD leader gestured at his companions, "were witnesses. Interview them now."

"Finnhandlerr, it's just me and Ben here on Sundays. We can't get into anything complicated like an investigation. Have the woman and your witnesses write out statements and I'll be there in the morning. Is your caretaker, Klapprott, still there during the week?"

"We understand perfectly, Sheriff," Finnhandlerr said, his voice under iron control. "Crimes against Germans are not important in this county."

"There's no need to be upset," the Sheriff said, his weasel words sounding falsely ingratiating to Harold's ears. "I'll be out to Nordland in the morning."

Finnhandlerr filled out the incident report form which the Sheriff handed him. While the big man was laboriously writing English sentences Harold glared at Acton and the bump on his head. *I gave him that knot on his head with the steel bar I took away from him. I sure as hell hope it hurts. But, but, but...whose side am I on? Are the Germans of Yorkville now my friends?*

The three men returned to their auto. As they pulled around the corner Everhardt, from the back seat, yelled out, "there it is!"

Harold looked where he was pointing. In a driveway behind the courthouse, hidden from all but Everhardt's sharp eye, sat a brand-new black Ford pick-up, with a shattered rear window.

"You know, Max," Harold said, "Sheriff Acton was already at Nordland today. He led the raid, and there is the truck that proves it."

"You are right Harold," Finnhandlerr said, anger dueling with resignation in his voice. "Regina said she bit her captor on the neck, at the exact place the Sheriff was wearing a bandage. Acton did not want to come to Nordland today. He could not face Regina!"

CHAPTER SIXTEEN

DECEIT AT NORDLAND

THE CITY ROOM WAS quiet. The last edition had been put to bed and everyone went home, everyone but Aaron, who chose the quiet time to call in Apple and O'Rourke. When they arrived he left them to stew in his office while he went upstairs to talk with the big shots. Harold looked at his partner, quietly dozing in the chair next to him. He picked up the latest edition of the paper from his boss's desk and scanned the front page.

Not much from Germany, just an amendment to the Reich citizenship law. Hitler is loosening the standards for being Aryan; only two grandparents are needed now. Harold scratched his head. *Lotta secrets in German closets, including the Fuehrer himself. You could make a lot of money in Germany now, selling Aryan ancestors. Getcha great-grandpa here, Heini Fogelschmidt, guaranteed descended from Arminius.*

At the bottom was an article about Macy's big parade. *The stores are predicting their best year since the Depression started. I sure hope so. The market's up.* Then Harold saw the story he'd been looking for, tucked in under a photo of the big Krazy Kat balloon from the parade—Pat's latest about the Yorkville stoning. *I wish I wrote the headline. I would have called it MURDER IN NAZITOWN.*

The only light in the city room came from the open door of Aaron's office, where Harold and Pat were waiting for their boss to return from talking to his boss. The erstwhile Nazi had the paper spread out on the table in front of him while his friend was leaning back, his feet up, his eyes closed, and his hair leaving a greasy stain on the glass front of Aaron's bookcase. Before he'd gone upstairs, the editor had told them, "We're making a big investment in this story. We need to get a lot out of it."

What kind of newspaperman ever thinks about money? Harold thought. *Only Aaron.*

The skinflint in question entered his office, dropping heavily into the padded chair behind his desk as if he bore the cares of the world on his narrow shoulders. Harold nudged O'Rourke awake. "OK boss, what'd the big shots say about the Nazi story? Did you tell them we're wasting too much money on it?" But Harold knew that the editor wasn't going to pull the plug on his story. News about Nazis, especially local Nazis, sold papers. "Pat, tell the boss what you found out this week in New Jersey. It'll knock his socks off."

"Last Sunday night Harold came to see me at home." O'Rourke was wide awake now. "He found this wallet at the scene of the kidnapping. There was ID for one Benjamin A. Butler, deputy sheriff, in the billfold, along with ten crisp fifty dollar bills."

"Why was this guy, this deputy, losing his wallet during an attack on the Nazi camp?" Harold said. "And why was he carrying so much money?"

O'Rourke bent over the editor's desk and continued. "I set off for Sussex County the next morning. I wanted to find out why the deputy, and probably the Sheriff to hear Harold tell it, had been involved in the raid on the camp. At the city limits I passed Roscoe's Gas N Go. I went a quarter mile past the garage, stopped, and opened my hood. I loosened the distributor wire connections with the spark plugs and tried to start the car. It whirred but wouldn't catch. I poked a hole in the radiator hose with my pocket knife, just in case, then put the roadster in neutral and pushed it back down the road to the gas station. This old timer came out of one of the service bays when I finally got to the gas pumps."

"Something wrong, young feller?" he said.

"'Sure is. It up and died on me a little way down the road. I'm on my way to Paterson, and I'm already late for work. Can you take a look at it?'"

"He said he would and introduced himself as Roscoe, just like on the sign. He spat tobacco juice on the ground, just beyond his old work boots. I jumped back half a step."

"Name's O'Malley, I said. I don't use my real name when I'm on an investigation. Told him I was passing through after spending the weekend at my uncle's cabin in the Poconos, and that I worked at the Royal Shoe Company in Paterson. I like to establish my story when I'm investigating. Pretty good, huh. Then I asked him if there was some place around I could get some breakfast."

"The old man told me about a place called Gimpy's, just down the street, towards the courthouse. You'll get a good breakfast, he said, and when you come back your roadster will be ready."

"I walked back into town. Gimpy's was the only restaurant near the courthouse. It was a dark kind of place to match the overcast day outside. The only light was at the bar. I slid onto an empty stool, between a hefty, red-haired woman and a youngish man wearing overalls. Next to the redhead was a slim brunette. They were talking and I was listening."

"I told him not to carry all that money, but he never listens to me, complained the large lady to the attractive brunette. Now he's gone and lost it, and no more coming in for a week."

"Maybe he'll find it, Missus Butler, said the brown-haired girl."

"Not likely, if I know that man, said the stout woman. She

finished her meal, mopping up the remaining gravy on her plate with a piece of toast. I've got to get to work, Em, she said. Someone in the family has to earn some money."

"Miz Butler got up and ponderously made her way to the end of the bar. I looked across the empty stool at the girl. She was dressed in a plaid skirt and a white blouse, like a schoolgirl's uniform. But she was no schoolgirl."

"I was suddenly jostled by the young man in overalls on my right. Hey darling, he said to the brunette, now that Martha Butler is gone why don't you slide over and spend some time with me?"

"Not likely, Clint, Emma said to Overalls, What would your wife say? Besides, this gentleman doesn't want to move. Her voice had an edge that said to me, please stay."

"I don't want to come between you and your friend, Miss, I protested mildly, hoping to give Clint the idea that I would, indeed, relish the opportunity to come between them."

"Oh, Clint's just leaving, the girl said, thanking me with her eyes."

"Finish your drink and go back to work, Clint, before I tell Denise you're trying to pick up every young thing in the bar. She had an edge in her voice that made the unkempt young man gulp his beer and beat a hasty retreat. The two of us were almost alone in the rapidly emptying tavern."

"Thank you, stranger, the girl said. If you hadn't been here Clint would've gotten mighty uppity. My name's Emma Acton. What's yours?"

"Glad to help Miss. Old Clint looked a few sails to the wind."

"Clint's harmless. We went to high school together. I must admit he usually doesn't start drinking this early. Must be having some trouble at home."

"That's too bad for him, Emma, but good for me. I got to meet the prettiest girl in the county. My name's Pat, Pat O'Malley, by the way. I was driving through town when my car broke down.

Roscoe, up at the garage, said he could fix it in a couple of hours so I walked over here to get some breakfast."

"I'm glad your auto broke down Pat, Emma said smoothly while sliding onto the vacant stool between us."

"'Your name's Acton?' I asked. Where have I heard that name before?"

"You've probably heard of my daddy. He's Sheriff of Sussex County, Emma said with pride. He's going to run for the state legislature next year."

"Ha. You're a politician's daughter. You must be very proud of him. Hey, who was the lady you were sitting with before? She sounded like she was upset with her husband."

"Oh, that was Martha Butler. Her husband is my daddy's deputy. Do you believe, the man just went and lost five hundred dollars in brand new currency? He said it fell out of his pocket but doesn't know where. Martha is hopping mad about it."

"Where would a sheriff's deputy get all that money?"

"He did a special job for some people from New York. I couldn't get any more out of her. Do you want to go for a walk Pat? Emma had an inviting tone in her voice. Your car probably won't be ready for hours. Old Roscoe is so slow."

"Don't you have to go to work, Emma?"

"Nope, I don't have a job, Emma said matter-of-factly. Since my ma died all I do is take care of Daddy."

"Outside, Emma took my arm. This girl is not shy, I thought. We walked past the courthouse to a street of large homes. Why don't you come in? I'll make some coffee, she said. She led me onto the porch of a large, freshly painted yellow frame house."

"Your house is the same color as my roadster. Are you sure your father won't mind me coming in?"

"Emma laughed like not even her father told her what to do. He's not here. He went to look at some cottages that were vandalized over the weekend. At the Nazi camp. Have you heard about the Nazi camp?"

"Sure. A guy from my neighborhood goes there all the time. Is it around here?"

"It's near Andover, by the big munitions plant, Emma explained. Those guys really make my daddy mad. They're always complaining about something; they want to be treated like little *fuehrers*. What makes them so special? We've got lots of camps in the county, kid's camps, an Italian camp, even a nudist camp. No one complains like the Nazis. I wish they'd all go back to Germany."

"Emma opened the door and a quivering ball of brown fur bounced into her arms. 'Down, Henry. Down boy," she yelled at a little wire-haired terrier. She took my hand and led me to a light, airy kitchen, sat me down at an old wooden table, and went about making coffee, filling a percolator with dark grounds from a canister on the stove. The dog was yapping at her feet as she said, Pat, tell me all about yourself."

"Tell her all about myself? I hadn't even told her my real name. But Boss, I liked this girl. I didn't want to lie to her. I said, not much to tell, Emma. I majored in business at college and afterwards got a job as an office manager at a shoe factory. Basically, the same lie I told Roscoe. Then I said, and I'm single, which is the truth. I was saved from saying anything else by a commotion in the front hall. The dog was jumping up and down and barking like nobody's business."

"Who could that be? Emma said."

"Is anyone home? a male voice yelled from the hallway."

"Daddy, what are you doing back so soon? Emma said to the big burly man who came into the kitchen. Have some coffee."

"Yeah, coffee. Emma, I saw what I had to see at that damn Nazi camp, so I left. I don't like being around those people, anyway. The Sheriff spied me sitting quietly behind his daughter. His eyes narrowed. Who is this? he said suspiciously."

"Daddy, this is Pat O'Malley. He was driving through town when his auto broke down. Roscoe's fixing it and you know how slow he is. Pat will be lucky to get out of town tomorrow. We met at Gimpy's. Pat was very gallant when Clint got a little forward. So I asked him back here for a cup of coffee. That was all right, wasn't it?"

"Em, you know damn well you're going to do whatever you please, whether you ask me or not."

"Sheriff Acton spoke with a mixture of affection and exasperation, but then he turned to me. Mr. O'Malley is it? Well, you're obviously not German, so you're all right."

"Emma's eyes widened. Daddy, what happened at the Nazi camp?"

"Ahhh, the same old stuff. Talked to their caretaker, Klapprott. That guy is the most superior acting shit I've ever met. Even worse than the ones from New York. But I'm sure Mr. O'Malley doesn't want to hear about this stuff."

"On the contrary, Sheriff Acton. I agree completely. This guy who lives on my street belongs to the Nazi Bund, and he's just insufferable. If the Germans are going to act like that then they should all go back to Germany."

"Well, that's the way I feel, too. Just not officially, understand? The Sheriff turned to his daughter. Em, I've got to go back to the office but some men are coming over at 3 o'clock. Call me when they show up. Pleasure meeting you, Mr. O'Malley."

"Now we won't be able to finish that walk, Emma complained. Do you want to call Roscoe and ask when your car will be ready?"

"The roadster had completely escaped my mind. I picked up the telephone from the kitchen counter and asked the operator for Roscoe's Garage."

"The car won't run,' Roscoe apologized. 'The radiator was dry so I filled it, but all the water leaked out. I found the trouble, a small hole in the hose. I fixed that but the engine still wouldn't turn over. I want to call in another mechanic. Might take a day or two."

"Go ahead, I told the old man. It suited my purposes to be trapped in Newton overnight."

"I asked Emma if there was a place to stay in town because she was right about Roscoe. He was slow."

"Pat, stay here tonight, the Sheriff's daughter said. We've got a spare room with the bed all made up. I couldn't bear the thought of you in one of those fleabag rooms at the tourist cabins."

"DING, DING, DONG. The doorbell rang and the dog went wild. Hold Henry please Pat, Emma asked. She scooped the pooch up and handed him to me. DING, DING, DONG. Whoever was there wasn't the patient type."

"Emma opened the door. Two men were standing on the porch. Emma quickly ushered them in, past me and the yelping dog, into the parlor. She retreated to the kitchen, pulling me with her. She picked up the telephone. 'Daddy, your friends are here.' And she said to me in a whisper while listening to her father, they creep me out. Are all Germans like that?"

"I snuck a peek into the parlor. The men were standing in the middle of the room, arms at their sides, looking grim. One was tall and blond, with an angular face, and the other was short and stumpy, with nondescript brown hair and a red, wet-looking nose, as if he suffered from a sinus condition. They both wore dark suits and expensive looking overcoats. I retreated to the kitchen."

"Emma hung up the telephone. Daddy will be here in a few minutes. I'm glad you're here Pat. I don't like being alone in the house with them. She shuddered then whispered to me, they're from the German consulate in New York. I moved closer to the girl. I didn't want to miss any of what she was going to say. The tall one is Captain Hans Thorson, the military attaché, and old red nose is Heinrich Mayer, some kind of official. Don't tell anyone about this. No one's supposed to know they're here."

O'Rourke stood up, took a few steps to Aaron's desk, and leaned over, face to face with the editor. "I don't know what to do Boss. It's a good story. But I like this girl. If she finds out I wrote about her daddy then I'm finished with her."

"You didn't use your real name Pat," Aaron reassured his reporter. "She won't figure it out."

"I'm going to tell you what else happened. I tiptoed into the front hall, still holding Henry, who was a very good dog, by the way. Didn't make a peep. I stole a look out the door. There was a big black Mercedes in the driveway. It looked official, probably because the rear windows were curtained for privacy. I remember thinking, 'if they want to be incognito they picked the wrong car.' Then I saw Sheriff Acton stalking up the driveway, a worried look on his face. I retreated into the kitchen, carefully closing the door in hopes the dog would continue his mild-mannered ways. Your father's coming in, I told Emma."

"Acton came in and went straight to the parlor. Emma opened the kitchen door a crack so we could hear. From their grim voices I imagined that the Germans kept their frozen expressions."

"Let me tell you what we did yesterday. Acton was speaking. He sounded apologetic. And at the same time, he sounded as if he didn't give a damn. I don't know how he pulled that off. We broke every window we could reach, he said, but we couldn't get into the main building. There were Germans in there, lots of them. Every time the sheriff talked about *Germans* his voice dripped contempt, which was actually funny because the men he was talking to were *the Germans*."

"You did not do what you were paid to do, barked Thorson. You were to leave Nordland a shambles!"

"You told me there would be no one there, not even the care-taker, countered Acton heatedly. We ran into a young woman wandering in the woods. That was the first thing that went wrong. We tied her up and left one man to watch her, but we must have been seen because someone hit him over the head and helped her to escape."

"Acton paused but the two Germans were silent so he continued. We were breaking up the cottages. We left the woods to go up to the main building. That's where the Nazis met us. They chased us down the hill and through the woods. We were lucky to get away. It would have been awful if they'd caught any of my men. I would have had to arrest them and the whole thing would have been a damned mess. There's gotta be a way to get the Bund camp out of the county, but I'm not going to break any more laws for you guys."

"America is so backward, Mayer complained under his breath to Thorson while I strained to hear. Only a racially pure country can be great."

"Shut up, you fool, Thorson said in a brittle voice. America is powerful. The Fuehrer knows that. He doesn't want to upset Roosevelt. If a few foolish *deutscher aussiedler* have to be sacrificed to please the Americans so be it."

"After listening to the byplay between the diplomats, Sheriff Acton grew suspicious. I don't know what you gentlemen are plotting but maybe the FBI would understand better than I do."

"I didn't know if the FBI would be interested, but I sure was. It sounded like official Germany was unhappy with the Bund. I hoped the three men would keep talking."

"Sheriff, Thorson said calmly, we would be very pleased if the *Bund* left your county. They are an obstacle to good relations between the United States and *Deutschland*. We do not know how to remove that obstacle. That is why we asked your help. We defer to your judgment. Are there any legal methods to accomplish our joint goal?"

"I don't know, Acton said, placated by the reasonable tone of the diplomat. Maybe I should call in the Feds. I'm just a country sheriff who's getting in over his head. Say...wait a minute. Maybe there is a way. New Jersey passed this Anti-Hate Statute last year. It outlaws any public display of foreign uniforms. Acton looked sharply at the pair of Germans. Maybe that's why you're not in uniform today, Captain Thorson. I seem to recall the law also prohibits hate speech. Sounds like it was designed for the German Bund, huh Captain? The sheriff had a good laugh at his own wit. But the law hasn't been tested in court yet, Acton continued. It might tie up our friends over at the camp in an expensive legal battle. Would that suit your purposes gentlemen?"

"Hmmm, yes, that might be satisfactory. I do not think the *Bund* has unlimited resources and, if I understand correctly, lawyers in America are very expensive."

"That makes more sense than scaring the *Bund* away when they don't have the sense to be scared. Acton seemed pleased with himself. I'll go in to Nordland when they're having one of their big meetings and arrest the speaker and anyone in uniform. All perfectly legal. Can I trust you fellows to let me know when their next meeting will be? I don't want any more screw-ups like yesterday."

"Acton escorted his guests to the door. Emma and I rushed to a window in time to see the Germans hurry to their car. With Mayer driving and Thorsen in the back seat, they backed out of the driveway and roared off towards New York."

"I have to go back to the office, Emma, yelled the Sheriff. I'll be back for dinner. And he shrugged into his coat and followed the Germans out the door, a sly smile upon his face."

"I was confused. I turned to the Sheriff's daughter and asked. What side is your father with, the German Nazis? Or does he secretly support the American Nazis?"

"Pat, can I trust you?"

"This wasn't a question I was expecting to hear. I had only met the girl a couple of hours ago at Gimpy's. I gave her my reporter's answer. Yes Emma, you can trust me."

"I'm going to tell you something that absolutely cannot leave this house. My father might be in danger if the Bund found out. Daddy is working for the Dies Committee."

"The House Un-American Affairs Committee? That Dies Committee. I was thinking to myself, I've hit the jackpot. International intrigue and Martin Dies, too. Pretty good for a police reporter."

"Yes, Emma said. The Dies Committee in Washington."

"I had to get the background on this. What could a small-town sheriff have to do with a Washington committee?"

"And Emma told me everything. Two years ago the Bund bought an old farm and turned it into a camp, she said. Soon after, an FBI agent showed up and asked for help in watching the Nazis. Some people in Washington think we're going to wind up fighting the Nazis, and, if that's the case, then Sussex County is strategic, because of the Hercules plant and the New York reservoirs. Then, a year ago an investigator from the Dies Committee, a Mr. James Gilbert, came by. He had learned from the FBI that Acton had an eye on the Germans and might be able to give him some information. The Sheriff has been working with Mr. Gilbert ever since."

"How did the guys from the German embassy get involved?" Aaron asked.

"Emma told me that six months ago Captain Thorson drove out from the city to make her father a proposition. He wanted Nordland closed and he didn't care how it was done. Acton reported this strange request to Gilbert, who told him to go along and find out what the real Germans were up to. Acton has been taking German money ever since, making small raids on Nordland, while trying to figure out the Nazis' motive. Mayer just cleared up the mystery."

"When my car broke down this morning, I told Emma, I never thought I'd wind up in the middle of international intrigue. Why did your father tell you all this? You could be in danger. I didn't like the look of those German fellas."

"Oh, I know everything Daddy does, Emma boasted. He can't keep secrets from me."

O'Rourke stopped talking. There was silence in the puddle of light which leaked into the darkened city room while a broad smile grew on Aaron's narrow face. It was the kind of story he loved—intrigue, spy stuff, real skullduggery—and just a dash of sex to liven it up. "How long will it take you to write the story, O'Rourke?" the editor asked, sure that the answer would be 'no time at all.'

"Boss, I don't want to write this story."

"You're writing the story," Aaron roared.

"If I do then Emma and her father will get in trouble, big trouble."

Aaron alternated sputtering and fuming at his reporter, but Harold looked thoughtful. "Could you write it without mentioning the Sheriff?"

It was O'Rourke's turn to look thoughtful. He quickly rewrote the story as he had it in his mind, deleting all mention of Sheriff Acton or his lovely daughter. "Get me a typewriter," he shouted.

"Use mine." The editor jumped out of his chair.

O'Rourke pounded on the machine for a few minutes while his editor stalked up and down from the far side of the city room to his lighted office. Harold sat and thought, *come in from the dark boss, come in from the dark.*

O'Rourke pulled the paper from the typewriter. 'Officials of the German Consultate in New York have been paying locals in Sussex County, New Jersey to vandalize and otherwise disrupt the serenity of Camp Nordland, the rural retreat of the German American Bund...' it began.

Aaron grabbed the sheet and read, "...Sunday, inside the main building of the camp, Bund members listened to speakers praising Adolf Hitler, while outside, paid agents of the Nazi government were vandalizing camp cottages. This strange turn of events is being closely watched by investigators for the Dies Committee and the FBI."

"Pat," Harold said, "you've got a good story there and with no mention of Sheriff Acton. It's more powerful that way and it leaves the Bund boys guessing." *I don't think they'll guess that I'm the spy in their midst, not after I helped save Regina.* Except, who knows what that weasel Everhardt is thinking?

Chapter Seventeen

A DIPLOMATIC SOLUTION

A NGER WAS PALPABLE in the ballroom of the Yor-kville Casino that night. Bund members, arriving for their regular meeting, were aghast at the news, reported in the *World Journal*, that the German government was behind the troubles at Camp Nordland. 'German Consul-General Plans Vandalism at Nazi Camp' screamed the headline. The target of the outrage was Dr. Johann Mendelsohnn, lead German diplomat in New York. "Let us march on the Consulate," cried the crowd as they surged toward the speaker's platform. Uniformed OD joined hands to hold them back.

"We are not barbarians," *Ortsgruppleiter* Stubble cried, his anger at the unsophisticated masses barely controlled. "We do not march against fellow Germans, we talk. I have arranged a meeting with Mendelsohnn tomorrow. I will be there. *Bundesfuehrer* Kuhn will be there."

~§~

The Bund members simmered to a low boil as they straggled back to their seats. Committees made their reports; old business and new business were heard. Stubble announced that the date for the trial was January 23. And the Christmas Fair was set for December 10th at the New York Hippodrome. Harold stood at his usual place in back of the hall, guarding the door against the Jewish hordes.

No trial for two more months, Harold thought. *That's a long time. No telling how many Jews the Bund can kill in two months.*

The hall still buzzed with talk of the treachery of the diplomat. "The *Fuehrer* knows nothing of the actions of his Consul," one pint-size man said.

"He will have to be told," an old woman said.

As the meeting ended Stubble was besieged with advice on what he should say and do when he saw the diplomat. "Threaten him," someone said.

"Smash his office!"

"No. Be polite, but write to his superiors." The argument continued as the members filed out onto the street.

Harold walked home with Willknecht. An overcast sky hid the moon and stars. Gloomy streets, puddled by the dim light of the streetlamps, matched their mood. In the super's eyes Harold saw the collapse of faith in *Fuehrer und Volk*, an erosion of belief that was utterly predictable. *Nazism is built on sand. This is just the start.*

"Reinhold asked me to join the delegation tomorrow," Willknecht said. "I do not know if I will."

If Georg wants to remain a Nazi not going with the delegation is the smart thing. The more he hears of the German lies the more disgusted he will become.

❦

Pat O'Rourke had returned from the country determined to find out what was going on in the Consul-General's office. "I made up an excuse to interview Mendelsohnn," he told Harold over the phone that night. "It was a good excuse and might be a story idea. Last week was the anniversary of the **Deutschland** incident. Have you heard of it? It happened in 1933. Hitler hadn't been in power that long but he was already pissing off the rest of the world with his talk of German rearmament and his repression of the Jews. The **SS Deutschland**, the flagship of the Hamburg-American Line, was the biggest passenger liner in German hands. The ship docked at Pier 31 right in the middle of a big dockworkers' strike. The passengers carried their own luggage ashore but there was also perishable cargo in the hold, German cheese if I remember correctly. The crew unloaded the cheese even though the stevedores had set up a picket line. The dockworkers were so angry they stormed the ship and ripped the swastika flag from the stern. It became a major diplomatic incident. Hitler was so mad that he made the swastika the official flag of Germany. Before that it had only been a party symbol."

"That's a great story, Pat," Harold said. "Did you talk to Mendelsohnn about it?"

"Yeah. I went to the morgue and got all the old stories, then went to Mendelsohnn's office looking for reaction to the fifth anniversary. But when I asked him about it he didn't know anything. Look, I know he wasn't here five years ago but shouldn't a top diplomat know about important stuff? I read up on it; he should have too. Damn, he didn't even want to talk to me. He is a lazy man, with no sense of how to deal with the press or people in general. While I was there though, I buttered up his secretary, a very good-looking *fraulein*. Before she knew what was happening, we were having drinks at that lounge overlooking the ice skaters at Rockefeller Center. Two double martinis were too much for her. She told me all about who really runs the consulate. Your old buddy, Gestapo Captain Thorson, has all the power. He reports directly to SS Chief Heinrich Himmler, bypassing Foreign Minister Von Ribbentrop.

❧

Later Willknecht called on Harold at his little apartment. "Friend Harold, I know it is late, but I have to ask you for a *grosses geschenk*, a great gift. Will you join our delegation tomorrow? "

"Has *Ortsgruppenleiter* Stubble approved? I do not think he likes me after I brought Regina to Nordland. Will Max be in the delegation? If my OD leader wants me I will join." *Georg just asked me to join an official delegation without approval from his superiors? That is unheard of in the top-down Bund.* Willknecht turned and trudged down the stairs, his dejection apparent in his slumped shoulders. *I've got to talk to Sally. Maybe she'll tell me what to do.* The reporter put his coat back on and went down to the street, to the closest pay phone, in front of a nearby pharmacy.

Sally answered on the first ring. "Harold do you know what time it is? Everybody is sleeping but me."

"I know it's late, but I had to talk to you. I wish I was there right now."

"You should be glad you're not here. The other night Saul told Mom and Dad about Christiana. I've never seen my father so furious. He's not talking to Saul. He walks around the house muttering, 'a *shiksa*, a *deutsche shiksa*,' under his breath. And he blames you, if he's not blaming me for bringing you into the house. Mama's mad too, but compared to Daddy she welcomes the new daughter-in-law."

"The only wedding in the family is going to be you and me," Harold said, tapping his finger against the dial with each word. "I'll talk to your father and Saul too."

"Please Harold, but when?"

"I want to come Sunday. There is so much craziness going on here in Yorkville I can't get away before then. Oh Sally, did you see the paper this afternoon?"

"Do you mean the story about Nazis beating up on Nazis at Camp Nordland?" Sally asked. "That sure is crazy."

"You know what's crazy? My Nazis are going to meet the real

Nazis, the ones from Germany, tomorrow at Rockefeller Center. They're all mad, but I worry about the real Germans more—they've got power. By the way, has my uncle said anything about getting the family out of Germany?"

"Rose Nathanson's husband, the immigration lawyer, is working on it," Sally replied. She sounded upbeat.

Harold decided not to worry about the family in Germany. He had enough to worry about right here in New York. "If things get too hot around your house Sunday, we can sneak off for a walk. Don't worry about your Dad and Saul, though. They just need time to cool off. I'm going to bed now, Doll, and dream of you."

Instead, Harold's dreams were of Saul's wedding to Christiana. The bride's father was in full Nazi regalia; Sam Brown Belt, swastika armband, and his Iron Ass Cross from the last war was worn proudly. All the men from Yorkville were in brown uniforms. The Jewish men were all dressed in long black coats, with white yarmulkes and tallit. Harold was also dressed in brown, with the swastika on his arm covered by his blue and white tallit. The bride wore white, a traditional wedding dress, but the groom wore a brown shirt uniform with his tallit and skullcap. The wedding canopy was crafted from a swastika flag. He woke with a vision of Willknecht's beefy face and the Horst Wessel Song ringing in his ears.

Harold dragged himself to the newspaper, the images from his nightmare still vivid in his mind. The first thing he did was tell Finnhandlerr that Georg wanted him to join the delegation to see the German consul that afternoon. To his surprise, the head storm trooper agreed with the super.

"We need someone newly arrived from Germany to help present our case, someone who understands the path that National Socialism is taking, and that someone is you, Harold Appel," declared the storm troop leader.

Damn, more danger, Harold thought. *Let's hope nobody asks my opinion.*

Harold and his supervisor left work early for the short walk to the Consulate. Approaching the office, Finnhandler pulled a swastika armband from his pants pocket and put it on over his white shirt. "I am the commandant of the *Ordung Dienst*. I must wear the uniform when I meet the officials," he stated. "Do my pants retain their crease?" The OD leader did not notice passersby staring with hostility at him and his crooked cross.

"Yes, my *leiter*. You look like a soldier of the *Reich*," Harold replied. "But what of me? I wear my work clothes."

"That is good," Finnhanderr said. "We are a party of the people."

Stubble and Willknecht were already waiting in the anteroom of the consulate, accompanied by Rudolf Franz. They all wore dark suits.

"Ah, our delegation from the newspaper," Stubble exclaimed. "We await only *Bundesfuehrer* Kuhn before we march on the Consul."

At that moment Fritz Kuhn, in all his imposing bulk, was striding up Sixth Avenue toward the office building where his followers waited. He was dressed as a civilian yet his imperious manner caused pedestrians on the street to grant him deference. He entered the building and let his companion, a short emaciated-looking man in a baggy suit, press the elevator button while he waited with his nose in the air.

As Kuhn entered the consulate, the receptionist jumped from her seat, something she had not done for the rest of the German party. "*Herr Bundesfuehrer*," she said reverentially, "the Consul General is waiting for you." She ushered him into the richly furnished office of the diplomat, followed by the small, thin man and the rest of the Bund party. Harold brought up the rear and was almost left in the anteroom by the woman swinging the door shut. He jumped to avoid getting swatted in the rear.

Consul Mendelsohnn sprang to his feet with a crisp Nazi

salute, and an equally crisp, "*Heil Hitler.*" The Consul acted with deference, giving Kuhn the respect due the *Fuehrer* of America.

Kuhn returned the salute with a limp wrist like the *Fuehrer* himself, with a well-mannered "*Heil,*" neglecting the obligatory Hitler. Finnhandlerr was meanwhile dragging a large chair from the side to the center, so Kuhn could dominate the room.

An impressive performance, Harold thought. *Kuhn can command a room when he wants to, like a junior Hitler. And who is the shrimp who came in with him? They look like Mutt and Jeff.* The reporter turned to Willknecht, who was standing next to him, and whispered, "who is that small guy Kuhn came in with?"

"That is the lawyer," Willknecht whispered back, "*Herr* Kergan. He is always with Kuhn these days, preparing him to testify."

Harold looked up at the other inhabitants of the room, a tall blond SS officer whose black and silver uniform reeked of Aryan superiority and a nondescript man in a brown suit. *Those guys must be Thorson and Mayer,* the reporter thought, *just as Pat described them, although Thorson wasn't in uniform in New Jersey.*

Kuhn dropped into his large armchair, leaving the diplomat standing for a long instant before he sat behind his desk. "*Herr Doktor,*" Kuhn began, "you have seen yesterday's report in the *World Journal.* We are here to determine if there is any truth to the charges made in the newspaper. Has the German Consul General, the representative of the *Reich*, been plotting against the foremost German organization in America? Or...is it a spurious lie fabricated by the sensation mongering press? I hope it is the latter because we are prepared to contact certain individuals high in the party if we are not satisfied with the answer."

Kuhn has turned this meeting into a trial, Harold thought, as he stood close to the giant Finnhandlerr, hoping to gain a measure of anonymity. *Mendelsohnn is the defendant and Kuhn is the judge, and jury too, if they have such things in Germany. Now let's see how the diplomat is going to play it.*

"*Herr* Kuhn, I have seen the newspaper, and if there is any truth to the charges it is beyond my knowledge. The purpose of my office is to help Germans in America, not to harm them."

That's a weak response, Harold thought. *Yet it could be true, especially if this is a project of Thorson. He wouldn't tell Mendelsohnn anything. Still…point for Kuhn.*

"*Herr* Consul-General, I am Reinhold Stubble, leader of the Yorkville *Ortsgruppe*. It was my daughter who was abducted at Nordland. I demand you investigate! We are German! We serve the *Fuehrer*!" Stubble barely contained his rage.

Another point to the Bund. How are you going to get out of this, Mendelsohnn? Harold thought. *You're dealing with fatherly love here, except Stubble didn't love his daughter until she got kidnapped. Poor Regina, misunderstood by everyone.*

"Do you! How do you serve the *Fuehrer*?" Mayer, the invisible man to the left of the Consul, suddenly lashed out at Stubble and Kuhn and all associated with the German American Bund. "By turning America against us! By playing into the hands of the Jews! Do you work quietly and shun publicity? No! You march and murder on the front pages! And you, Kuhn, you are a common thief."

That's how the diplomats are going to get out of it, the reporter thought, *by turning loose Mayer, the attack dog.*

Kuhn was on his feet in an instant, eyeball to eyeball with Mayer. "The charges against me are false," he shouted. "It will be proven in court. Apologize now!"

"Never!" thundered Mayer. "I will not say I am sorry to a man with no honor!"

Honor? thought Harold. *Both of them have stains on their souls. A five spot to the first guy who finds 'honor' here.*

"And what of the charges we make against you, kidnapping and common vandalism?" Kuhn roared at Mendelsohnn, an easier target. "I do not hear any denials. I know how you got your job, Consul-General. Your friend Ribbentrop took pity on the failed academic. You like it here, do you not? You had better protect the Bund or you will not be here much longer."

The meeting became a shouting match. "Betrayal!" yelled Kuhn. "Thief!" hollered Mayer.

"Slander," chipped in Kergan, the lawyer.

Thorson stood aloof, eyeing the proceedings with distaste. He pounded on Mendelsohnn's mahogany desk, his large fist creating a cracking sound that took all by surprise. There was silence. All eyes turned to the SS Captain. "Consul-General, there will be no investigation, not when the German people are at war. Not when facing an enemy as clever as the International Jew."

I can't believe it, Harold thought. *Thorson is blaming the Jews.*

"We agree," Kuhn said loudly as if he was starting one of his speeches at Yorkville Casino. "It is the Jew who is our enemy." A wily look passed over the face of the *Bundesfuehrer.* "The provocateurs who deigned to destroy Nordland were in the pay of the Jewish conspirators. But where are the German diplomats who are tasked with protecting the Bund, the best hope of Germans in America?"

The Bund members hung on Kuhn's every word but Thorson was made of sterner stuff. "The Consul-General represents the Reich, not those who deserted Germany for America and who like to play at dress up." The SS Captain pointed at Finnhandlerr in his Sam Browne belt and swastika armband. "I have my orders, Herr Kuhn. Desist making a public spectacle or we will take steps to eliminate the problem you represent." Thorson strode from behind the desk, brushed past Harold, and went out the door. Mayer followed.

Kuhn blamed the Jews too, just what I would expect from the big buffoon. He probably can guess at the truth, just as Thorson knows the truth, but what of my friends from Yorkville? Harold looked around the office, trying to gauge the effects of Thorson's angry words on the gullible group of Bundists. Stubble and Willknecht looked disturbed, although he didn't know if they were scared of Jewish perfidy in their midst or of Thorson's veiled threats. Finnhandl-err looked OK but the big man usually wore equanimity on his sleeve. Kuhn should be most upset; he knew that Thorson wasn't faking. The SS man would take out the Bund organization without a second thought. But Kuhn wasn't quaking in his boots. He had a thoughtful look on his face. He was planning something. Kuhn must know people in Germany to counter Thorson.

With the departure of Thorson and Mayer, Mendelsohnn was left to face an enraged *Bundesfuehrer* all by himself. "I appeal to the comradeship of the German *volk, Herr* Kuhn. Do not listen to the hot heads who work for me. All will be right."

"I have been insulted and belittled," Kuhn fumed. "This cannot be official policy. My friend Adolf would not allow it. *Herr Doktor* Mendelsohnn, I will excuse you, but you must control your underlings."

"But...but...but...what about Nordland?" stammered Stubble.

"I pledge there will be no interference with Nordland from this office," the Consul-General promised.

The Bundists took Mendelsonn's words as a solemn vow. They could return to their membership with guarantees they had come for. No mention need be made of the hostility they had encountered at the outpost of the Fatherland.

Harold knew better. *Mendelsohnn's assurances are worthless. He's a figurehead. Thorson's hostility toward Kuhn rules in the New York consulate,* he thought, as he retreated with his friends toward Sixth Avenue.

On the street Harold and the others were warned not to speak of what they had seen and heard. "We all take the same line," Stubble said. "The Consulate had nothing to do with the attack on Nordland and strongly deplores all attacks on Germans."

The members of the delegation left the Consulate in a foul mood, feeling betrayed by Germany and persecuted by America.

The stateless persons headed for the subway. They wanted to drown their sorrows in beer or something even stronger.

The Bavaria Inn, their destination in Yorkville, was dark after the harsh light of a day which had exposed the Bund and its leader to ridicule and threats. Kuhn was the center of attention, as he had been at the Consulate, but here he was among friends. Here his bombast was appreciated and admired.

Several Bund members had been in the bar when Kuhn and his group arrived. More arrived as the *Bundesleiter* held court. But only the members of the delegation realized that the supremely confident, larger than life, Kuhn of Yorkville was not the leader he appeared. *Am I the only one here who sees the real Kuhn?* Harold wondered to himself. *Am I the only one who sees the false front he puts up? Maybe his friendship with Hitler is a sham, too.*

Harold had a larger audience than the Bund in mind. The story in the Monday edition of the *World Journal* would begin, 'Nazis berate Bund. Diplomatic representatives of the German Reich have warned leaders of the German American Bund to keep a low profile in the coming months, to avoid antagonizing the American public. They want a stop to the buffoonery which they claim has characterized Fritz Kuhn's leadership.' *I'm safe filing this one,* the reporter thought. *Kuhn and the rest will believe Thorson or Mayer talked to the press.*

Impromptu court could not continue if throats were not well lubricated. The innkeeper brought a big bottle of whiskey, enough shot glasses to go around, and beer chasers for all. The men filled their glasses and Stubble proposed a toast. "To our leader, may his troubles wane and his pleasures increase. And to our party, may it grow ever stronger as our enemies grow weaker."

Harold downed a shot in honor of the enemies of the Nazi Party.

"So you are this Appel I have been hearing about from every-one," a low voice sounded in Harold's ear. The reporter turned quickly to catch the lawyer Kergan standing close behind him. "I'm Bill Kergan. My son told me about you. And Finnhandlerr and Willknecht both say you're a tireless worker for the Bund. How long have you been here Mr. Appel? One month? You've made quite a reputation for yourself."

"It is all because of the justice of the Nazi cause, Mr. Kergan." Harold looked nervously at this little man with the ferret-like face, so unlike his big athletic son, and wondered if his cover was blown.

"So you believe in justice, Mr. Appel," the lawyer said. He turned away before slyly adding, "You'll have to tell me someday all about Nazi justice."

CHAPTER EIGHTEEN

A SHIVA VISIT

IT WAS SUNDAY, a chilly midmorning, when an emissary from another world, a land of mighty words, of forceful leaders and faithful followers, appeared in the old neighborhood. Harold Apple, apprentice Nazi, wandered up Davidson Avenue, lost in thought. *If Hitler hadn't lived, I wonder…would there be another leader? Is Hitler, or someone like him, inevitable, a product of anti-Semitism, Nietzsche, and the Treaty of Versailles? Which came first, the leader looking for followers or followers searching for a leader?*

"Hello there Mr. Apple, nice day isn't it?" said the flower seller on the corner. Harold often bought Sally a bunch of daisies or a red rose on Sunday morning but today he walked by in a daze, not noticing the old man's words.

What if… Harold thought, as he bypassed the elevator and slowly climbed the steps to Sally's floor, *Izzy didn't hate the goyim? At least I understand Izzy. The gentiles have mistreated us for centuries. No wonder he doesn't want a shiksa in the family.*

Sally opened the door at Harold's knock and flung herself into his arms. Their kiss was long, passionate, and surprising. *I don't deserve her,* he thought. *I've been unfaithful. No...not unfaithful, uncaring. I've been a good Nazi. I don't deserve a good fiancée.*

Sally had been up for hours, bathing, dressing, primping for her man. Her hair and clothes had to be perfect. Harold came so seldom that she made every visit an occasion. Her mother had helped with her hair, washing it; drying it in a fluffy towel, combing it out, and fixing it in a fashionable flip, all to be ready for her man.

"Come into the kitchen darling, and I'll make you some break-fast," Sally said catching her breath after disentangling. "I want to hear about everything you've been doing."

"Sure Doll, I haven't eaten yet. Is anyone else here?" Harold was positive this visit was going to end badly. Saul had told his folks about Christiana, and the reporter was going to be blamed for bringing a *shiksa* into the family.

"Mother is in the kitchen, Saul is still sleeping, and Daddy is at the store—thank G-d. He's been spending more and more time there. He must be driving Lois batty."

Harold was glad he wouldn't have to face Izzy right away. *I can take on Sarah now and maybe have an easier time with Izzy later,* he thought. "Lois? Who is Lois?" he said to Sally as they went into the kitchen.

"Lois is the girl who works at the store," Sarah said over her shoulder as she stood in front of the stove and cracked eggs into a bowl. "And am I ever glad we have her. I don't have to go to the store so much."

"Daddy is happy because Lois is a hard worker," Sally said, "and she's happy to have a job. Kids are having a hard time finding work these days."

"To tell you the truth, Sarah," Harold interjected, "I'm relieved Izzy is at the store. I wasn't looking forward to talking to him about Saul and Christiana."

"As Israel sees it, Saul has to stop seeing that girl, immedi-ately," Sarah said to Harold while whipping the yolks and whites together with a little cream and a pinch of salt. "I know that will never happen, of course. My son is stubborn, as stubborn as his father. I don't know how I put up with those two." She poured the eggs into a frying pan and waited patiently as the edges browned.

"What exactly did Saul say about Christiana?" Harold asked.

"We were talking about you, Wednesday night at dinner," Sally explained. "How you seem to have mixed feelings about the Nazis, hating them and liking them at the same time."

"I don't like them!" Harold was vehement, but his thoughts were different. *Am I that transparent? I can't help liking some of them, like that old shoe Willknecht. And even the rest, when they're not playing Hitler boys, are a decent lot, trying to make a living like anyone else.*

"That's not the impression Saul has," Sally said. "He says you like some of them. That's when he told us about Christiana. Daddy was sitting quietly through all of this, so still I didn't even notice how mad he was getting. When Saul said he wished your assignment for the paper would be over so he could bring his girl home to meet the family, Daddy blew up, his steam spewing over all of us but scalding Saul the worst. 'I don't have a son anymore! I don't have a son who brings home a *shiksa*! I don't have a son who brings home a German, a Nazi! Ahhhh!' And Daddy stormed out of the room. He hasn't talked to Saul since."

"Saul didn't say anything so bad," Harold said. "He didn't announce his marriage. Maybe something else is bothering your father."

"You may be right, Harold," Sarah said, "but Saul could simplify the problem by giving up the *shiksa*. I'm not going to force him. He's at an age where his independence is more important than family. It's a new world out there." She gestured widely out the window. "Jews and gentiles meet as equals, and children expect to make their own decisions. Who would have thought it?"

"Yeah, but Izzy's not living in this new world," Harold said.

"I know Izzy," Sarah said. "He'll come around."

Water ran in the bathroom. Saul was up.

"Hmm, ten-thirty. He's up early for a Sunday," Sarah said. "Harold, why don't you wait a few minutes? Join Saul for breakfast."

"Sure, I'll wait Sarah. Sally, do you know if anything else is bothering your father?" *I don't have to ask Sally to know something is wrong with Izzy. He's having trouble at the store, maybe with that girl he hired. My future father-in-law would never tell his family. Izzy's old fashioned. There are problems you just don't speak about with women and children. I wonder if Sally has figured it out yet.*

᪅

"Good morning Ma, Sis. Hello Harold," said Saul as he came into the kitchen, still in his pajamas. "That was a good sleep. What's for breakfast?"

"We've got some good whitefish, but only if you go put on your robe," Sarah said.

"Aw Ma."

"Rules of the house," Sarah said. "You know that. Look, we're all dressed."

"OK Ma," Saul said, but as he was going back to his room he called out to Harold. "Cristiana invited me to the Christmas Fair they're having on Saturday."

Damn that girl, Harold thought. It's a*nother chance for Saul to get in trouble with the Germans, and to get me in trouble.*

"He should go to *shul* on Saturday, not some Christian fair." Sarah was upset. When Saul came back in the kitchen, wearing his robe, she started to yell at him.

Saul cut her off immediately. "Ma, Ma, I'm not going to become a Christian. I'll go to synagogue in the morning just like always. The Christmas Fair is just a big bazaar. They hold it every year, just like we do before Purim, and it's in the afternoon."

"I'll be there," Harold said. "I'm sure Saul can be of some help to me." *He can help by disappearing with Christiana, like he did at Nordland.*

"Oh, all right," Sarah said. "Just don't tell your father."

Harold ate the last bit of flesh off his whitefish, leaving only the head to tell the tale. "If Izzy asks where Saul is, say he's helping me out," the reporter told Sarah. He turned to Sally and said, "Let's go visit Uncle Frank, Doll."

∽

It was noon when Harold and Sally knocked on the Appel's front door. "Ah, the young people," Uncle Frank said. "Come in, come in."

"Uncle Frank, it's been a while. How are you and Aunt Annie?"

"We're all right. Your aunt is in the kitchen, fixing food of course."

"Uncle Frank, you've got to hear about Harold's trip to the German consulate," Sally said.

Aunt Annie came out with coffee and cake and settled down next to her husband to listen. Harold had to tell the story again, about two sets of Germans with the same loyalty to Hitler, behaving in diametrically opposite ways. "Well, my Nazi nephew, those diplomats are out of their minds, antagonizing their natural allies like that," Uncle Frank said. "It's very amusing though, and typical of the Hitler government; one hand doesn't know what the other is doing. You say there's a story in your paper about it? I don't usually read the *World Journal*, but I'll look for it."

"Uncle Frank, you've got to read Harold's paper," Sally said.

"Other papers have better international coverage, and that is what I look for." Uncle Frank was pessimistic about the situation of the Jews in Germany. "The Jewish position is precarious and our government is not helping. The boycott of German products isn't working and the Roosevelt administration won't apply tough sanctions. Untermeyer and the Non-Sectarian Anti-Nazi League are really upset with the President. On the positive side however, Nathanson says we'll have visas for Hiram and Simon and their families by next month. The fact that they have three brothers who are American citizens evidently swayed the State Department."

"That's great," Harold said, a smile spreading across his face. "How long will it take them to get here?"

"They'll have to buy exit permits from the Nazis. That will cost a lot but as long as the Nazis are willing to sell their Jews, we're buying. I've cabled Hiram to liquidate everything they have left after the business was destroyed, but the burden is going to fall on us here in America. Do you have any savings, Harold?

"I've got a little bit saved up. I'll help as much as I can." *Goodbye to the honeymoon cruise to the Caribbean.*

After leaving the Appel's, the cruiseless couple went to the Drabinsky house, where the plumber's face still presided posthumously from the parked pick-up. "Dare I mention to Ida that she should sell Moe's truck?" Harold asked Sally.

"She knows," Sally said. "I visit them every few days. Ida and Cynthia are taking it well, but Howard is a mess. He gave up going to class. In fact, he rarely leaves the house. Ida was keeping the truck for Howard, but she knows now he'll never use it. She did manage to get him out day before yesterday. She took him to a psychiatrist."

"He sounds bad," Harold said. "I haven't seen him since the funeral and he wasn't in such good shape then."

"He's worse now. On the other hand, Cynthia is better. Do you remember how frivolous she used to be, only interested in clothes and boys? Well, she's changed. She's a Zionist now, just like her father was. When I visit all we talk about is the new life the Jews are living in Palestine."

"It sounds like Cynthia is honoring her father," Harold said. *Tragedy has different faces,* he thought. *I've got my own way—revenge!*

Sally rang and Ida, still wearing black, answered the doorbell.

"It's good to see you, my darling girl, and you brought Harold, how wonderful. Come in. Cynthia," the widow called out, "look who's here, your friend and her fiancée. You got here just in time. My girl has to go out in an hour. Zev Jabotinsky is speaking at the Workman's Circle tonight."

Cynthia came into the deeply curtained living room. Her long dark hair was pulled back. She wore no makeup. *She looks radiant,* Harold thought. *It's her eyes—so bright. And I've never seen her dressed like that—khaki pants, khaki shirt. Like a uniform.*

Sally hugged her friend. "Your ma says we got here just in time. You're going to hear Jabotinsky tonight?"

"It's so exciting," Cynthia said. "He's going to talk about the Jewish self-defense forces in Palestine. Just think, Jews not in the ghetto. Jews emancipated from fear. No dictators, no pogroms, no stoning of fathers. I want to go to Palestine and be a part of it."

For Harold it was as if Moe had come back to life in the body of his daughter. Ida seemed to feel the same way, deferring to her older child as she had to her husband. *Of course, Moe wouldn't have gone to Palestine to fight Arabs,* Harold thought. *Ida can't be happy with that part of Cynthia's plan.*

His gaze wandered around the room while the women talked, finally alighting upon a form in a shadowy corner of the dim room. *Is that Howard scowling at us? No one said he was here. Do Ida and Cynthia take his condition so for granted that he becomes invisible? And what is his condition? He looks terrible.*

Howard's dark visage marred the visit for Harold. Always silent, he kept to his chair in the corner, his eyes on the floor. *Is this the lively boy I knew?* Harold thought. *I remember playing ball with him and Saul in the summer. And oh, the arguments they had over who was better, Ruth or Gehrig.*

❦

Their visit at an end, Harold and Sally walked back though the pale light of late afternoon to Davidson Avenue. They stopped in front of Harold's building and embraced. "We have an hour before my mother serves dinner. I can't imagine what we're going to do with a whole hour," Sally teased. She squeezed Harold tight, and then jumped back out of his grasp. "Do you have any ideas, honey?"

Harold lunged but Sally eluded him and ran in the building. He fumbled for his keys and followed. He opened his door under a hail of kisses, tumbling into his apartment to escape the storm. Sally shrugged out of her coat and pulled her sweater over her head. She stood in the middle of the room, holding her arms over her head while fluffing her brown hair. "Such pretty hair, so soft and fine," Harold murmured while drawing her to him.

Afterward they lay entwined with one another, in no hurry to end their time together. "Harold," Sally whispered, "I don't want you to go back to Yorkville."

"And I don't want to go back, except..." *There's always an 'except,'* Harold thought. "...except, I've got to see this through for Howard. A few stones in Nazi hands can end a life, or ruin a life. I've got to go back." Seeing Howard cleared his mind. All the stuff he'd been going through, the hell he'd been putting Sally through; it wouldn't mean anything if he couldn't destroy the Nazis. The joy he just had with his doll baby wouldn't be worth anything if the Nazis won. "I've got to go back, for all of us."

"Hello, I'm home," Izzy called as he took off his coat in the front hall. "Is anybody here?" He followed his nose to the kitchen, pursing the rich odor of Sarah's chicken soup. She was at the stove while Saul was at the table, his head in a book. *Probably that Steinbeck he's been reading the last couple of days,* Izzy thought. Saul slowly lifted his head, his mind still in the dust bowl, and watched his father greet his mother. Sarah accepted a peck on the cheek from her husband and turned back to her soup. Suddenly Israel grabbed his wife by the shoulders, turned her around, and kissed her full on the lips.

"What has gotten into you, old man?" Sarah said, surprised and pleased with the unexpected attention from her husband of thirty years. "You haven't kissed me like that in ages, and in front of the boy, too."

"I'm glad he's here," Izzy said to Sarah. "Saul, will you forgive me?"

Saul was dumbfounded. In this family, forgiveness went the other way, from son to father.

Izzy continued. "I thought you were denying your Jewishness to follow a *shiksa*. But you are not denying anything. You're following your heart. And...you're a man now. You make your own decisions. When I said you were not my son, I was doing what my father would have done. But...I'm not my father. Times are different. Let's meet the *shiksa*."

Father and son embraced briefly, awkwardly. Saul had been anguished over his father's silence, and his happiness now knew no bounds. Yet there also lurked a thought in Saul's head. *I've won!* It was the first time Izzy had accepted a choice, a decision, he had made. It was the first time his father had accepted Saul's status as a man.

Sally and Harold returned to find Izzy and Saul talking as if nothing had happened between them. The next day Sally asked her mother what had caused the reconciliation. "Your father told me that he had to fire Lois because she was making advances toward him. Harold was right. Something was bothering your father. I'm glad he had the character to solve the problem himself. I'm too old to live without him."

CHAPTER NINETEEN

REGINA AGAIN

HAROLD STOOD AT the corner of 43rd Street and Sixth Avenue, feeling ill at ease among the throngs of New Yorkers doing their Christmas shopping. Not that he objected to Christmas shopping; he'd grown up with it. Public Square in Cleveland was a December fairyland—capped off by Higbee's famous windows.

No, it was the intensity of the New Yorkers, as if they had to find the perfect presents for all on their lists. Jews were not immune from this New York craziness; Hanukah presents had to be bigger and better than last year. In front of Harold stood the Hippodrome, site of this year's December angst for the reporter. The outside of the hall was dressed in holiday colors, with wreaths hanging in every window, and strings of light bulbs climbing marble columns. A banner across the entrance read **Weihnachtsfair von das Amerikadeutscher Volksbund**, announcing to midtown that Germans did Christmas shopping the New York way.

And still...I know the words to all the carols. And this year I'm supposed to be German...and Christian. Why can't I enjoy myself, like everybody else? I could even have a tree. It's not a religious symbol. It's pagan—like the swastika. I've got a swastika armband in my closet, why not a tree in my parlor? Why not go all the way and get a picture of Arminius? Hey, wait a minute, Arminius fought the Romans and so did the Maccabees. Germans and Jews aren't so different after all.

Harold started up the steps of the Hippodrome. He entered the big double doors and was surrounded by green—pine, fir, and holly laced with red ribbons. The colors of the German forest, salted with the crimson of German blood. *All natural symbols,* he thought, *fitting in with a natural view of the city.* He then remembered what was artificial about the German world view. *Premature death—death by stone, death by blade, death by bullet—all unnatural.*

He passed through the entrance lined with decorated Christmas trees to the big hall filled with booths selling Christmas crafts, gifts, and food. All around were friendly celebrating people, children and adults, out to have a good time. And green and red were colors, only colors. He found himself standing before a large fir decorated with candles, twinkling magically atop dense greenery. Fire, another Nazi symbol: He was collecting symbols today. Over the loudspeaker came a song: ***O Tannenbaum, O tannenbaum, wie treu sind deine Blaetter.***

Against the walls was advertising from businesses supporting the fair. Their names, Hamburg American Line, Foreign Exchange Bank, *Deutsche Tonfilms,* were power, German power. Small businesses were there too—Terlotz Jewelers, Rinder Cleaners, Europa Theater, Yorkville Pork Store, Bavaria Inn, all familiar names from Yorkville. All meant money, German money. *Wealth in time of depression,* Harold thought. *Germans have money, they don't need Jewish money. But they want it. At least the Nazis do.*

Looking down a row of booths selling food and drink, Harold saw Saul and Christiana standing in front of a sign saying *Hofbrauhaus,* waiting for a *fraulein* to draw mugs of beer. He worked his way through the crowd toward them. "Get me one also," he said. "Are you enjoying the *Christ fest?*"

"It's for little kids to see *der Weinachtsmann,*" Christiana said, pointing to the other end of the hall where a roly-poly Santa Claus was sitting on a high throne, with green-suited elves lifting children to his lap.

"I've never been to a German fair in New Jersey. I love it," Saul said. He gave his girl a squeeze on the arm. "I love the food. I love the shopping. I wish I had enough money to get a present for everyone in my family."

"You said you have an older sister, Solly. I'd like to meet her," Christiana said as the two wandered off into the depths of the fair.

Another thing to worry about. Christiana wants to meet Sally. Harold contemplated the complications caused by his masquerade. *I'm not going to be able to keep this up very much longer.* He absent-mindedly went over to a stall displaying *lederhosen,* and continued down a row of booths selling such things as intricate embroidery and souvenirs of the *Vaterland.* He greeted people he knew from Yorkville and paused to listen to a chorus of the *Madelschaft,* the girl's youth group, sing Christmas carols. *German is a guttural language,* he thought, *but those girls are melodious. It must be the music. It's so familiar. Stille nacht, heilige nacht, alles schlaeft, einsam nacht... I'm actually having a good time.*

And then the good times ended. Harold turned away from the carolers and came face to face with the heroine of Nordland, Regina Kergan, wearing a short silver fox coat over a red and green dress. *Very festive,* he thought. *I wonder if her mood is anything like her clothes. I hope so.* Next to her was a walking pile of packages. "Tom Kergan, is that you?" Harold shouted, over the singing. "Hello Regina, *frohe Weihnachten,* merry Christmas."

Grateful for an excuse to interrupt his wife's shopping, Kergan dropped his packages on an empty table and slumped in exaggerated exhaustion. "Appel, how have you been? All I've heard for the last two weeks was how wonderful you were at Nordland. Thank you for saving my wife from who knows what fate."

"Harold did not save me Tom," Regina quickly corrected her husband. "It was that friend of his, and the Willknecht girl. I never thanked that boy. I remember he has red hair. What is his name?"

"His name is Solly, Regina. Solly O'Rourke. He's Pat O'Rourke's brother."

Kergan looked at Harold thoughtfully. "I met Pat's brother once, years ago. I don't remember him having red hair."

"God damnit!" thought Harold. *There goes the whole act. Shoulda stuck with the neighbor boy story. Aaron's gonna be pissed. I better find Saul and get outta here."* He looked Kergan straight in the eye. "Yes, it's kind of dark red, I guess. I never really noticed." *Maybe that will satisfy him, or maybe I can distract him.* "Tom, I met your father last week, at the German consulate."

"Oh yes, I heard about that meeting; sounded quite unpleasant for everyone." Regina was pulling on Tom's overcoat. "Wait a minute. I almost forgot to tell you, my wife is pregnant."

"You're going to have a baby? That's wonderful! When did you find out?"

"Just last week," Kergan said. "But it must have happened before I sent the two of you off to Nordland. Your friend saved a pregnant lady."

"I'll tell him," Harold said. "Congratulations to the both of you. *Herzlichen Gluckwunsch*, Regina."

"*Danke* Harold," Regina said. And Tom picked up his packages and they were off to do more Christmas shopping.

That's strange, Harold thought, as he set off to find the redhead who might be the end of his career as a German. *Kergan wasn't excited about being a father; he seemed burdened. Burdened by a Nazi wife and a Nazi kid. Come to think of it, he wouldn't have told me if Regina hadn't made him.*

The reporter spied Saul and Christiana through the crowd.

They were looking at a display of goose-down quilts, probably imported from Germany, maybe the same kind sold in Uncle Hiram's store. Harold hurried over, pushing jovial Germans out of his way.

"Solly, we have to leave now," Harold yelled through the throngs of merrymakers.

"Harold, I don't want to leave," Saul complained.

"Say good-by to Christiana and let's go." Harold looked over his shoulder, fearing he'd see the Kergans approaching, but the crowd did not part and they were left in comparative solitude, with only the salesgirl peddling quilts paying attention.

"Christy was just about to buy me a quilt," Saul said. "Can't you wait a few minutes?"

"Yeah, what's the hurry, Harold?" Christiana asked, her mouth turned down in a pout.

"Solly, I don't have time to argue," Harold hissed. "Remember where we are!"

"Can Christiana walk out with us?" Saul asked.

Harold unhappily nodded his ascent and turned toward the exit, down the long row of German merchandise.

"Hey, what about this quilt?" the salesgirl yelled.

"Hold it," Christiana snapped. "I'll be back."

Harold propelled the two young people toward the nearest exit, on the Sixth Avenue side of the building. In the lobby Saul gave the girl a quick peck on the cheek. "I'll call tomorrow," he said.

"Solly, what kind of good-by is that?" Christiana grabbed the boy's face and gave him a long smack on the lips. Harold fidgeted while Saul returned the kiss with enthusiasm.

The two separated and Harold led Saul outside into the dusky late afternoon. At the top of the steps, Harold stopped short, brought to a halt by the familiar scene laid out below. What he saw was a group of a dozen anti-German protesters, holding signs saying 'Boycott German Goods' and 'Hitler Kills German Jews.' And nearby, a group of twenty or so men, not in uniform—but presumably German—were pelting them with stones. Harold squinted through the deepening twilight from his perch at the top of a long flight of marble stairs, to see who the rock-throwers were. *There's Everhardt,* he thought, following a very well thrown rock from his hand to its target, a young woman carrying a sign that said 'Don't Buy German' in big black letters. *And there's Finnhandl-err, directing the action. My friends, my comrades, stoning Jews again!*

"Harold, look over there," Saul shouted over the sounds of melee going on below them. "Who's that coming around the corner? Don't I know her?"

Harold looked where Saul pointed. A woman in a silver fox coat led a man burdened with packages onto Sixth Avenue. In the seconds it took for the sight to register with Harold, they were in range of the rock-throwers. "It's Regina," he cried.

Harold and Saul, descending several steps, were close enough to Regina to see her look of horror when she realized that rocks were flying at her. *Oh no,* thought the reporter, *it's Berlin all over again. I hope Tom can protect her.* A sharply thrown rock, perhaps from the arm of Everhardt, hit the young wife on the forehead. She stumbled backwards, into her husband, who was blinded by the packages he was carrying. The carefully wrapped presents, all glittery gold, shiny silver, with reindeers prancing before the *Weihnachtsmann,* went up in the air, only to shower down upon the fallen *frau.* Then Kergan, knocked off balance, fell atop the pile of presents.

A roar started in Harold's head, a chainsaw sort of roar, as if all the German forest was being cut down and deposited on Regina. *And she can't hear the roar because she's muffled in her fur coat.*

Harold stood still, rooted in place by his second stoning in less than two months. Not so for Saul. He charged down the steps, into the midst of the rock-throwing men, yelling, "No! No! No! No!"

The roar in Harold's head was replaced by silence. *It's like an old two-reeler,* he thought. *Lights, camera, action, but no sound. There goes the hero, chasing the bad guys. All it needs is the tinkle of a piano. Why can't I move? I want to chase the bad guys too.*

Two police cars, big black Chevys with officers riding on running boards, careened to a stop at the curb. As if by magic, the attackers melted away at the sound of the sirens. All that was left was Saul kneeling over the pile of packages that covered Regina Kergan, with her husband lying nearby, Harold standing rooted near the top of the stairs, dazed demonstrators picking themselves up off the wide sidewalk, and the typical crowd, which always formed when the police showed up.

Harold looked at the signs laying in the gutter—No Nazis in America, Boycott German Goods, Non-Sectarian Anti-Nazi League. *How are we going to boycott German goods when we can't boycott German rocks?* Harold thought as he numbly watched the police helping victims to their feet, greeting ambulances, and pushing the crowd out of the way. He raised his eyes from the crumbled signs and saw a policeman questioning Saul. *I better get down there before Saul starts talking.*

"Tell me what happened," an officer was asking Saul as Harold ran down the steps. The redhead was bent over, his breath coming in ragged gasps.

"We were coming out," Saul wheezed. He pointed up the steps to the entrance of the Hippodrome. "People were on the ground. Hooligans were pelting them with rocks."

"Can you identify the rock-throwers?" the policeman asked.

"No. It all happened so fast. I ran down the steps, yelling at them to stop. Then I heard the sirens and they all disappeared."

"Do you have anything to add?" the officer asked Harold.

"No sir, I was way up there." Harold pointed to the exit at the top of the stairs. *I'm such a liar,* he thought. *But suppose I tell the cops who did it? Then my story will be over, dead, kaput. I don't want to get revenge on a few storm troopers. I want to bring down the whole damned Bund. Besides, no one was hurt.* He glanced over at the handful of demonstrators the police were hauling to their feet. *Everhardt, you get a pass on this one.*

"All right, no one hung around for us to arrest. Give me your names and you can go."

"I'm Harold Appel. I live in Yorkville. This is Solly O'Rourke from New Jersey."

"Hey Sarge, we've got a body over here," cried one of the cops.

The officer stalked up the sidewalk. Harold and Saul followed.

"Willya look at this Sargent! This woman's husband was following her with an armload of presents. She tripped and fell onto him, and all the packages landed on her. It looks like she was killed by Christmas presents to the head."

Regina lay on the sidewalk surrounded by gaily wrapped parcels. Her head rested in the street, off the edge of the curb at a steep angle. Kergan sat by her side, his feet in the street by her head, and his own noggin held in his hands between his legs.

Regina, why is your head like that? Harold thought. "The woman's father is inside," he said. "I'll get him."

"That would be a big help," the policeman said.

"Wait here, Solly. I've got to find Regina's father." *No one knows a rock hit Regina,* assumed Harold, *no one except the thrower and me. Who was the thrower? Let's see,* the reporter mulled it over as he trotted back up the steps. *Regina and Tom had just come around the corner, about fifty feet from the picketers. The OD was on the sidewalk, another 50 feet further down. And the rock was well thrown. Which of the storm troopers can throw like that? Only Everhardt. But did he know it was Regina? Maybe he only saw a woman in a fur coat. I bet there's more to it than that. Who ordered the stoning? Geez, my head's spinning. Poor pregnant Regina, in the wrong place at the wrong time, again.*

Harold returned to the din of the Hippodrome. A brass band

was playing. It sounded out of tune to Harold. *All these people,* he thought, *and I can't find Stubble. What should I tell him anyway? Your beloved daughter was killed by the OD. You'll never be a grandpa now.* He stumbled down a crowded aisle between booths selling framed pictures of the German countryside and others selling photographs of the *Fuehrer.* The goose down quilt stand was nearby. *German girls always give goose down to their lovers. Willknecht told me. I bet Tom Kergan has a quilt at home. He'll never use it again.* Tears filled his eyes and he started stumbling into people.

"Harold! Harold!"

Someone was yelling in his ear. Harold stopped moving and swayed in place. He saw Christiana's face rotating—up, down, sideways. He fell backwards.

"What's the matter, Harold!" Christiana was kneeling over him.

Harold's eyes opened wide at the sound of his name. Red and green swam in front of him. His view steadied. He was looking at a swastika flag surrounded by green boughs and red ribbons. Around the flag were concerned German faces. He recognized Helga Willknecht. He sat up and stammered to her, "It's Regina Ssstubble. Sixth Avenue. Police!"

Harold got to his feet. He led the crowd to the Sixth Avenue lobby, Christiana and Helga steadying him on either side. Outside the hall they met Saul coming up the stairs with a policeman. Christiana abandoned the reporter to stand at the side of the redhead. At the curb was an ambulance. Tom Kergan was climbing in the back.

"What happened, officer?" Helga asked.

"Are you a relative of Regina Kergan?" the cop replied.

"I'm a good friend of her father."

"Is he here?"

"We are looking for him now. What happened to Regina?" Helga was insistent on knowing why the police were looking for Stubble.

"She was killed, Madam," the officer explained. "She was already dead when we arrived. We've got her husband in the ambulance with her. He'll make ID at the hospital. Someone should meet him there. He's pretty shook up."

"What hospital?" Helga asked.

"St. Anselm's, Madam."

"We will have someone there."

The policeman went down the wide stairs. Helga watched him go, no emotion visible on her face. "Thank you for telling us, Harold," she said in a flat voice. "We will take care of everything now."

Christiana grabbed Saul's arm when she heard about Regina. Tears welled in her eyes. "My mother needs me now," she whispered to him. She rejoined the Germans as they set off to tell Reinhold Stubble the bad news.

Harold and Saul were left alone. They walked off, heading for a subway and the safety of The Bronx. "No emotion, none at all," the reporter said. "What's the matter with these people? They acted as if Regina was a dog who got run over in the street. They probably would have been more grief stricken if she had been a dog. All but Christiana. She was the only one who showed any emotion."

"Harold, when we walked out those doors and saw people being stoned, my mind went blank. Then all I could see was Uncle Moe lying at my feet, his head all bloody red pulp. I went crazy, started yelling, and rushed down the stairs. I didn't know what I was going to do." The boy looked for an instant like he was either going to break out in tears or an angry tirade to match his flushed face. But instead he asked Harold, "Why did we leave at that moment? Did you know what was going to happen?"

"No. No. No!" Harold was upset that his future brother-in-law could accuse him of such heinous knowledge. "Do you want to know what happened? I ran into Mr. and Mrs. Kergan after I saw you. Regina wanted to thank you for rescuing her but couldn't remember your name. All she remembered was your red hair. I told her you were Pat O'Rourke's brother. Her husband piped up with 'I know him—and he doesn't have red hair.' I decided to get out before they saw you and gave me some explaining to do."

Harold and Saul descended to the tracks of the IRT at 45th and 6th Avenue. Pushing through the Saturday shopping crowd on the platform, they boarded the train for The Bronx. As they settled into their seats, the reporter was thinking of Finnhandlerr, and why he'd dressed the storm troopers in mufti. *I don't think the big man is foresighted enough to consider them wearing street clothes. Nah, he would have had them in uniform. That order had to come from Stubble. Smart, very smart. The OD melts away into the crowd. No uniforms, no trouble, no newspapers. But one newspaper will have a story. 'The Non-Sectarian Anti-Nazi League peacefully protesting the unlawful sale of German-made goods outside the New York Hippodrome yesterday was attacked by rock-throwing storm troopers of the German American Bund. The attackers, in civilian clothes, melted away down side streets at the prompt appearance of the police, who rescued twelve protesters. One woman was killed.' That ought to give Stubble something to think about. His own daughter was killed. And of course, no by-line. I'm in mufti too.*

CHAPTER TWENTY

THE
WEIGHTLIFTING CONTEST

"IT'S BUSY IN here," Harold said.

"Hey kid, it's the week before the Interborough," Allie said from behind his desk, the only part of the room not crowded with sweating Germans. "Everyone wants to win; your buddy, Finnhandlerr, most of all."

"Yeah, he sure has a fixation," Harold said, looking around Albrecht's Gym at all the bodies drenched in perspiration. Big men, little men, in between men, all were at work, saturating the air with a sour scent. "Allie, tell me the story again, how Max lost the contest last year."

"Hey kid, it's revenge Max wants," Allie said. "A year ago he beat all the other heavyweights. He out-lifted the wops, frogs, pollacks, and niggers. He beat that fancy boy, Vandereedt, from the Rich Man's AC. He beat 'em all until the finals. Now, the other guy in the finals was a *yid*. You know how Max feels about *yids*."

"But he lost, Allie, he lost," Harold said. "How did that happen? Max is so strong." *Yeah, strong and stupid,* the reporter thought. *And he did something completely boneheaded.*

❧

Harold had heard the story before. Willknecht had told it to him for the first time one night when they were sitting in his kitchen drinking *schnapps*. Helga was sewing and Christiana was reading a movie magazine. *That girl always has her nose in a book or magazine,* Harold had thought. *Gotta admit though, the conversation around here is dull, dull, dull. Only two things Georg talks about—how good it was in Germany before the war and how bad the Jews are making it for everyone now. I wonder if he knows any Jews, besides me?*

"Max and the Jew had mounted the stage together and taken position by the weights," Willknecht said that night. "One of the judges repeated the rules." They were allowed two lifts in each of three categories—flat bench press, curl, and clean and jerk. They had the option of declining the second lift. The contestant who lifted the most weight on either the first or second lift would win the category. Wins in two of three categories were necessary for victory.

"Max was ready," Willknecht said proudly. "He stood in a slight crouch. His knees were flexed and his arms hung freely. He looked ready to explode. A fine mist clung to his bare arms and legs, haloing his whole body in the spotlights. The blood red AV symbol, crowned by a black swastika, leapt off his white tunic. He overawed the upstart *yid* beside him."

"Max lifted first," Willknecht said. "Four hundred and fifty pounds in the bench press. Applause filled the hall. The Jew took two turns and couldn't match it. There were hoots of derision. One category to Max. The *Yid*, straining for all he was worth, man-aged three hundred pounds in the curl. Max bested that by twenty pounds. The *yid* asked for more weight on the bar for the second lift, forty pounds. If he didn't make this lift he lost the champion-ship. But the damn Jew made it. Max could end it if he made the next lift. He asked for thirty pounds to be added to the bar, more than was necessary because he wanted to show up the Jew. The hall was silent, the audience breathless. Max stood before the bar; his hands looked slippery on the weight. He lifted—and lost his grip on the bar."

Score one for the good guys, Harold thought. *If Adolf knew Max forgot to chalk up he'd be drummed out of the German race.*

"The audience was on the edge of their seats for the last set. Max lifted first. He added weight then stooped to take the bar in his big hands. Chords of muscle stood out on his shoulders, his neck knotted, his face screwed in a mighty frown. He lifted the impossible mass, one smooth movement from ground to shoulder-high, then a power-jerk above his head. Five hundred pounds, a new city record, everyone in the hall roared approval."

Much of weightlifting is psychological, Harold thought. *The crowd makes a difference. Still, you have to lift the weight.*

"The Jew looked ashen," Willknecht continued. "He bent to the weight, waving away officials who wanted to add more pounds to the bar. He lifted to his shoulders, but could not bring the weight above his head. Spotters jumped up to help the defeated man lower the massive load gently to the floor. A judge turned to Max, asking if he wanted to attempt to better his record with a second lift."

Christiana looked up. She had been following her father's story after all. "Uncle Max strutted around the stage, circling the other lifter and the official," she said. "Some in the audience shouted, 'lift again,' while others hollered, 'you have him beat.' Uncle Max faced the judge and said, 'My first lift stands; no weak-kneed Jew can beat it.' What a stupid thing to say. Shubnik, for that was his name, straightened up from a loser's posture. You could see a light come into his eyes."

Finnhandlerr wasn't content to be a sportsman, Harold thought. *The dummy made it personal.*

The Jew wanted more weight now," Willknecht said. "He wanted to lift more than Max. Anger gave him power. In one motion he lifted the bar to shoulder height and jerked it above his head to stand, quivering but triumphant.

᧞

I bet the same thing happens this year, Harold thought as he listened to the elderly owner of the gym inveigh against the Jews. *Finnhandlerr, or one of his boys, will say something, just stupid enough to get the other guy mad. Then the Yorkville crowd can go through another year of agony, longing for revenge against Yid or Negro. It doesn't matter who. There's always someone to wrong the poor heinie.*

"He must have been hopped up," Allie said. "Ain't no Jew can lift that much weight."

"Huh, what's that Allie?" Harold said.

"That Jew was on drugs," Allie said. "I don't know what kind but that lift wasn't natural."

"Shubnik was not on drugs, Allie," Willknecht said as he pulled up a stool to sit by the two men. "He was mad, and we know he will be back this year. We got a list from the AAU. If Max does not say anything stupid he will have a chance for revenge. Then everything can get back to normal."

Ha, normal! As if being a Nazi is normal. Harold considered the foolishness of it all. *Germans sweating their brains out, not for themselves, which I could understand, but for revenge on a Jew, hoping their leader—their Fuehrer— will be proud.* "I have had enough weightlifting today," he announced to his companions. "Christiana and I are going to a movie."

"What are you going to see?" Georg asked. "Not one of those mindless romances or silly musicals she loves."

"We are going to see the new German film at the Garden Theater, Unsere Fahne Flattert Uns Voran."

"Georg, there is hope yet if young people are going to see good German films," Albrecht said.

Harold took leave of his friends, wondering why Georg seemed so strange today. Pulling his coat close around him, he decided to ask Christiana when he saw her.

It was seven o'clock when Harold knocked on the Willknecht door. "When should you be home?" he asked Christiana as she pulled on her coat.

"My ma doesn't care when I come home," said Christiana. "It's every woman for herself in this house."

Harold and Christiana walked to the movie house at 87th and Third. It was a cold evening but the crowds on the sidewalks ignored the temperature. It was December and people were in a good mood. *Santa Claus is coming soon,* Harold thought. *Hell, I feel good. I can even put up with two hours of German propaganda.*

"I hope this isn't too boring," Christiana said as they settled into their seats in the darkened theater.

"I thought you wanted to see this film," Harold whispered as the credits started to roll.

"I wanted to see you, alone, and thought this was something that would appeal to you."

"Huh?" Harold practically shouted in the half empty theater.

Shushing came from all sides. "Shhhh, Harold, the movie is starting," Christiana whispered into his ear as she took his arm.

Oh no! Harold thought. *She's got it bad for me. What will Saul say?* He sat stiffly and watched the movie. *Our Banner Flies Before Us, a well done bit of film-making,* he thought when the movie was over. *Clean cut Hitler Youth triumphs over disreputable Young Communist in pre-1933 Germany. It's the kind of story that makes Nazi hearts go pitter-patter.*

"What a lousy film," Christiana said as the lights came up. "But there was some good acting, especially that adorable Klaus Klausen as the Hitler Youth leader."

If Georg and Helga had stayed in Germany that might be Christiana on the screen, Harold thought. *Poor but proud young girl joins*

Madelshaft, fights commies in the streets, falls in love with Hitler Jugend leader, and builds future Reich.

"Can we get a bite to eat?" Christiana asked. "I'm famished."

"Yes. There's a coffee shop on the next block. But I have to be up early in the morning so let's not stay long."

Only a few people were in the restaurant this late. Harold and Christiana sat in a booth across from each other and gave their orders to a tired-looking waitress—a hamburger with pickles and onions for her and a slice of apple pie for him. Only then did she look him square in the eye. *Uh-oh, here it comes,* he thought, *the main course of the evening.*

"*Herr* Harold Appel, I know who you really are."

"What do you mean? I am me."

"I know what you're doing in Yorkville, Mr. Jewish Reporter," Christiana said in a low voice. "I think it's wonderful. You're fooling everybody. It's so much fun!"

"Now wait a minute. How do you know this?" *Saul!* Harold thought frantically. *The fool kid must have blabbed. Can I brazen it out, convince her she's wrong? This is not fun!*

"I guessed it," the girl said, almost gaily. "First of all is Solly. Do you remember when I said he's not like the German boys I know? He's kind and considerate and knows things, like poetry and music. And I never met anyone from New Jersey who likes the Yankees, either. They're all Giant fans."

"So he likes the Yankees. So what?"

"Second, there's you," the girl continued. "You came from out of nowhere, and all of a sudden, stories began appearing in the *World Journal*, stories that only someone who knew a lot about the Bund could write. And you work at the *World Journal*."

"That's just an accident," Harold protested.

"What's an accident," Christiana said, "is that none of our *uber* smart Nazis have figured it out." The food came. The girl stopped talking while she devoured her burger. Harold picked at his pie until she started again. "The third thing which helped me figure it out was Regina."

"What about Regina? She's dead." Harold couldn't believe this was happening. *Out of insubstantial evidence Christiana had unraveled his secret. If she could do it so could her father, and Finnhandlerr, well maybe not Finnhandlerr, and the rest. I'd better not go back to Yorkville tonight. It might be dangerous. But why is Christiana telling me all this, if there was going to be an ambush? She's no Nazi. She wouldn't tell on me. She said so herself—she's having too much fun.*

"Regina is better off dead," Christiana said. "Anyone who knew her would tell you that. But she liked you, genuinely liked you, and she didn't like anyone, not even her husband. I ran into her when I first got to the *Weihnachtsfest*, before I met Solly. She asked me about you, whether you were going to be there. That got me thinking. If you were who you said you were, you would have heard of the crazy woman in Yorkville, the daughter of the *Bundesleiter*, and would have stayed away from her, not gotten to know her well enough so she would go asking about you. When I talked to Solly later that night, I told him what I was thinking. I told him something was wrong. Why wouldn't he give me his phone number? He confessed the whole thing last night."

It was Saul. How can I ever trust him again?

"Harold, what you're doing is wonderful," Christiana said. "This Nazi business is so awful. I don't hate Jews, or Negroes, or anyone. My parents and their friends are foolish to hate people who haven't done anything to them. Your secret is safe with me, Harold."

What is Christiana saying? Harold wondered. *That she wants to betray her parents and everyone she knows?* "Listen little girl," he said. "I like your parents. I even like some of the others. But I'm going to bring them down."

"It serves them right."

"You sound like a Jew."

"Harold, I've been living all my life with these crazy people.

Don't you think I know them? Besides, I'm in love with Solly, uh, Saul is his real name. If my parents knew that do you think they would give a damn about me?"

✦

The next few days were surreal to Harold because they were so normal. By Friday, when Finnhandlerr was still talking to him and the boys at the gym were still preoccupied with the coming contest, he realized that Christiana had been talking from the heart. She was probably even in love with Saul. Still, he avoided the Willknecht house, spending all his free time after work at the gym, encouraging Finnhandlerr to lift greater and greater loads. *I hope he gets a hernia,* the reporter thought.

Harold talked to Saul Thursday night, speaking from the pay phone at Jaeger's. "Christiana figured out you were a reporter," the boy said. "But she was sure you were working with the police or FBI and were planning on arresting all the Bund big shots. She was positive that I wasn't from New Jersey and suspected I was Jewish, probably because of my circumcision. So there it is, Harold. You're not mad, are you? She won't say anything."

"What's done is done," Harold said. "Don't worry about me; worry about Christiana. She says she loves you and that you feel the same way about her."

"I do Harold, I do." Saul said, sounding like he really meant it.

Saul my boy, are you ready for love? Harold thought. *I don't know if I am.*

✦

Saturday morning dawned wet and raw; a chill rain had fallen all night. Harold jumped over puddles in the cracked sidewalk as he made his way to the large building next door to his loft. He and Willknecht were leaving early for the Interborough, sent as scouts by Max Finnhandlerr, who wanted to know the layout of the New

York University building where the weightlifting contest was being held. The OD leader had a plan to pack the auditorium, especially key places such as the aisles and near the doors. "We have to be ready for anything when dealing with Jews," Finnhandlerr had said Thursday night, meeting at Georg's apartment to explain his scheme.

Paranoia, Harold had thought.

All over Yorkville, Bund members were rising with first light. They had to arrive at NYU early to grab the vital seats. Identifying those seats was Harold's job. So here he was, a spy again for his little Fuehrer. *The other night I told Saul not to worry about me, but maybe I was too confident. People are going to get hurt if Finnhandlerr has his way.*

Willknecht came bounding down the sidewalk, splashing through puddles with great abandon. He gestured with his rolled up umbrella, showing Harold and the curtained windows of York Avenue what he would do to Jews who dared to attend the contest. On the subway, the garrulous janitor told Harold about the retribution Finnhandlerr would have on the *yid,* Shubnik. *He's back to his normal Jew-hating self,* thought Harold. *At least Christiana hasn't told him that I'm a Jew.*

Just when Harold was beginning to like the man, Willknecht turned hateful. *Is there a character defect in Germans of a certain age?* the reporter wondered. *No, there are young and old Nazis. Still, Germans who lived through the war must have feelings of inferiority. They must want revenge. But who made the Jews their enemy? My Uncle Hiram fought in the German army. Is he their enemy?*

⋰

The two men climbed from the subway and walked the block to Washington Square. The sky was lighter now; the storm breaking up, the sun silvering the clouds. Standing at the edge of the park, they faced the auditorium, a neo-classical building dominating the southeast quadrant of the square. They climbed the sweeping steps to the entrance, where Harold turned to face the giant arch at the base of Fifth Avenue—so reminiscent of the *Arc de Triomphe* in Paris. The sun was illuminating the top of the arch and nearby trees. Water dripping from bare branches haloed the monument with rainbows. Here, in this square named for Washington, Finnhandlerr was planning his revenge on the Jews of New York. *I don't think George would approve,* Harold thought. He remembered that the First President belonged to the Bund's pantheon of heroes, along with Hitler and Frederick the Great. *I know George wouldn't approve.*

Willknecht punched Harold hard on the arm, interrupting his reverie. "Come, my friend. We have a task to complete."

The Amateur Athletic Union, organizers of the Interborough, gave each group sponsoring weightlifters fifty tickets. "That is not enough," Finnhandlerr had said. "We work in a printing plant. We will forge tickets." The OD leader found ticket stock of the right color and weight, set the type exactly as the originals, and printed 400 extra tickets, good enough to fool the ticket takers of the AAU. "With more support from the crowd, our German boys will lift harder and longer."

"Some real ticket holders will not be able to get seats," Harold had pointed out.

"So what! We will win the Interborough and prove we are the superior race."

Finnhandlerr's scheme was for Harold and Georg to string velvet ropes around big blocks of seats, so that early arrivals would sit elsewhere. But the two men had to gain access to the auditorium. The front doors were locked. Back down the steps they rushed, looking for another entrance. Down an alley on the east side of the building they found an open door. An aged Negro janitor challenged them as they entered. "Hey, you gentlemen cain't come in. We don't opens the doors fo' another hour."

"We are here to arrange seating for today's event," Willknecht said. He produced a membership card in the Custodial Union of New York City. He held up a big bag, taking out a crimson strand of velvet rope, so the old man could see what they were about.

"I'll show yo'uns where to go," the old janitor wheezed.

"I did not know you were a union man, Georg," Harold said as the two followed up steep steps from the bowels of the auditorium.

"Hmmph, some union, we are just a bunch of supers from buildings in Yorkville. We get together every now and then to drink and grouse. But we had the cards printed up and they are useful sometimes." Willknecht started pulling rope from his bag as they entered the hall. "We have to hurry. It is a big hall, it must seat a thousand, and they will be opening the doors soon."

At nine, the old janitor unlocked the doors and people began to trickle in. Competitors went to the backstage area reserved for them, where they received last minute instructions from officials. Their friends and families found seats in the auditorium, but not the seats Willknecht and Harold had roped off for Germans. When Bund members arrived Willknecht and his little band of storm trooper assistants directed them to special seating inside the ropes. He put the women and children in the front row, where their cheering would be most effective. He assigned the men to the aisle seats, to control access to the entire room. And he put the OD, who were not in uniform but stood out by their erect bearing, in the back to control ingress and egress if necessary. He did this all without the knowledge of the contest organizers, who were puzzled by the number of people they had to turn away. In fact, there were numerous arguments at the entrance concerning the lack of seats and the fire regulations. Cornelius Gilderman, chairman of the New York AAU, was seen screaming at committee members about printing too many tickets. Harold, sitting in the back with his OD comrades, was witness to many ticket altercations. *Finnhandlerr's plan succeeded,* he thought. *The house is packed with Germans. Now what?*

By midafternoon the heavyweights were lifting, two by two, slowly winnowing the field. Loud applause filled the hall whenever a Bund member took his turn. It had been that way all day long, with the Germans filling almost half the hall. They vociferously supported their representatives, cheering madly for Strauss, who won the lightweight division, and for Everhardt, who won the middleweight crown. Now they were yelling in support of Finnhandlerr, who responded by crushing all his opponents, whether they were Slavs from Flushing or Spaniards from Flatbush.

Joe Shubnik was also advancing. The Jew from Pelham Bay defeated a patrician representative of the New York Athletic Club and a Negro from the Harlem Youth Center. If Finnhandlerr and Shubnik continued at the present pace they would once again meet for the championship of New York City. Harold was on the edge of his seat, straining to see one of Shubnik's lifts, when, out of the avalanche of sound sweeping across the auditorium, someone yelled his name.

"Hey Apple, how's it hangin'? What ya doin' here?"

Harold knew that high, nasal voice, which could cut through any crowd. It was Morty Zucker, sports reporter for the *New York Evening Post*, whom he had last seen the previous June at Yankee Stadium. Zucker was coming up the aisle from the front when he spied Harold sitting one seat over in the last row. *If there's anyone who looks like a Jew its big-nose Zucker,* Harold thought. *Damn it, I'm trapped.* His storm trooper seatmates had heard too. They stared at Zucker, coming up the aisle, then turned and glared at Harold. *If looks could kill I'd be dead.*

"Apple, they got you on sports now?" Zucker, as loud and obnoxious as Harold remembered him, stopped at the end of the last row. "I thought you covered politics. Why are you with these apes?" The pudgy sports reporter gestured broadly at the big blond men on either side of Harold. "Hey Klaus, hey Hermann, where do ya keep your guard dogs?"

"Do you know this miserable excuse for a man?" Gustav Zollner, the OD man on Harold's left, asked menacingly. Wilhelm Schroeder, who sat to the right, was more direct. He leaped up, grabbed Zucker by the collar, and pulled him down over the back of his seat. In the pandemonium of the moment, as Shubnik defeated his last opponent to reach the finals, no one seemed to notice the altercation at the back of the auditorium or hear Zucker's muffled cries.

"How does this pig, this fat Jew with a press card in his hat, come to know your name, Appel?" Schroeder yelled in Harold's ear. Other storm troopers pressed around the reporter. In an instant they were transformed from comrades into mortal enemies. Harold tried to stand but Zollner pushed him back down.

"We have our two finalists in the heavyweight division!" The excited voice of the announcer boomed throughout the auditorium. "Max Finnhandlerr and Joe Shubnik will fight it out to see who wears the championship belt." Everyone in the hall was on their feet, applauding madly. In the tumult Harold stood and leapt over his seat, reached over the seat next to him and grabbed Zucker's arm, and dragged him through the exit which had been abandoned by the OD, who were all cheering for their leader.

In the lobby, Harold shoved Zucker toward the front door while yelling, "Get out of here, Morty!" Big blond men were flowing out of the auditorium so Harold ran back in. *They didn't see me,* he thought as he ran down the aisle. *I hope Morty was frightened enough to listen. Those guys would just as soon kill him as say hello. And now I'm in the same cockroach class, except it's worse, because I marched with them, I fooled them.* He allowed himself one moment of satisfaction while thinking of all the ways he'd bamboozled the Nazis, then he turned and saw two OD re-enter the auditorium, obviously looking for him. *Once word passes that I'm an enemy, I'm finished. There are so many Germans in here. But there is one spot of safety—with Shubnik's people. And I know where they are.*

Harold went down the center aisle. He and Willknecht had done a good job packing the place. German faces were everywhere—wolfish faces, predator faces. *I'm going to be eaten alive.* Panic rose in his chest until a large group of men near him erupted in applause. He glanced at the stage in time to see the Jewish weightlifter lower a heavily laden bar onto the curl stand. *This is the place. There are friends over there, past the Germans on the aisle.* He pushed into the row, stepping on the feet of two friends of Willknecht's, who he knew slightly. *I've got to get as many people as possible between me and the OD. I've got to reach the Jews.* He pushed past a few more people, stopping as a short, muscular young man stood to get out of his way. To him he said as urgently as he could, "The Nazis want to kill me. Hide me!"

The man looked at Harold like he was crazy, then he turned and saw a dozen hard-looking men coming down the aisle. He saw a purpose in their eyes and made a quick decision. "Crouch down in front of me." He signaled the men around him to stand, hiding Harold from the aisle. The men started to cheer, "Joe! Joe! Joe!" as the announcer called for the last set of heavyweight lifts.

"Who the hell are you, and why are those thugs out to get you?" Harold's benefactor hissed between cheers for Shubnik.

"I'm Harold Apple. I'm a reporter for the *World Journal.* I'm doing a story on the Bund."

"You came to the right place, Harold," the man said. "We hate the Bund. I'm Abe Kaplan."

"Abe, what's happening on stage?"

"That guy with the swastika on his chest is lifting first. Looks like he's doing four hundred pounds. Joe can do more than that."

Harold knew that was near Finnhandlerr's limit. Willknecht had said Max did five hundred last year, but Harold hadn't seen it. He imagined the big man bent over the bar, straining, straining, and finally not able to lift that much.

"He got it up," Kaplan said. "Now Joe is lifting four hundred twenty…and he's got it." The hall roared, all except the Germans. "Harold, we've got some of your German friends talking to the men on the aisle. Now they're looking this way. Keep down!"

Harold curled up on the cold floor at Kaplan's feet and listened to the sounds of the contest. The audience grew very still. He imagined that the OD leader was preparing to lift four hundred and twenty-five pounds. The hush was broken by a hoarse grunting. *That's Finnhandlerr, all right,* Harold thought. *He always sounds like a broken down locomotive when he's lifting a heavy load.* Suddenly there was a thunderous crash and a shrill cry of pain.

"What happened?" the reporter hissed at Kaplan. The crowd was silent as cries of pain from the stage filled the auditorium.

"The Nazi collapsed under the weight," Kaplan said in a little more than a whisper. "He had it up to his chest when his legs gave out. He went straight down with four hundred and fifty pounds on top of him!"

Good lord! Four Hundred Fifty! Four Hundred Fifty! The amount Finnhandlerr had tried to lift went racing through Harold's mind. *I've seen him do four hundred; never any more.*

Over the loudspeaker the whole auditorium could hear confusion on the stage. "Get an ambulance! Get the doctor! For Christsakes, I didn't know a body could bend like that!" The microphone shut off only to come back on a moment later with the voice of an official. "There has been an accident. Attention! There's been an accident. Max Finnhandlerr was hurt on his last lift. He is receiving medical attention. Our heavyweight champion, Joe Shubnik of the Pelham Bay Hebrew Association, has asked that we forego the ceremony to proclaim the winner. Under the circumstances we are complying with his request."

With that word the audience shifted their attention from the stage to the exits. They stood at their seats, looked around, and prepared to leave. In the midst of the sizable clump of Jews from Pelham Bay, in the middle of the auditorium, Harold stood also, unfolding his cramped legs and lifting himself to his full height which was a head above the diminutive Kaplan. Over the excited hum of voices he heard a shout. "There he is! Get him!"

Wilhelm Schroeder started down the row. He waved what looked like a bloody nightstick in his right hand. With his left he pushed people out of the way. Harold glanced at the other end of the row. Nazis were blocking any way out. In the confusion of the slowly emptying auditorium no one noticed the coming assault in the middle of the hall.

"Good lord Harold, what did you do to them?" Kaplan asked breathlessly. "They want your blood!"

"Yeah, I kinda made fun of them," Harold said. Now there was no way out. Now the Nazis knew he was not one of them. He felt relief and a sense that he wanted to hit some Germans, even as they wanted to beat on him.

"Harold," Kaplan said quickly, as Schroeder nearly was within reach, "we've got twenty weightlifters from Pelham Bay, all of whom would relish a dust-up with some Nazis." He yelled to his friends all around, "Guys, we've got some Nazi butt to kick!"

The Pelham Bay boys held their ground as the seats around them emptied. Schroeder stopped advancing when he saw the muscular men surrounding Harold. *He's waiting for reinforcements. And here they come.* Forty men leapt over empty seats to form a ragged square around Harold and his new-found Jewish friends.

In front of Harold stood the men he knew best from the Bund. Willknecht and Stubble, even Everhardt, fresh from his triumph with the weights, were there. Their eyes spoke of betrayal.

Only Willknecht, he who had the most reason to feel betrayed, did not look at Harold with hate. His eyes looked disbelieving. *Poor, simple Georg.*

Harold thought of Sally, and felt determined to live. "Harold Appel, our quarrel is with you, not with these other men." Stubble had to yell to be heard over the departing crowd. "Come with us. We can settle this privately."

"Not likely, Reinhold. With all the hotheads in the OD I'd wind up in the hospital or, more likely, the morgue."

"Are you really a reporter Harold?" Willknecht called out, disappointment loud in his bitter, bitter question.

"Yes Georg," Harold answered honestly. "To you, and you only, do I express sorrow."

Schroeder lifted his arm in rage. "Appel, you slimy creature, come get what you deserve, just like your reporter friend." Stop hiding with these Jew bastards. Be a man." The big blond, his face flushed with anger, jumped over a row of seats and pushed Harold hard with his bloody nightstick. The reporter fell back, tumbling over a seat behind him. Abe Kaplan caught Harold then struck at the storm trooper, but the Nazi eluded him.

That was the signal for the Germans, from all sides, to attack the Jewish men. The Nazis had an advantage in numbers but the Jews had the better position, fighting back to back. The Pelham Bay boys gave out more than they received, whether straight up fist to fist or kicking and clawing. Only Schroeder had success among the Nazis because he was the only one in the melee with a weapon. He caught Kaplan across the head, knocking him down at Harold's feet. He clubbed Harold across the left shoulder, raised his stick for another blow, but stopped short when police whistles shrilled and men in blue uniforms entered the auditorium.

The Germans drew back. As the police approached they filed out. The men from Pelham Bay watched stoically, their only injury the gash to Kaplan's forehead. As Schroeder went by he shook his fist at Harold and yelled, "This is not over, dirty Jew!"

"Is everything all right in here?" a policeman called to the people on the stage.

The head judge shaded his eyes against the spotlights. "We

have a severely injured weightlifter up here. But he's receiving medical treatment and the ambulance is on the way."

"Okay. We've got trouble outside, so we'll get back to it," the police officer said.

Harold yelled out, "What happened officer?"

The policeman turned toward Harold. "Who are you?"

"I'm a reporter with the *World Journal.*"

"I guess I can tell you. We found a body on the steps, looks like he fell or was pushed."

Harold powered his way past the Jewish men who had saved him. "Was there any ID on the body?" he asked.

"Let's see," the officer said, calling out to one of his fellows. "Hey Al, you got any identification on the dead guy?"

"Yeah," the answer came back. "His name is Morty Zucker. He's carrying a press card from the *Evening Post.*"

The OD had killed Morty, fat Morty with the big mouth. The storm troopers pushed him down the long flight, tumbling down marble steps to his death. Harold walked out of the auditorium and watched the police, down on the street, load Morty into the ambulance for his last ride. The OD had their blood this day. It seemed to Harold that they had blood most days he was around. Kaplan came up behind the reporter, holding a ragged towel to his head. "I know who killed him," Harold said to the man who had saved him. "They're going to pay!"

CHAPTER TWENTY-ONE

THE ACT IS OVER

SORROW GAVE WAY to anger. Harold had many stops to make that night. The first was the precinct house on East 8th Street, right off Washington Square. He went, accompanied by Kaplan, to ask about Zucker. "I demand the body be examined," Harold said to the police officer in charge. "I saw the bloody stick Zucker was killed with."

"Ah, you reporters see a homicide around every corner," the policeman complained.

"Look at my shirt," Harold yelled. He held his coat open. "Look at the cross. Schroeder painted it with Zucker's blood. Then he told me he'd killed Zucker."

"I saw it," Kaplan exclaimed. "A big man—blond hair, blue eyes, twisted face—pushed him in the chest with a bloody nightstick, the kind you cops use. I'd recognize that man anywhere."

"Who the hell are you?" the officer demanded of Kaplan.

"A friend," Kaplan stood his ground. He had heard Schroeder's boast. The cop took their information and promised to be in touch.

The young weightlifter, a third year law student at City College, had his own Nazi story. "My grandparents live in Heidelberg but they're Polish citizens," he told Harold as they left the sta-tionhouse. "The Nazis had my grandfather fired from the univer-sity, where he taught biology. The last I heard he was going to be deported, my grandma too. I thank God my father left Germany when he did."

How many awful stories do I have to hear, thought Harold as he said good-bye to Kaplan. *As many as there are Jews in Germany, I wager. Uncle Hiram times so many. I want the stories to stop. Maybe I'll wake up in the morning and there won't be any Nazis. Yeah, dream on Harold.* He pulled his coat around him and hurried to his next stop, the newspaper.

When he arrived at the office, he called Aaron at home. "Boss, there was another murder, at the weightlifting championships. I got the story, but had to scramble to save my life. My cover was blown. They found out I'm a reporter and a Jew. I can't go back to Yorkville, so I want a byline on whatever I write."

"God damn it, Harold! How the hell did that happen?" Aaron bellowed into his reporter's ear. "That Nazi stuff was good, good, good! All right, put your name on it, but do it fast; you're at dead-line. Call Scudari to save space on the front page. Now let me get back to my dinner party."

"Yeah, we'll save a two column box and room for a three point head," Scudari said when Harold reached him just before the edi-tion was put to bed. "But make it snappy or else you'll have to set it yourself."

Harold made a final call before starting on his column. "Mr. Finnhandlerr is out of danger but in serious condition with a ruptured spleen and broken leg. Who did you say you were? His brother? Who's going to pay for his treatment?" the nurse at Bel-levue Hospital spat. The reporter hung up.

'A reporter died at the city weightlifting championships yester-day afternoon,' Harold wrote, 'another victim of the Nazi plague sweeping the city. Fighting broke out as the Nazi heavyweight lifter, Max Finnhandlerr, was seriously injured attempting to defeat the defending champion, Joe Shubnik, of the Pelham Bay YMHA. It appears the reporter, Morton Zucker of the Evening Post, fell or was pushed down a long flight of steps while fleeing the Nazis. Zucker and this reporter were in an altercation with storm troopers prior to the incident.'

I didn't say outright that the Nazis killed Zucker, because I didn't see the deed. But you don't have to see something to know it's true. Harold called Aaron again, received approval on the story, and ran it down to the printing plant. He had to set the type himself because the regular crew had gone home. *Last time I'll set type for this rag,* Harold thought, *except they're going to be shorthanded with Finnhandlerr hurt. Maybe they'll need me to come back for a while.* He bade farewell to Scudari, who had waited to make sure the story made the morning edition.

Harold ran back up to the city room to use the phone. He dialed Sally's number and Saul answered. "Sally's not home right now, Harold. I'll tell her you called. But Harold, I called Christiana earlier and her father answered. He wouldn't let me talk to her. Did he find out you were a reporter? He called you a damned dirty Jew."

"I bet that's not all he called me. Yeah Saul, the masquerade is over. My cover was blown, by another reporter who glad-handed me at the Interborough, while I was sitting with some storm troopers, but I managed to get away. Tell Sally I'm OK, but you should stay away from Christiana for a while. The story will be in the paper tomorrow morning. Look for my by-line."

✍

Harold stumbled into his apartment after midnight, not in Yorkville but back home in The Bronx. He pulled some old blankets from a closet, took off his shoes, and sprawled on the couch. He awoke in the morning light, on the floor, tangled in blankets, wondering where he was. He remembered. He was home.

The party's over, Harold thought. *I'm not a German anymore.* He took a shower, washing the Nazi dirt off in long, steamy celebration. He found a change of clothes that was not brown. *No more wide leather belts for me, no more uniforms, no more armbands, no more Hitler salutes, no more crooked crosses. No more play-acting.*

Harold walked around the corner to Sally's, where she greeted him with relief. She had read the morning paper so she knew what the rest of New York knew, and she was glad to have him home for good. They embraced, but in the middle of a tender kiss Harold stiffened. "What's the matter darling?" she asked, leaning back and tenderly touching his cheek.

How could he tell her, he had thought of Zucker in the middle of their embrace? How could he tell her if he'd gone out the front door with the sportswriter he'd have spent last night on a slab in the morgue? Harold's stomach clenched. *I sent him out that door. I killed him.*

⁊

Monday morning, Harold showed up for work at nine. He went to the printing plant to make sure Scudari knew about his foreman. "I know about Finnhandlerr because I read your story this morning," the plant boss said. "You're a better writer than you are a typesetter, but I still hate to lose you. We're shorthanded with Max out."

"If you're really in a bind call me," Harold said. "I liked working here." He would miss the guys, the deadlines, even Finnhandlerr. Serious and strong, the giant never made mistakes and didn't let anyone else goof up either. Harold liked that part of him, the worker, the perfectionist. Too bad the big man couldn't carry that work ethic over to his job as OD Leiter. He couldn't enforce discipline. Too many of the men were ruled by hate, the stone-throwing

Everhardt, the bully Schroeder. *I wonder if Finnhandlerr will be the same when he recovers. Injury can change a man.*

Back at the city room Harold went straight to Aaron's office, where the editor was settled in with his first cup of coffee. "Boss, the masquerade is over and I'm lucky to be in one piece. Zucker wasn't so lucky. And you know something? He didn't even know they were Nazis. He was in the wrong place at the wrong time, looking too Jewish." He took a long look at Aaron, hook nose, high forehead, balding in back. He noted his boss looked Jewish too. *Looking Jewish, what is it? Frizzy hair, bulbous nose, long cheek-bones? Everyone in New York looks like that. I know the Nazis think Jews have that Der Sturmer look, the mookie look. Oy veh, I can get it for you wholesale. Did Morty Zucker die because he was fat and had a big nose? Roosevelt has a big nose. Oops, bad example. The Nazis already think he's Jewish.*

Aaron's office seemed to be getting smaller. The editor, with his Jewish face, occupied more of it than seemed reasonable. Harold tried to be cheerful. "I've got material for more stories, Boss. Lots more. I want to cover the stoning trial. There will be an investigation of Zucker's death where I'll probably be called as a witness. I'm so happy to be back." *Am I? He* wondered. *Do I long to be surrounded by Aryan faces, straight noses, tight lips, blond hair and blue eyes? I can pass as German. I did pass.*

"Hallelujah, just what I've always wanted—a rotten apple in the city room," Aaron joked as if Harold hadn't heard it thousands of times before. "Harold that was a very good story you wrote yesterday," he continued in a more serious tone. "Damn shame about Zucker though. I didn't know him." He bowed his head in respect. "Ahhh, we've all gotta go sometime. Tell me about the Bund stories you've planned. And before you leave the office remind me to call accounting and put a stop on your rent in Yorkville. Do you need any help getting your stuff out of there? Better give me your key."

"Here's my key, Boss. Yeah, I can't go back in that part of town without a police escort. I slept in The Bronx last night, on my couch, because my bed is in Naziville."

"I'll send a truck to get your stuff," Aaron promised. "Can't have you sleeping on a couch. I want my reporters well rested."

There was a loud knock on the door. Pat O'Rourke, well dressed as usual in a grey hounds tooth jacket and red bow tie, was very impatient when Harold opened the door. His toe tapping made him look as if it was his birthday and he was late for cake. Aaron motioned him in. "What is it Pat? Tell us fast before you explode."

"Chief, am I that transparent? I don't mean to look anxious." O'Rourke paused for a minute to straighten his tie and let the flush leave his face. "Harold, I've been looking all over for you, ever since I read your story. Tom Kergan called last night. He wants to see you."

"Kergan wants to see me," said Harold, looking puzzled. "Why?"

"I don't know," O'Rourke said. "He can see you tomorrow night, at my dad's bar."

⤥

The two reporters left the newspaper at six o'clock the next evening. In no time at all, thanks to Pat's driving, they were sitting down to dinner with the entire O'Rourke clan. "Told ya it wouldn't take long," O'Rourke said. He nudged his friend in the ribs.

"Oh yeah, I'm lucky to be alive, the way you throw that roadster around," Harold complained. He was still feeling out of sorts and it wasn't all because of the thrill ride from the city. *I know why I'm worried. It's the threat from Schroeder and his friends.*

"May God bless this bread we eat today," Frankie O'Rourke said quickly as his mother and sister brought out big platters of pot roast and potatoes. "Harold, what's Saul been up to?" Frankie asked between mouthfuls of meat. "Is he still seeing that *fraulein*?"

"I'm kinda *persona non grata* with the Germans, Frankie. Saul is too. Christiana's father won't let her talk with him on the phone."

"Pat tells me you're meeting the Bund lawyer tonight," Henry O'Rourke said. "Do you have any idea what he wants?"

"It's probably about the Zucker murder," Harold said. "I'm a witness to what went on right before he was killed."

"Harold and I went to the precinct house this afternoon, Dad," Pat said. "They found a witness—some guy who saw the whole thing. Zucker was beat up and pushed down the stairs. The police held a line-up, and wouldn't ya know it, the witness picked the right guy, the same one that Harold fingered. Our story will be in the paper tomorrow. We think that's what Kergan wants to talk about."

"The police were very efficient," Harold said. "We think that the fact there were Nazis involved set off alarms. Dewey has a standing order to be notified of any violation involving Bund members. Mayor LaGuardia is interested too. Tuesday morning a warrant was issued for Schroeder's arrest. They found him at his job on the docks, not trying to hide, as if the murder of a Jew didn't matter. I guess he found out he's not in Germany anymore. And I didn't even have to see Schroeder. I just had to repeat my statement and agree to testify at the trial. It was swift and pain-less for me but not for that damn storm trooper. I hope they've got him in the deepest, darkest dungeon in Manhattan, the arro-gant bastard." *That's the way I felt about most of them, the damn OD. But how did I tolerate being with them for so long? Maybe it was the camaraderie, the locker room atmosphere, being around the guys. There's not too much of that in the rest of my life. Except with Pat; I've gotta tell him he's replacing the storm troopers.*

"You have a dangerous job Harold," Pat's sister Mary said, "being around all those Nazis. Of course if you hadn't gotten the Bund job Pat would never have met Emma."

"Emma? Oh, you mean the girl from the country, the sheriff's daughter. How is Emma, Pat?" Harold gave his friend a knowing wink.

O'Rourke's face turned red. His sister was embarrassing him, not because he was anything but head over heels in love with the wisp of a brown-haired girl, but because he had a reputation to maintain with his buddies as a lady's man. Harold knew this. *Pat understands what it means to be one of the guys. We all want to be in the club. But he's got to learn what it means to be in love. It shouldn't take him long.*

After dinner Harold and Pat and the elder O'Rourke donned their overcoats for the short walk to the tavern. On the way, Pat's father told Harold exactly what he thought of the English collapse at Munich. "It was disgraceful the way Chamberlain toadied to that Nazi bully. We're going to fight them eventually, but the English, in their eternal spinelessness, took the easy path."

Arriving at the tavern, Henry took his usual place behind the bar, amidst the glitter of bottles filled with amber spirits, sparkling glassware, and the gaiety of a Christmas tree set atop the leather-covered counter. He quickly became the center of attention in the room as he dispensed both drinks and social commentary. It was a normal Tuesday evening at the Manhattan Avenue Bar and Grill. *Everyone is in the club,* Harold thought, *the guys club.*

The two reporters made themselves comfortable at a table against the far wall. Precisely at nine Kergan pushed through the doors. *I'm amazed that he looks so good. If I lost Sally I'd be a wreck.* Kergan stopped and squinted through the smoky room. Harold stood and waved until the lawyer saw him. "Hello Tom. Sit down and have a drink, then we can talk."

"Hello Pat, Appel." Kergan sat facing the reporters.

"My name's not Appel anymore. It's back to Apple. But what is this all about Tom?" Harold said. "Did your clients ask you to see me?"

"They're not my clients anymore, Apple." Bitterness edged Kergan's voice.

"I had better go get those drinks," O'Rourke said and hurried off to the bar.

"What happened?" Harold looked at Kergan, thinking, *Good God, the man does have emotions.*

"Nothing. I quit," the lawyer said flatly. "Let my father have them." O'Rourke returned with a bottle of Irish whiskey and three shot glasses. He poured for each of them. Kergan downed his and Pat poured again. "I'm confused, Apple. I saw your story and realized you might be the only one who could tell me why I feel so bad, why I've got this grief, this sense of loss, over Regina—and at the same time I feel relief that she's gone"

"Tom, you didn't believe any of that Nazi crap, did you?" O'Rourke asked. "Because, when we were at your house that night, I got the impression that you were just humoring Regina."

"No Pat, that's not it at all," Harold said. "Tom's talking about losing people you thought you knew well. It's a dilemma for me too. I thought Willknecht was my friend, now I know he was a friend to my Nazi persona. But it hurts, right Tom?"

"No Apple, that's not it. I really thought you would understand." A scowl passed over Kergan's face. "After Regina's funeral, a bunch of us wound up at Stubble's apartment. Now, I never had any use for my father-in-law, but he was family. What he said that night was so puzzling, so bothersome, that I haven't been able to sleep since." Kergan paused, a courtroom pause, as if he was presenting a case. "We were drinking, like at an Irish wake, except most of the people there were celebrating, celebrating Regina's death, and the happiest one was her father. It was a lot like my wedding, when Reinhold thought he was getting rid of her. Stubble was sitting on the very same chair I was in when I first laid eyes on Regina, when I first saw the most beautiful girl in the world, and he says, 'if we were in Germany the problem would have been solved years ago. Send her to the institute and never see her again.' Even I knew he was talking about euthanasia. Then he goes on, 'but we did it our own way, and no one is the wiser.' And everyone laughs. Tell me Apple, did I just hear Stubble confess to killing my wife—his daughter?"

Harold was not shocked. "I've heard rumors that the Nazis sterilize defectives but I've never heard of killing them," the reporter said. *Can't tell Tom that the Nazis do kill their crazies. The poor fool has suffered enough.*

"Poor, poor Gina! I loved her, I hated her, but I always treated her with respect," Kergan cried, tears rolling down his cheeks. "And the baby! What about the baby?"

Harold drummed his fingers on the table. He sipped his drink while Kergan dried his eyes with a sodden napkin. *He doesn't know I was there. I saw Everhardt throw the stone. I'm an eyewitness! And there's no masquerade anymore, no reason to hold back.* "Tom, I've gotta tell you something."

CHAPTER TWENTY-TWO

THE TRIAL BEGINS

A MONTH PASSED. Christmas came and went but winter stayed and there was snow on the ground. Harold wrote a flurry of Nazi stories at the end of the year and then his typewriter fell silent. He gave a statement to the police about Regina's death, and in January grew busy with other stories. He covered a garbage worker's strike in Brooklyn and a factory fire in Queens. Sally kept him occupied with preparations for the wedding. After some time, days went by when Harold did not think about Nazis or his time in Yorkville.

All good things, even forgetfulness, end. The Yorkville Stoning Trial, as the papers dubbed it, began the last week in January and Harold was forced to remember the days of November and the men he had liked and hated; the Willknechts, the Finnhandlerrs, the Stubbles, the Kuhns, the Everhardts. He remembered all he had done, all he had written, the fears he had felt, and yes, the bonds he had formed. And he remembered Moe Drabinsky, Regina Kergan, and Morty Zucker—the victims he did not want the city to forget. *Time to unlimber the writing muscle.*

❧

"Hear ye, hear ye, the Superior Court for New York County, State of New York is now in session," the bailiff called. "All rise for the Honorable Dominic Giordano, presiding."

The judge entered from behind the bench. *He looks tough,* Harold thought as he examined the short stocky fireplug of a man with wavy gray hair framing a severe looking face. *Black horn rims, black robe, and grey hair; yep, he's a hanging judge, at least that's what O'Rourke says.*

"Opening arguments in the case of the State of New York versus Werner Everhardt and Klaus Groening, being tried for second-degree murder, docket number NYSC 108-39, will now be heard," the bailiff announced.

District Attorney Tom Dewey, the well-known foe of the isms of Europe, assumed the prosecutor's role for himself. The well-compensated William Kergan spoke for the defense. The first task was jury selection. The judge, the defendants, and the spectators on both sides watched the lawyers tap-dancing around potential jurors, the defense seeking a panel free of Jews and their opponents looking for good Americans. O'Rourke left after Kergan's first challenge excused a little white-haired lady named Clara Cohen. "This is boring," he complained. "Call me when they run out of challenges." And he noisily pushed past a row of reporters, to the great displeasure of the judge.

As O'Rourke reached the door of the courtroom, Judge Giordano barked out, "You reporters stay in your seats or I'll throw you all out." O'Rourke stopped for an instant then pushed through the big double doors, letting them slam behind him. A whole row of reporters cowered meekly in their seats, trying to look invisible.

He doesn't give a damn about courtroom etiquette, Harold thought about his partner. *He gets away with bad behavior, because he's the only one who dares it while the rest of us suffer in silence.* Harold looked around at his fellow gentlemen of the press. *I wonder where the bastard is going.* The reporter returned his attention to the front of the courtroom, where Dewey was interviewing another potential juror.

O'Rourke returned late in the afternoon. "You missed all the fun," Harold said. "We've got a jury with ten guys named Smith and two gals named Jones."

"You missed some fun too," Pat said, sounding extremely satisfied. "I had lunch with an assistant DA. He told me all about Dewey's strategy. He's putting the whole damned Nazi Party on trial for the death of one Jew. In effect, he's trying the Germans for *Kristallnacht.* And the publicity he's going to get doesn't faze him at all, because he wants to run for governor next year."

"I don't care if he runs for President," Harold said, "as long as he puts Everhardt and Groening in jail."

The next day the courtroom was packed for the opening arguments. Fiorello LaGuardia was there, to the delight of reporters, who always enjoyed quoting the mayor. "The wrong people were charged in this case," he said. "It should have been the Nazi bigwigs. I mean Hitler and his cronies. But I guess we'll take what we can get. One Nazi in Sing-Sing is worth a dozen on the street." Several reporters scurried for the exit, anxious to call in this quote before the judge arrived to confine the Press to their courtroom prison.

"It looks like LaGuardia is talking to Dewey," O'Rourke whispered to his partner as they settled into their hard wooden chairs while waiting for the judge to appear. "That's the prosecution strategy."

The local Nazis, in the courtroom in strength, scowled in unison at Mayor LaGuardia's words. Stubble, Franz, and Willknecht, along with others who Harold recognized, rose to their feet, their arms raised, their fists made. Only Fritz Kuhn sat passively, his face devoid of emotion. The bailiff took a step forward, right hand gesturing to the NYPD officers in the room to be alert. Kuhn, at the front of his delegation, raised his arm in a familiar gesture and quickly, emphatically, lowered his hand, telling his angry people to sit and shut up.

Kuhn's like Arminius, always another battle to fight. But look who's coming in now. He poked O'Rourke. "Here are Mendelsohn and Thorson. This ought to be fun."

The Germans are gathering, Harold thought. *This is the first time I've seen Willknecht since the weightlifting contest. Only Finnhandlerr's not here; he's still recovering.* But the reporter knew what was going on in Yorkville. Christiana had been keeping Saul informed ever since he showed up at her school and pledged his undying love.

"Or something like that," Saul had told Harold. "Her parents are not coming between us ever again. Christiana is eighteen, of legal age. Besides, her father has problems of his own. He and his friends are afraid of this trial. They're afraid of District Attorney Dewey. They think the Government is going to come after Germans, like they did during the War."

The Germans were outraged to see Harold sitting with the other reporters at the trial. Stubble marched up to him, swearing in German that reporters all belonged in the deepest hell the devil could devise and that went double for Jewish reporters. He exchanged a hostile glance with Willknecht that seemed downright friendly compared to the bile spilled on him by the others.

The opening arguments began. His hair slicked back, his brown eyes gleaming, his pencil mustache waxed to a fare-thee-well, District Attorney Thomas E. Dewey spoke first. "Honorable Judge, ladies and gentlemen of the jury, we live in a forgiving country, a land that ignores our origins if we live together in peace. The crime with which we are faced today is repugnant to Americans. The motivation behind the 'Yorkville Stoning' was not passion, greed, or any other easily explainable motive to our countrymen, but anti-Semitism arising out of European prejudices, race hatred embraced by the National Socialist Party of Germany, and championed by Adolph Hitler. I intend to put on trial not only the two defendants in the 'Yorkville Stoning' but also the foreign ideology, which also led to the atrocity of '*Kristallnacht*,' because this ideology respects no national borders, and has caused crimes in Europe and the United States."

"How did these two men become Nazis? Americans value free speech and free association, except where these rights are used to conspire to kill other Americans. Our Founding Fathers did not foresee the rise of the perfidious isms, Nazism and communism, which undermine our constitution. If they were alive today they would deny these ideologies the protection of law. Congress has established an Un-American Affairs Committee to root out these beliefs from our society. Can we in New York City do any less?"

"I was elected District Attorney on the Republican ticket, but the fight against Un-American beliefs is non-partisan. President Roosevelt, speaking in Chicago last October, said, 'Landmarks and traditions which have marked the progress of civilization toward a condition of law, order, and justice are being -wiped away. An epidemic of world lawlessness is spreading.' The President recognizes the threat inherent in the behavior of the Nazis. I recognize the threat. All Americans should recognize the threat. Nazis roam the streets of Europe, doing their dirty deeds. We cannot permit the contamination to spread to New York."

"In conclusion the State will prove that Morris Drabinsky was killed by rocks thrown by the defendants and that others were injured in the same incident. The rock throwing incident was inspired by the foreign ideology of Nazism, as propounded by the German American Bund, and that those who participate in Nazi activities in the United States are guilty of subversion. And those who participate in throwing stones are guilty of murder."

Dewey sat down. Sweat ran off his brow as he accepted congratulations from his associates. O'Rourke was already dashing for the exit, along with a dozen other reporters, heading for the telephones in the press room down the hall. The judge half-heartedly banged his gavel, but nothing was going to stop the gentlemen of the press. *Dewey will get front page treatment, but he barely mentioned Everhardt and Groening, and not by name. Is that any way to convict criminals? He sure as hell talked about Nazis. I hope his strategy works.*

Kergan stood and asked permission to approach the bench. It was hot in the courtroom despite the weather outside. Men loosened their ties. Women fanned themselves with newspapers. Sweat beaded the forehead of the defense attorney as he came up to the judge. He suddenly turned and looked at the defendants. Harold's eyes followed his. *Groening has a haunted look, like he's on the verge of a nervous breakdown. Everhardt, on the other hand, looks calm.*

"Mr. Kergan, how do your clients plead?" asked the judge. Despite the heavy robes he wore, Judge Giordano seemed the coolest one in the courtroom.

"My clients plead not guilty, your honor."

"Then proceed with your opening statement, Mr. Kergan."

"Ladies and Gentlemen of the jury, Judge Giordano, a man died on the afternoon of November 11, 1938, at the corner of Lexington Avenue and East 85th Street. But what did he die of? The medical report says a blow to the head, and goes no further. Everyone presumes that blow was delivered by a thrown rock, but no one offers solid proof. An autopsy was not performed on the victim. He could have had a heart attack and we would not know."

"Rocks were thrown, we know that as fact. The question I put to the court is how, out of the hundreds of people at the corner of Lexington and 85th that afternoon, did the prosecution pick my clients as the killers? Did the police take fingerprints from the rocks? Is the prosecution going to offer the rocks as evidence? The answer is, no."

"The District Attorney just now stated that he is prosecuting my clients because of their Nazi ideology and membership in the German American Bund. That is guilt by association. Nowhere in the charges against my clients does it say anything about the Nazi Party or the Bund. The Nazis aren't charged here, two men are charged, charged with a specific crime which they did not commit."

As Kergan took his seat the courtroom erupted, cries of 'no Nazis' competing with raucous applause. The judge gaveled for order. "We will recess for lunch," he announced, "and resume at two o'clock."

Harold made his way through the crowd to the press room, where he had to wait for a telephone. What he phoned in, 'Defense attorney claims storm troopers innocent,' was expected in a criminal case. The rewrite man would combine that with O'Rourke's report on what Dewey had said, Hitler is guilty, for a story in the five o'clock edition, a story which would convey little of the outrage Harold felt. *I know Everhardt is guilty,* he thought. *I was there. I'd be willing to testify to what I saw, if only the damned DA would call me. Dewey's making a big mistake. Kergan won the first round.*

O'Rourke came into the room. "Let's have lunch. I know a place the other side of City Hall Park with a great view of the bridge." They put on their overcoats and left the courthouse.

The two reporters cut across the northwest corner of the park, which looked lifeless, dead brown grass, stunted leafless trees, trash all over the sidewalk. The grey government buildings loomed over the little park like giant mausoleums. Downtown was dead in winter. Harold felt depressed as they crossed Broadway to the restaurant. *I bet there is no justice here, no green shoots of truth.*

"Here we are," O'Rourke said, opening the door with a flourish, "the Brooklyn Bridge Café." He gestured at the headwaiter. "And this is Ralph."

I've been in this joint before, Harold thought. *But I don't know the maitre'd. Pat does. He knows everyone in this town who can get him the best table, dress him in the latest fashion, and introduce him to the crème de la crème. Am I jealous? Not really. Pat's Pat. I don't want to be like him, just bask in his glory once in a while.* He followed as a fawning waiter led Pat to the finest table in the house, by the window. They sat and gazed out on City Hall and beyond it, the Manhattan end of the prettiest bridge in the world.

"Pat, you bastard," Harold said. "How do you always get royal treatment, the best of everything?"

"Attitude, my friend, attitude. I have a good one and it shows. Harold I want to tell you something about the lineup of witnesses. I got an updated witness list from a secretary in Dewey's office. You know most of these guys. Maybe you can make some sense of the order Dewey is calling them. Leading off is Fritz Kuhn. I know who he is, but next is Levi Sobidor. Who's he?"

"He's president of the Glusker Young Men's Association. Drabinsky was at the parade with them."

"Then we have Anton Goldwasser."

"He's an official of the Jewish War Veterans. Those two will establish that Drabinsky had a legit reason to be at the parade. That shouldn't take long. Who else?"

O'Rourke hesitated, and said in a low voice, "Saul Schwartz."

"I knew Saul was going to testify," Harold said. "He's been talking about nothing else for weeks. My future brother-in-law looks on this as an opportunity to avenge Drabinsky."

"The next witness's name was blacked out on the list," O'Rourke said. "Either Dewey changed his mind or there's a problem. We'll just have to wait and see."

The reporter's talk was interrupted by the arrival of their lunch, two platters of spaghetti and meatballs, with sides of garlic bread and onion salad, the specialty of the house. "After this lunch," said Harold, "all we have to do to end the trial is breathe on the judge."

"Speaking of the judge," Pat said, "isn't that him over there in the brown suit?"

"I think it is." Harold had to squint to see the man seated in a dim corner of the dining room. "Hey Pat, can you make out who's with him?"

"No. It's kind of dark back there. Small guy though."

"Pat, I think it's Kergan."

"Yeah, you're right, Harold. But why is the Judge having lunch with the defense attorney? Wait a sec, you don't think the fix is in?"

"If Hitler could get himself named *Time Magazine's* Man of the Year, then he can fix a trial for the Bund," Harold said.

Harold felt queasy after lunch. He took his seat in the courtroom, barely paying attention to O'Rourke telling him about the rest of the witness list. *Kergan and the Judge together were enough to get me sick,* he thought, *but then I had to eat that greasy food.*

"Sheriff Acton follows…" O'Rourke said.

"Pat, I'm sick! I've got to get to the can!" Harold ran for the exit, only to find his way blocked by Fritz Kuhn.

"Appel, you filthy Jew, and a reporter too; how disgusting." The big man spat, hitting Harold in the eye as he pushed his way past.

Harold stood in the bathroom. He could still feel Kuhn's spittle, even after scrubbing his face a hundred times, because he had sat with his eye clouded and sticky all the time he had emptied his bowels. *Nazi spit—it stains the soul. I got it in the eye on the way to the shithouse. My family got it in the streets of Frankfurt, in their houses, in their store, in their hearts.*

The *Bundesfuehrer* was already on the stand when Harold returned to the courtroom. "What did I miss, Pat?" he asked.

"Kergan moved for dismissal on grounds the prosecution wasn't addressing the charges, but the judge dismissed the motion. And Kuhn was just sworn in.

Dewey was speaking. "Mr. Kuhn, what position do you hold with the German American Bund?"

"I am the national president, the leader, putting myself at the forefront for all to follow." Kuhn spoke calmly yet forcefully, as if his position was known to all.

"In German is your position known as *Bundesfuehrer,*" Dewey asked, "and is that comparable to *Reichsfuehrer?*"

"Why yes, it is." Kuhn was pleased with the initial questioning. Dewey was playing to his vanity by comparing him to Hitler.

"Now, was the parade on November 11th an event with which you were involved in any way?"

"No. It was organized by the *Ortsgruppe* Yorkville." Kuhn was hesitant in his answer.

"Did you address the gathering on that day?"

"Yes I did, at the request of the local leadership."

"And do you remember what you said?" Dewey asked quietly.

"Do I remember? That was over two months ago. I give many speeches each week. I can't remember each one. I was speaking on the anniversary of the Armistice. I probably talked about the valor of the German troops."

"Do you remember talking about anything else, Mr. Kuhn? Perhaps about *Kristallnacht?*"

"I do not remember."

"He's lying!" Harold hissed in O'Rourke's ear. "It was in the wake of the biggest pogrom in German history. He told his storm troopers to do what their German brothers had done and attack the Jews." Harold's slowly recovering digestive track suddenly knotted in pain.

"Harold, your face is green!" O'Rourke said.

"I've got to get to the can again," Harold grunted through clenched teeth. He flew down the row of reporters, stepping on feet, knocking knees, and ignoring looks of annoyance and anger.

The judge stamped his foot. "You're out of here mister," he said to Harold's back as he staggered out of the courtroom. "Don't come back."

Harold stayed in the stall a long time, emptying his bowels of dinner, breakfast, lunch, and all encounters with Nazis for the last three or four months. Men came and went. Toilets flushed, water ran. Until the door opened again and he heard a familiar voice, "Kergan has the fix in. We have nothing to worry about."

Another voice started to say something. A toilet flushed, obscuring the response. *Who was that?* Harold wondered. *It sounded like Willknecht.*

When he finally emerged the courtroom was emptying, the trial adjourned until morning. He met and exchanged a few words with the Drabinsky women, assuring them the trial was going very well, despite how it was actually going. He had a sour taste in his mouth when he entered the pressroom and saw O'Rourke and the other reporters writing their stories, unaware that the trial was over according to the unknown but very familiar sage of the bathroom. "What happened while I was gone Pat?" Harold asked his partner.

"Kuhn finished testifying. He was evasive, as you heard. Kergan declined to cross-examine. Why should he? Kuhn said nothing to incriminate the storm troopers, in fact he barely mentioned them, only saying they were there for crowd control. Harold, do you know why Dewey is handling the case this way?"

"Maybe he figures it's the only way to win," Harold said. "He needs a big case with lots of publicity to turn this judge around. I heard something while I was sitting in the stall, Pat. Someone said, 'The fix is in.' I know that voice, from Yorkville, but I can't put my finger on who it was."

"Damn it Harold, do you think the Germans can fix the jury too?" Pat's voice echoed his partner's outrage.

"I don't know," Harold said with resignation.

CHAPTER TWENTY-THREE

THE TRIAL CONTINUES

AT DINNER THAT night Saul told the family what he would tell the court in the morning. "Mr. Drabinsky was felled by rocks thrown from the German side of the street. I can't say any more than that. I hope it will be enough."

The entire family rode the subway downtown in the morning. Izzy had shuttered the candy store last night, something almost unheard of. Sally took a holiday from the dress factory and Saul skipped school. They arrived early and stood shivering in front of the Criminal Court Building. When it opened at nine they entered the formal lobby and made their way to the wood-paneled courtroom.

The morning papers spewed the news of Kergan calling for a mistrial based on lack of evidence. His clients, as well as the other Nazis, were cheerful as they filed into the courtroom. They anticipated a quick and easy dismissal. The prosecutors wore grim expressions as they entered. Dewey had the darkest face of them all.

Who's that sitting off in the corner? Harold scanned the room as he took his seat in the row of reporters. Off in the corner he spotted a familiar face he couldn't quite place. Then it came to him. It was Sheriff Action from New Jersey and his daughter Emma.

Pat had mentioned the sheriff was going to testify. Harold looked closely at the attractive girl his partner was so smitten with. *She doesn't look like a schoolgirl now; she looks like a vamp in that slinky dress. Oh my Pat, you've got a good one.*

Judge Giordano looked grim as he entered. The whole world was watching the Manhattan courtroom, waiting for American justice to deliver its vaunted fairness. The papers reported that Hitler dismissed the trial as evidence that America was a mongrel country, the races hopelessly mixed. There was no doubt the judge was being buffeted by political winds. Harold's reporter's instincts were aroused. He had to find out if the fix was in, which meant finding out more about the judge. Where was he born, Italy or the U.S.? Where did he go to school? Who did he associate with?

The prosecution didn't waste any time getting down to business. The first two witnesses, Goldwasser and Sobidor, established that Drabinsky was on Lexington Avenue that afternoon. "Morris was a strong man," Sobidor said sadly. "He went despite the danger. Who would think that in New York City, one could be killed for being a Jew?"

"Dewey is setting the scene," whispered O'Rourke to a melancholy Harold, who was deeply affected by Sobidor's testimony. Kergan declined to cross examine and the prosecution prepared to call the next witness, Saul Schwartz.

"Please state your age and where you live," Dewey asked Saul after he was sworn in by the bailiff.

"I'm seventeen years old, eighteen on April 21," Saul said in a firm voice. ""I live in The Bronx, 186th Street near Jerome Avenue."

"Do you go to school Saul?"

"Yes. I'm in my last year at The Bronx High School of Science. I hope to go to Columbia next year."

"Did you know the victim?" Dewey asked gently. "Did you know the man who was murdered, Morris Drabinsky?"

"Objection," cried Kergan. "It hasn't been determined that anyone was murdered."

"That is what I am doing right now, your honor," Dewey protested, "proving that a man was criminally assaulted, killed by stones thrown by the defendants."

"Objection sustained," growled the judge, irritation evident in this voice. "The Court should not have to remind the District Attorney that nothing has been proven."

"Very well your Honor, let me rephrase the question. Did you know the man who was allegedly killed?" Dewey was angry.

"Yes I did Mr. Dewey," the redhead answered, loud and clear. "Mr. Drabinsky was my father's best friend."

"And you were with him the afternoon of November 11th?"

"Yes."

"Will you tell the court, what the two of you were doing, how you came to be there, and who you were with?

"Earlier that week my folks and I went to a meeting called by the Jewish War Veterans to announce plans for a protest to the Nazi Armistice Day march," Saul recounted. "No one felt it was right that Nazis should be celebrating, especially after what just happened in Germany. I wanted to go. I really wanted to go. My parents weren't going to let me go on my own, but Mr. Drabinsky—Uncle Moe—said I could go with him. He was going with the Gluskers, my father's *landsmanschaft.*" Saul paused, as if he expected another interruption, but the room was hushed. He continued in the same strong voice, "We met around noon at the synagogue, about twenty of us, mostly men my father's age like Uncle Moe, except two of my friends from school were there. *Kristallnacht* was on all our minds. We took the train downtown and got off at 79th and Lexington. It was one o'clock. We were standing around, waiting to join the parade, when I saw my sister's fiancée. He's a reporter for the *World Journal* and was posing as a Nazi."

There was a rustling from the row of reporters. This was news. A reporter, posing as a Nazi, had been at the site of the murder.

"What is this reporter's name?" Dewey asked Saul.

"Harold Apple," Saul said. There was a gasp from the spectators.

The judge gaveled once, twice. The courtroom quieted. O'Rourke whispered to Harold, "They remember your by-line."

"Is he in the courtroom now?" Dewey asked Saul.

"Yes. There he is." The redhead pointed back to the section where the newsmen were penned. The reporters around Harold, even O'Rourke, shifted an inch or so away from him, as if they didn't want to be contaminated.

"What happened when you saw Mr. Apple? Did he say anything to you?"

"He said there might be trouble, and he was right," said Saul.

"Will you tell the court about this trouble, Mr. Schwartz?" Dewey asked.

"We were marching up Lexington, past the intersection of 85th. There was a line of police on our right, and beyond them I could see lots of people. There was noise, music, people shouting. I could hear snatches of German. Then it started, at first just a few, but moments later there was a hail of rocks. The men I was marching with, the Gluskers, were falling all around me. A big stone, bigger than a baseball, hit Uncle Moe on the side of his head. I know because it bounced and I caught it. Moe stumbled while crying out to me, 'Cover your head.' I saw more rocks hit him. They left his head all bloody." Saul paused, tears welling up in his eyes. "I went to him. I wanted to protect him. I was too late."

"No further questions, your honor," Dewey said.

It seemed that everyone in the courtroom let out a collective sigh, a release, a blown breath of tension. The judge sharply rapped his gavel once, looked to his right, and said, "Mr. Kergan, your witness."

Kergan approached the witness stand. "Mr. Schwartz, did you see where the rocks came from?"

"All I could see was a lot of rocks coming from the right, over the police line." Saul paused, and said, "Something else, the police were all facing us, as if we were the trouble makers." There was a gasp from the spectators and a rap of the gavel.

Kergan plowed right through the noise. He had a point to make. "You did not see the defendants throw any rocks, did you?"

"No sir."

"No further questions, your honor," Kergan said.

"Please call your next witness, Mr. Dewey," said Judge Giordano.

District Attorney Dewey conferred with the bailiff, who loudly called out, "Harold Apple, come forward."

Harold remained rooted in his seat as faces turned toward him. The Nazis glared at him with murder in their eyes. *Why wasn't I on the witness list,* the reporter wondered? *Did Dewey know it would get out?* He slowly rose and walked to the front of the room. The bailiff escorted him to the witness stand, beneath the judge's bench, next to the jury box, and directly opposite the defense table, where Everhardt and Groening speared him with hateful looks. Further back were the public galleries. Sally sat on the edge of her seat, looking proud and anxious at the same time, her brown pageboy flying as she turned from her father to her mother. Saul sat contentedly smiling, as if aware that he had done his part and was now waiting for Harold to carry on. All the cast, the Drabinsky women, the Gluskers, O'Rourke and the other reporters, Willknecht, Fritz Kuhn and assorted Nazis, Sheriff Acton, Consul Mendelsohnn, were in the room waiting for Harold to speak. All the faces swam before him, his loves and his hates, those he had tricked and those he had confided in, expecting him to be an actor in the drama. "Do you swear to tell the truth, the whole truth, and nothing but the truth?" the bailiff asked.

"I do."

Dewey began the questioning. "Please state your name, age, place of residence, and occupation for the court."

"My name is Harold Charles Apple. I'm twenty-six years old. I live in The Bronx and am employed as a reporter by the New York *World Journal.*"

"In your job, did you have an assignment involving the German American Bund?" Dewey was the soul of reasonableness as he began the questioning, but he had an intense look in his clear eyes, as he paced in front of Harold, back and forth, back and forth.

"Yes," Harold answered, then began to tell of his experiences as a reporter posing as a Nazi. "On the morning of Armistice Day I went to work at the printing plant. Max Finnhandlerr was my foreman. He was also the head storm trooper of the Yorkville branch of the Bund. Finnhandlerr told me that morning about the Jewish march. He learned about it from someone at the Yorkville police precinct. Of course, the Bund was marching at the same time. That is when he ordered me to spy on the Jews."

"Did you?"

"Yes."

"Did you write of this in the newspaper?" Dewey's eyes narrowed as he asked this question. He examined Harold closely.

"Some. Not all. Nothing about the spying. My editor and I knew there would be legal action, this trial, and we didn't want to prejudice the outcome." *I don't think the DA likes reporters,* Harold thought. *He probably puts us in the same class as Nazis, interlopers in his neat little world.*

"So what you are going to say has not been aired in public. Precede, Mr. Apple."

"When Finnhandlerr asked me to be his spy he also said he wanted to smash some Jewish faces."

"Was that the first time you suspected the Bund was planning violence?" Dewey asked.

"Objection." Kergan was on his feet, his forehead beaded with sweat. "The District Attorney is leading the witness."

"Overruled," the judge said calmly. "Answer the question, Mr. Apple."

"Yes, that was the first time I had heard anyone in the Bund clearly advocate violence, but I'd heard a lot of anti-Semitic talk. Everyone seemed to hate Jews."

"Objection," shouted Kergan. "That's not pertinent."

"Sustained," said the judge. "Strike the last statement from the record. Mr. Apple, we're not interested in opinion. Just answer the questions."

"Continue with your account of that afternoon, Mr. Apple." Dewey patiently led Harold back to the narrative.

God damn, we're talking about Nazis here, Harold thought, still upset with Kergan for his interruption. *Everyone knows they hate Jews.* He took a deep breath to calm himself, then began speaking again. "I took a subway up to 79th and Lexington after I left work. It was about noon. There were very few people on the street, even though that corner was supposedly the starting point for the Jewish parade. I felt confident in reporting to Finnhandlerr that the German parade would be much bigger. I started walking toward 85th and York where I'd arranged to meet him. He was standing with Fritz Kuhn and Reinhold Stubble when I got there and reported that there wasn't much of a Jewish presence on Lexington Avenue. Kuhn was very excited. I think he wanted to run his own pogrom."

"Objection," Kergan quickly piped up. "That is editorial opinion."

"Sustained," said the judge. "Stick to the facts, Mr. Apple."

"Well," Harold continued, "I remember Kuhn told Finnhandlerr to 'let the OD have a little fun' with the Jews."

"And the OD are the storm troopers?" Dewey asked.

"Yes, the *Ordung Dienst,* the Service Order, patterned after

Hitler's SA. And Kuhn unleashed them on what he thought was a small Jewish parade." Anger rippled in Harold's voice.

"Where were you when the violence erupted, Mr. Apple?" Dewey said.

"I was standing by the platform set up on the sidewalk in front of the Turnhall. The German marchers were coming up 85th toward Lexington where they were stopped by the massed OD in front of the stand. Behind the storm troopers the police had Lexington blocked off for the Jewish parade. It was very noisy; lots of band music, lots of shouting, lots of singing. Kuhn was starting to speak when I looked over my shoulder for some reason and saw these disciplined, uniformed men, members of this so-called Service Order, reaching into their pockets for rocks. There were more than a hundred of them throwing rocks over the heads of the police into the heart of the Jewish parade. It went on and on for, it seemed like, hours. Then they rushed through the police line into the middle of the Jews. Most were on the ground, cowering under the hail of rocks."

"Mr. Apple, you said you saw all of the storm troopers throwing rocks," Dewey said. "Did you recognize any of them individually?"

"Earlier, I saw some I knew."

"Did you see either of the defendants?" Dewey asked.

"Yes. I saw Werner Everhardt in the back row minutes before they began throwing the rocks." Harold looked at Everhardt. The storm trooper, not so frightening in a red tie and ill-fitting brown suit, was halfway to his feet, his face red with rage. He was being restrained by Kergan.

"Did he go anywhere, leave the storm trooper formation, at any time before the rock throwing incident?" Dewey questioned.

"No, I would have seen him leave. What I did see was all of the storm troopers throwing rocks, Everhardt among them," Harold said.

"And what of Klaus Groening?"

"No, I did not see him. I did not even know him at the time."

"Your honor, I wish to submit the police report of the incident as Exhibit 1 and the medical report from New York Hospital on the treatment of Morris Drabinsky as Exhibit 2. I have no more questions of the witness at this time," Dewey said, surrendering Harold to cross-examination.

"The court notes the exhibits. Your witness, Mr. Kergan," said the judge. "Do you wish to cross-examine?"

"Yes I do, Judge. Mr. Apple, you are a reporter. Is that correct?"

"Yes."

"And you are also Jewish," Kergan continued. "Is that not so?"

"Yes."

"Would you say that a Jewish reporter who has infiltrated the German American Bund is going to be an objective reporter?"

"I don't see what objectivity has to do with my job," Harold said. "I was a reporter on assignment. My job was to find out what was going on inside the Bund and report on it. There was certainly no lack of material." *Come on Dewey, object,* thought Harold. *The judge wouldn't let me mention pogroms, but Kergan makes snide anti-Semitic remarks with impunity. Real fair trial!*

"Did you report on what was good in the Bund?" Kergan asked.

"No, of course not. My editor wasn't interested in things like that, only in the evil, like the prevalent anti-Semitism and the authoritarian, anti-democratic structure of the leadership." *He's fishing,* Harold thought. *He doesn't know where to attack my testimony and I even got in something about anti-Semitism. Not that it will make any impression on this jury but it makes me feel better.*

"How long had you known the defendant, Werner Everhardt, before you saw him at the parade?" Kergan asked.

"I met Everhardt on Wednesday night at the Yorkville Casino. The parade was on Friday. I knew him two days."

"Was he wearing his uniform when you met?"

"No."

"Did you have a conversation with him at the time?"

Harold glanced up at Everhardt, who had a smirk on his face. "No, we didn't talk on Wednesday night."

"What were you doing at the Yorkville Casino that night?" Kergan asked.

"I went there with a friend to have a drink."

"Mr. Apple, you say you recognized Werner Everhardt among the OD at 85th and Lexington after meeting him only once, when he was not wearing his uniform, and you had been drinking. Are you sure that was Werner Everhardt you saw?" Kergan asked. There was triumph in his voice.

"I never said I met him only once," Harold said. "I ran into him, in full storm trooper uniform, in front of the Germania Bookstore, not more than one hour before I saw him and his fellows stoning the Jewish parade."

Kergan quickly relinquished the witness and Harold stepped down. *Guess I gave the little coot more than he could handle.* He glared at the Bund lawyer. Kergan glared right back.

Dewey gave the bailiff the name of his next witness. The bailiff exited the courtroom and returned a few minutes later with a frail looking woman, her grey hair wrapped in a bun. A deputy helped her walk, with halting steps, to the witness stand. She took the oath in a high, thin voice.

"Please state your name, age, place of residence, and occupation for the court," Dewey asked.

"My name is Bertha Mae Goldtwaith. I'm seventy-one years old. I am a retired teacher and I live at the corner of 85th and Lexington." There were gasps from the spectators.

Is this Dewey's big surprise? Harold thought, watching the trial from his old seat next to O'Rourke. No one objected when the reporter came in and sat with his fellows. But Bertha was sequestered, kept separate from the trial. All the other witnesses had points of view, for or against. What will Bertha have to say from her perch above the Turnhall?

"Where were you on the afternoon of Friday, November 11th?" Dewey asked.

"I spent that day at home, looking out the window. There were parades going on, you know."

"Please tell the court exactly where you live and what view you had of those parades."

"Yes Mr. Dewey. I live at 116 East 85th Street, second floor, directly opposite the New York Turnhall. I've lived there for 10 years, since the building was new. I have a corner apartment and my living room has windows on both Lexington and 85th. That is how I was able to watch both parades. I had my window on the Turnhall open a bit so I could hear the speeches. I don't know but a few words of German but I love to listen when it's spoken. The language sounds beautiful and authoritative at the same time."

"Mrs. Goldtwaith, you witnessed the incident known as the Yorkville stoning. Tell us about it."

"I was looking across the street at that fat man, who was speaking in German." Mrs. Goldtwaith pointed at Fritz Kuhn, sitting in the midst of his followers. "I was surprised out of my wits by all those rocks flying through the air, right in front of my nose. I looked down and saw all these boys in uniform—I thought they were boy scouts—throwing rocks at the other parade. I noticed one boy with bright red hair sticking out from under his cap. I love red hair on boys. My husband had red hair."

"Mrs. Goldtwaith, just tell us what you saw," Dewey said gently. "The red haired boy, was he throwing rocks?"

"He threw a rock. I watched it arch over the police and hit a man standing in the middle of Lexington. He was standing right next to another red haired boy, who caught the rock after it knocked his friend down. I looked back to my other window and saw the first redhead and his friend, right next to him, throw two more rocks. They hit the same man as before, on the head, and down he went. Then the boys in brown uniforms rushed right past the police and into the other parade."

"Mrs. Goldtwaith, do you see anyone you described in the courtroom today?"

"Why yes I do, Mr. Dewey. There is the first boy, the one who was in uniform. I couldn't miss his bright red hair." The old lady pointed at Klaus Groening, whose face turned as red as his hair. "And his friend is sitting next to him," she said, pointing at Werner Everhardt, not looking up at the witness but instead examining his fingernails.

"Did you see what happened after the men in uniform rushed the police, Mrs. Goldtwaith?"

"I saw one of the red-haired boys, the one in uniform, cut by flying glass. I'd moved over to my other window to watch and was leaning out when, right beneath me, a store window—it was a dress shop I frequent—exploded. It must have been hit by a rock or maybe someone ran into it. The redhead was running by. I saw him put his hand to his neck and blood spurted out. I was scared by the flying glass so I pulled my head back in and closed my window. I pulled my drapes and didn't see any more."

"Thank you, Mrs. Goldtwaith," Dewey said. "I have no more questions." He smiled at Kergan as he relinquished the witness.

Now I remember where I saw Groening before, Harold thought. *It was at the hospital. I saw a redheaded Nazi bleeding from his neck and being a big baby to the nurse who was trying to help him. Finnhandlerr would have thrown him out of the storm troopers if he had seen the way Groening was blubbering and carrying on, just like his name.*

"Do you wish to cross-examine, Mr. Kergan?" the judge asked.

"Yes, your honor. Mrs. Goldtwaith, did you tell the court that you are seventy-one years old?" Kergan, a scowl on his face, was not happy.

"Yes sonny, I certainly did say that very thing."

"And would you say that you have all your faculties, madam? I notice you wear spectacles."

"Objection," Dewey said.

"Overruled," the judge replied. "Witness will address her vision."

"Nothing wrong with my vision, Judge," Mrs. Goldtwaith said. "I may move a trifle slower than I used to but I wasn't doing much moving, maybe window to window, but the glass was clean and my eyes are good."

"But with all the excitement that afternoon and you looking on from a distance might you have misidentified the defendants, Madam?" Kergan asked.

"Sir, I was as far from those two that afternoon as I am now," the witness said, pointing at the pair slouching at the defense table maybe fifteen feet away from her. "The only difference is that I was above them that afternoon. They were standing on the curb, in front of my window, when they threw those rocks. I identified them in a police lineup and I can identify them now."

"I have no further questions," said a frustrated Kergan.

"Call your next witness, Mr. Dewey," said the judge.

The bailiff retrieved the witness from the sequestration room.

"Please state your name, age, occupation, and place of residence to the court," said Dewey.

"My name is Diane Eudora Dimpelkoff. I'm thirty-one years old and am employed as a nurse in the emergency room of New York Hospital. I live in Long Island City, Queens."

"Were you on duty in the emergency room the afternoon of November 11, 1938?" asked Dewey.

"Yes, I was on the swing shift that day. I came on at three in the afternoon."

"Did you treat a young man named Klaus Groening that afternoon?"

"Yes. He came in with a bunch of people, some seriously injured, right after I came on duty. He had a deep gash on his neck and some lesser cuts on the side of his face. I understood that he had been hit by flying glass and that someone at the scene had stopped most of the bleeding with compression. He was very upset and abrasive towards me," recalled the nurse.

"Your honor, I wish to submit the medical report on the emergency room treatment of Klaus Groening as Exhibit 3," Dewey said. "I ask the court to note that the defendant has scars on the left side of his neck and face. Are these scars consistent with the type of injury you treated, Miss Dimpelkoff?"

"Yes they are."

"No further questions, your honor."

"Mr. Kergan, do you want to cross-examine?" Judge Giordano asked.

"No, your honor."

"Very well, Mr. Kergan, Mr. Dewey, we will continue after lunch. Court is recessed until 2 o'clock."

Decorum dissolved as the court recessed and the spectators, reporters, and lawyers rushed for the one exit. "What do you think of Dewey's strategy now?" O'Rourke asked Harold, as the two, caught in the mass of bodies, struggled toward the exit.

"I don't like it," Harold said as he pushed toward Sally. "Let's see what tricks Kergan pulls before we celebrate a victory. Maybe it's Dewey, maybe it's the judge, maybe it's because I know the defendants and their crowd so well. Kergan has an angle somewhere. I feel it." At the exit Harold met Sally and they left the court building arm in arm. He was still sweating right through the January chill. *I testified against the Bund,* he thought with some alarm. *Can they get revenge?*

⁂

It was shortly before two o'clock and the courtroom buzzed with conversation. Precisely at two, Judge Giordano entered, bearing an armload of papers, and the room hushed. "Superior Court is now in session," The bailiff announced.

"Over lunch I received a friend of the court brief from the House Committee on Un-American Affairs," the Judge said, gesturing at the papers he had deposited on his desk. "I conferred with Mr. Dewey and learned that it pertains to the testimony of his next witness, so I will allow it to be entered and a synopsis will be read later."

"What does a Congressional committee have to do with this trial?" Harold whispered to O'Rourke. "Are they investigating the Bund?" The dapper reporter shrugged.

The bailiff knew that law enforcement officers were not sequestered. He strode forward. "Will Sheriff James T. Acton of Sussex County, New Jersey come and be sworn in."

"You have responded to many complaints from the German American Bund at Andover, New Jersey—is that correct, Sheriff Acton?" Dewey asked.

"Yes I have."

"Do you know the defendant Werner Everhardt?"

"Yes."

"Will you tell the court the circumstances of your last meeting with Everhardt?"

"It was right after Thanksgiving, Monday, November 28th, when I saw Everhardt last," Acton said. "The day before several Nazis, Everhardt among them, came to my office to file a complaint about vandalism at their camp. They also said that a young woman had been abducted but had escaped her captors. Now, we don't have a lot of crime in Sussex County, not like here in the big city. On Sunday we only have one deputy and myself to cover the entire county, so when I heard that it was just some broken windows and the only victim had already escaped, I told those guys I would be out Monday morning to investigate. Their leader, a big guy by the name of Finnhandlerr, accepted that, but Everhardt was upset. I'd seen him before when I was out to the Bund camp, even learned his name because I figured he might be a troublemaker."

"Objection," Kergan said.

"Sustained," Judge Giordano agreed.

"I like to know who might cause trouble in my county. Sometimes it comes in handy. In any event, Finnhandlerr got that hothead calmed down and they left."

"What happened on Monday, Sheriff?" Dewey asked.

"I went to Andover Township first thing Monday morning with one of my deputies. When we got to the camp we found about a dozen men, all bundled up against the cold, throwing stones at a bulls-eye they'd nailed to a tree about twenty yards from the main building. Well, we didn't think nothing of it, so Ben, that's my deputy, and I walked right on by, looking for the caretaker, a fellow named Gus Klapprott. He took us to look at the broken windows in some cottages down at the bottom of a hill. There was some furniture broken up too. I looked around for evidence but didn't find anything, just some dead leaves trampled and some tire tracks where someone drove through mud on a back road out of the camp. Me and Ben trotted back to the main building where Klapprott gave me written statements from the lady who was abducted and from Finnhandlerr. We walked out the front door, stopped for a minute to catch our breath, and watch the fellows throwing stones. They were good. Almost every throw hit the target. Everhardt himself hit three bullseyes in a row. He was talking, all loud and boisterous, boasting about his fastball. He said the target wasn't far enough away, how he'd cut down that old Jew on Lexington Avenue at a longer distance. Now the newspapers had been full of stuff about the Yorkville Stoning. It had happened about three weeks before. And being that I was in the War, I was interested. I knew that the Everhardt guy was indicted in the case so it didn't take much effort to know he'd just made a confession. I called District Attorney Dewey and told him what I'd heard."

Dead silence in the courtroom was broken by Dewey. "The state rests." Everhardt jumped to his feet, reporters scrambled for the exit, the spectators burst into babble, and the judge gaveled for order.

"Your witness, Mr. Kergan," the judge said, after pounding his gavel for five minutes to get some order in the court.

"Sheriff Acton, you are the chief law enforcement officer of Sussex County, New Jersey. Is that correct?" Kergan asked.

"Yes, that is right. I am the sheriff."

"As such, do you expect the court to trust you, to take you at your word?"

"Yes I do."

Kergan stepped back and cocked his head as if he couldn't believe what the sheriff had said. "How do you explain your role as perpetrator of the criminal acts you were ostentatiously investigating at the Bund camp? You, and your men, broke up those cottages and kidnapped that woman."

Dewey was on his feet. "Objection your honor, Sheriff Acton is not accused of any crime."

"Let me rephrase my question, your honor," Kergan said. "Sheriff Acton, you told the court of some remarks you claim the defendant Everhardt made, and you overheard, while you were at the Bund camp investigating kidnapping and vandalism. I contend you never intended to pursue this investigation because you and your cronies had committed the crimes. Your revelation of Everhardt's supposed boast is a red herring, designed to draw attention from your own nefarious activities. Whether you are prosecuted is not relevant to this proceeding. But I ask you, ladies and gentlemen of the jury, how can you believe this supposed enforcer of the peace who may stand accused of breaking New Jersey law?"

Audible gasps came from every corner of the courtroom.

Reporters stampeded for the telephones. Judge Giordano pounded his gavel, the tightening of his jaw visible. "Bailiff, bar the door. Do not let anyone into the hallway. Mr. Kergan, to elicit information from the witness you have to question him. I, for one, wish you would get on with it. Before you continue however, now is the time to read this Friend of the Court brief which I received from James Gilbert, Chief Consul of the Un-American Affairs Committee of the U.S. House of Representatives."

"Ah ha," said Harold to O'Rourke, it all makes sense now. This is why Sheriff Acton was willing to expose his activities at the camp. He's got support from Washington.

The crowded courtroom hushed. "Mr. Gilbert says that Sheriff Acton is working for Chairman Martin Dies of the Committee on an investigation relating to the German American Bund but not focusing on the matter before this court," Judge Giordano read from a paper in front of him. "The illegal activities of the sheriff were undertaken as part of this investigation with the full knowledge and approval of the FBI. The Chairman does not wish to reveal any more information about the subject of the investigation, but an announcement will be forthcoming in the very near future. Mr. Gilbert goes on to say that the content of this announcement will have no bearing on this proceeding. He concludes by saying that Sheriff Acton is a fine man. Mr. Kergan, does this information pertain to the questions you were about to ask the Sheriff?"

Kergan looked stunned. "Y-yes y-your honor," he stuttered. "C-can I have a recess?"

"Considering the lateness of the hour, I believe now is a good time to adjourn for the day," said the judge. "We'll resume at ten tomorrow morning."

CHAPTER TWENTY-FOUR

GUILTY OR NOT

THE DEFENSE BEGAN to present its case in the morning. Harold slumped into his seat, big bags under his eyes, as Stubble made his way to the witness box. O'Rourke looked at him skeptically. "What the hell is the matter, Harold? You look awful."

"I didn't get any sleep last night," Harold said in a low voice.

"Why not? More tummy troubles?"

"No. I'll tell you later."

Kergan strode confidently forward to question Stubble. "How many uniformed OD were there in front of the Turnhall that afternoon?"

"There were one hundred men lined up in ranks before the platform."

"Did they all begin throwing rocks at the same time?"

"No. None of them threw rocks."

"None of them," Kergan feigned surprise. "We've heard testimony that rocks were thrown."

"Maybe, but not by my men," Stubble said.

"Do you know the defendants, Everhardt and Groening?"

"Yes, I do."

"Did they throw rocks?" Kergan asked.

"No."

"No further questions, your honor," Kergan said.

The man has no conscience, thought Harold. *He laughs at his daughter's funeral and he lies now.*

"Your witness, Mr. Dewey," said the judge.

"Mr. Stubble, you said the defendants didn't throw any rocks. How do you know?" Dewey asked.

"I ordered that there be no violence." Stubble sat in the witness chair ramrod straight, his chin pugnaciously thrust forward. "It would dishonor the memory of fallen German soldiers."

"Yesterday we listened to Sheriff Acton testify that he heard the defendant Everhardt boast about the killing."

"Objection." Kergan was on his feet, his face red.

"Sustained," said the judge. "Mr. Dewey, we are in cross examination, not final arguments. It appears you're talking to the press, the jury, the spectators—anyone but the witness."

"Your Honor, I am addressing the witness and the rest of the court. May I continue?" Dewey's face was as red as Kergan's had been.

"By all means, Mr. Dewey."

"Mr. Stubble, you say you ordered the storm troopers not to throw rocks. Yesterday we heard several witnesses say that rocks were thrown by storm troopers. Have you considered that the men disobeyed your order? Storm troopers have been known to throw rocks."

"They threw no rocks," Stubble insisted.

"I'm through with this witness for now," Dewey said, a disgusted expression on his face.

"Will you get the next witness from the witness room?" the Judge asked the bailiff.

A short man, looking uncomfortable in a crisp blue suit, his close-cropped gray hair crowning a meaty pug-nosed face, lurched his way to the front of the room. His ill-fitting pants, too long by over an inch, forced him to dance down the aisle, hopping from one foot to another.

"Who could this be?" O'Rourke said in a low voice. "An eyewitness, a character witness, a clown?" He gave Harold a crooked smile.

"I guess Kergan still has some surprises left," Harold whispered back.

"Will you please state your name, age, occupation, and place of residence for the court?" Kergan asked.

"My name has been Magnus Xavier Shaughnessy for the past fifty-eight years. I'm proud to say I've worked for the Pennsylvania Railroad for forty years, thirty of them as a brakeman. But now I'm slowing down so I'm only working half time, going out one week and staying home the next."

"And where do you live Mr. Shaughnessy?"

"I live at 116 East 85th Street, number 311."

Shaughnessy lived at the same address as Mrs. Goldtwaith, across the street from the Turnhall. *I know exactly what his story will be,* Harold thought. *He'll say he saw no rocks thrown the afternoon Moe died.*

"And I was home the whole week when Armistice Day rolled around," Shaughnessy continued. "I was getting kind of restless after not working all week so I was looking forward to watching the German parade. It was something to do, you know."

"Where exactly is your apartment in relation to the Turnhall?" Kergan asked.

"I'm on the third floor, right across the street."

"Your honor, I've prepared a diagram of the intersection of 85th and Lexington. With the court's permission..." Kergan displayed a large chart, like an engineering site plan, showing

Shaughnessy's apartment, marked in bright green, directly opposite a large red box, representing the reviewing stand. There were black swastikas, yellow Jewish stars, and a line of blue police dots representing the actors in the drama.

"What a waste of time," Harold whispered to O'Rourke.

Kergan turned to his witness. "Mr. Shaughnessy, what were you doing on the afternoon of Friday, November 11, 1938, between one and three? Were you in the apartment marked in green on the chart?"

"Yes sir, I was in my apartment watching the parade."

"Mr. Shaughnessy, will you tell the court what you saw when the speeches started, particularly the speech by Fritz Kuhn." Kergan pointed at the swastika in the center of the red square on the chart, then at the real Kuhn, seated in the first row of spectators directly behind the defense table. "Do you remember this man?"

"Yes, I remember him. He was wearing a uniform that day. Just as he started speaking the wind died down. Without the wind his voice positively boomed out. I don't understand German but I listened anyway; there was something about the way he spoke that made me listen. I peeked out my window to see if other people were listening as hard as I was and I saw the brown-uniformed men, all crowded together like a forest."

"That's a popular Nazi image," Harold murmured to O'Rourke. "On You Brown Battalions, on like Teuton's endless forest. I bet Shaughnessy was coached."

"That man," the witness pointed at Kuhn, "stopped speaking, just as everyone shoving from down the street broke up the police line and pushed the cops out of my sight onto Lexington Avenue. I didn't lean out the window, not even a little, because I didn't want to risk a three story fall. I watched over 85th for a while but I guess all the really exciting stuff was going on around the corner. It sounded like it anyway. The men on the platform disappeared. I suppose they went into the Turnhall. That's all I saw."

"Thank you Mr. Shaughnessy," Kergan said, sounding confident in the story his witness told. "Did you see any rock throwing?"

"No sir."

"Are you sure?"

"As sure as you're standing there, sir," Shaughnessy confirmed loudly.

"No further questions, your honor," Kergan said, relinquishing the witness.

"Mr. Dewey, your witness," said the judge.

Dewey approached the witness stand while thumbing through a thin file of papers he held in his left hand. "Mr. Shaughnessy, I have in my hands the reports on the interviews the police conducted with residents of your building on Saturday, November 12, 1938, the day after the Yorkville stoning. I will submit your report as an exhibit to the court in a few minutes, after I find it again. Ah yes, here it is. It seems Detective Knapp came to your door at nine that morning. Do you remember that?"

"No."

"You don't remember talking to the police at all?"

"Well...maybe," Shaughnessy said hesitantly.

"Did you tell the detective the same story you told the court?" Dewey asked the witness, who was now visibly sweating in the heat of the courtroom.

"I don't remember what I said to the cop. I don't remember talking to him at all."

"Did you have any other contact with the police?"

"No."

"Mr. Shaughnessy, I'm interested in how you came to testify before this court if you don't remember an interview with the police. Can you explain?"

"I don't remember talking to no cop. That doesn't mean my memory is bad. When Mr. Kergan came around, a week later,

I told him what I saw that day, just like I told everyone here," Shaughnessy said belligerently.

"Mr. Shaughnessy, I want to read you what Detective Knapp wrote in his report after seeing you." Dewey paused for a moment, twirled his pencil mustache, and continued. "And I quote, 'Occupant of Apartment 311 came to the door in an obviously inebriated condition. When questioned about the events of yesterday, subject claimed to have been home all day, but to have seen or heard nothing unusual. Subject was quite intoxicated, appeared to have been drinking for several days, and will be of no use to this investigation.' I wish to submit this police report into evidence, your honor."

"So noted," said the judge.

Turning back to the witness, Dewy asked, "Do you deny being drunk the day of the parade and the stoning incident?"

"Yes sir. I was not drunk. I only had a few that day."

"No further questions, your honor."

"I wish to call German Consul-General Johann Mendelsohnn next," Kergan said.

"Is Consul-General Mendelsohnn present?" the bailiff called, knowing that foreign officials were not under the same rules as citizens, and would be in the courtroom.

The diplomat leveraged his bulk out of a seat amongst the spectators and lumbered toward the witness stand. The bailiff swore him in.

"Consul Mendelsohnn, were you on the reviewing stand in front of the Turnhall the date of the parade?" Kergan asked the florid-faced diplomat.

"I was sitting in the second row, directly behind *Bundesfuehrer* Kuhn," said Mendelsohnn. "I was there in an official capacity, honoring the noble German soldiers of the late war.

"Tell the court what you saw of the incident, sir."

"The platform was not in the best position for speech-making, most of the people were off to the left, jammed together as they marched into a dead end. To our right the police had Lexington Avenue barricaded so the Jewish parade could pass. *Bundesfuehrer* Kuhn rose to speak, blocking my view of the *Ordung Dienst* and everything in front of the platform. During his speech I did see, off to my right, that the weight of the people packed into the street had breached the police line, creating a chaotic situation. Those of us on the platform withdrew into the Turnhall at this time."

"Did you see any stones thrown?"

"No. The *Bundesfuehrer* was blocking my view, of course. He is a rather wide man, as you can see." There was tittering from some sections of the courtroom, where Germans sat. "All I saw was, to my left, gallant German soldiers in dress uniforms and their lovely ladies, all pressing forward to hear the words of their leader, and to my right, members of the equally gallant *Ordung Dienst* being forced through the police line by the press of bodies."

"Despite your seated position behind the standing Fritz Kuhn who, as the court will note, is quite ample, don't you think you should have seen rocks flying through the air?"

There was laughter in the courtroom as Kuhn himself stood and bowed to the defense attorney, demonstrating his girth for all to see.

Mendelsohnn harrumphed as if he resented the attention of the court being drawn elsewhere. "Yes, one would think I would have seen rocks. However, I saw none."

"Based on your observations," Kergan asked, would you say that not many rocks could have been thrown?"

"Objection," cried Dewey. "Counsel is leading the witness."

"Sustained," said the judge. "Mr. Kergan, you're putting words in the mouth of the witness."

"I'm sorry, your honor," Kergan said, not sounding apologetic at all. "I have no further questions of the Consul-General."

"Your witness, Mr. Dewey," Judge Giordano said as the pros-ecutor stepped to the railing of the witness box.

"Consul-General, you represent the Government of the Third Reich in New York. Will you tell the court of your background and how you came to be appointed to this important post?" Dewey eyed the corpulent diplomat coldly, his jaw set, his mouth tight, his thin moustache bristling.

"I was a professor of modern German history at the univer-sity in Berlin when Foreign Minister Von Ribbentrop asked me to serve the Fuehrer," Mendelsohnn said, disdainfully returning Dewey's frigid stare. "I want you to understand Mr. Dewey that I am here willingly. I cannot be forced to participate in American judicial proceedings."

"The people of New York appreciate that you are here volun-tarily," Dewey said, smiling slowly. "All that we are doing in this court is trying to arrive at the truth. You can further that quest by answering a few questions. Number one, is it true that Foreign Minister Von Ribbentrop is a boyhood friend of yours?"

"Yes, that is no secret."

"Number two, why is it that your boyhood friend person-ally ordered you to testify for the defense at this trial?" Dewey was happy to give the diplomat something substantial to sweat about.

"W-w-why, because the defendants are German," stam-mered Mendelsohnn.

"Wrong. They are both naturalized American citizens," said Dewey. He turned to address the judge. "Your honor, I wish to sub-mit as exhibits three cables between Consul-General Mendelsohnn and Foreign Minister Von Ribbentrop, all dated in November of last year. In the first, dated November 15, four days after the ston-ing incident, the Foreign Minister asked whether Mendelsohnn was present at the Turnhall, and if so, what he saw. The second, dated November 23, from Mendelsohnn, is the most important. In it the Consul-General states that he saw the beginning of the incident, with all the storm troopers throwing rocks, before he left the reviewing stand with the other dignitaries. The last cable is from Von Ribbentrop. It is dated November 28, well after the indictments for Everhardt and Groening were handed down. It states that Mendelsohnn should contact the defense attorney and offer to testify that he saw no rock throwing."

"Enter them into the record," the judge told the court reporter. "Mr. Dewey, will you tell the court how you came to be in possession of these documents?"

"Your honor, I do not wish to divulge my sources in public. The documents are genuine and I will tell you in private, if you wish, how they came to me."

"I object," Kergan shouted.

"I overrule you on this one, Mr. Kergan. Proceed with the cross-examination," said the judge.

"They walked right into it," O'Rourke whispered to Harold. "Dewey knew Mendelsohnn would ask Kergan if he could testify."

"But where did those cables come from?" Harold asked his friend.

"I gave them to the District Attorney."

"But where did you get them? Oh no, from Mendelsohnn's secretary, right?" Harold smiled for the first time since the trial had begun.

Dewey continued the questioning. "Consul Mendelsohnn, do you remember the cables in question?"

"Why…yes, vaguely. I do recall something." Mendelsohnn was now perspiring freely.

"Why do you suppose the Foreign Minister, your friend, would ask you to perjure yourself? Do you think he did it on his own initiative or after discussions with others? Perhaps he consulted with Adolf Hitler. Maybe the Nazis are embarrassed by the Bund."

"Objection, your honor," Kergan said, trying to gain his witness some time to catch his breath. "The Consul-General is a guest in our courtroom and the prosecutor is overwhelming him with hostile questions."

"Sustained," Judge Giordano agreed. "Please slow down, Mr. Dewey, and keep your questioning pertinent."

"Consul Mendelsohnn, how many of the storm troopers did you see with rocks in their hands, throwing them at the Jewish parade?" Dewey asked.

"All of them," said the diplomat.

"No further questions, your honor."

"This is a good time for a break," said the judge. "We will reconvene after lunch."

"Court is adjourned until two o'clock," the bailiff announced.

Dewey is crafty, Harold thought. *He lured Mendelsohnn into admitting a lie.*

❦

The two reporters had lunch at the courthouse cafeteria. "Why didn't you get any sleep last night, Harold?" O'Rourke asked. "Did Sally keep you up?"

"No, I was burning up the transatlantic cable. I found out that our friend the judge has family in Italy. His brother is high up in the Fascist Party, real buddy-buddy with *Il Duce*."

"How the hell did you find that out?"

"You're not the only one with sources in this town. I've got a friend who knows Judge Finkelstein."

"Chief Judge of the Superior Court—I'm impressed."

"Yeah, put that together with what I overheard in the john yesterday and I'm sure the fix is in. But what can we do about it? Not a damn thing. Giordano will be subtle. He'll entertain objections when he should overrule. He'll let Kergan get things in that the jury shouldn't hear. He'll slant instructions. This jury isn't going to be sympathetic to an old, dead Jew anyway. Not the way it's set up. Imagine, a million Jews in New York and not one fit for jury duty."

Before returning to court Harold phoned Sally at her office. "Hi honey, Dewey cross-examined Mendelsohnn before lunch. O'Rourke held out on me. He gave Dewey some documents which really embarrassed the fat slob."

"Saul and I want to be there when the verdict comes down, Harold. When is it going to the jury? Should we come tomorrow?"

"It depends on how things go this afternoon. We'll talk about it tonight, Doll."

The judge entered the courtroom as the afternoon session came to order with the defense still presenting its case. "Proceed with your next witness, Mr. Kergan," he said.

"Your honor, my witness is just entering the building," said Kergan. "It will take him a few minutes to get up to the courtroom."

"That is reasonable," Judge Giordano said. "Court will recess for ten minutes."

Harold stood and stretched. *Who will the witness be? Someone who saw the parade, no doubt, although only those who had been near the reviewing stand had been able to see everything. Maybe Kergan has discovered another overhead witness.*

O'Rourke nudged Harold in the ribs. "Do you know this guy coming in with Kuhn?"

"Of course!" Harold cried. "It's Max Finnhandlerr. He was there." The head storm trooper moved gingerly down the center aisle. The big man, diminished by his injuries, was no longer larger than life. He settled painfully into the witness chair.

The judge returned to the bench while Kergan conferred with the bailiff. "Court is now in session," the official announced. "Max Finnhandlerr is on the witness stand."

"Please tell the court your name, age, occupation, and place of residence," Kergan said.

"My name is Maximillian Finnhandlerr. I am thirty-eight years old. I was chief foreman at the printing plant of the New

York *World Journal* until recently. I live at 7157 York Avenue but soon will be returning to Germany."

"You have been hospitalized for over a month with injuries received in a weightlifting competition and have to return to the hospital when you are finished testifying. Is that correct?"

"Yes," said Finnhandlerr.

"Sir, I will try not to tire you," Kergan said in a gentle, sympathetic manner. "Do you hold an office with the German American Bund?"

"Yes, I am the leader of the *Ordung Dienst*, the Service Order."

"What are your duties?"

"I am the leader of the OD. The men take their orders only from me."

"You said you worked at the *World Journal*. That is the same newspaper that employs Harold Apple, who testified at this trial earlier. Do you know Mr. Apple?"

"Yes. He worked for me in the printing plant during the month of November. He was a good workman and I thought he was a good German. I had no idea he was a reporter...and a Jew." The storm trooper spit out the last word, as if it left a vile taste in his mouth.

"What was his role on the afternoon of Armistice Day?"

"He had joined the OD so he was under my orders. I told him to watch the Jews and report back to me. They were coming to our neighborhood and we wanted to know what to expect." Finnhandlerr started coughing violently.

Kergan looked up at the judge and said, "Patience, your honor."

"Of course," Judge Giordano said. waving his hand as if to indicate they had all the time in the world.

After a few minutes Finnhandlerr composed himself and began speaking again in a weak voice. "And, and, and that despicable reporter came to me and told me that the Jewish parade was very small, almost beneath our notice, and I need make no special preparations to meet it."

"What do you mean by 'special preparations,' Mr. Finnhandlerr?"

"If I had known there was going to be such a large crowd confronting us on Lexington Avenue, I would have positioned my men differently and cautioned them not to confront the Jews."

"Then you did not order the men under your command to throw rocks?" proposed Kergan.

"No. Whoever threw stones did on their own."

"Do you think Apple acted provocatively in not telling you the truth about the Jewish parade?" Kergan asked loudly.

What! Objection! Objection! Harold half-jumped to his feet before O'Rourke caught his arm and pushed him back down while slapping his other hand across his mouth to stifle the outcry that might get him thrown out of court. "That wasn't how it happened," Harold whispered to his partner. "Kergan is blaming me for the rock throwing."

Finnhandlerr continued. "Yes. If I had known that so many Jews were there I would have ordered my men not to provoke them."

"I have one more question. Did you see the defendants, Everhardt and Groening, throw any rocks?"

"No. They were standing in the first row of the formation, right in front of the reviewing stand. I saw no one in that row throw anything," Finnhandlerr said emphatically.

"No further questions, your honor."

"Why, oh why, didn't Dewey take the trouble to interview me?" Harold whispered dejectedly to O'Rourke. "I remember talking to Finnhandlerr at Jaeger's, after I returned to Yorkville from Moe's funeral, and he all but admitted to ordering the OD to carry rocks."

"Maybe Dewey did make a mistake not talking to you,"

O'Rourke replied. "But I don't think it will make any difference. The defense case is so full of holes that those two are all but in jail."

"I hope so," Harold said, gripping the armrests of his chair. "But I still feel the fix is in. Here comes Dewey. He should rip Finnhandlerr apart."

Dewey approached the witness. Finnhandlerr smiled wanly, as if he was ready for the cross-examination to end before it began. *What a strange look for him to have on his face,* Harold thought. *This isn't the pugnacious giant I know.*

"Mr. Finnhandlerr, you are the leader of the storm troopers; is that not correct?" Dewey asked.

"Yes, I am the leader of the *Ordung Dienst,* the Service Order."

"Now as I understand the Nazi leadership principal, the *fuehrerprinzip* I believe you call it, all authority devolves from the top, from the leader. Is that correct?"

"Yes."

"Yet you say that the few rocks that were thrown, were thrown on the initiative of underlings, men operating without orders, 'on their own' as you put it. How could that be?" Dewey was incredulous, astonished at this breach of Nazi discipline.

"That is the way it happened," Finnhandlerr woodenly replied.

"I suggest that you ordered your men, all your men, to carry rocks in their pockets and to throw them at a prearranged time. No rocks would have been thrown otherwise. You are responsible for the death of Morris Drabinsky, although you have not been charged. You were acting on orders from your superior, the leader of the German American Bund, Fritz Kuhn, who wanted to emulate his German master, Adolf Hitler, by having 'a little fun' with the Jews!" Dewey roared out his indictment of Hitler, Kuhn, and the Nazi Party. "That is the way it happened, is it not?"

"Well...I do not know. I cannot say," Finnhandlerr mumbled, intimidated by the suddenly ferocious prosecutor.

"Where were you when the rock throwing began?" Dewey asked, his words dripping with venom.

"On the platform, listening to the *Bundesfuehrer*." Finnhandlerr looked weary; his diminished strength was deserting him.

"And did you retreat to the safety of the Turnhall at that time?"

"Yes."

"Yet you claim that Everhardt and Groening threw no stones. Could they have thrown rocks after you left the platform?" Dewey asked, his voice no longer hostile, but almost friendly.

"No...uh, I mean yes, yes, it could have happened that way," Finnhandlerr said, confused by Dewey's suddenly reasonable manner.

The District Attorney pounced. "You first claim the defendants threw no rocks, then admit leaving while the throwing was still going on. Which one was it?"

"I can't say." Finnhandlerr looked confused, not the decisive giant Harold knew but a shriveled, injured man who should not have left the hospital.

It appeared Dewey saw he would get no more from a sick man. "No further questions, your honor."

"Mr. Kergan, do you have any more witnesses?" the judge asked.

"I have no more witnesses, but I wish to submit one exhibit," Kergan said. "It will take several minutes to prepare and will require the assistance of the defendant, Klaus Groening. Do I have the court's permission to retire to a private room for a short time?"

"Objection," Dewey said in a perfunctory manner, as if he knew he would be overruled.

"Objection overruled," the Judge said and he continued, "the request is unusual, but this has been an unusual case. Permission granted. The court will recess for five minutes."

An excited babble rippled through the courtroom as Kergan, his client, and a guard exited. The judge sat at the bench staring stonily ahead. Harold noticed Stubble reaching across a railing to give the other defendant, Everhardt, a pat on the shoulder. "What kind of trickery is Kergan up to now?" O'Rourke asked.

A door creaked slowly open. Everyone turned. There, in the entrance, stood Groening, in full storm trooper regalia. He goose stepped down the center aisle, jackboots creaking loudly in the silence that otherwise enveloped the courtroom. Kergan followed. The two stopped in front of the bench, Groening at attention. Kergan spoke. "Your honor, the defendant is wearing the formal uniform of the *Ordung Dienst*, the same uniform worn at the parade on Armistice Day. Ladies and Gentlemen of the jury, I want you to imagine one hundred men dressed in the same uniform, in formation on 85th Street. Now think of the difficulty in identifying any one member of that group. Please note that Mr. Groening is wearing a campaign hat, which covers his red hair completely. The only question I have to ask, is how did any witness follow a red-haired man throughout all the melee of that day, when that man was wearing a hat which hid his hair and she was looking down from a second floor window? The defense rests."

The courtroom was in an uproar. The Nazis applauded the ploy of Kergan. Others moaned. Reporters choked the exit, trying to get to a telephone. The judge banged his gavel.

"Closing arguments in the morning," Judge Giordano shouted. "Court is adjourned."

As the jury filed out, plaintive voices could be heard from the spectators. "What does it mean? Are they guilty? Imagine the nerve of that lawyer parading the swastika in court."

Harold and O'Rourke made their way to the pressroom. "Those two storm troopers are going to fry," said a man from the *Daily Mirror*.

"Don't be so sure," a *Post* reporter cautioned. "Juries do strange things, especially in a strange case like this."

◆

In the morning Harold, Sally, and Saul traveled downtown together. They met O'Rourke in the corridor outside the courtroom. "Pat, I want to sit with Sally and Saul today," Harold said. "Can you carry on alone?"

"Sure," Pat replied. "I'll take care of the story. You guys take care of yourselves."

Sally and Harold followed Saul down to the first row in the public gallery, where they sat with craned necks, watching the spectators file in for the verdict, the hoped for rending of the Nazi Bund. The Nazi contingent entered. Kuhn, Stubble, and Willknecht were there, joined by Consul-General Mendelsohnn. Kergan stood at the open door and motioned for them to take seats to the left, away from Harold.

Minutes later Ida Drabinsky and her two children entered the courtroom, all dressed in black. Howard looked stiff and uncomfortable. Harold hadn't seen him in months, since just after his father's death. "Is this the first time Howard has been out?" he whispered to Sally.

"I think so," Sally said, astonished to see the boy with his mother and sister. "I hope this will be the end and Howard can get better."

The defendants, faces as pale as their white shirts, filed in, accompanied by the bailiff. They were followed by Thomas Dewey and his prosecution staff. The jury filed in. The judge, black robe billowing, took his seat behind the bench. The bailiff called out, "Hear ye, hear ye, Superior Court of New York County, New York State, is now in session, his honor Judge Dominic Giordano presiding. All rise."

The short thickset Judge tapped his gavel and everyone sat. "I take it that the prosecution and defense are finished presenting witnesses. Is that correct, Mr. Dewey, Mr. Kergan?" Both attorneys nodded ascent. "We are ready for closing arguments. Mr. Dewey, if you please."

"Your honor, ladies and gentlemen of the jury, the defendants are charged with second degree murder because they did not plan to murder Morris Drabinsky. What they did plan was to sow mayhem among a group of peaceful marchers. The murder was the result of that. The Jewish War Veterans had a legitimate purpose in planning their parade just as the German American Bund had every right to march. Our Constitution guarantees the right to 'peaceful assembly.' Note the word—peaceful. When that right is disturbed by violence Americans should feel assaulted. When that disturbance is combined with vicious race hatred, all Americans should feel violated."

Dewey is enjoying this, Harold thought, as the prosecutor paused for breath. He was that kind of politico. Defending American values—free speech, right of assembly and so on—gave him a warm feeling. *But he didn't do his job. He didn't prove Everhardt and Groening killed Moe.*

"Over the last two days," Dewey continued, "we have seen the facts of this case. Morris Drabinsky, exercising his rights of free speech and assembly, was cut down by two thrown rocks, as witnessed by Saul Schwartz. Harold Apple witnessed a group of uniformed men, the Service Order of the German American Bund, all throwing rocks. He identified the defendant, Werner Everhardt, among that group. Bertha Goldtwaith witnessed the red-haired Klaus Groening, whom she also identified in a police lineup, as one of the men who threw the rocks that killed Drabinsky. She also said that Groening was not wearing a hat that covered his red hair, and that he and Everhardt were together all throughout the incident. We heard a nurse who corroborated Mrs. Goldtwaith's identification of Groening. We heard Sheriff Acton of Sussex County, New Jersey testify to Everhardt boasting of his role in the incident, saying that he killed Morris Drabinsky. We heard that Consul-General Mendelsohnn of Germany saw all the uniformed storm troopers throw rocks. The medical evidence shows that Drabinsky died from blows to the head. Saul Schwartz witnessed those blows."

"There is no doubt as to the guilt of these men. The only question is, why did they do it? What is there about Nazi ideology that turns men into cold-blooded killers? The jury is asked to find the two defendants guilty of murder, as is appropriate, but no charges have been brought against those really responsible, the leaders of the German American Bund and their Nazi masters in Berlin. These men, led by Fritz Kuhn in America and Adolf Hitler in Germany, have instilled hatred into their followers, making them willing tools in a campaign to Nazify the United States. The State of New York is asking you, the jury, to send a message to the leadership of the Bund and the Nazi Party, and find the defendants guilty as charged, guilty of sowing hate and discord in the fabric of American society. You have the opportunity to uproot this abomination by finding Werner Everhardt and Klaus Groening guilty of second-degree murder." Dewey turned from the jury to face the Judge. "Your honor, the prosecution is finished."

So Dewey is sticking to his guns, Harold thought, *prosecuting the Nazis for their ideology as well as their crimes. It'll never work.*

"That was a good speech, wasn't it Harold?" whispered Sally, not sounding sure of herself at all. "I don't understand why Mr. Dewey is making such a big deal about what the Nazis think. Everyone knows they hate Jews."

"That's exactly what I'm worried about; Dewey is going for the hate and ignoring the killers," Harold said. "There's a good case there but Dewey hasn't found it. I hope the jury can. Some of them were frowning while Dewey spoke and one actually looked like he was sleeping. Here goes Kergan. I think he's just begun." Harold leaned forward and returned his attention to the drama.

Kergan stood by the jury box, leaning on the rail in front of the foreman, and spoke in a conversational tone of voice. "Ladies and gentlemen of the jury, we are at the end of a trial for murder, a trial of two men who were arbitrarily picked for persecution simply because they were nearby when the victim was killed. There were one thousand people at the scene of the killing, yet none of them has been accused, only the two defendants. How did the District Attorney know that Klaus Groening and Werner Everhardt are the killers he wants? I do not know!" With his last four words, Kergan raised his voice in protest.

"Mr. Dewey has presented witnesses who claimed that all of the *Ordung Dienst* threw stones. I have presented witnesses who claim that none threw stones. I will not go so far as to call those who testified for the prosecution liars. I am sure that they testified truthfully, to the best of their ability, as have the witnesses presented by the defense. But perceptions differ, and in a mob scene like the one at 85th and Lexington on November 11th, with one thousand people packed together like sardines, I am frankly surprised that any observer had a coherent picture of all that took place. As Mr. Shaughnessy testified, some of the action took place around the corner, out of his field of view. No one person saw everything, and I firmly believe that no one person can paint a complete and accurate picture of the events which led up to Mr. Drabinsky's death. For the prosecution to pick Werner Everhardt and Klaus Groening out of one hundred *Ordung Dienst* members present that day and say, 'You are responsible for this man's death, you two, and you alone,' is ridiculous. What's more, it is irresponsible, a perversion of justice."

Kergan paused for a moment before continuing. "One witness for the prosecution testified, not about events on Armistice Day, but about a conversation that occurred weeks later. Sheriff Acton claimed to have overheard Werner Everhardt, who he admittedly considers a troublemaker, make an incriminating statement. But I do not understand how Mr. Everhardt could have known he was responsible for Drabinsky's death, since he was on one side of the police line and could not possibly have seen the victim fall. Everhardt was boasting, not stating facts, and is not a murderer. In conclusion, I ask you to find my clients not guilty. The evidence the prosecution has presented does not alter the presumption of innocence to which Mr. Everhardt and Mr. Groening are entitled." Kergan bowed slightly to the jury, nodded to the Judge, and walked slowly back to his seat at the defense table.

Harold did not even listen to the Judge give his instructions to the jury. "Damn, damn, damn," he muttered softly to himself. "He lost it. Kergan and the judge don't have to do a thing. Dewey lost it, all on his own."

"Harold, please have some faith," Sally whispered back. "The jury will do the right thing."

Saul overheard his sister. "Harold, we've gotta be positive." He patted Harold on the shoulder.

Harold shook off the touch. *They don't know. They're innocents. My father would know. Izzy would know. Jews don't get the breaks.*

The afternoon dragged on while they waited for the jury to make their decision. Harold and Sally played word games. Saul read 'Romeo and Juliet' for English lit. O'Rourke, who had moved over from the press area, when most of the reporters adjourned to a poker game in the pressroom, polished his stories, one version for innocent and one for guilty.

At two o'clock, after deliberating for three hours, the jury sent a note to the Judge to clarify his instructions.

The waiting continued, too long for Sally and Saul. "Harold, we're going home," Sally said. She rubbed her big brown eyes, reddened by the dry heat of the courtroom. "Call me if they reach a verdict tonight."

"I'll call if it's not too late," Harold promised.

"Good-bye, my darlin'," O'Rourke said playfully as Sally squeezed by him to the aisle. "If I don't see you tomorrow, I'll see you at your wedding. He shook hands with Saul and turned to Harold. "Where do you want to go to dinner now that the women and children are abandoning us?"

At that moment, with Harold kissing Sally good-by in the half-empty courtroom, the prosecution and defense tables both empty, and the judge absent, the Foreman led his fellows out of the jury room, into the courtroom, and announced to the sleepy bailiff, "We have a verdict." The official, startled awake by the news, rushed off to find the judge.

The defendants were the first to return, followed into the courtroom by their Nazi supporters. They were led by Kergan, marching confidently to his place in front of the bench. Everhardt came in, his head held high, arrogance in his stride. Groening followed, looking less confident. Kuhn, Stubble, and the rest straggled in, faces expressionless, except for the looks of hate they directed at Harold.

Hard on the Nazis' heels were the members of the fourth estate. Alerted by the noise in the corridor, eleven reporters abandoned their card game, and rushed in to join their colleagues in the courtroom.

Over the next few minutes, spectators returned, called in by the bailiff or the guards. Cynthia Drabinsky came to sit next to Sally while her mother, unable to control her emotions, stayed in the ladies lounge. Finally the district attorney arrived, trailing several young aides. Tight-lipped, his thin mustache bristling, Dewey quickly stepped to his place at the front of the room, nodding curtly to Kergan as he took his seat. The bailiff, back from his hurried search for court officials, announced in an out-of-breath voice, "All rise for the Honorable Dominic Giordano."

The judge entered from the back, sat down with a rustling of his robe, and motioned everyone else to do likewise. "Mr. Foreman, do you have a verdict?"

"Yes," the foreman replied. "The jury has found the defendants not guilty."

The Nazis whooped and hollered. The judge pounded his gavel. The reporters scrambled for the telephones. Sally sobbed quietly. Saul's face grew hard with anger. But it was Cynthia Drabinsky, her face an emotionless mask, who put the trial in perspective when she said, "The only justice for a Jew is among our own."

Chapter Twenty-five

RALLY AND REVENGE

THE NAZIS WERE celebrating George Washington's birthday with a rally at Madison Square Garden, and New York's finest were prepared. Wooden barricades were strung out along 49th Street to the south and 52nd Street on the north. Entrance to the area in between was restricted to rally ticket holders. Police Commissioner Lewis Valentine spoke on radio station WOR that afternoon. "I'm going to have 1,500 men there. That's the largest contingent of police assigned to any event in the city's history. If anyone makes trouble they'll be arrested so fast their heads will spin."

Harold heard the broadcast in the city room, where reporters, re-write men, and copyboys crowded around the battered old Philco by the teletype machines. *Good,* he thought, *the police aren't taking any chances. Who knows what could happen?* Shaking his head, Harold pulled on his gloves, pushed open the door of the World Journal Building, and headed uptown for the rally.

Harold met O'Rourke at a pre-arranged spot on the way. Caught in the crowd of Nazi ticket holders surging up the sidewalk on Eighth Avenue, the two reporters fought to the curb near

West 50th, outside the Garden. They clambered over splintery sawhorses and sprinted across the wide avenue, dodging potholes, automobiles, and the attention of mounted officers on the corner. On the far side they huddled against a boarded-up storefront, hands deep in their pockets against the cold. On the other side of the street they could hear the buzz of German being spoken, or rather roared, as many *Seig Heils* rang out, while police horses snorted and whinnied. The rhyming chant of many voices shouting anti-Nazi slogans could be clearly heard.

"I'm staying out here," O'Rourke yelled over the din. "It looks like there'll be a lot of action. You go inside."

Harold looked at O'Rourke. In the shadowy light thrown by the street lamps his partner's nostrils flared and his steamy breath exploded into the cold air. *He's a police reporter,* Harold thought. *He craves action. Long speeches aren't for him.* "Okay. Go see what's happening down there." He pointed down the block to where a knot of mounted officers confronted a large group of protestors on the other side of the barricades. "That's why Aaron sent two of us. I'll meet you at the office later."

O'Rourke ran off and Harold pulled his hat down to hide his face, crossed the street, and handed his ticket to the attendant, who was dressed in the hated uniform of the OD.

Harold hadn't been eager to cover the Nazi rally. "I've done my time, boss," he'd said when Aaron asked him. "Let O'Rourke do it. Better yet, let that new guy, Krumbein, go to it. He knows German."

"You know the Bund, Harold," Aaron had said. "You have to do it. I can't let you go on living in a dream world. Are you worried about your safety? Is that it? What happened to the reporter who'd do anything for a story?"

"That reporter has changed Boss. He's getting married next month." But Harold had heard, from Christiana, via Saul, that the Nazis weren't thinking of him anymore. He had been defeated.

Kergan was smart, I've gotta admit. The hat thing ruined Dewey's case. He moved with the crowd into the cavernous arena, past officious storm troopers, all wearing their campaign hats. *Mrs. Goldtwaith didn't testify about hats. Why should she? Groening's hat didn't cover his hair. But the jury didn't believe that, especially after Kergan's trick, showing off Groening with his hat pulled way down.*

Harold stood inside the hall, staring at the spectacle before him. There were flags plastered everywhere, above the high-rising seats, on the facing of the balconies, even hanging from the dimly lit rafters: Old Glory next to the Nazi banner. Rows of folding chairs, set up on the floor of the arena, stood before a large platform dressed in red, white, and blue. On the wall behind the platform were three gigantic banners lit by spotlights, dominating the hall. The center flag bore a full length portrait of Washington. The father of the country was flanked by two enormous black swastikas, on round fields of white, with blood red backgrounds. Old George was dressed in Continental uniform, blue frock coat with gold epaulettes and piping, white tights and black boots. He was holding a black tri-corner hat with a blue and white cockade.

It's a heroic picture, Harold thought. *But it's not the familiar Washington, the friendly George from the dollar bill, the guy with high forehead and arching brows over clear eyes. No, the Nazi George is a cruel character. Look at his squinty eyes and hard mouth. Personally, I think it's the company he keeps.* Harold let himself be carried by the crowd to the front of the hall.

The press section was guarded by a small cadre of storm troopers, half a dozen young men in well-creased brown uniforms, all wearing campaign hats, standing at attention around a rope barrier. Harold scanned their faces as one examined his ticket. *I don't know any of them,* he thought with relief. He pulled his floppy hat down some more and turned up the collar of his overcoat, as if he was feeling a chill. "Brrr, it's cold in here," he said to the OD man in front of him as the trooper gave him back his ticket. Storm troopers ringed the arena, standing every few feet around the perimeter of the hall. On stage they stood shoulder to shoulder. He saw faces he knew. *Up on stage, there's Everhardt. He looks arrogant as ever. There's Groening. I bet he hasn't had that hat off since the trial. Who's that next to him? The big guy, wait, he's turning around. It's Schroeder. He must be out on bail till the Zucker trial. God, I'd like to wipe that sneer off his face.*

The press gallery was almost full, with reporters from local and out-of-town papers competing for seats. Haywood Broun, the well-known columnist, was saving two seats in the front row. "Buzz off, Apple. They're mine." Harold retreated to a seat in the next row, nodding to friends as he sat down.

From his seat in the front, Harold turned to see the Nazis thronging the arena. From all over the city they came, ordinary looking men and women loudly proclaiming their love of Fatherland and *Fuehrer*. The room shook with their shouts—*Seig Heil, Seig Heil, Seig Heil!* The sound eddied and swirled around him. The air shimmered with the noise. *I can cut it,* he thought, *cut it with a dagger.* He looked at the seats above him. Thousands of boys were yelling and holding daggers, the daggers they were presented upon joining the Hitler Youth.

Precisely at eight o'clock the lights dimmed. A lone spotlight shone on the stage and a black clad figure appeared. Shards of lights reflected off silver trim. *He's wearing the eagle of an OD Leiter,* Harold thought, squinting at the familiar insignia, trying to make out a face beneath the brim of that high peaked hat. The figure's hand came up, palm out. Nineteen thousand throats roared then quickly fell silent as the leader stood at attention.

The only sound, other than thousands of people breathing deeply, came as a door opened directly behind the stage. The spotlight shifted a few feet to illuminate a pair of women, one plain and one stunning. Harold recognized the ordinary one but only had eyes for the superb blond, dressed in a red evening gown, her bare shoulders shaking with laughter. "Hush, my dear, hush," he heard Dorothy Thompson—for she was the plain woman—say, as the pair moved into the auditorium toward where Harold was sitting, transfixed.

"Over here girls," Heywood Broun yelled loudly. "Our seats are right here." The two women moved to the row before Harold and sat. The spotlight returned to the black clad figure on the stage.

What is Dorothy Thompson doing here? Who's the gorgeous dish she's with? Why are they both with Haywood Broun? These questions roiled Harold's mind as he closely studied the bare neck and shoulders and back of the beautiful woman sitting right in front of him. Miss Thompson had a reputation but compared to the beauty she was with, she was invisible. *That's it!* A consideration grew in Harold's mind. *She wants to be invisible. Everyone knows Dorothy Thompson hates the Nazis. Ever since her interview with Hitler in 1931, when she called the Fuehrer a 'little man,' she's been persona non grata with the Nazis. She would be taking her life in her hands if she waltzed in here alone, but in the company of a beautiful woman she goes unnoticed, and can report on the rally. Not that she's ugly or anything, but that blond with her is va-va-voom. It's a better trick than my masquerade.*

Harold's own masquerade had become well known since the trial. All the papers reported on it, of course, much to the annoyance of Aaron, who felt Harold's charade belonged to the *World Journal*. But Harold hoped that in the month since the trial he had been forgotten. He jammed his hat over his ears again.

Attention in the arena returned to the stage when the spotlight left the women. The storm troop leader introduced the first speaker, Hermann Schwinn, leader of *Gau* West, the West Coast department of the Bund. *So this is a Hollywood Nazi,* Harold thought. Schwinn was matinee idol handsome, tall with straight black hair and an aquiline nose on a square-jawed face.

"I was born in Berlin in 1904," Schwinn was saying, "too

young to fight in the war, but not too young to know of the humiliation of peace. My parents wished to forget, however, so they brought me to America in 1919. Now, you may ask yourselves, why am I a leader in the Bund, when I am so young, when I speak unaccented English, when I am, so obviously American. I will tell you. *Ich bin ein Deutscher.* I have never forgotten who I am and why I am here. I am German!" The building shook with applause.

Schwinn continued. "We all know who planned the humiliation endured by all Germans in 1918, the same brutes who run the city I call home. Hollywood must be liberated from the filthy Jew bosses, just as our *Fuehrer* has liberated Germany. I abhor the influence Jews have on America, not only because I am a proud German, but because I am American. George Washington warned of entanglements with foreigners, yet in this century the United States has allowed itself to become entangled, nay, ruled by a race of outsiders, the most foreign of the foreign, who only care for their own power. The mission of the *Amerikadeutscher Volksbund* is to alert the American people to the Jewish conspiracy. We will not be silent!" Wild applause swept through the arena.

The next speaker, Eduard Wheeler-Hill, secretary of the national Bund organization, began talking about the radio priest, Charles Coughlin. "Father Coughlin is the only one on the radio today who speaks the truth," he bellowed out for all of Madison Square Garden to hear. "Radio is dominated by the likes of Winchell and Cantor, Benny and Bernstein, Jews all. Jews run the newspapers. Jews run Hollywood, producing all the movies our children see. Jews are bastardizing the American people. Do you want your son to marry a Jewess? Do you want your daughter to marry a nigger? Of course not! The only way to combat this creeping bastardization is by enrolling your boys in the *Jugendschaft* and your girls in the *Madelschaft*, so we can give them the antidote to the poison which surrounds them in the air of America." This speech drew cheering, louder and wilder than anything that had come before. A band began playing a stirring march, one Harold recognized from meetings at Yorkville Casino. Fritz Kuhn, dressed in his finest *Bundesfuehrer* uniform, rose and marched to the podium.

"Herren und frauen, comrades, I am so happy to see you here today. Your presence, in such great numbers, leads me to believe that the swelling tide of National Socialism will soon overtake this great nation, just as it has overwhelmed the Fatherland. I know that George Washington would approve." A tidal wave of applause washed over the platform, lapping at every nook and cranny of the hall, and deafening the occupants of the press gallery. Kuhn paused. An enormous smile split his broad face beneath his tiny campaign hat. His massive belly quivered with pride under his brown jacket decorated with silver lightning bolt insignia and gold trim.

The hall gradually grew silent. Thousands of enraptured listeners awaited the next words of their leader. "The Bund stands accused of being un-American, but it is our detractors who are un-American. We stand for purity, purity of the people. Our enemies would mongrelize the people. Our enemies, led by the Jews, seek power over all aspects of American life. George Washington would spin in his grave if he knew of the terrible things that Roosevelt and his Jewish clique have planned for this country. Washington owned Negro slaves. His successor, Roosevelt, wants to elevate Negroes in his government to rule over white Americans. Washington believed, rightly, that the lesser, darker races were made to serve the white race. Jews are the demons of America. They pose as white men, yet have the souls of niggers. Jewish carpetbaggers turned loose wild niggers on upright white women after the War of Northern Aggression. Today Jews control all the newspapers and movies, centralizing their devilish message to all the good people of this land."

Nineteen thousand throats roared their approval of Kuhn's words. Only one protested. A rich, full belly laugh rose above the clangor of hate spewing from Kuhn's lips. The high-pitched sound spread to every nook and cranny of the Garden from the first row of the press section, where Dorothy Thompson was convulsing with uncontrollable laughter. An alert technician focused a spotlight on the woman whose sniggering, cackling, and gurgling, had smothered Kuhn to dumb silence. A dozen storm troopers leapt from the stage and advanced menacingly on the still chuckling woman. An expectant sound, like thousands of tiny whispers, shrilled through the hall. Heywood Broun stood up in front of Miss Thompson but was crudely thrust aside. "It was funny! What he said was funny!" protested the woman in a piercing voice as two burly storm troopers picked her up by the elbows.

A dozen men in dark blue uniforms rushed down the aisle towards the confrontation, breaking through the brown barrier around the columnist. "Gentleman, we will escort the ladies out," a police sergeant announced loudly to the storm troopers. Tense looks were exchanged until the Nazis backed off. Miss Thompson slowly stood on her own two feet, shook herself off, and slowly walked down the main aisle, the center of a clump of blue. She was accompanied by her friend in the red evening gown with Mr. Broun trailing behind. The press gallery relaxed. The last thing the reporters wanted was a riot, with them at the center. Harold was stunned by the quickness of the incident. *I've gotta see what happens,* he thought. He pushed past a startled storm trooper and ran up the aisle, battling through waves of sound that threatened to knock him off his feet with their intensity.

SEIG HEIL! SEIG HEIL! SEIG HEIL!

Several reporters followed Harold. There was a small exodus from the press gallery, right in the middle of the leader's speech. Kuhn glared at them but kept talking.

⁂

The scene that greeted Dorothy Thompson and her escort when

they reached the street was chaotic. The protestors had breached the police lines further up the block and were now taking a position across the street from the Garden. Some of them were testing the police with forays onto the pavement. The police horses were getting skittish at all the activity.

Miss Thompson and her friends came flying out the door right into the arms of Pat O'Rourke and Captain Wells, commander of the police on the west side of the building. They'd been surveying the threat posed by a dozen young protestors taking turns running onto Eighth Avenue carrying a large American flag.

It was a game on the street. One young man, overcoat flying, would dash out, dodging the sparse traffic, holding the flag high. A mounted officer would try to catch him but the protestor was too fast for the horse, which had to maneuver among the cars. "We've got to close off the street," Wells was complaining when he caught an armful of young woman wearing a bright red evening gown. "Is this high society come to watch the fun?" he said,

"God damn Nazis chased us out," Thompson cried. She caught O'Rourke's arm to stop from tumbling to the sidewalk. "I must have lost my heel. Hey, I know you."

"Pat O'Rourke at your service, Miss Thompson," the reporter said, bowing with a flourish. He grinned at the laughing policeman, who was cradling Miss Evening Gown in his arms.

"That's good of you, O'Rourke," Thompson replied, brushing a strand of hair out of her eyes. "We need a taxi. Miss Wolf wants to go home. Then I want to go back in there." She hooked a thumb over her shoulder.

"Maybe I can help," Captain Wells said. "Let's walk to the corner, Miss Wolf. We'll find you a cab there." Winking at O'Rourke, the officer took the well-proportioned blonde by the arm and led her away.

"What's going on in there, Dorothy?" O'Rourke asked, while

watching as his friend led the young woman through a line of police toward West 50th Street.

Dorothy Thompson squinted at O'Rourke, adjusted her skirt, and said, "It was funny in there Pat, it was really funny. There they were, those Nazis, strutting around in their fancy uniforms, like peacocks, enjoying all the free speech of Americans, while they were boasting about how they would abolish those rights when they took over. I couldn't help laughing. And then those goons manhandled us. It turned frightening in a hurry."

Heywood Broun appeared at the entrance to the Garden, Harold by his side. "Dorothy, come back in," he called. "I told the Nazis that if they don't let you back in they'll get a black eye with all the papers in New York."

Dorothy Thompson gave O'Rourke's hand a squeeze. "Don't underestimate the power of the press, Pat. See you later."

"Yeah, see you later, Pat," Harold called out as he turned and followed Thompson and Broun inside.

O'Rourke turned back to the street just in time to see a mounted cop finally catch one of the flag-wavers, a young woman dressed like a sailor in blue bell-bottom pants and a navy pea coat. The policeman, a frenzied look in his eyes, grabbed the flag away from the girl and, leaning over in his saddle, began beating her on the head with his nightstick. She fell to her knees and a dozen of her friends rushed into the street. They surrounded the officer's horse and tried to pull him to the ground. Three more mounted men galloped up as police on foot ran to meet the demonstrators. *A riot's brewing out here,* O'Rourke thought. *It'll be better than the one inside.*

⁓

What was happening inside was a one-sided assault on the absent. Kuhn beat on Jews and Negroes until they were bloody. "These *untermenschen* claim the same rights as honest citizens yet they do no work," the *Bundesfuehrer* was saying. "The rich *Kikes* live off the work of Aryans. The poor niggers live off the dole. The niggers and the *Yids* should live together. They can clean up each other's filth."

Harold only half listened to the monotonous refrain spewing from Kuhn's mouth—subhuman, sheeny, mongrel, monkey. Kuhn had been flaying the Jews for almost an hour and the reporter was bored, tired, and half-deaf from the Nazi cheers. He looked around the auditorium, trying to pick out interesting people and how they were reacting to the venomous tirade. There was one young man who, with his *frau,* looked well-bred, he in a brown double-breasted business suit, she in a tailored green skirt with sequined white sweater. They were sitting on the aisle, across from the press gallery, and the reflections from the wife's sparkly sweater were getting in Harold's eyes whenever a roving light captured her. *Spotlights and noise are the hallmarks of Nazi rallies,* the reporter thought, recalling an article he'd read about the Nuremberg party rallies. *But those two sure don't look like most of the people filling the hall. What hold can the Nazis have on such a stylish couple? They don't look like greenhorns right off the boat. I wonder how many people like them are here?* He started looking people over more closely, at least those sitting nearby, seeing how they were dressed, whether they were young or old, even if they looked like Germans. *I should know who's here, for my story.*

Turning in his seat to inspect more of the audience, Harold saw a shadowy figure running in a crouch down the center aisle, toward the glare of the platform. The young man in the double-breasted suit had a better view. He started to yell.

Then Harold heard Double-Breasted's shout through the roar. "Watch out! He's got a gun!"

The young man jumped to his feet. His wife, a look of horror on her face, grabbed his coat and held him back. "Hermann, no! You will be killed," she wailed, cutting through the noise in the arena. Kuhn stopped speaking. A spotlight rotated off him to the drama that was unfolding just a few feet away. The gunman stopped running. He lifted his Lugar for all to see. Thousands of hands were frozen in mid-clap, thousands of throats were frozen in mid-scream. The gunman aimed and fired at Kuhn. Three familiar storm troopers stood at the edge of the platform between the gunman and Kuhn. One had bright red hair sticking out from under his campaign hat. Harold could see the arrogance in the second one's eyes. The third wore what looked like a police billy club stuck in his belt. They all faced the pistol at point-blank range. **BANG...BANG...BANG,** three shots in quick succession, three storm troopers fell. The gunman bounded onto the platform.

For a long second the echo of the shots reverberated through the hall. The gunman stood on the stage, pointing his pistol at the podium where Kuhn was lurching from side to side. Storm troopers rushed him, hoping to get there before he fired again.

But time stood still for Harold. He knew the fallen storm troopers. Everhardt and Groening hadn't escaped punishment, and Schroeder had died with them, saving New York the expense of trying him for Morty's murder. A fitting fate for a trio of ruthless men. And the author of their fate was—Howard Drabinsky. Harold recognized Howard when he leaped onto the stage. *Where did he get the Lugar and how'd he learn to shoot?*

Time moved again in the arena. Howard was wrestled to the ground. Kuhn was on his feet over the fallen young man, kicking the gun away. "Strip him," the *Bundesfuehrer* snarled to the closest storm trooper. "Let us see if he is Jewish scum, like that one in Paris."

Howard's pants were ripped from him. Storm troopers grasped him by the arms and legs and paraded him around the stage so all Germans could see his circumcised penis. Howard's bearers stumbled over a storm trooper body and dropped him—right next to where Everhardt lay, lifeless eyes staring upward.

The bullet had punched through Everhardt's forehead, leaving a hole which oozed blood. His mouth was untouched, still curled in a sneer. A small trickle of blood flowed from one downward-pointing corner. Howard hit the floor facing Everhardt. He took one look at the wide-eyed face of death and spat. Nazi blood and Jewish spit mingled on the raw pine boards of the stage.

Police rushed into the auditorium. They fought through the storm troopers to find Howard lying on the floor, naked from the waist down. Kuhn stood over him, pointing at the young man's penis, a mad look on his face, a cackle coming from his lips. *"Jude, Jude, Jude, Jude…"*

The reporters were on their feet, trying to see. Harold stood on his chair, with the best view of all. Howard, wrapped in red, white, and blue bunting from the waist down, was dragged from the stage and up the aisle by the police, while the Germans jeered. *That's it! All wrapped up and tied with ribbon,* thought Harold. *That's the end of Everhardt and Groening, neat, clean, and with Schroeder thrown in for good measure. Howard got his revenge. But at what price? His life is over, done, '30', behind bars with nineteen thousand witnesses. Then again, he didn't have much of a life. It ended the day his father died.*

CHAPTER TWENTY-SIX

THE END OF A LONG JOURNEY

MARCH 19, 1939. Europe marched in lockstep towards war. German-Polish negotiations broke down, as the Nazis charged that Germans in Poland were the victims of abuse. Hitler, in a towering rage, cried out, "I am not responsible for the outcome if affronts to German dignity do not end." And Harold and Sally were getting married.

Harold, getting dressed for the wedding, was thinking, *what a dismal world. All the wars, Japan and China, and who knows what Russia is going to do?* A big battle is going on right now on the Manchuko border between the Soviets and Japan. They say it's the biggest tank battle ever. Sure are a lot of 'biggest' these days. They all involve war. Killing is easier these days. The Nazis kill Jews whenever they get the chance. Howard Drabinsky kills. He goes into a nest of Nazis and cuts down storm troopers as easy as one, two, three. And the Nazis try to gin up another Kristallnacht over it. Revenge seems to be the order of the day. Howard has his and now Tom Dewey is casting around for a target. He indicted Kuhn for tax evasion, again. Let Dewey have his pound of flesh; he deserves it after what Kergan did to him. *And, in the middle of all this uproar, Sally and I are getting married.*

Harold, humming the wedding march, was adjusting his tie when there was a loud knock on the door. His father and father-in-law-to-be, wearing dark suits and white carnations in their lapels, had come to escort him to synagogue. "Well Harold, today's the day," Izzy said.

"How is Sally doing?" Harold asked.

"She's fine," Izzy said. "A little nervous, but that's to be expected."

"Harold today is a special day," Sam said with pride in his voice. "We have a wedding to celebrate, but also, today is the day our family is out of Germany."

"When is Uncle Hiram getting here?" Harold asked, eager to meet this mythic figure, a man who knew the camps.

"He's in London. We heard late last night," Sam said. "Your uncle Simon was so excited when we got the telegram. He thought for sure the Nazis would detain Hiram again."

"Simon is going to be at the wedding, isn't he? I'm eager to meet him too."

"Yes, he's probably at the synagogue already," Sam replied.

Amidst all the talk of family refugees there was one person Harold had forgotten about. "Where's my best man? Wasn't he supposed to be here with you? Where's Saul?"

"He left early on some mysterious errand," Izzy said. "He said to tell you he'd be at the synagogue on time."

Harold held out his arms and his father helped him don his short, white *kittel*, the traditional wedding robe. He put his suit coat on over it. He put on his hat and the three men left for the wedding.

In the bright, clean air of the first spring-like day, Harold looked at the sparse Sunday morning traffic, the grimy faces of winter-weary apartment buildings, the melting piles of dirty snow in the gutters, and realized The Bronx had survived the winter intact and so had he. After all that time in Yorkville, he was getting on with his life, and the thing he had to do now was marry his beloved. He raced ahead of his father and Izzy, straight to the synagogue and the basement hall where the preliminary festivities were taking place.

❧

Harold sat at the head of a long table. Flanking him were his father and Izzy. Down the table, which was laden with sweet cakes and wine, were the dignitaries of the wedding. Arnold Aaron had a place of honor. Uncles Leo and Frank sat beaming at their newly arrived brother, Simon, who looked uncomfortable in this strange synagogue full of Glusker customs. Before the Nuremberg laws he hadn't been religious; it had taken Hitler to make a Jew out of him. Next to Simon were his teenage sons, Gunther and Carl, and his nephew Manfred, Hiram's oldest son and the only German Appel who spoke passable English.

On Israel Schwartz's side of the table were many of Sally's cousins and the officers of the Young Men's Association. All were waiting for Rabbi Kabakoff to bring the *ketubah*. Everyone was there except Saul.

On the other side of the room, behind a head-high screen, the women of the wedding were honoring the bride. Sally—beautiful in a long flowing white gown with seed pearls at her neck and white lace sleeves pushed up a bit, leaving her forearms bare—was sitting on her throne, a high-backed chair. Her feet bounced along with the fiddle player in the band, off in a corner of the room, playing *freilech,* happy music for the wedding.

Harold began his *d'var Torah,* demonstrating to the world that even at this, the most joyous of his life, he remembered G-d. Israel had helped him select a portion from Isaiah. "It is proclaimed that all flesh is grass, the mighty, those who raise themselves on high over the Jews, shall fall, and wither like grass in the field." Harold's voice was high, sing-song, almost drowning out the music from the other side of the room.

Harold paused and the Gluskers interrupted, breaking into song: "One, unitary and unique, is G-d, sought out by the pure in heart, who desire only good for Israel, Hallelujah." Harold attempted to continue his sermon but was interrupted every time, after he said a few words. Izzy had warned him not to be upset. It was customary.

Amidst the confusion Rabbi Kabakoff entered. He bore a large, hand-lettered scroll which he unrolled in front of Harold. Taking a seat, he said, "mazel tov," hugging first Harold then Izzy. "Please sign your Hebrew name." Harold signed *Hayyim* and the rabbi signed *Sara* for Sally. The *ketubah* was then witnessed by Levi Sobidor and Arnold Aaron, two devout men not related to the bride or groom.

The short afternoon *mincha* service was read as soon as the *ketubah* was signed. After *mincha* the men and women were free to mingle for a while. It was one o'clock and Saul had not appeared. The twin demons of nervousness and hunger began to gnaw at Harold's stomach. *Where was Saul?* He had the ring.

Pat O'Rourke appeared. "Sally my friend, you and Harold are really getting hitched." He gathered his small entourage around him to introduce them to the bride. "Sally, you don't know my brother, Frankie, but Saul does. And this is my new fiancée, Emma."

"The sheriff's daughter," Sally exclaimed. "Congratulations to both of you. We'll be going upstairs in a few minutes, Emma. The men don't sit with the women in our synagogue, so let me introduce you to my friend, Cynthia. She'll show you the way."

The time for the veiling of the bride was at hand. The band played *Va Yehi Bi Yeshurun,* Betrothed Forever. Harold broached the barrier and approached Sally. Sarah handed him the veil and he pinned it to satin ribbons in her hair.

The wedding party went up to the sanctuary, with Harold leading the way. The band continued playing as his parents escorted him to the *hupah,* the wedding canopy. Finally, Saul rushed up the aisle, hair tousled and out of breath. "Where have you been?" hissed Harold.

"I had to get my date," Saul panted. He pointed to the women's section, where, among the people filing in, Harold saw Christiana Willknecht, her face flushed, with excitement or trepidation the groom did not know. All that mattered was she was here, this Nazi daughter, at a Jewish wedding in The Bronx.

"Shhh," Rabbi Kabakoff murmured. "We're about to begin."

The band, upstairs now, began playing the wedding march as men took their seats and Sally began her processional. Upon reaching the *hupah,* she circled Harold seven times, and took her place at his right.

The rabbi stood facing the bride and groom. A step behind stood the two sets of parents; then Saul, the best man, and Cynthia, the maid of honor. The rabbi lifted a cup of wine from a small table and toasted the couple, "*Baruch atah Adonai, borey p'ri ha-gafen.* Blessed are You, O G-d, who sanctifies Israel through *hupah* and *kiddushin.*" First Harold, then Sally, sipped the wine.

Harold asked Saul for the ring and passed it to Rabbi Kabakoff, who asked. "Is this yours?"

"Yes," replied Harold.

"Is it worth a *perutah*?" the rabbi asked the best man, thus establishing the value of the ring and the wedding.

Harold took it with his right hand, as G-d gave Torah to Moses, and slipped it on Sally's right forefinger, the finger closest to her heart. "Behold, you are consecrated to me with this ring," Harold said softly to his bride.

The rabbi read the *ketubah* out loud and passed it to Harold who passed it to Sally. He filled a wine glass and said seven blessings over the couple. He drank from the cup and passed it to

Harold, who took a long drink and passed it to his bride. She finished the wine and handed it back to the rabbi, who wrapped it in velvet and placed it by the foot of the groom. By reflex, Harold raised his heel, ready to stomp the glass to smithereens. "Not yet," cried Sally and Rabbi Kabakoff together. Harold, red-faced, lowered his foot.

"Do you, Harold Apple, take this woman, Sally Schwartz, to be your wife according to the laws of the State of New York?" the rabbi asked.

"I do!" Harold said.

"Do you…"

"Yes, I do!" Sally said emphatically. Harold took her in his arms and they kissed.

"Harold, now." The rabbi grinned and pointed down at the wrapped glass. Harold stomped hard and the tinkle of breaking glass filled the room.

Mazel tovs filled the synagogue.

Now we have to go to the yichud, Harold thought, *the place where we symbolically consummate our marriage.* Harold took Sally's hand and they skipped from under the *hupah* to an inconspicuous door at the rear of the room, greeting well-wishers as they went.

The door of the *yichud,* a small room, closed behind Harold and Sally. They sat on the only piece of furniture, a loveseat, and continued their kiss. After a few minutes they stopped, breathless, and sat hugging each other. "We're only supposed to stay in here a little while," Sally said. "We have to greet our guests."

"I know Doll," Harold said. He stood and had his hand on the doorknob when he turned and asked, "Sally, did you see that girl with Saul?"

"Yes, who is she?" Sally said as she gathered her gown around her.

"That's Christiana," Harold replied. "And Saul brought her to our wedding. I wonder if they're getting serious. And what's your dad going to think?"

"But Harold, you know Daddy and Saul worked that out months ago."

"Still…"

"Harold, forget about it," Sally said. "It's OK." She lovingly fondled his cheek,

Harold knew Sally was right, he should be focused on them. *Why am I upset?* Harold thought. *I know Christiana. She's good people. After all I've been through, I'm still thinking like a Nazi. Let it go, Harold, let it go!*

Applause greeted the couple as they descended the stairs to the basement room, which had been rearranged for the wedding meal. A screen still separated the men from the women but the head table crossed the boundary so Harold could sit next to Sally. Music was playing as they made their way to the place of honor.

Levi Sobidor and a bevy of Glusker men were dancing madly in circles. They surrounded Harold and Sally, lifted them in their chairs, and began whirling around the room. The women joined in, and soon everyone was dancing except the newly-arrived German Jews and the non-Jews, the O'Rourke's, Emma, and Christiana. Pat and Emma, then Frankie and Christiana joined in and the only ones still in their seats were the Germans, wondering what strange people they had come to be among.

"Enough, cry uncle," laughed Harold. He didn't know if he was dizzy from dancing in circles or from hunger. He and Sally were set down at the head table.

"Before dinner can be served you have to say the *motzi*," Sobidor shouted, "and we're all so hungry."

"*Ha motzi lechem meen ha'oretz,*" Harold said, tapping the loaf of challah twice, breaking it in two, and passing half to his new wife, who broke off a piece and daintily devoured it. The band broke into a tune and waiters began shuttling from the kitchen with platters of food. The wedding guests formed a line in front of the head table to congratulate the newlyweds.

First in line was Saul. He leaned over the table to give his sister a big kiss on the cheek and introduced his companion. "Christiana, meet my sister, Mrs. Harold Apple," he said, trying Sally's new name for the first time.

"Congratulations to the both of you," Christiana said. "It was a lovely wedding."

Is this the same girl I knew in Yorkville? Harold thought in wonderment. *She is so quiet, so demure.*

"Harold, my father sends his greetings."

Harold was shocked. Willknecht, the Nazi super, was sending a message of good will to Apple, the Jewish reporter. *I accept Christiana being here,* Harold thought, *but for her father to send me greetings, is just bizarre. Maybe she was telling a fib, just to be polite. Still, Georg was acting disillusioned by the Nazis. I hope I get to talk with the girl later, before Saul spirits her away. It looks serious between those two.*

Sally did not have the same mental baggage as Harold. "Hello Christiana," she said, smiling sunnily while grasping the Nazi daughter's hand. "I would love to talk with you later. Thanks for coming."

The O'Rourke party filed past. "Have you set a date yet?" Sally asked Emma.

Harold did not hear Emma's answer. He was busy fending off a bear hug from Pat which threatened to overturn water pitchers and platters of food. "You did it, old friend," Pat cried jovially. "You got married the week of Sally's birthday and you didn't let any old Nazis stand in your way."

"Nothing was going to stop this wedding," Harold declared. "Not even Nazis." He gestured in the direction of Saul and Christiana holding hands on the other side of the room. "My brother-in-law has changed since Aaron assigned me to Yorkville."

"A lot of people have changed Harold, a lot of people," O'Rourke said. "Our stories touched people. "We can be proud of ourselves."

"Yeah, but where's our Pulitzer?"

"They haven't been awarded yet, you big jerk."

Next in line were Rose Nathanson and a dark, handsome man who had to be David, her lawyer husband. Sally leaned across the table to give Rose a kiss while Harold shook hands with the man who had reunited his family. "Mazel tov, old man," Nathanson said. "You've got yourself quite a gal."

"I know, David, I know," Harold said. "And you've given us the best wedding present."

"It was a struggle but Frank Appel is a very persistent man. The problem wasn't in Germany, believe it or not, Hitler will give us all our people we can pay for. The hang-up is in Washington. The State Department is full of anti-Semites who don't want another Jew in the United States. But your father and uncle are tenacious. They even enlisted Senator Taft to help.

The line of well-wishers dwindled and the couple got to eat a bite or two, enough to ward off starvation, before the dancing started, women with women and men with men. Sally went twirling off with her girlfriends. They all wanted a chance to be with the bride, because they were already married and wanted to give advice, or because they were still single and wanted some of Sally's luck to rub off on them.

The men gathered around Harold, who motioned for the newly arrived Appels to join them. Manfred came over. "Cousin, we are all so glad to have you here," Harold said. "Tell us what it is like in Germany."

"The whole family is overwhelmed by your wedding, Cousin Harold," Manfred said. "No one from the outside has shown us kindness in so long. Life in Germany has been hard for the Jews;

the Nazis were never satisfied. They kept on taking things away from us. Then there was the terror of November."

Manfred paused for breath, and continued in a firm voice. "I will never forget the night of November 9th. We had a small apartment on *Turringer Strasse,* in the heart of the Jewish district. We had been forced to move there just months before. I had lost my job with the city government in the last wave of firings of Jews, in 1937, when the Nuremberg Laws began to be widely enforced, and was teaching history at Hirsch, the only school for Jewish children in Frankfurt. It brought in a little money, enough to buy milk for the baby, and kept me busy, out of my wife's hair. Eli had enough troubles in her life, trying to find food for three people and working as an emigration counselor at the Jewish Center. It was her connections at work that made it possible for our family to get the first visas issued after your *Herr* Nathanson persuaded the United States Government to open the quota."

The men around Manfred stood hushed, spellbound by his story. "I digress," the young man said. "It was on the night of the ninth that the final destruction of our lives as Germans began. I was on my way home from school, escorting four children who lived in our building, when someone ran by, shouting, 'They're smashing *Herr* Shapero's shop!' Shapero was the only kosher butcher left in Frankfurt, and many people depended on him for whatever meat they could buy. My family had never kept kosher so it was easier for us; we were able to eat whatever we could find, which was never very much. The children and I ran a block to see what was happening. There were shards of glass all over the street. Three big men carrying clubs came out of Shapero's butcher shop. They weren't running, they did not look over their shoulders in fear. They just strolled away without a care in the world. We looked in the door. *Herr* Shapero was sitting on the bloody floor, ruined meat all around him, bruised head in his hands. He was moaning, a horrible sound. On the corner a policeman was standing, watching, without interest. I knew the man. We had played together as children. I called out, 'Klaus, arrest those men. They have wrecked Shapero's store.' But I knew deep in my heart that he would do nothing, so much had people changed since Hitler came to power."

"But Klaus talked to me. He said, 'Manfred, go home right now,' in a low voice, looking around to see if there were any witnesses to him addressing a Jew. 'If you are at home you won't be hurt, but if you are on the street in an hour do not complain to me.'"

"We ran home, four more blocks, past my father's store, which was burning. The proud sign, *Appel und Sohn*, was torn down and lying in pieces in the gutter, along with broken glass from the display windows. There was merchandise scattered all over the sidewalk. I saw some of the employees scrounging for clothing, sheets, and bedding, but when I confronted them, they turned away. As I ran past one of them yelled at my back, 'Your father was arrested and you should be too.'"

"The children were wide-eyed. We were all used to taking verbal abuse from our German neighbors, but to see so much physical damage was too much for them. Their lives were being turned upside down. To tell the truth, I felt the same way." Manfred continued, his voice breaking at the memory. "We moved trance-like down the street, picking our way through broken glass. Shadowy figures were running in and out of Jewish shops, taking what they wanted and smashing the rest. I was numb but I had to get the children home, so that is what I did."

"Some of the cousins had gathered at my apartment," the young man continued while tears welled up and trickled down his cheeks. "They looked to me because I was the oldest, but I could offer nothing. There was no hope of ever returning to a normal life in our homeland. I had to look to my wife, with her ties to the American Counsel in Frankfurt, for salvation. We sent everyone home, although no one has far to go—we all lived in the same old rabbit-warren—and sat down to assess our situation. My father had been arrested by the Gestapo and taken who knows where. The older people, my mother, aunts, and uncles, were all paralyzed with fear. My wife and I had a small baby. All my brothers and cousins were clamoring to get out of Germany. It looked hopeless, so we went to bed, to find escape in the sleep of despair. But there was no escape. We were awakened by the sounds of crackling flames and timbers falling. We looked out the front windows to see the Boerneplatz Synagogue, across the street, burning swiftly in the bright night. The brisk wind captured the embers and swirled them high in the darkness, as if to send a message to the heavens. Your house is burning, the Nazis were telling God, and no one will lift a hand to save it. The fire brigade sat on the corner, alert for sparks starting fires on other buildings, but paying no heed to the centuries old synagogue burning to the ground.

The men clustered around Manfred were silent. The band played and the women danced all around their side of the room. "I am so sorry to say all this at a happy occasion, a wedding, but I am still overcome with grief at the life we have lost," the young man said. "I am sure I will learn to laugh again in this land of America."

Music played and laughter floated around the room. The bride and groom were not laughing, however. Harold was absorbed in Manfred's tale on his side and Sally was deep in conversation with Christiana on hers.

"I am so glad you came," Sally was saying. "Saul talks of you all the time."

"Yes, he wanted me to come and I wanted to see Harold get married. And I wanted to meet you. But your customs are strange." Christiana shook her head. Her hair cut fashionably short after a lifetime of being long and in braids, shook loosely about her face.

"There have been many changes in my life since Harold came and went," she said. "But the strangest thing I've seen is women sitting apart from men."

"Mostly to please my father, because this is the way he's always done it," Sally replied. "The sexes are mixed in modern synagogues. But you know about parents. Don't yours cling to the old ways?"

"They used to. They always believed in *Vaterland und Volk*. When Harold came he seemed authentic but different. He had respect for others. He didn't have that all pervasive hate which most Germans have. I could see it and evidently my parents could too, after a while. There were other things that helped. My father has non-German friends from that superintendents club he belongs to. He doesn't go to Bund meetings anymore, instead he spends time with supers from across town. My mother even let me cut my hair and I can listen to the music I want to. It's like living with different people. They've met Saul and they sent a present for you and Harold."

"That's wonderful. I didn't know Harold was so persuasive. Maybe we should send him to Berlin to work his magic on Hitler."

◈

From the men's side of the room came ringing. Saul was tapping a spoon on the side of a water glass. The Gluskers removed the screen and he spoke to one room. "I want to toast the bride and groom. They deserve all the happiness in the world. Let us drink to them and pray that they'll have the time to enjoy each other."

That's a funny toast, Harold thought. *But Saul is a funny fellow. Still, you never know. Maybe Sally and I do have to live for the moment. The Nazis have Europe on the brink of war and we could get in on it. Sure we could.* He remembered his *d'var Torah. God says, "All flesh is grass." Maybe I could be fighting Nazis again.*

ACKNOWLEDGEMENTS

I FIRST STARTED writing Shadows of Shame over thirty years ago, when I was still a young archivist. I have to thank everyone I worked with at that time at the National Archives who listened to me talk about the work, the records I drew my inspiration from, and the process of learning to be a writer. In particular I want to thank the late Ed Hill, my boss, who assigned me to describe the records of the German American Bund, records seized by the Alien Property Custodian at the start of World War II.

I want to thank my wife, Denise Cassens Ashkenas, who suffered with me when I lost the completed first draft for fifteen years (no computers back then) and gave me the space to do more drafts after I found the first. I want to thank my daughter, Sam Ashkenas, for being my first reader along with my wife, and for being a good writer herself. I also want to thank my son, Adam Ashkenas, who lived with me during the time I labored on the first draft.

I want to thank other readers who have helped me along the way. Robert Blake Whitehill, author of the Ben Bradshaw series of thrillers, who gave me my first blurb which follows these acknowledgements. Les Bergen for the technical help; Rabbi Jack Moline; E.A. Aymar, author of the Dead Trilogy; Jim Cassedy;

Bruce Busman; Howard Ross; Anton Merbaum; and my brother Ron Ashkenas.

Thanks go to the people at Damonza who designed the interior of the book and the cover.

Thanks are due my editors, Shelly Stinchcomb, Holly Kammier, and Jessica Therrien of Acorn Publishing, who with their prodding and poking have made me a better writer.

A Review

Shadows of Shame is a brilliant work. Bruce Ashkenas has crafted a spy story, a romance, and a courtroom drama about a dark period in world history, when Nazis roamed America with arrogant impunity. Harold Apple, newsman, single, Jewish, risks his life to infiltrate the Nazi Bund in late 1930s New York City on behalf of his paper. In search of the real story, he witnesses brutal cruelty of a hate-filled paramilitary mob. Apple walks readers through historical events, and introduces them to real people who played crucial roles in the unfolding drama when America flirted with fascism, and Germany was seduced by it before WWII. In reading *Shadows of Shame* there is no way to prepare for the shock of the story's whipsaw turns. Through it all, Ashkenas writes with warmth, with heart, and with a grace rarely found today. He loves language, and knows how to flail a human soul with his words. I stand awestruck by his keenly honed talent. Yet there is nothing mawkish about Harold Apple's journey. Simply put, this is not a book. It is a literary experience you will never forget.

Robert Blake Whitehill
— Author, Screenwriter, The Ben Blackshaw Series,
www.RobertBlakeWhitehill.com

ABOUT THE AUTHOR

Bruce Ashkenas retired from the National Archives ten years ago. Since then he has published three young adult novels, *Auntie's Ghost, Sick Street,* and *Aglow in The Bronx. Shadows of Shame* is his first book for adults. Mr. Ashkenas lives in Fairfax, Virginia with his wife, daughter, and two dogs.